THE MARKET

A Steamy Victorian Romance Series

Sorcha Mowbray

D1559622

AMOUR PRESS

Published by Amour Press 2021, First Edition

ISBN: 978-1-955615-08-2

CONTENTS

LOVE REVEALED

BOOK 1

DEDICATION

Thank you to Kristen Koster and Elise Hepner for your early comments and encouragement. I would also like to thank my beta readers Shelly Munro, Andrea Haywood-Gray, and Jarrah Dale. Without all of you and the Decadent editors this book might still be sitting on my hard drive.

CHAPTER ONE

Heath's shoulders ached as though the weight of the world rested upon them. Well, the weight of Christine's future anyway. His niece needed a husband. As her guardian, he had to ensure she made the best possible match. His brother would have expected nothing less. He ran his finger along the collar of his shirt to relieve the sensation of slow strangulation.

It was hard to say which was more choking—delving back into society in order to marry off his ward, his shirt and cravat, or the duty of filling in for his dead brother.

Absorbed in watching the young buck escorting Christine into the next dance, he missed his opportunity to avoid the pack of women bearing down on him. Lady Albright and her winsome daughter lead the charge, followed smartly by Ladies Winthorp and Rollings, widows of dubious reputation.

Gritting his teeth Heath bowed as the gaggle came to a full stop before him. The pungent mélange of their perfumes punched him in the face. "Good evening Ladies, Mademoiselle."

"Good evening Lord Heathington." They chorused back to him and curtsied. The two widows dipped so low he thought they might not make it back up. There was also the very real possibility one of them might dislodge a precariously perched breast. Heath struggled to control the curl of his upper lip.

Clearing her throat, Lady Albright shoved her daughter forward. "You remember my daughter Clarisse? You met her in the spring at your cousin's house party."

Repressing a long suffering sigh, he nodded. "Of course. How do you fare, Miss Albright?" A stealthy glance around the room held no salvation.

"My lord, I am well." Her limpid smile and shy darting glances were off-putting under the best of circumstances.

Elbowing the poor girl out of the way, the wicked widows pressed their bosoms against each of his arms. "Lord Heathington, we missed you at the Hampton house party last month," Lady Winthrop purred and pressed closer. Lady and Miss Albright stood by, mouths agape. Not unlike the trout he sometimes fished for at his country estate.

"I'm afraid I had another engagement that required my attention." He stepped back and attempted to disengage from the slavering pack of women. "I believe I see my cousin, please excuse me." He made his escape.

How much was one man expected to contend with?

He was at cross purposes with every matchmaking mama and horny widow in the immediate vicinity. Marriage was of no interest, and dalliances too risky. No, he'd continue to manage his sexual needs at The Market, with a woman who could handle his baser desires. It worked better that way. No chance of miscalculated expectations ruining things, or of terrifying an unsuspecting lady, and no chance Christine could be tainted.

"Heath." The soft voice of his cousin's wife intruded on his brood. "You look upset. Is anything wrong?" Cassandra asked, a worried furrow forming between her eyes.

"Not at all. I was just mulling over a few things after a quick escape from a gaggle of enterprising ladies. I am pleased to see you here. I take it Dorian is with you?"

"Here I am, Heath." Dorian joined them. "I see my wife has found you again. I wonder if I ought to be jealous." They all laughed at that silly idea. Heath and Cassandra attempted making a match of it years ago, before he recognized his darker sexual needs. Then she met Dorian and fell in love.

"No, I am just glad to see you here. You know how much I enjoy these occasions." He flashed a wry smile and clapped his cousin on the back. "Shall we go find ourselves and the lady a drink? I believe Christine will be busy for the next few dances."

They proceeded to the main ballroom and looked around at the swirling mix of gowns. The wave of heat slapped Heath in the face, followed in rapid succession by the less appetizing odor of bodies and perfume. A sudden burning need gripped him, the need to inhale the scent of Kat. Her smell always lingered on him for hours after they were together at The Market.

Tonight she would be his, nobody else's.

His jaw clamped shut as the idea of her in the arms of another man annoyed him. Shaking off the foolish notion he excused himself and edged around the ballroom. Fresh air might be in order.

As he neared the potted plants in the corner, Heath spotted Lady Drummond. Rather plain, with her simple bun, pale cheeks, and brown eyes. Forever alone in the corner, it was rare that she danced. In fact, he wasn't sure he had ever seen her dance. Doomed to be left withering on the fringe of society, she was too old to be among the girls vying for husbands, and too young to be welcomed by the matrons who eyed her with suspicion. Not to mention the general scandal of her husband's death. He pitied her, often spent time discussing plants with her so she might feel less alone. It was time well spent in kindness to her and to himself.

He sidled up next to her and dropped to the bench she occupied. "Lady Drummond, I see you're taking a break from the crush." He nodded toward the dancers whirling past. A faint but familiar scent teased his nose. Sweet and soft. Carnations. Kat. His fixation with the mysterious woman was starting to bleed into every aspect of his life. He gave himself a mental shake and focused on the isolated widow at his side.

"Lord Heathington. Yes, I needed to catch my breath."

She lied. Her very calm even breathing and dry brow indicated the truth. Being a gentleman, he let her keep her dignity by accepting her statement in silence. "Did you attend the last lecture at the Botanical Society? Dr. Luden holds some interesting views on the hybridization of roses."

Dorian and Cassandra drew his eye as they weaved past to join the other dancers. The starched woman next to him recaptured his attention as her crisp accents broke through his distraction.

"I did. I was most disappointed in his lack of interest of splicing plants together to make the most of their strengths. Why wouldn't you want a rose that could grow in cooler climes and resist pests? Why must everything always be about superficial wants? Why not make a better quality flower? A stronger one? Not just a pretty thing to look at."

Heath noticed a sparkle in her eye as her passion for plants broke through her reserve. She bordered on pretty. That was not how he saw her under normal circumstances. "I completely agree. Strength is more useful than beauty alone. It is very short sighted of Luden." *And men in general.*

Lady Drummond nodded in agreement and they fell into a comfortable silence as they observed the dancers go by. The music ended and he rose.

"It was lovely to chat with you, as always, Lord Heathington."

"I do enjoy our botanical discussions. Perhaps you would be inclined to continue them on the dance floor?" To be honest, he could not explain why he asked Lady Drummond to dance. Maybe he was intrigued to feel her in his arms? Curiosity got the better of him. Would she light up while dancing as she did when discussing plants? He wanted to know.

Surprise flitted across her features. "You want to dance? With me?"

"I don't bite, my Lady," he assured her as he stood with his hand out.

Her brow creased in confusion before her manners reasserted themselves. "Of course not. Thank you." A blush turned her face a rosy shade of pink, which made her look rather pretty. Again, his perceptions of her were challenged.

A waltz was starting as they walked toward the floor. A gentle tug on his arm indicated her hesitation. Ignoring her reticence, he shifted them on to the floor and swept her into his arms. Her lips parted, cheeks still a bit flushed. *Might she look similar in the throes of passion?* Her soft scent of carnations teased him again as the music began. He reminded himself he was heading to The Market later to see Kat. Perchance he needed an extra visit this month, without a doubt he was in need of some release.

Katherine looked up into the soft gray eyes of the Earl of Heathington and tried to imagine what was running through the man's head asking her to dance. What could he possibly want with her? Then he spun them into the lilting flow of the waltz. He swept them around the floor with effortless ease despite her awkwardness. She had not waltzed with a man since her dead husband had courted her, normally she was lucky to dance a Quadrille on occasion. Wary of her partner's motives, she held herself away from his body with an unnatural stiffness.

"Do you enjoy the waltz, Lady Drummond?" His warm baritone caused her heart to skip a beat.

"I do, my lord, but I am afraid I neither dance often nor with a partner as capable as you." Where had those words come from? The flames of mortification licked at her cheeks. Tucking her head down, she caught notes of lime and sandalwood. She breathed deep, absorbing the entrancing scent.

"Thank you. I find few women are capable of truly giving up control of the dance to their partner. Without trust, the waltz is but a battle of wills instead of the beautiful exchange it is meant to be."

Peeking up, her breath caught at his sensual smile. It was not the one she'd seen—always from across the room behind the plants—bestowed on countless ladies. This one held a warmth, an honesty, his usual grin lacked. Yet, it was too brash to believe he might intend anything but friendship. The rigidity eased as he continued to sweep her around the floor. "I appreciate the chance to experience such mastery of the dance."

"I always find you are full of excellent conversation, which only enhances an excellent waltz."

The heat sweeping across her cheeks had little to do with the exertion of dancing and everything to do with the kindness paid her by her dance partner. And still, she waited for the criticism or backhanded comment that inevitably came from her peers. Nothing. No rude comment or dry observation about how solid she was, stony. Instead they returned to their previous discussion of hybridization.

They made one last sweep around the floor before the music ended with a flourish, followed by a handsome bow from the Earl. Katherine dipped a curtsey, resting her fan over her breasts shielding them from view. Holding her body rigid in an attempt to hide her ridiculous thoughts, she rested her hand on his arm as he led her back to her bench in the bushes.

"Thank you for an exquisite waltz." She could not look up at Lord Heathington from her seat. Her gaze stayed glued to her hands in her lap. A flood of awareness and angst caused her to shrink back within her shell.

"You are welcome. I hope you enjoy the rest of your evening." Then he was gone.

Enjoy the rest of her evening? Not a probable scenario as the remainder of it would be split between the bench she occupied at present and the retiring room. His departure was for the best. She had no desire to forfeit control of her life to a husband ever again, not even to have someone to wake up next to in the morning. Men were not to be trusted. They wooed you, charmed you, lured you in and then like a Venus Flytrap devoured you. Regardless, it was a non-issue when the lone man who spoke to her was Lord Heathington, and he was nothing but an acquaintance.

He danced with her. He talked plants with her. He didn't court her. He showed no interest in courting anyone for that matter. So the chances of her ever rolling over to look into his soft gray eyes in the pink haze of dawn was somewhere south of her becoming Queen.

An independent widow, her life was filled by books and research. When her physical needs became too great, she would sneak off to The Market to find release. The shame she experienced her first time had come close to paralyzing her. She had lain like limp cloth as the masked man above her rutted until he came.

Fortune smiled when she stumbled across The Hall of Windows.

Behind each pane of glass a set of curtains could be opened allowing the occupants to display themselves. Transfixed by the first couple, she had stared until her eyes burned with the need to blink. The woman writhed beneath the man as he pumped his cock into her body. Then suddenly they shifted, and she was straddling his hips bouncing up and down as her breasts followed.

It was erotic to watch.

With cheeks flaming she had fled, but soon after returned with the desire to experience the kind of pleasure that couple had shared. The Market had become her secret shame and greatest pleasure. Nobody would believe the retiring Lady Drummond enjoyed the pleasures of the flesh, and she intended to keep it that way.

A glance around the ballroom reminded her there was no reason for her to stay. She was invited out of some strange loyalty to her dead parents, or perchance morbid curiosity. Attending the few events she was invited to, gave her a chance to be out. However, over the years it seemed she was more tolerated than welcome. Maybe it was time to cease the charade and skip society all together? Well, except for the Clarendon's dinner. She'd at least attend their small gathering since they were such close friends of her parents.

The exit of the ballroom was in sight when she collided with a gentleman.

"Excuse me, Madame." As he turned to look at whom he had bumped into, recognition flashed before his face drew blank.

"No, it was—" before she could finish her mumbled words, he turned his back on her and walked away. No pleasantries, it was a simple and succinct cut once he recognized who she was.

Lord Drummond's proclivities were not precisely a secret, but his failing health had been impossible to hide. That he had contracted syphilis became the best-known secret in London. Of course, it was assumed she had the disease, too. Her apparent health was no deterrent to a juicy bit of speculation by the Ton. As though they expected her to suddenly leap off a balcony and wrench her hair out raving like a lunatic. She was aware of the truth. The visions appeared at the end when the victim was too weak to do much of anything but mumble in their delirium.

Resigned, she forged ahead gaining the foyer of the house where one matron, standing near the ladies retiring room, whispered to another. The damning words husband and syphilis floated on the fetid air of too many bodies packed into too small a space. It was cloying. Suffocating. More so than the truth of what she had known but refused to acknowledge.

Katherine needed to escape more than ever as the horrid suspicions of her peers nipped at her heels.

Outside, she gained the cool night air and drew in a fresh, cleansing breath. As the burst of oxygen hit her lungs, all she wanted was to forget. Forget society, forget her dead husband, and forget who she was. The Market was where she turned to do that, and she was due there tonight. She tried not to be a frequent visitor. It would be easy to become addicted to forgetting, and that was something she could not afford to do for long. Remembering was important if she were to avoid making the same mistakes again.

Thankfully her carriage appeared, allowing her to escape into its dark confines. She would be more careful in considering which events she attended in the future. Indeed, it was quite obvious her invitations stemmed from morbid curiosity.

The coach rolled on as she allowed her depressing notions to float around her. She was alone in the world, her parents dead before her husband. For five years she'd had no one to turn to but herself. Independence was easy when there was no other choice.

CHAPTER TWO

K atherine shivered and huddled deeper into her hooded cloak. A damp London mist hung heavy in the night air as the hackney bounced, jostling her with a comforting gentleness. A dull, achy throb built between her thighs, intensified by the ride. Another bump had her sucking in a breath. Sensation rippled through her, heightening her anticipation.

She was on her way to meet Sir. Submission to Sir was unlike any other encounter she had experienced at The Market.

His dominating presence was a natural extension of who he was. It flowed off him in overwhelming waves. When she was with him, nothing intruded on the pleasure he bestowed.

The hired coach jerked to a halt, swaying back and forth for a moment. She struggled to contain her need to escape the interior of the carriage. Alighting with practiced grace, she attained the sidewalk and floated through the rear entrance. One of the girls awaited her arrival to show her to a dressing room for the evening.

Once enclosed in the small space, the girl helped her shed the layers of cloak, gown, petticoats, and corset. Her short chemise and regular pantalets were all that remained. Deftly, she laced up the working style corset cinching it in front. A maid's uniform was provided; though no maid of her experience had ever worn such a low cut bodice. It would not have been practical. Not when her breasts threatened to spill from the top if she bent over. The last touch to her toilette was her mask.

It covered the top half of her head, lacing in the back for a snug fit and offering a significant amount of anonymity. The Market maintained a strict standard of privacy, which included masks to protect its client's identities. It would be uncomfortable in society if one looked across the ballroom and saw the man you'd flogged the night before as he approached dancing on the arm of a fresh-faced debutant.

The mask also allowed her to shed her prim exterior in exchange for her inner sensual self. Anonymity made it easy to keep the men at a distance, using them only for the pleasure they offered.

Kathleen took a quick look in the mirror and opened the door. She stopped and curtsied as she entered, keeping her eyes down like a maid.

"Sir, you rang for me?"

"Come here." His rich velvety voice came from across the room.

Standing next to the fireplace, his face was cast in shadows. There was no need to look up to know his features were shrouded in a half mask similar to the one she wore. Without a word, she proceeded across the room to stand before his six-foot frame. He was athletic, well put together. Bulging muscles under bronze skin made it clear he had worked more than a day's manual labor in his life. Despite his physique, he was refined. Not rough.

"Were you responsible for polishing the banister today?" His brow quirked up in question.

"Yes, Sir." Kat kept her gaze focused on the shadows hiding his eyes. His finger traced the edge of her scooped bodice, dipped into her cleavage as it advanced along the landscape. Chill bumps rippled across her chest, her body reacting of its own accord.

"You shall need to try again tomorrow." He frowned.

"Yes, Sir." She waited in supplication for him to decide what would come next. Punishment or pleasure? To her relief, he pulled her into his arms. Firm masculine lips compressed hers as his tongue swept into her mouth. Invading. Claiming.

This was what kept her coming back to this place. To this man. The feeling of strong arms wrapped around her and a demanding, yet delicious, devouring of her person.

The tips of her breasts pebbled, straining against the restricting fabric of her bodice. He raised his lips from hers and looked down. She followed his gaze and found he could see the relief of her nipples against the black of her dress. He flicked a finger down across one, and then the other.

Her breath caught in her throat. He paused, stared at her intently, but said nothing as he stepped toward the lone chair in the room. A comfortable wing back seat placed before the fire.

"Pour me a glass of whiskey and then you may remove my boots, my valet seems to have disappeared."

Without a word she poured two fingers of amber liquid and then made her way over to where he sat. There she held out the glass to him. He took it, and used his free hand to stroke her hip through her dress. Devoid of all of the normal petticoats, the warmth of his touch burned through the material.

Still silent, she turned and slung one leg over his, and raised his booted foot. The motion lifted her skirts and exposed her calves. Bent over, her backside on display to him, the first boot slid free. She progressed to the next foot and repeated the process. This time he placed his hand across her bottom to help shove. The boot slipped off and she stumbled forward, unaccustomed to the task.

Kat stood and placed her prize next to the first by the chair. Without warning he hauled her into his lap. At first she struggled, shoving against his chest in feigned surprise.

"Hush. Kat, you'll do as I say." He adjusted her position across his thighs.

"Sir. The housekeeper will dismiss me." She pressed against his chest, attempting to free herself from her captor.

"Only I can dismiss you." His hand delved into her bodice. He captured a nipple, again rolling it with his thumb and forefinger.

A low moan escaped as the telltale wetness seeped from her body. She couldn't hide her desire, though she must play out the scene for Sir. For her ultimate pleasure.

"Sir! I cannot. I am a good girl!" She leapt from his lap.

He inhaled sharply. It seemed like he could smell her arousal, except the fire must be covering the odor of her lust.

He pointed, an imperious gesture, at the bed. "Sit."

Now. This was when she was to give in. Let him have his way with her. She sucked in a breath and went to the bed. He stalked toward her, shedding his clothing one article at a time except for his cravat. Jutting from a nest of dark curls, his cock stood proud, thick with veins and a purplish tip. She squeezed her knees together with lady-like decorum, feet dangling over the edge of the bed. The pressure eased the ache between her thighs.

An unconscious gesture, her tongue slid past her teeth to moisten dry lips. His bulbous head slipped into her view and hovered, waiting for her to grasp it in greeting. Her hand shifted upward to clutch it. A reflex she stopped before it could complete its path. Her gaze darted to the silk material dangling from his fingers, then to his face.

"May I?" She begged, already desperate with the need to have him within her body any way she could. Her mouth. Her pussy. It didn't matter.

"You may, since you asked so nicely."

Eager for him, she slipped her mouth over his head and swallowed him. He was neither over long nor too thick. In her mind, he was perfect. A bit of a stretch to swallow him whole, but not so much she couldn't enjoy having him fuck her mouth or her quim depending on his fancy.

"Excellent, Kat. Take me deeper, as deep as you can and then pull back." He dropped the material on the bed before his hand fisted in her hair.

Drawing back, she allowed her tongue to trace the vein on the underside of his cock before she sank back down on him. His balls tightened up and quivered just before he withdrew from her moist warmth. With a groan, he yanked her top down to expose her breasts.

Ripping, the material hooked below her cleavage plumping and lifting her already generous breasts. He dropped to his knees and sucked one nipple into his mouth. Tracing the whorl of her aureole with his tongue, he flicked the crest and bit down. Her body spasmed in response. With a satisfied grunt, he relocated to the other breast and repeated the caress.

He caught her watching his tongue feather across her peak. She drew a deep breath when he smiled a predatory smile that made promises his body would keep. He tipped her back across the bed with a gentle prod and hauled her skirts up to her waist. Undeterred by her pantalets, he found the slit and wrenched them open with a tearing noise that made her heart leap with desire.

"You have a beautiful mons, my dear." His fingers slipped through her curls to part her wet folds, and then his tongue dove in. He ran the edge up the length of her heated sex to flick her clitoris with ruthless determination. Her legs shifted, a restless movement, until he pinned her hips down on the bed with his arms.

"More, Sir. I need you inside me." She clutched the sheets in distraction.

He lifted his head from her thighs. "Touch your nipples. I want to watch you while I feast."

Grateful for a focus, she grabbed each nipple between her fingers to roll and pinch until he was satisfied she was following instructions. When he returned to devouring her, she gasped as he inserted a finger into her tight channel. Greedy for more, her body rippled around it. His tongue flicked her clit again as he inserted a second digit. She cried out in ecstasy as his fingers curved upward catching the spot that always made her crazed with lust. His insistent tongue and fingers continued working her until she believed she couldn't stand it any longer. Finally, as she balanced on a knife's edge of pleasure, her body broke and pure bliss rushed in to rack her in spasms.

"Sir! Oh, sweet heavens."

Slowly, her body calmed as he continued lapping at her honey. Once she settled again, he rose from her thighs.

"Slide back." He loomed over her, his cock even harder than it had been before. Purplish and swollen, it looked painful.

Kat was quick to inch her body backward until he commanded her to stop with a simple touch. Then he knelt between her legs and took her wrists in one hand. Picking up the forgotten cravat, he lashed her hands together and pinned them to the bed over her head. Panic assailed her as he loomed over her helpless form. She closed her eyes and focused on breathing.

It is Sir. He would not hurt me. Breathe.

She opened her eyes and focused on the face hovering above her. He took his rod in the other hand and rubbed it in the wet crease of her body. Her fear faded as pleasure jolted through her. Merciless, he massaged her clit and teased her opening with the engorged tip until the need to cry out was more than she could contain.

She broke. "Please." It was more a whimper than anything.

"Please what, Kat?"

"Please, take me. Fill me as only you can, Sir."

On a grunt, he plunged into her body and seated himself to his balls. She could feel them squashed to her backside as he ground his pelvis against her. Then he withdrew until just the tip sat inside her body. He drove into her again, but drew back without hesitation. He continued the pattern stopping every so often to grind against her.

Her body fluttered around his cock, always trying to draw him closer. Deeper. They both neared their climax as he continued to thrust into her, as he held her wrists not letting her go. She cried out, her hips rising to meet his as her world broke apart again. Her body screamed its release as pleasure swamped her senses causing her to lose touch with the corporeal. Coherence returned, and she found him pumping into her body one last time. Withdrawing, he came on her breasts milking his body, running his hand up and down his cock.

The skirt of her maid's uniform was used to clean off her chest, then her bindings were loosened before he collapsed next to her. After a few minutes, he sat her up and divested her of all her clothing. Naked, he picked her up and settled her under the covers of the massive bed and climbed in. He doused the lamp next to them, leaving the low glow of the fire to light the room. Kat sighed, exhausted and content. Despite her initial fear at being tied up, she had found the restraint freeing. It left her with no choice but to feel and to enjoy. Then sleep stole through her limbs, dragging her down into its restorative depths.

Sometime later, groggy from her nap, she roused to the feel of his erection entering her still wet body. Her core opened to him, welcomed him as he slid into her. This time he was gentle, careful with her. It did not take long for them to find release. Her first, then he dragged his rigid flesh out and spilled on her stomach. Again, her dress was employed to clean up his cum and then he tugged her into his arms where they slept a bit longer.

Kat awoke again to the gentle pressure of him nudging her arm.

"It is getting late. The sun will be up soon if you wish to leave before daylight."

"I should go. Thank you," she said, voice husky from sleep. Rising and seeing her clothes were a terrible mess, she walked nude across the room. With the snick of the door closing behind her, her chest ached a little. It was always a little disturbing to slip away in the night as though she were taking something not given of someone's free will. With a resigned sigh, she set about dressing so she could return home. Back to reality. She tucked the mask into her cloak pocket when she left.

CHAPTER THREE

H eath sat in the dining room reading the morning paper as he sipped his coffee. A deep sense of contentment warmed him from the inside out. It was always the same after an interlude with Kat.

Christine sailed in, greeting him with a huge smile. "Good morning, Uncle Heath. You look well considering you were out all night."

All the blood drained from Heath's face. His sense of well-being evaporated like a fine mist. What did she know? "What makes you think I was out all night?"

"I heard you come in this morning just after dawn. I couldn't sleep after having such a wonderful evening." Her grin widened, if that were possible, and she spooned a mound of eggs onto her plate.

"I was returning from my morning ride." He folded his paper and set it aside striving for his usual calm.

"In your evening wear? Come now, Uncle, who is she?" Christine pressed.

Dear God, when had she gotten so blunt? So worldly? "Ladies do not ask such questions."

"But you taught me to speak my mind. Why would it surprise you I listened?"

"*Touché*. I suppose I am not accustomed to being the subject of your inquisitiveness." He took another sip of coffee. He might have been remiss in not taking a wife after his brother died leaving her in his care. No doubt she was more of a bluestocking than he had meant to raise.

"I suppose not. But you, dear uncle, have still not answered my question. Who was she?"

"That is none of your business, my too-curious niece. Now, what are your plans today and this evening?"

"Eleanor and I plan to visit this new milliner who is making the best bonnets of the season. Later we will be joining Marian and Sarah at the Denton musical. I do hope Sarah leaves that awful cousin of hers behind." She shuddered.

"What is wrong with Sarah's cousin?" Heath quirked an eyebrow at his ward.

"She talks incessantly. I swear we won't be able to hear Caroline Denton sing over the chatter."

"Perhaps she is simply nervous? Remember not everyone has your confidence and advantages," Heath urged.

The bright sound of Eleanor's greetings to the butler sounded in the hall causing his niece to jump up from the table, peck his cheek and dash into the foyer.

Alone, he realized he had an unexpected free night. Without question he would be heading to The Market to see if Kat was available for the evening again.

The Market consisted of three row houses. The main house in the center contained the common rooms and Madame Marchander's offices. From the street, the house on the left was for the average customer who was there to see one of the girls. The right side catered to those with less average desires and the income to indulge them. Kinks of all kinds could be found on the right side. Voyeurs were given something to watch, floggings could be both given and received, domination abounded, and orgies were not uncommon occurrences.

Heath donned his mask and entered the plush main rooms. He glanced around for Philippe, the guest liaison who was always lurking about to see to any guest's needs. Spying him across the salon, he approached.

"Philippe, I was wondering of you could tell me if Kat is available this evening?"

"I will check for you, Sir," he responded in his broad Yorkshire accent.

The man disappeared behind a tapestry masking a door to Madame's office. Every member signed their membership agreement in that office. It covered the house rules such as the masks, penalties for exposing someone's identity against their wishes, and other rules designed to protect the patrons of The Market. Heath walked over to the fireplace and stood staring at the crackling flames. It seemed like an eternity before the liaison returned.

"Sir, I am afraid Kat is unavailable this evening. However, I did take the liberty of checking and Solange is at hand if you are so inclined."

Heath's stomach tightened. Not available. She might be there, in the arms of some other man. That thought had his jaw hardening as his hands clenched in an unconscious forming of fists. It took a moment to rein in the inexplicable reaction. This was a house of pleasure. She was either a resident or a patron. He had no claim on her. "Solange will be acceptable. Thank you."

Heath followed Philippe to a room on the right side of the house and into the spacious bedroom and sitting room where Solange was already waiting for him. He studied her as she rose from the chair by the fire and knelt down. She had served him before and remembered his preferences. That or, the diligent Philippe had reminded her.

"Come here, Solange."

"Yes, Sir."

He tracked her smooth motions as she rose and approached. Her golden hair glowed in the orange light of the fireplace limning her form. She wore a transparent robe and nothing else.

Stopped before him, she waited for his command. His cock lay flaccid as he looked into her deep green eyes. Peeling her robe open, he tweaked a nipple until it grew hard and then pinched the other one. Still his staff was less than interested. Desperate to push Kat from his mind, he leaned over, drew one of the pebbled tips into his mouth, and suckled. His eyes closed as he sought to savor the feel of her nub on his tongue. Instead, his closed lids acted as a backdrop for images of another woman, a dark haired woman with beautiful brown eyes. Kat.

Releasing the peak, Heath stepped back and groaned in frustration. Solange looked at him as though she recognized something was disturbing him. Her eyes held a question he did not want to answer. Without a word, she dropped to her knees before him and worked the fastenings of his trousers until she released his soft member.

A gentle stroke preceded more determined efforts. The warmth of her mouth encompassed him with ease. Then her tongue worked up and down his disinterested length and flared around the head to dip into the slit at the tip. Still no response. It dawned on him how futile this effort was, and how unfair to the woman before him. With a nudge, he slipped his cock from her mouth and tucked it away into his pants.

"Sir? Was it something I did or did not do?"

"No, Solange. It is apparent I was mistaken in thinking another would do in the place of the one I want. It is a situation I will remedy immediately. Thank you for your efforts, and I apologize for my body's ungrateful response." Heath helped her rise and retied her robe before kissing her on the forehead and leaving the room.

He arrived back in the common rooms and found Philippe again.

"I need to see Madame Marchander. It seems I have some business to negotiate with her." He needed to figure out what it was about Kat that drew him, or he needed to exorcise this fascination so he could move on.

"My lord, I will see if she is available." Phillipe bowed and disappeared again.

A short while later the redoubtable Madame Marchander appeared in the common room. Her aqua satin gown made her blue eyes stand out in striking contrast to her blond hair. She was a stunning woman, and she wielded her power with a careful stratagem that would have made Wellington proud.

"I understand you would have a word with me, my lord"

"I would, Madame, let us speak in private."

"Of course, please accompany me." She slipped her arm in his and led him to the door behind the tapestry. They entered a smaller room, which held a delicate desk and chair with two comfortable wing back seats set across from it. Behind those seats crackled a warming fire. With a swish of her skirts, Madame Marchander settled behind her desk, for without a doubt it was hers, and indicated one of the seats for him.

"Now, what is it I may do for you?" she asked, all but purring the question.

"I find I'd like to establish an exclusive arrangement with Kat, one of my more frequent partners here. I'm prepared to offer generous terms in return for exclusive rights to her time. I want her available to me whenever I choose and she will entertain no one else for the duration of the agreement. You understand the nature of my preferences, but we will stay true to the rules agreed to by all members. Whatever the fees are, send me the bill. I will cover hers as well if she is a fellow patron."

Madame Marchander sized him up from across her desk. Perused him head to toe as though assessing his offer, and even his manhood. After a long drawn out silence, she spoke. "My lord, as you are a member in good standing with no warnings in your file, I will entertain your request to arrange a contract. I will need to relay your request to the lady in question and determine her interest and if the terms are agreeable. This will require a few days' time."

"I don't wish to wait. Contact me tomorrow with her response." Heath stood and stalked toward the door. A few days were a few too many. He wanted her. Now. Madame Marchander would make the arrangements. That he did not doubt.

"My lord, do not confuse me with one of your women. The lady will have sufficient time to consider your offer. I will contact you with her response as soon as it is delivered." Her eyes had turned ice cold. He overstepped his bounds. He should know she was not a common servant to be ordered about. It grated against every fiber of his instinct, but he acquiesced since he had no other option.

"Very well. A speedy arrangement would be greatly appreciated, and well rewarded." She was, after all, a businesswoman at heart. He nodded and left her office.

Katherine sat in her morning room and reread the note for the third time. Her hands trembled and her heart raced. Madame Marchander, proprietress of The Market, penned the missive with remarkable elegance. It relayed an offer from Sir. For the next six months he wanted her to be available to him at all times, she would see no other men during their agreement, and her body would be his to do with as he chose. In exchange for this agreement, he'd cover her fees at The Market and of course see to her pleasure. He wanted to meet her that night. A delicious shiver ran up her spine as she remembered how he had bound her wrists the last time they were together. It was as though he recognized her, what she wanted, even needed, practically before she did. Her nimble imagination made the leap, picturing her submitting to Sir's attentions on a regular basis. Their encounters were always satisfying, and the contract was only six months. Besides, as a patron she had the right to sever any contract if she was unhappy with the arrangement.

She walked to her writing desk, tucked in the corner of her morning room, and retrieved fresh paper and ink. Dipping the pen in the well, she paused for a moment. Then wrote, explaining to Madame that while the arrangement was welcome, her availability required twenty-four hours' notice. She would normally need time to be able to arrange her schedule in such a way it would not be too disruptive to the rest of her life. She still had responsibilities to be managed and could ill afford any further damage to her tattered reputation. However, she agreed to the requested meeting later in the evening. With a satisfied nod, she folded the note and handed it to her butler to give to the waiting messenger.

Heath sat in his library, impatience riding him hard as the clock ticked like a racing turtle. When would he hear from Madame? The waiting made it impossible to get any work done. The rather large stack of correspondence in need of his attention sat on his desk in silent reproach. Around mid-day a message arrived. He read the reply and request for a day's notice and had to consciously stop grinding his teeth. The appeal was reasonable considering it was clear his Kat, and she was his now, had a life of her own to manage.

Quick to reply, he indicated his acceptance of her terms then folded the letter and passed it back to his man. Heath stood, walked over to the whiskey decanter, and poured himself a drink. He swirled the amber liquid that reminded him of Kat's eyes when the fire caught them. Anticipation coiled in his stomach and caused his groin to tighten when he pictured her spread out beneath him as he claimed her body. It would be a fierce claiming, no gentleness that first time. He wanted her, wanted her to know she belonged to him. He'd fuck her and claim her in the most basic of ways, and he reveled in the expectation.

All that was left was to plan how he would plumb her boundaries and test her strength. He suspected her inner strength; the question was what would she bear? How far would she go? Did she trust him? How much? How would she take to punishment? Had she ever been spanked? Would she let him take her backside? Would she enjoy restraints as much as he wanted to restrain her? She had responded well to being bound their last time together.

He needed answers to those questions. Always, he wanted to test people, explore their limits. It was part of him. A part he worked hard to keep in check as dictated by Victorian society, but part of him nonetheless. He feared letting it out, feared what may happen to a woman if he didn't control the beast within. However, Kat was different, somehow with her he could be his true self, and she would neither shrink away nor be hurt. She was resilient, strong, beautiful, and now she belonged to him.

Mine. Of course, not in any permanent or meaningful way. But for now, for this moment she was his. And, that gave him great satisfaction. Enough that he was able to settle in and focus on the neglected correspondence. If he didn't get through it all, Chelmsford, his secretary, would grow very disapproving; which was a strange and uncomfortable experience. Preferring to avoid any such unpleasantness, Heath made notes for each of the letters indicating a reply. It was a tedious business, but necessary and with the reward of a night with Kat looming over the horizon it was much easier to accomplish.

A few hours later, Heath rose and stretched, working the kinks out of his back. He glanced at the clock and decided he needed to get out, stretch his legs and burn off this restless energy. A ride through Hyde Park seemed just the thing.

She was fidgeting. She never fidgeted. It wasn't her way. She'd always advanced through life with a calm serenity. Today she couldn't find it in her to control her own body. Sitting across the desk from her man of affairs as he explained a new investment, her leg bounced in the most unladylike fashion. Absently, her fingers drummed in an appalling and rude manner that had the man staring. Giving up all pretenses, she stood and paced his office.

He very carefully set his pen down, his body rigid with frustration, and gave her an expectant look. As though he waited further direction. She paused in her meanderings and stared at the man. Hair ruffled from the slide of his fingers, and his crushed, rumpled clothes told of a long day. "Lady Drummond, is there something you need to attend to?" His measured tone reminded her of one a parent might use with an errant child.

The rolling chimes of the grandfather clock in the hallway burst into the room. Two in the afternoon. She resumed pacing the length of his office, skirting her maid tucked in the corner. "No. Why do you ask?"

"My apologies, my lady. You seem distracted today. Perhaps we should resume our conversation tomorrow?"

"I have nothing else to attend to at this time. I apologize if I am not my normal, calm self today. I have had exciting news that will resolve itself later. I am afraid it has made me twitchy," she offered as she made another pass in front of his desk.

"Very well. I take it you understand the proposition I'm explaining to you?"

"Quite well. I can't sit still, I didn't grow deaf. Please continue explaining this mining operation to me." She waved him back to the conversation even as she continued her route. The harried man, ever persistent, explained the viability of an investment in mining as technology continued advancing. Close to thirty minutes later she stopped and turned to her adviser. "No. Not more coal. I wish to invest in steel. It is the common thread across this industrial surge. No matter the fuel used to propel something; that something is usually made of steel. Find me a steel mill to invest in. When you have a few prospects, you may present them to me, and I will decide on any further investments." With a decisive nod of her head, Katherine turned and departed her financial adviser's office.

She marched down the stairs and clambered into her carriage, trailed by her little companion. A swift rap on the roof was followed by a succinct, "Hyde Park, Ralph." She was able to settle back and allow her mind to wander to the evening's adventure to come. She belonged to him, to Sir. The myriad of possibilities of what he might do to her both tonight and down the road were damn near overwhelming. She understood he'd be commanding. Demanding. But might he also be playful? Adventurous?

She'd seen many things when she first visited The Market. Could she learn to trust him enough to explore the possibilities? He had been careful with her when he bound her wrists, and he was her favorite partner. A wave of anticipation rolled through her.

Having arrived at Hyde Park, she exited the carriage to walk along a deserted Rotten Row. Yes. She would let him bind her wrists again in order to experience the pleasure they had shared. It wasn't as if he stirred her emotions. Besides, the idea of the physical restraints held a strange appeal. No decisions to make, her sole responsibility to feel. It was taking their role play, his demanding nature, and her deep buried desire to surrender to a whole new place. She laughed and reined in the urge to spin, the need to let her skirts swirl around her while her arms thrust out from her body.

Heath was pounding along the riding path when he spotted Lady Drummond walking with her maid trailing behind. He trotted over and dismounted.

"Why, good afternoon, Lady Drummond." He greeted her, happy to see a welcoming face.

"Good afternoon, my lord." She seemed to thrum with a vibrancy he had not seen before. Her normal prim exterior had a crack in it. A pleasant and intriguing fracture.

Her eyes sparkled in the afternoon sun, taking on a cognac shade in lieu of the usual brown. "You seem to be in high spirits today."

"I am in excellent spirits. I have received tremendous news and in a few hours shall see everything set in motion."

Heath's breath caught in his throat. She sparkled. Her hair was still pulled back in a simple bun, but her cheeks were flush with color and her eyes seemed to entrance him. Where was the reserved Lady Drummond? "I find I too have received good news recently." He couldn't control the grin splitting his face.

"Well, it seems we both have something to be pleased with. I just left my solicitor's and felt the need to go for a walk. Is it normal for you to ride at this hour?"

"No. I missed my early morning ride and then worked most of the day."

It happened fast; perhaps she stepped on a rock. Lady Drummond stumbled, but he reached out and caught her before she fell. He found her cradled in his arms, not unlike when they waltzed. Only closer. Without warning, a profound awareness of her curves sent him reeling. This cognizance was followed by a familiar scent that teased his nose. Carnations. An image of her flashed through his mind. Naked and lashed to his bed, she cried his name as he entered her willing flesh. His uncontrollable body responded in the blink of an eye, when for weeks now Kat alone had stirred his interest.

He was insane with lust. There was no other answer. Was there?

"Oh dear. Thank you, Lord Heathington." Her hands pressed against his chest as she tried to right herself.

"Are you unhurt?" He clutched her to his chest, unwilling to let her pervasive warmth go.

"I-I'm fine. I should pay more attention to where I step." Her husky tones sent shivers down his spine.

"Yes, you should. At least I was here to catch you." He tried to temper his desire to scold her.

"Perhaps you should let me go now?" The question penetrated his haze and he realized that besides clasping her in an intimate embrace, he was doing so on a public thoroughfare. And there was no doubt she was aware of his body's reaction to her proximity.

"Yes. Just making sure you were safe on your feet." He cleared his throat as he set her from him.

"Thank you, my lord. I think I shall head home now." With those soft words she spun and fled to her carriage at the nearby entrance.

He stood on the path watching her drive off, a raging erection straining his trousers, and a swirl of questions in his mind. Could the straitlaced Lady Drummond be his Kat? It was hard to reconcile the two women as one. But, his physical reaction to Lady Drummond, combined with the sparkle in her eyes and the tantalizingly familiar scent of carnations, all made a rather convincing argument that they were, in fact, the same.

CHAPTER FOUR

K atherine's carriage halted and the door swung open. She stifled her naughty mind, filled with questions of what to expect from Sir, and exited the vehicle. As she sailed in through the front door, her butler greeted her with a salver bearing a note. She plucked it up and stopped dead in the foyer. It was a man's writing. It must be from Sir. The script was so clean and bold, only a man as disciplined and commanding as he would have handwriting to match his persona. Smiling, she dashed to her chamber to peruse the note uninterrupted

There, she unfolded the heavy paper and read her instructions for the evening. She was to use her regular perfume, but she was to wear no cosmetics—anywhere on her body. Her hair should be down so it might hang from beneath her mask. She could wear whatever she might like to The Market, but once there she'd change into the provided garments. Madame Marchander had taken care of ensuring everything would fit. His last instruction relayed that she should plan to stay until he was prepared to allow her to leave. She should make any arrangements she needed to make certain that was possible.

A soft gasp escaped her at the last of the instructions. It seemed Sir had intentions on keeping her busy for a while. She hesitated. Was this what she wanted? A warm tingle settled low in her belly as her core grew slick at the thought of him keeping her through the next day. Yes, she wanted the pleasure she knew he could bring her. She glanced at the clock on her dresser and realized she needed to bathe and prepare. Her hair must look its best if she was to leave it down.

A few hours later, clad in a simple but elegant gown of bronze satin and armed with an extra douche to prevent any mishaps, Katherine left for The Market. Delayed by her preparations and then finding a hack, she worried about keeping Sir waiting. No, she decided it would put their exchange on the right foot if he understood that he did not control her mind. He merely had the use of her body.

The drive was short, as it was still premature for the usual traffic associated with partygoers and other revelers attending to the social season. This allowed her to be ensconced in what was to be her dressing room for the duration of the arrangement long before the normal patrons were about. Katherine glanced around the room and found a lavender box with a large dark purple bow sitting on the chaise lounge.

On the dresser lay a new mask. It was similar to The Market's usual masks except it had the back cut out so her hair could hang free, and it was made of very soft leather. It still laced in the back, but the strap would be lost within the mass of her wavy hair. She turned to the box with the bow, her heart pounding. This. This would be her first insight in to what the night (and perchance day) would hold.

With a delicate touch she raised the lid of the box and found a corset, stockings so sheer it was scandalous, garters, and a matching robe. A note rested on the contents instructing her to leave the robe on the chair when she entered the room. She wasn't to have it on when he arrived. She dressed, first sliding on the black stockings and securing the deep purple garters. Next was the corset. As she picked it up she realized it was an under bust corset that would expose her breasts for his delectation. Her nipples puckered as though a cool breeze had swept through the room.

Nibbling her lower lip, she put the corset on and laced it from the bottom to the top. The garment, covered in beautiful purple brocade, glowed in the gas light. The cords extended to the top, just below her breasts, so she tied them off into an easy to release bow and left them dangling. She was pleased with the effect. A soft knock at her door made her grab the robe to give some little modesty.

It was a maid sent to see if she needed anything and to let her know Sir was ready and waiting. Kat kept her face averted from the maid. "Thank you. Please tell him I am almost ready. Perhaps another five minutes."

The maid nodded and headed down the hall. Kat snapped the door closed, placed her mask on and ran a brush through her hair. A moment later another knock sounded. It was the maid again. This time she entered before Kat could arrive at the door. "Sir directed you were to be ready now. He wants you in place when he comes in. If you will follow me." The pretty girl walked to the other door opposite the hall and entered the chamber.

Kat remained where she was, assessing her own reaction to his demand. Part of her insisted she get dressed and leave. He was already changing as all men did once they had what they wanted. The rest of her was curious about what he might do next. She knew spankings and other rougher activities could be included in the sexual pantheon. Perhaps Sir was more of that persuasion than he had previously shown. Curiosity won out and she followed after the maid.

A cheerful fire crackled in the fireplace across from the massive bed. It could have slept four across with ease. In the center of the bed's headboard were a set of padded wrist restraints.

"Oh," slipped from Kat's lips, more an exhalation of air than an actual word. Her heart pounded as she came face to face with the reality of what she had committed to.

"Sir wants you restrained on the bed, miss."

"Yes. Of course he does." Kat dropped her robe on the chair, walked to the bed, and positioned herself against the pillows so her arms were above her head in as comfortable a position as was possible. The maid buckled the straps around each of her wrists as tight as she could without causing pain and left the room.

Strapped to the bed, Kat found herself licking her dry lips as she waited. Had this contract gotten her into too deep waters? She glanced up at her wrists. It was too late to turn back.

Heath paced his chamber as though it were a cage at the zoo, and he a tiger. He was restless, eager to claim his prize and deal with her little display of independence. He must have terrified the poor maid who had come to tell him the lady would be another five minutes; but he was having none of Kat's nonsense. He'd get to the bottom of her game right at the start and correct any silly notions she had of asserting herself in the future. That was not how this arrangement was going to play out.

Two taps on the hall door let him know Kat was ready. He took a deep breath, checked the tie on his robe, and entered the room. There, just as he had envisioned, she lay on the bed. Restrained. Her body swathed in black and purple silks, arms pulled over her head causing her breasts to lift and collide, plumping them for him. Her nipples were erect, straining against the air. Her hair cascaded down over her shoulder and across the pillow behind her, a river of chocolate silk. She was as beautiful in that moment as he had ever seen her.

He took a slow breath to steady himself. The tie of his robe loosened with a smooth tug releasing it to join hers on the chair by the fire. The weight of her gaze rested on him as she followed his every move. His throbbing erection jutted from his body in a near vertical position.

If he were honest, he had not been this excited in a very long time, not since allowing his need to control to rule him unchecked. It had ended in disaster. Avoiding a repeat of that experience drove him to The Market where he could choose his partners with calculated caution. He approached the bed and stood over her.

She stared at his cock and licked her lips in anticipation.

"Kat." His voice sounded husky, as though rusted from disuse. There was no denying now what he had discovered that afternoon. The delectable woman restrained on the bed was Lady Katherine Drummond. How he had missed the connection before now was unimaginable. "Why is it you were compelled to make me wait when you were aware I was here and ready? This is not how we should start this arrangement."

"I was delayed." She met his gaze, hers teamed with desire, hope, defiance, and perhaps even a tinge of fear. Mostly promising reactions, the defiance would need to be addressed.

"You will of course be punished." He paused. "When I am ready."

"Yes, Sir." Her eyes lit up with his pronouncement.

"Not when you are, and it is clear you are." Yes, Kat was the exact woman he needed in his bed. She fit him, was a perfect foil for him, for his base compulsion. No. He must be caught up in the moment. She was no more than a desirable woman.

He sat next to her on the bed and caressed the outer edge of one breast. "It was good of you to tell me the truth, Kat. You must always tell me the truth, just as I will always tell you the truth. Do you understand?"

"I will always be honest with you, Sir." Surprise flitted across her features as the truth of her vow rang through her words and warmed him.

"Do you trust me, Kat?" Curiosity got the better of him.

She hesitated, her thoughts whirling like crazy behind her beautiful eyes. "No." She finally responded and dropped her gaze. He stopped caressing her soft flesh.

Trepidation reared its head before logic squashed the anomaly. His pulse thrummed through his veins. "And yet you let me restrain you. Perhaps you trust me more than you think?"

She glanced up at him. "Maybe a little."

"Do you trust that I won't physically harm you?" He let his fingers trail from her wrist down her arm in a light caress.

"Yes."

Relief washed over him. "Do you trust that I will not do to you anything you do not wish?" His touch now slid across her collarbone, tracing the delicate line.

"I do."

"Then we have a point upon which to build. It is my responsibility to earn your trust from there." He leaned over and kissed the tip of her masked nose. Something about her seeming innocence tugged at his heart. "Good. Now, I want to know what you have experienced or might like to experience within the confines of our arrangement." His hand returned to stroking her breast, dragging a slow sensuous trail toward her nipple.

"Spanking, but not flogging. I shouldn't like that." She glanced up at her wrists. "I think I like this. Yes, I like this quite a lot. I also like to watch, I'd like for us to watch another couple...." She gasped and arched up when he took her nipple between two fingers and rolled it.

He groaned and kissed her. His tongue plunged into her mouth, seeking. Ravaging. Claiming. He broke the kiss, lowered his mouth to her free nipple, and continued to roll the other with his fingers. He bit, a gentle nibble, on the distended nub and her skin rippled in response. So responsive. With a silent groan he left her nipples and shifted down her body, crawled between her thighs. He parted her folds and watched her juices continue to flow over her pink center. He wanted to bury his tongue in her. No, he needed to taste her. Feed his craving for her.

Without further delay, he feasted on her. He slid his tongue up the length of her slit and flicked the pearl at the top again and again. She moaned. The metal links of her restraints clanked, holding her in place. Her hips arched into his mouth and his tongue plunged into her channel, dragged out, and plunged in again. He wanted her to explode on his tongue, to mark him with her scent in the most basic of ways. He would be hers as much as she would be his. Her body clamped down on his tongue. He drove it into her again, and stayed, working her nub with his thumb while he lapped at her honey. She cried out with the intensity of her orgasm. He loved the taste of her, wanted to stay there making her come until she was senseless. But, he also wanted to bury himself inside her.

With a growl, he lurched up, and holding her legs over his arms, placed his shaft at her opening. She was so wet he didn't hesitate. He drove into her body allowing his need to take over. He pounded into her body, fucking her hard and fast.

"Sir," she cried out.

"Yes, Kat. You're mine. Mine to do with as I please," he ground out, his body continuing to piston hers in a relentless rhythm.

"Yes! Harder, Sir! Harder," Kat cried and gripped her restraints while trying to meet his powerful thrusts into her body. He dug deep and drove harder, harder than he ever had allowed himself with any woman. His fingers dug into her buttocks, securing his grip on her body, and he sank into her core. Like a vise, her body clamped down on his cock, and she arrived at the breaking point. She shattered, but he continued to push her ecstasy. Not far behind her, he impaled her over and over. A strange and heady mix of power and something like love swept through him. Then physical sensation surged, pushing the foreign sensations aside. His balls tightened and he pulled out to finish on her breasts. His legs quivered and he gasped for breath until his pleasure subsided. She lay there glowing from her release, a goddess. Right after he punished her for her tardiness, he planned to worship her all over again.

First, the punishment.

Kat's breathing slowed once his body reared off hers. She was lost, everything he did to her was diametrically opposed to who she believed herself to be now. How could she enjoy his dominance when it was the very essence of what she had avoided in marriage? Why did this feel so good?

Her haze cleared and she realized he was cleaning himself. Next he wiped his semen from her chest then set the towel aside so he could release her restraints.

"There now. Give your arms a shake. Massage them a bit to get the blood flowing again." He smiled at her, a gentle upturn of his lips. There wasn't any pain; it was more discomfort as feeling returned. Within a few moments it had passed.

"All better now?"

Kat nodded. "Quite. Thank you." This was why it worked for her, because in his dominance lay care and concern. Most men would have not taken the time to see to her sexually, much less after.

Sir handed her a glass of wine, which she was grateful to accept. She emptied half the glass before he took it back. He was no longer smiling. Her stomach knotted.

"It is time to deal with your punishment. Follow me." He sat on the bench at the foot of the bed, plenty big enough to support his huge frame and hers once she joined him. "Come. Lay across my lap."

Kat draped herself over his thighs, her hips crossing one of his legs. Her backside was turned up to him, and her face was down. Fear edged near the surface, scraping at her sensitized skin. He smoothed his warm palm over one cheek. She baulked.

"Ah. Ah. Ah. No flinching. You earned this." He chided her just before the first smack rang out.

Crack.

Heat bloomed in her backside. His hand landed on the other cheek. Now both sides were warm as though she had stood in front of the fire in her bloomers. Two more quick spanks, one on each side rained down. Then he slid his hand along the inside of her thighs and slipped a finger into her slick sheath. The fear had made a hasty retreat.

"Oh yes. You do like the spankings. I wish you could see this. Your backside is so rosy and your pussy is drenched."

Moisture welled in her eyes as the need for more than that single finger left her stunned. She wanted more. Needed more. Two more slaps popped off across her bottom, and he slid in a second finger. She moaned and surged back in to the penetration.

"Now, Kat. Are you going to ever keep me waiting again?" Sir demanded as he held just the tips of the two digits at her opening, teasing her.

"No, Sir!" She was desperate now. Needed those fingers back inside working her, wanted a third if he would give it.

"Good girl," he said and slid three fingers back in her channel. She mewled in pleasure as he worked in and out of her body. He popped her on the bum again, lighter this time. Just enough of a smack to sting a little and heighten her pleasure. "Tell me, have you ever taken a man here?" He thrust a finger against the muscle of her rear passage, not enough to penetrate, but to illustrate where he meant.

"No, Sir." He slid those wonderful, slick fingers back in and out, then stopped.

"I want to take you there at some point. Will you let me?" He shifted her to lay across the bench as he knelt next to her.

"Yes." He could do anything he wanted if he would make her come. She was close to telling him, but bit her tongue. It was too much for him to know. He pushed his fingers back inside, then out and dragged them to transfer her wetness to her rear entrance. A single digit slid inside her pussy and gathered her moisture before deserting her. The three fingers returned to her slick channel while his lone finger worked past her tight rear muscle.

Kat had never experienced anything like it, her body spasmed and released in instant response. He worked the three fingers in her pussy in concert with the digit in her backside until she exploded. Her muscles pulsed around his fingers and lights danced across her closed eyes.

"Sir. Don't stop!" He continued working his fingers until her climax calmed. Limp. Spent.

Sir rolled her over and gathered her in his arms. He carried her to the bed and bid her sleep for a bit. She protested when he didn't find release, but he assured her his time would come again. He kissed her and settled next to her on the bed.

A loud snap and pop from the fireplace woke Heath. He rolled over and found Kat still asleep. Unwilling to consider the odd sensations from earlier, he concentrated on the sleeping form snuggled in the bed. Waking a woman was one of his specialties. He stood and stretched before he slipped the covers off her body. She still wore the corset and one and a half of the stockings. Gentle with her, he untied the front lacing and slipped the garment from under her body. A sound sleeper, her even breathing continued undisturbed. Next, he worked the stocking that had fallen down her leg off her foot. Finally he released the garter on the other leg and dragged the stocking off.

Now that she was nude for him, his cock reared its head. He leaned down and spread her thighs with the gentlest touch. Her wet quim was exposed, and its dampness declared the general subject of her dreams. With a self-satisfied smile, Heath ran his tongue up her center to gather what dew he could find. She stirred. As he parted her folds and caressed her clit with his tongue, a moan escaped from the still sleeping Kat.

The combination of a finger working in and out of her body while his tongue worked on her nub was what drew her to a fully wakeful state. She half rose from the bed, but he held her pinned with his weight and his free arm.

"Oh," she said, surprise written all over her face. "I believed I was dreaming." She smiled and settled back on to the bed.

"Hhhmmm, I think you were. I was being helpful." He smiled at her and dove back into his labors.

A second finger paired with a few more flicks of the tongue and she moaned his name as her orgasm crashed over her in waves. Loving the light and sweet taste of her, Heath continued to lap at her pussy. He rose up and laid his mouth across hers, letting her taste her juices on his tongue and lips. His cock throbbed as she kissed him, slicking her tongue across his lips to gather her own taste from him.

"I love my taste on you." The words slipped out as a low sexy purr that shot straight to his groin.

"I love tasting you, so it works well for both of us," Heath agreed, inching down to flick her nipple with his tongue. She shivered in his arms, and he liked it so he did it again.

"Mmmmm. I want to take you in my mouth, the way you have me." She shoved against his chest, but he chose not to move.

"No. Not this time. I wouldn't last, and I have plans for you."

He rose up and took her with him. They stood next to the bed wearing nothing but firelight. He smacked her bottom and pointed at the bed. "I want you on all fours."

With a nod she crawled back on the bed and assumed the commanded position. She was stunning. He found her more and more beautiful each time they were together. Each boundary they explored made him appreciate her more. He ran a hand up her right thigh, like he did when inspecting a thoroughbred. The muscle quivered in response to his touch. He slid a finger through her folds to ensure she was still moist, and found her wetter than when he'd left her a few moments before.

Without further delay, he climbed behind her on the bed and nudged his head against her opening. He surged forward until the thickness of his cock was nestled inside of her body.

"I'll not be gentle. I need to claim you again." His gravelly voice grated on his own ears, like the grinding of the millstone at his country home.

"Yes, Sir. I need to be claimed by you." She glanced over her shoulder and met his gaze with her own. He realized she meant what she said, and so he plunged into her body in one swift filling stroke. He took her. Used her. And then he spent his seed on her backside.

CHAPTER FIVE

As the sun filtered in to the room, a knock on the door preceded a maid who wheeled in a table for two laden with breakfast.

"Will there be anything else, Sir?"

"That will be all. Thank you." He rose from the bed as the door shut behind the maid. "Come, Kat. We must eat to keep our strength."

"Mmm. I could eat a rasher of bacon." She stretched and smiled unconscious of her semi-nudity.

"Put your robe on or I may not last long enough to eat this delicious breakfast without having you again," he rumbled as he tied his own robe closed.

"Yes, Sir." She smiled. And once robed, settled in the chair he held out for her.

He pulled the other wing chair up and settled across from her delightful, but rumpled, form. He fixed her a plate after asking what she preferred, and then fixed his own. "May I ask why you agreed to my offer?"

Her fork paused halfway to her mouth, then continued on. She chewed her food slowly, stalling for time.

"Remember your promise to be honest," he urged.

"I do." She drew a slow breath. "There are things I have seen done here that I would like to experience myself. I have enjoyed our times together. You have always been a considerate partner, so I decided to try this. I am no slattern who revels in jumping from bed to bed; the arrangement you offered appealed to my desire for more consistency in who I lay with."

"Marriage offers the same consistency for far longer terms." His heart thundered against his ribs.

"Marriage also makes a woman vulnerable." She stabbed the eggs on her plate.

"It can make a man equally as vulnerable."

She snorted. "You know our society only allows a married woman those rights granted to her through her husband. A husband has no onus to be faithful beyond being a man of his word. Women are far more vulnerable in marriage. Whereas with our arrangement, I can end it any time I see fit, and you have no domain over me beyond that which *I* grant within these four walls. That is what appealed to me. Why did you make the offer?"

Her question surprised him, though it shouldn't have. She was proving to be a challenge in bed and out. "I have found myself drawn to you with increasing strength over the last few weeks. I feel a connection with you I wished to explore further. You have not shrunk in distaste from my baser side when it has appeared. You are present in mind as well as in body when we are together. And, you are beautiful." His lips tipped up in a smile.

She blushed and focused on her plate.

"You are uncomfortable with the compliment. Why? Do you not see your own beauty?"

"I have never been accused of being a beauty. I have been called many things, but never beautiful. Thank you." She laid her fork down and started to rise.

He reached across the table and stayed her with a hand on hers. Their eyes met. "Kat, you are beautiful in both a physical and intellectual sense."

Her gaze dropped to their joined hands..

"Who has led you to believe differently? Your husband?" He worked to keep his voice calm, even.

"My dead husband was always disappointed by me. I was never enough, in any capacity. It took me a few years to figure out why, but by then I suppose the damage was done." A tear slipped down her face as pain etched itself across her features.

Heath rose and pulled her up, gathering her to him.

Katherine trembled in his arms as she realized she must tell him the truth. She owed this kind man the full truth, even if it exposed her identity. He had a right to make a choice to continue this arrangement or not.

"Sir, I must tell you something." Her words came out muffled against his chest.

"Go ahead. You can tell me anything."

She pushed back from him. Choosing to deny herself the comfort of his arms. "My late husband had—certain proclivities." She began pacing.

"All men have proclivities, did he prefer heavier women? Boys? Men? Did he like to be whipped?" He looked pained, even as he tried to make it easier for her.

"Men. He preferred men. He often spent days lost in the stews fucking anything that would hold still and was male."

"It is not uncommon—" He tried to placate her, but she cut him off.

"He had syphilis. He contracted it before we married and it killed him in the end. I am clean though...." She drew a ragged breath. "We never consummated the marriage since he couldn't muster the interest in me physically." It felt as though she had ripped her soul out and laid it bare before this man.

Sir vibrated with rage. His jaw ticked uncontrolled, even as he held himself in check. Panic flared. She was a fool. How could she have let the intimacy of sex make her believe she could expose herself like this to him?

They had a physical connection, nothing more. But it was too late to call the words back.

"If he were not already dead I would kill him for what he has done to you. How he has made you suffer. I can only thank God he never touched you." His words came out harsh, the leash on his anger still tenuous.

Stunning. She couldn't comprehend that his anger was not aimed at her, but on her behalf. "I'm so sorry I did not tell you sooner. I knew I was not infected, but still you had a right to know in light of our agreement."

He crossed the room to where she had stopped and hauled her into his arms. His lips crashed down on hers and his tongue demanded entrance. He swept inside and ravaged her mouth until she could not speak. Withdrawing, he slowed his breathing and held her chin forcing her to look into his eyes. "Thank you for trusting me enough to tell me your truth. I am moved you cared enough to tell me, even knowing I was not at risk." His hands reached up and loosened the lacings of her mask.

"What are you doing?" Horror bloomed as she swatted at his hands. "No!"

"Katherine, I know who you are. The mask is pointless." He pulled it from her face.

Fear squeezed her heart. She should never have trusted this false sense of security. She should never have trusted him. He would reject the mousy Lady Drummond like all the others. How could he want her now, when he knew who she was? "I knew I should never have told you. Blast it!" She pulled away from him and hid her face.

"Kat, I knew before you told me about your husband. I figured it out after yesterday's walk in the park together."

His words sank in and she felt her knees go weak. Before she could crumple, he was there catching her again. She looked up into the grey eyes of the Earl of Heathington. "How did I not know?"

"I think we each see what we expect to see, not always the reality." A beatific smile lit up his face before he pulled his own mask away.

"And you came anyway?" She couldn't hide the wonder in her voice as she reached up and traced his brow and then down to his jaw.

"Of course I came. I have found a woman who not only enjoys plants as much as I do, but she dances the waltz divinely, and she is a match for me in the bedroom."

"How did you guess? I never thought anyone would figure it out." She was still baffled by the truth.

"I found myself imagining Lady Drummond naked in my arms and couldn't explain why. I thought I was so desperate with lust for Kat, you, that I was imagining things. But then yesterday, as you scampered off, the pieces fell into place, and I realized you were her. Finding you here today on the bed confirmed what I already knew." He nibbled her lips and then pressed the kiss again. At some point he carried her to the bed and set her down. "Now, I believe the plan was to have dessert following breakfast."

They spent the day periodically fucking, with short intermissions for naps, conversation, and food.

In the dark of night Kat heard Heath rise from the bed. She levered herself up onto an elbow. "What time is it?"

He came around the bed and kissed her on the nose. "It is the middle of the night. Go back to sleep until you feel rested enough to go home. I fear I have worn you out."

She chuckled. "I dare say you have, but must you go?"

"I must. If I don't leave now I may never let you get dressed again."

"I don't recall asking for my clothes." She laid back down and pulled the covers up.

He groaned. "You are a temptress. But I will do the honorable thing and give you time to rest. I will see you in a few days and then there is the botanical society in a few weeks with dinner after."

She sat up again. "You wish to meet in public?" What could he be thinking?

"Yes. I know we will both attend, why not sit together? We speak often enough at other social events." His gaze held hers, warm, steady, and confident.

"You know what they will begin to say about you." She looked down at her lap.

"The gossips wouldn't dare. And if they do, it will only last until the next big scandal." He tipped her chin up to look at him and smiled. "Now, I will send around the dinner invitation later today. As for the meeting, I will pick you up at eleven."

"Oh, no I must run some errands that morning. Why don't I just meet you at the hall?"

He looked doubtful but acquiesced. "Very well. I will meet there. Sleep well, my sweet, until we can meet again."

He kissed her once more before disappearing through his connecting door.

The morning of the Botanical Society meeting Katherine rose early, unable to sleep. She was eager to see Heath again. It had been a few days since they last met at The Market, and though he had stopped by her home briefly, they had not spent any length of time together. The last few weeks with him had been full of wonder and pleasure. They were growing closer with every meeting.

Despite her anticipation of the day ahead, she could not help but wonder about their coming evening. During his visit to her home, he had been so gentle and caring in a nurturing way. Different than the demanding lover she knew from The Market. She liked this new side of him, but not as much as she liked his serious, domineering side. It was a difficult thing to admit to herself. Where did the real man lie, between the two? The man she had yet to meet. Resolute in the banishment of such dangerous questions, she focused on her coming day to be spent listening to a lecture at the Botanical society.

A strange desire to show herself to best advantage took hold leaving her rushing to arrive on time. As she alighted from the carriage at the Society's hall, she glanced around hoping to find Heath waiting. He was nowhere to be seen. With a little deflated sigh, she progressed inside. At the door of the lecture hall she scanned the half-full room of men and women.

Focused on finding the man she sought, she was startled by the smooth, dark voice sliding over her right shoulder.

"Are you looking for someone in particular, Lady Drummond?"

With a small exhalation she turned and found Heath looking at her as though she were a sugared almond to be popped in his mouth.

"We never said where we'd meet to hear the lecture." Heat crept up her cheeks as her voice trailed off under his assessing gaze.

"We did not. I'd hoped to arrive before you and escort you inside. But it seems you have arrived on time, rather unusual for most ladies of my acquaintance. I should have known better with you."

The warmth of his smile made Katherine's knees wobble as though they would give out right there. She wavered, leaned in to his warmth, but managed to recover herself before further embarrassment ensued. The arc of awareness between them was intense. Trying to ignore the blood now pounding through her veins, Katherine picked up the thread of the conversation.

"Oh well, I am sorry I missed you, but we're here now. Shall we go in? I am very much looking forward to the discussion on plant classifications by

Lord Pemberly." She tried a bright smile to cover her own awkwardness.

Lord Heathington held out his arm, "Of course. Do you prefer the front or the back of the seating?"

"Oh, without a doubt, the front is best. I don't want to miss anything." Her eagerness slipped past her caution and caused a smile to grace his lips. She faced forward so she wouldn't trip while staring at the mesmerizing man she was fortunate to be with. She couldn't fathom how she'd gotten so lucky. The question remained of how long such providence might hold.

"Did you manage to accomplish all of your errands this morning?"

"My errands?" Her mind drew a blank.

"Yes, you would not let me bring you because you had errands to run." His eyebrow quirked up.

"Yes. Those errands. I um—managed those quite nicely. Very busy morning." She smiled, hoping he did not notice her fib. She needed to hold him off. He was somehow invading her entire world, not just the bedroom.

Soon the lecture started, and the debate became quite heated. Those staunch botanists who seemed unable to march forward with the times, with the rest of Europe, were still clinging to the Linnaean system of classification. Many of the botanists in the room were adamant in defending the Sexual system, which Lord Pemberly was arguing against. A handful of the others, including Katherine and Heath, were firm in the opinion it was time to move past the sex of the plant and follow the Natural system of classification as first created by Antoine-Laurent de Jussieu. The problem was, naturalists couldn't agree on all of the definitions and principles.

As the heated debate closed, they rose to exit the hall. Still discussing the division of the naturalists, they arrived on the street.

"Perhaps we should get a cup of tea? It is a gorgeous afternoon, and we could stroll down the way to a little tea shop if you would like," he suggested as he waved his arm to his left indicating the direction in a general sense.

"That would be lovely." She agreed as they turned to stroll.

Upon arriving at the tea shop, Heath ensured they had a seat in the back so Kat wouldn't feel too exposed. They ordered their tea and biscuits, and then resumed their discussion.

"I simply don't understand why they cannot progress beyond the Sexual system of classification. In truth the number of stamens and pistils should not matter in the classification of a flowering plant," she said, her voice growing rough and firm as her passion took hold.

Heath perceived a hint of the Kat he recognized from The Market under the false shell of Lady Drummond. His cock stirred to life. Transfixed by the flash in her brown eyes, he absorbed her passion, listening as she railed against the strictures and mores of Victorian England. Her rant veered away from botany and into deeper, more personal territory.

"Truly, it is wrong that I'm painted with the same brush as the man I was married to. Why can I not be seen and judged as an individual rather than the property of a man?" Her eyes opened wide and her hand flew to cover her mouth as it dawned on her what she had said publicly in mixed company. Her face flushed a delicate shade of rose pink as the girl delivered the tea and biscuits.

Without batting an eye, Heath proceeded to serve her and give her a moment to collect herself. "One lump or two?" He clenched a sugar cube with the serving tongs over her cup.

"One, please. Lord Heathington, I must apologize for my outburst."

"No. Not if that is how you feel. I don't disagree with you in the slightest. I believe a woman should be allowed the same rights and freedoms as a man." He held her gaze with his as she took the tea cup from him. There was a brief moment of connection via porcelain that held them both in thrall. Then a crash of dishes sounded nearby breaking the spell.

They both chuckled and sipped the hot brew.

He pitched his voice below the hum of the crowd. "How are you faring these last few days?"

"As if we haven't visited. I am quite well, if a trifle tense." The pink stain returned to her cheeks.

"I am glad you are well. I am looking forward to this evening. I want to see you spread across a bed for me again."

Her pink tongue peeked out past her lips to swipe across them, coating them with a short-lived gloss. "Oh. My. That sounds promising."

His cock was now at full attention as her husky, desire laden voice rasped across his raw senses. He wanted to kiss her and promise her an eternity of pleasure. Wanted to beat his chest and yell. She was his woman. He needed to claim her, mark her as his. Not in the societal way of women as chattel, but in the most basic elemental way as a man and a woman.

She was still staring down at her tea cup as he managed to tame the emotions rolling through him. "It is a promise of pleasure to come."

"I am not sure I can wait." Her breath came in shallow gasps, proving she was as affected as him.

He leaned close, to whisper in her ear. "Before dinner tonight I want you to touch yourself, give yourself the pleasure you need. It will ease your tension until I can take proper care of you. Can you do that, Kat?"

Her wide eyes were glazed with need. "I can, but I will be wishing it were you."

Something inside unfurled and came alive with those words. He needed this woman to be a permanent part of his life. Settling back in his chair, he struggled to rein in his desire and regulate his voice. "I will see you at dinner tonight."

"Of course." She paused, disoriented by the change in conversation. "I'm looking forward to meeting your ward, and then there is the rest of the evening." Her smile was sultry and filled with desire.

CHAPTER SIX

K atherine sat in the bathtub soaking and reflecting on her afternoon with Heath. He was like a rose. Every time you plucked a petal there was another layer to discover. Today she had seen that mix of Sir and the urbane Lord Heathington. She remembered the charged conversation over tea and her need resurged. Her nipples puckered just above the water line as a dull ache burned between her thighs. Her hands seemed to move without a conscious decision on her part. Images of her time with Heath flashed through her mind. She cupped her breasts, squeezing her nipples. Sensation shot from there to her mons and the pressure built. One hand slithered down below the water line to cover the ache. She pressed her hand against the pulsing and rubbed. More. She needed Heath. Needed to be filled by him.

She moaned and pinched her nipple as a digit slipped between the lips of her pussy. The pad of her finger came in contact with her clit, causing a jolt of pleasure to skitter through her body. She pressed more, dragging her finger over that point of pure pleasure again and again. Her own moisture seeped out and helped slick her way. Moving her hand to the other breast, she pinched and rolled that nipple and her body warmed with need.

A low moan escaped her as she pictured Heath driving his cock into her from behind. She loved his rough and ready ways, not always wanting a gentle lover. Writhing against her hand, she dipped two fingers into her entrance and gathered more cream to lubricate her clit. Her fingers stroked languidly over the swollen nub. Then her need peaked and as she pinched her nipple hard, she raked her fingers over her clit again and again until she felt wave after wave of warm pleasure roll over her and through her.

As Heath had promised, it took the edge off her immediate need. What he hadn't told her was that it would heighten her desire to feel him buried in her, filling her.

Dinner was going to be interminable.

She rose and let the cooled water sluice down her body. Stepping out, she dried herself and set about dressing for the evening's entertainment. This was the first time Heath was introducing her to friends and family. It was another step toward building a public relationship. But, did she really know this complicated man who reveled in domination, yet seemed entranced by her intelligence and desire to learn?

A few hours later she stood on his doorstep, her knees knocking. The door opened and a youngish butler bowed and welcomed her. He took her cloak and escorted her into the front parlor.

Heath strode across the room and greeted her warmly. "Katherine. It is excellent to see you again. Please come and meet my family." He tucked her hand in the crook of his arm and urged her to where a man and two ladies stood talking.

"Dorian, you remember Lady Drummond?"

"Of course. It is very nice to see you again." He smiled and kissed her hand.

"Lord Tarkenton, it is splendid to see you again." Kat curtsied and then retrieved her hand.

Heath glared at his cousin, but moved on. "This is Dorian's wife, Lady Cassandra Tarkenton." The dark haired beauty curtsied and smiled.

"Welcome, Lady Drummond. It is a pleasure to meet someone Heath holds in such high esteem."

Kat's face warmed with the kind words. "It is delightful to meet you as well. I have heard much of your youthful exploits. I fear I am a bit jealous of your zest for life."

"Oh, I am sure whatever you heard was sufficiently exaggerated to warrant a correction in the future, and please call me Cassie."

"And this image of youthful decorum is my ward and niece, Lady Christine Tarkenton. Don't let her fool you." Heath grinned at her look of outrage.

"Uncle Heath, how could you. I was working so hard to act proper tonight. Lady Drummond, it is a pleasure to meet you. Although, unlike my aunt, I know nothing about you. My uncle has been very tight lipped lately." She slashed a grin at him, unmistakable in its challenge.

"It is very nice to meet you." Katherine glanced at Heath and the knot of tension eased as she realized how content he appeared. They chatted for a bit before the remaining guests arrived.

Not long after dinner, the guests departed for other entertainments including Dorian, Cassie, and Christine. Katherine found herself utterly alone with Heath.

"Kat, I have been dying to hold you all night." He hauled her into his arms and kissed her lips with incredible tenderness. Her heart skipped a beat. "Come with me." He took her hand and led her to the foyer. The butler waited there with their cloaks. Settled inside a rented hack, their thighs pressed together as they sat on the bench. Heath knocked on the roof and called out the address for The Market.

Alone, he pulled her closer against his side and wrapped an arm around her shoulders. "Did you do as you were bade this afternoon?"

Kat's face heated at his question. "Yes, Sir, I did."

"Mmm...very good. Tell me what you did."

His scent surrounded her. Intoxicated her to the point she could no longer remember why she should be ashamed. "I touched myself as I lay in the tub thinking of you. Thinking of us, together."

"Yes. Did you pinch your own nipples?" His voice rasped.

"I did." Her whole body flushed.

"Did you touch your pussy? Slide your fingers inside of your tight channel?" His breathing had grown labored, as had hers.

"Yes. I wished it was you; ached for you, even after coming."

Heath groaned in the dark beside her. "You will have to show me sometime. I would very much enjoy watching you touch your pussy."

Could she do that? Could she touch herself in front of Sir? Yes. Deep down Kat knew if he asked her to, she would do it. For him.

The hack stopped and he pulled her hood up hiding her face. He tied a mask over his own and led her inside. Kat thought she might not make it to their room before her need took over. Heath led her through his entry. A fire roared waiting for them as the chamber glowed with soft light. He pressed her against the wall, trapping her between his arms and ravaged her mouth. She opened for him, let his tongue invade her, taste her. Trembling with the need to feel his skin against hers, she reached up and pushed his coat off his shoulders. He dropped his arms letting her push the garment off. Breaking the kiss, he spun her around and pressed her against the wall.

"Don't move." His fingers began working at the fastenings of her gown. Soon she found herself nude and crushed against his fully clothed body. The sensation of her skin chafing against the fabric he still wore was like tiny jolts of electricity all over. His hands roamed over her form, touching her shoulders, breasts, hips, and then the globes of her bottom.

She moaned. How long would she have to endure such exquisite torture?

"Tonight I have something special in mind for you. Do you trust me?" The dark edge to his voice was intoxicating.

"I know you would never harm me. I trust you, Sir." The understanding of how deep her trust ran was shocking to her own psyche. Rocked to her core by the knowledge, she missed the transition from the wall to a tall bench at the foot of the bed. There he bent her over the surface with a pile of pillows under her hips and stomach to support her weight while allowing her to keep her legs straight. Then she watched him tie each wrist to a post of the bed, stretching her forward so her breasts hung free.

Kat had never been so exposed and vulnerable. Splayed out for their pleasure, she experienced a sense of peace and contentment that she could never have expected. Heath ran his hands over her backside, squeezing each cheek gently. "You have such a beautiful bottom, Kat."

"Thank you, Sir." Anticipation stirred deep in her belly, the waiting an intensifier of her need.

"Now, as I recall I owe you a spanking."

"You do, Sir?"

"You lied to me, Kat. You had no errands to run this morning did you?"

Unable to see his face in her position, she had no idea if he was truly angry. "I'm sorry, Sir."

"Why did you lie to me, Kat?" His hand stroked her right cheek down to her thigh. A gentle caress.

"I was afraid. This has happened so fast. I needed to still feel in control of something." She cringed at the hitch in her voice.

He said nothing, the silence stretched taut with waiting. "I understand. Do you wish to stop now?"

She heard the fear in his voice. It would hurt him if she wanted to stop, but he would release her. That knowledge alone reaffirmed her earlier revelation. "No. I understand now how much I trust you. Need you, Sir."

His breath released in a soft gush as though he'd held it. "I am gratified by your trust and understanding. It would devastate me if I harmed you physically or emotionally. You have become so much more than our contract." He pressed a soft kiss to her lower back. "Now, I must punish you for your doubt and deception."

"Please, Sir." Her heart hammered against her chest. The first blow fell. Heat bloomed in her backside as her core softened and heated. Three more blows landed and then he pinched and rolled a nipple, causing her to cry out in pleasure.

"What have you learned, Kat?" His velvety voice wrapped around her as he squeezed the other nipple.

"I shall not tell lies, Sir." A tremor of need rolled through her body.

"Very good." He plunged two fingers into her pussy. Her body clamped down on the penetration, squeezing him. He pumped into her channel, wreaking havoc on her overwrought senses.

She couldn't take much more of his attention without exploding. "Please, Sir."

"Please what?" He demanded.

"Please make me come, Sir." Her hips pressed back as much as they could on his fingers, but he withdrew.

"Not yet." She heard him step away from the bed, rummage in a drawer, and then he was back.

"It is time for your surprise. These past few weeks have given you time to adjust and now it is time to push your boundaries again."

Something thick and cool began coating her rosebud. Need had her clenching, trying to draw in his fingers. She wanted to be filled by him, craved it with a desperation she could not explain. Then her patience was rewarded, and he slipped two fingers past the tight ring of muscle. Mewling in pleasure, she again tried to push back against him. He worked them in and out of her backside, driving her closer to the edge. Just as she thought he was going to let her peak, he withdrew his fingers. She half lay there, her legs shaking with desire and her weight, as she came down from her near miss.

Dazed and foggy with desire, she reined in the impulse to beg. Begging would not sway this man when he was set on a course for their pleasure. Her pussy throbbed with the urge to be filled, nipples ached to be touched. And still he tormented her.

"I need you to relax, Kat. Are you ready?"

"Yes, Sir. I'm ready for you."

He chuckled, damn him. "Not me, sweet. I am going to stretch your bottom with this."

A jade dildo, beautifully carved, appeared before her eyes. It was Chinese with a dragon head carved in the hilt. The opposite end was a few inches of smooth stone that mushroomed at the tip replicating a penis. The dragon head was worn to rounded edges from a few thousand years of use. Her whole body shook with the idea of taking that within her body. Her juices dribbled down her inner thigh as he circled around and came between her spread legs. More of the thick, cool salve coated her hole before the tip of the hard cylinder pressed against her.

She took a deep breath and willed her body to relax. As the stone slid past the tight ring, she concentrated on relaxing around it. Focusing, she ignored the stretched burning sensation that came as it sank deeper into her body. Her backside felt so full, so uncomfortably full that she couldn't help but squirm.

"Dear God you are a sight. Do you know how you look bent over with that dildo lodged in your backside? Arms stretched out forcing your breasts to dangle as though begging for me to touch them?" His voice caressed her, even as his words pushed her desire up another notch.

His hands found her breasts, pulling and tugging on her nipples. Then he trailed his fingers down her spine to cup her cheeks, spreading them so he could see the toy lodged firmly in her derriere.

His breath hitched. "Now, I am going to have a sip of whiskey as you adjust."

Need leant a raspy quality to his voice and a jerkiness to the quality of his movements. The clink of glass came before the sound of liquid being poured. Then a chair scraped across the rug stopping where she was displayed. The burning had eased, leaving her feeling the contrast of the fullness between her cheeks and the emptiness in her pussy. It was pleasure and torment all rolled in to one. How could she let him expose her like this? How could she find such pleasure in having her weakness revealed? All sense of time slipped away. Her awareness narrowed to the male presence nearby, to the driving compulsion to please him.

"It seems someone is enjoying my surprise." His finger trailed up her inner thigh, collecting her moisture that had dripped down her leg. "Mmm. Sweet is the right name for you. Like ripe berries in summer." He repeated the scooping of her juice and held his finger in front of her. "Taste how sweet you are."

Eagerness had her licking his fingers hungrily. He pulled away, and to her great relief she heard his clothing rustling and then dropping on the floor. Then he was behind her, and the first slice of pleasure cut through her with a twist of the dildo before he pulled it out. His tongue plunged into her pussy while he slid the dildo back in her tight hole. Pleasure streaked through her, would have taken her to her knees but for the pillows.

He worked the long stone in and out of her body in sync with his tongue lapping at her honey. A scream reverberated off the walls around them when she shattered. Her channel spasmed around his tongue as her bottom clenched the invading jade. Wave after wave of pleasure swamped her until he gave her one last lick. "Thank you, Sir," she murmured. Gratitude swamped her, followed by a pleasant lethargy.

A light swat on her cheek got her attention. "We are not through yet, my sweet."

The swollen head of his cock slid through her throbbing folds. Still filled by the stone, the idea of taking him at the same time had her desire stirring again. He pushed into her in a long slow assault that had her crying out in pleasure. Filled to the brim with Heath's cock and the dildo, she thought she would expire from the bliss.

Then he pulled the jade back and pushed it in, while dragging his cock out of her pussy. He worked an alternating pattern that she found herself shoving back in an attempt to drive each cock deeper into her body. Wrapping her hands around the cravats lashing her to the bed, she gained some leverage to drive her body backward.

The first spark ricocheted through her Heath's iron flesh slamming into her body. Lost in the pleasurable assault of the man and the toy, her orgasm burst over her with a force that rocked her soul. Wave after wave of pleasure peaked and then lulled only to peak again with the continued thrust of his cock into her sheath.

With a shout, he withdrew himself and the dildo from her body, and spent his cum on her back and derriere, rubbing the head across her sensitized flesh. Both panting from the exertion, he slumped over her back for a moment.

Lost, she found her wrists released and her back cleaned. Heath rolled her over, and lifted her boneless body into his arms. She snuggled closer against him before the softness of the bed cradled her. Everything around her was a haze punctuated by Heath. A touch. A gentle murmur. A whiff of his essence. Then his big warm body cocooned hers and she slept.

CHAPTER SEVEN

Heath sat across the carriage from her, a calming presence. He was, as expected, a demanding lover. He'd taken her in all of the ways he promised he would, and in one he may not have intended. Katherine was afraid she was falling in love with him. She found it hard to credit herself, but despite all her best intentions he was razing her barriers a little at a time. With him, she felt protected. Safe. It was a feeling she was growing to revel in, and one she didn't wish to give up, even if it were to cost her freedom.

The vehicle halted. With a sigh she gathered her skirts and alighted with Heath's assistance. Amidst a swish of satin she entered the Carrington's home. Friends of her parents, she considered herself obligated to attend the rare dinner party they hosted. At least their invitations were genuine. She hoped no one would be too rude this evening; it would be a shame to upset her hostess.

Entering the salon on Heath's arm caused all eyes to swivel in her direction. Being the center of attention was unnerving.

"Breathe, Katherine. You look beautiful. The burgundy gown makes your eyes glow."

"Thank you, Heath." Her heart fluttered in her chest. Would everyone know they were lovers?

"Come, my sweet, I would like to introduce you to a few friends." He ushered her toward a clump of men.

Introductions were made, followed by an awkward exchange of pleasantries. Then Heath's cousins, Lord and Lady Tarkenton, appeared. "Good evening My Lord." She dipped into a graceful curtsy. Relief at the arrival of a pair of friendly faces calmed her nerves.

"Lady Drummond, how nice to see you once again." Lord Tarkenton greeted her and cast a sly look at Heath who remained serene in the face of his scrutiny.

"What a beautiful gown. Is that a Madame Le Fluer design?" Cassandra fingered the lace trim on Katherine's sleeve.

"It is. You have an excellent eye. I was afraid it might be over the top, but I so loved the fabric I couldn't resist when she showed me the design." They spoke for a bit when Kat excused herself to speak with Lady Carrington.

"Your gathering seems to be quite a success."

Her hostess grinned. "Once word got out that Lord Heathington would be attending, a slew of acceptances appeared on my doorstep. How are you faring? You appear to be recovering from your grief."

Kat hesitated, daring a glance at Heath from across the room. Her heart sped up. "Widowhood agrees with me."

"I dare say your parents would be pleased to see that considering how disagreeable marriage turned out to be. But don't let that rotten apple spoil the barrel. Men do have their uses." Lady Carrington quirked an eyebrow up and giggled as she sailed away to greet a newly arrived guest.

With another lingering look at the man who dominated her body and her thoughts, Kat sought out the fresh evening air. Alone on the veranda that overlooked a spectacular night blooming garden, she lost herself in the botanical splendor.

Disappointed that she could not explore the torch lit grounds on her own, it simply wasn't safe when one might be accosted by a rake, she determined to insist Heath take her for a walk before they departed. Absorbed by the notion of a stroll in the gardens with him, she didn't notice the man who'd stepped out on to the wide terrace with her.

"Good evening." He flashed a smile in the dark and nodded.

"Good evening, sir," she said, nonplussed by the stranger's unexpected arrival, and more so by his pleasant greeting. She realized he mustn't know her identity.

"That is a lovely gown you are wearing. The burgundy makes your eyes sparkle so much I could not help but notice you inside."

"Thank you for the kind words." The hairs on her arms rose in alarm at receiving such a compliment from a complete stranger. Flustered, she started for the doors to the salon. She wanted to find Heath, to stand near him and let him banish this person from her vicinity. Before she made it to the pool of light that spilled from the doorway, the man had latched on to her arm and hauled her into the shadows.

Katherine's heart pounded against her ribs so hard she swore a herd of stampeding horses plunged through her chest. Fear choked her as the iron band of his arms clamped down around her, imprisoning her between his body and the stone wall of the house. She clutched his jacket trying to fend him off, but to no avail. With a swift, menacing grace he lowered his mouth.

In a futile effort, her fists gripped his lapels and pressed against his chest. Heath. She needed him. Where was he? He would trounce the cad assaulting her in a trice, if only he would appear. Despite her inability to scream effectively, she fought until her arms ached with the strain. Her attacker's hands clamped down on her upper arms as he used his chest to crowd her against the wall. The stone, as unforgiving as it was uneven, left her with an aggressive male crushed against her, and a sharp brick jabbing into her back. The unforgiving wall paired with the manacles he called hands left no doubt she would be in a sorry state come the morning no matter how this ended. Anger at the indignity of the attack leeched into her muscles, renewing her strength.

The low murmur of male voices had him shift their tussle deeper into the shadows, drawing her away from the stone wall. His hands relocated, his arms wrapping around her, imprisoning her more capably while allowing him the access he needed to finally kiss her. Panic flooding her with adrenaline, she attempted to free herself again, but found her ribs crushed as he leaned in to fuse their lips. She jerked her head to the right and avoided the unwanted intimacy, crying out. "Stop."

Undaunted he tried again, his brutish kiss finding its target. He ground her lips into her teeth, cutting the inside of her mouth. Tears of rage and frustration seeped from her eyes once she realized there would be no stopping him. Resignation led to a full mental retreat while his tongue poked against her sealed lips and her back bent nearly in half. This was it. There would be no recovering from this socially and perhaps not mentally. No man would have her after this, not even Heath.

Then, all of a sudden, he was gone.

Heath's fist slammed into the cad pawing his woman. *His woman.* When he'd caught a glimpse of burgundy satin and realized the bastard had Kat cornered, his heart had nearly split his chest wide open.

Heath gathered Kat into his arms as his cousin picked up Mr. Richard Kemp, second son of the Baron Latimer, from the ground and proceeded to thrash him soundly. Not wanting her to be further traumatized, Heath eased her up from the ground and cuddled her into his warmth while she collected herself. She seemed distressed and much disoriented by the whole experience, not that he was surprised. Men just didn't attack women.

Dorian exchanged a few words with the cad. "Whatever possessed you to attack a lady?" The question was punctuated with a sharp jab to the man's chin.

"I figured she was as hungry for sex as I am. Since I've been infected with the pox no woman will lie with me. She seemed the answer to my prayers when I overheard some of the old ladies talking about her." He spit out some blood as he gripped his side and doubled over.

"Syphilis? Is that what they are saying about her? Because of her dead husband?" Dorian raised his arm to strike another blow.

"Cry off! I'm sorry I touched her. Please." Kemp begged then took the opportunity to limp off when Dorian hesitated.

Heath nodded to let him go and turned back to see that Kat appeared to have gathered her composure, although she was still very pale. "Dorian, please go find our cloaks and send my coach around to the back mews. She shouldn't have to face those people like this."

"Of course. I'll return in a moment."

Dorian was back within a few moments with their cloaks. Heath lifted her into his arms and caught a soft whimper when he squeezed her ribs. She was in pain. He wanted to drag the idiot back and thrash him again.

"I'm sorry. Here, let me loosen my hold a bit. Hang on around my neck."

He strode off the terrace and across the back gardens to find the stables in the rear mews. A few minutes later the coach rumbled up and he deposited Kat inside before climbing in himself. He settled next to her, tucking her against him so he could feel her. Neither spoke as they rolled through the streets of London. When they arrived at her home, he helped her out of the carriage and picked her up..

With her clutched to him, there was no mistaking the shudder that racked her form. Guilt settled like an albatross around his neck, straining his muscles in an effort to hold his head up with any dignity. She required a hot bath and bed without delay. He could at least see to this since he failed to protect her earlier. Her butler opened the door and stepped aside letting them enter.

"My Lady!" The horrified man cried out as he took in Kat's appearance.

Standing in the foyer Heath glanced around as various servants filtered in to see what the ruckus was about. "Which way to Lady Drummond's bedroom?" Heath demanded.

"My Lord, please, we'll take—" The butler tried to retrieve Kat from his arms.

"Kat, which way to your room?" The affable Lord Heathington slipped away, replaced by Sir.

Kat recognized and responded to him as she always did. "Upstairs, third door on the left, Sir." Exhausted, she rested her head on his shoulder.

His chest tightened, constricted with worry. What if he hadn't found her in time or someone else, less sympathetic, had discovered her? The desire to protect, to secure was overriding every other instinct he had.

Katherine's savior marched upstairs with an inexplicable energy and located her bedroom. Mrs. Willis, her housekeeper, hovered in the background, confused by his taking charge, and yet, unable to gainsay him.

He set her on the bed. "Your Lady requires a bath. Please have one readied straightaway. I suggest adding some oils to help her relax, and anything you have to help deter bruising."

Mrs. Willis nodded and disappeared.

Katherine's voice broke.

"Thank you, Heath. Thank you so much."

"God, Kat, I was almost too late. I damn near left you there thinking it was two lovers in need of privacy. Don't thank me."

Sore and shaken, she looked into his eyes and saw his torment. "No. You are my savior. You swooped in and rescued me."

"Lady Drummond's bath is ready. If you'll leave us...." Mrs. Willis trailed off.

"No. I will help her with her bath." Heath was implacable.

The housekeeper gasped.

"Mrs. Willis, Heath will assist me. If you would be so good as to bring up some tea and a snack, I think I could use a bit of something restorative." Katherine wanted to placate her loyal servant, but settled for keeping her busy.

"Very well ma'am." She left, disapproval plain across her face.

Heath helped her sit up and then played ladies maid and undressed her. Naked, she found herself scooped up and carried to the bathing room next door.

Once in the soothing warmth of the tub, she took stock. Her arms hurt, her sides hurt, and her mouth hurt. All in all not the best reckoning she could have hoped for.

"How are you doing?" Concern laced Heath's voice.

"I'll live. A bit sore and shaken up, but no lasting damage I think." She squeezed his hand.

He took the rag he had soaped and rubbed her back, then her arms, chest, and legs. His gentle touch was soothing to her sensitive skin. Her psyche had fared much better, bolstered by their weeks of intimacy and conversation.

"May I stay with you tonight? Hold you while you sleep?" His request came low, in a reverent tone.

If he stayed the night everyone would know. "I suppose it won't matter much now. You're already here in my bath taking care of me. And frankly, I would like nothing more than to sleep in your arms. But what of Christine? Won't she worry?"

"She will be fine. I will send a note around letting her know I have been unavoidably detained. The worst that will happen is she will demand once again to know who my woman is." His smile warmed her heart.

"And what will you tell her?" Curiosity egged her on.

"That she is cheeky and inappropriate. Of course she'll figure it all out eventually." He lifted her out of the tub and stood her up. With brisk, efficient movements he dried her off and whisked her to the bed. With her deposited between the sheets, he fetched a cup of tea and a small plate of biscuits.

Then, he proceeded to strip down and join her. The reassuring warmth of his body pressed to hers settled creating a sense of peace and safety.

A few days later, Heath waited for nightfall before departing for The Market. Tonight he would ask Kat to marry him. Unsure of her answer, even though he knew she cared, his nerves were twisted in knots. In his dressing room, each piece of clothing plopped on the floor as he crossed to the closet. Pausing, he reminded himself to slow down. Calmly sliding a robe over his arms, he lashed it in front and stalked to the door. Two people were moving around in the adjoining room. Pacing away from the door, he took a few deep breaths. The next time he approached and listened, all was quiet. He entered.

Kat was in the center of the bed, her arms restrained above by leather straps. She wore the outfit he'd provided for their first encounter after signing the contract. Her breasts were exposed, nipples hard with excitement. Her labored breath, drawn in deep gasps, served as a counterpoint to her hips writhing and squirming with need.

He growled in response to her obvious need and his cock rose to full attention. Shedding the robe as he stalked across the room, he arrived naked at her side. He stood over her, absorbing the glorious sight of her overwhelming desire. Despite his plans to be gentle, she was in no condition for it. And now, neither was he.

"Whatever has brought you to this state?" He stretched out and pinched one nipple causing her to arch up off the bed.

She remained silent, just scrutinized him with her big brown eyes.

"Answer me," he demanded as his inner beast surged to the fore.

Still she refused.

"Very well. You do know what this means?" He was angry at her refusal, but excited by the notion of punishing her for her disobedience.

"Yes, Sir." Her voice was husky to his ears, as though she had smoked a box of cigars.

Without a word, he released her hands and led her to a bench. There he took a seat and laid her across his thighs. With two quick strikes he smacked her once on each cheek.

"You know you're to answer me honestly at all times. Do you not?" Two more blows rained down on her pinkening backside.

"Yes, Sir." Her breathing had grown ragged.

He slid two fingers into her wet pussy as he spanked her four more times in an alternating pattern. She moaned low in her throat as he worked his fingers in and out of her slick passage. She was so wet he groaned knowing he would not be able to hold out from driving into her.

He spanked her more, harder, quicker. She cried out in sheer ecstasy.

A surge of love for the bold woman in his lap choked the air fighting to reach his lungs. Reining in the flood of emotion, curiosity remained. "Why? Why did you not answer me?" He withdrew his fingers until just the tips rested inside of her warmth.

"I wanted this." She glanced back over her shoulder as a tear slipped out of the corner of her eye and down her flushed cheek.

"Kat, you need only ask. Do you not understand I would do anything for you? For your pleasure." His voice was hoarse with feeling.

"Please. More." She begged and wiggled her backside. Lost to the pleading in her voice, he initiated a steady rhythm of spanking in perfect sync with the slide of his fingers in and out of her body. She moaned louder as the tension built. She was close. He withdrew his fingers and ceased the spanking. Her bottom glowed bright red, and he feared he'd come, prodded by nothing more than looking at her backside and hearing the heavy pant of her desire. Her body grew taut, as though she was working very hard to restrain a protest at his cessation.

This. This was the punishment and the path to even greater pleasure for them both. By denying his own body's demands while meeting hers' he could begin to cleanse his guilt, even as their individual quintessence blurred. Each of them a half of the greater whole. One heart. One soul.

He helped her to stand on legs as weak as a new foal and then rose himself. His cock pointed the way as they shuffled back to the bed. With her settled back in place, the restraints buckled snug around her wrists and held her in place. Cheeks flushed to match the glow of her bottom, her hair cascaded around her on the sheets. Her beauty robbed him of breath. Heath went to the wine decanter in the corner and poured a glass for them. He returned and offered her the rim, giving her one sip, and then another. He removed the glass, took his own sip, and set it aside.

Equilibrium restored and no longer able to resist, he leaned over and sucked a nipple into his mouth. Her silky skin held a faint sweetness that teased his taste buds. The pebbled tip of her breast swelled and teased him, entreating him to roll it around with his tongue, flick it over and over. Then, with a temperate force, he bit down.

"More please," she rasped as her upper body arched into him, burrowing her breast further into his greedy mouth. Desire lanced through his groin tightening his balls, but he refused to be weak. She deserved all the pleasure he could give.

Shifting to the other tip he delivered the same treatment, loving the feel of her nipple on his tongue, the taste of her skin in his mouth. As a groan tore from her, he rose up and glanced around the bed. He took the bolster from the foot and had her lift her bottom so he could tuck it under her. Placing her feet so her ankles rested against the bolster forced her legs to spread wide so he could both admire her pussy and have complete access. Content for the moment to just look, he settled at the end of the bed and sipped the wine.

He wanted to bury his tongue inside her, then his cock, and then he wanted to fulfill the promise he made her on the first night. He'd prepared her to take him, to let him push past her tight little rosebud. With his goal in sight anticipation threatened his tenuous control. The time had come to show her all the pleasure they could experience together.

He offered her the glass, but she shook her head no. Rising up, he set it aside again and came back between her legs. Licking her, tasting her was one of his favorite things to do. To do it with her restrained and exposed like this brought to life one of his darker fantasies. It was almost more than he could bear.

She was amazing, her strength and resilience were inspiring. It awed him that such a woman chose to give up control to him. Trusted him.

He let his tongue trace a lazy trail up her thigh to her soaked center. There, he used the flat span to lick a wide, wet, and warm trail up her exposed slit. She groaned in pleasure. He repeated the motion a few times and then drove so deep inside her channel he could reach no further. Her body attempted to squeeze him, to try to draw him deeper, but it wasn't possible. He withdrew and focused on her swollen clit, flicking it with the edge of his tongue as he worked two fingers into her channel again. Her hips started thrusting, trying to meet each sweep and stroke that carried her higher. . Heath considered letting her come like this, but he wanted to take her to even greater heights so he held back as her movements grew more frantic.

"No." She whimpered. "Please. I need you."

Heath's knees grew weak. Grateful he was not standing; he knelt over her panting as he worked at reining in his emotions. Total focus was requisite to ensure they wrung every granule of pleasure from their loving. A moment later, he collected himself and repositioned, as eager to be inside her as she was to have him there. In a single swift thrust, he was seated balls deep inside her. Her body clutched at him, worked his cock over until he worried he might not last for all he wanted to do. Through sheer force of will, he tamped his surging lust down and pumped into her body driving his cock deep into her warmth.

"Yes! Yes, Sir!" She cried out in joy as he pistoned in and out of her pussy. Clenching every muscle he had, he withdrew from her body as she neared her release. Her dismay, palpable and fierce, clawed at his restraint.

"I made you a promise I've yet to fulfill. We have worked toward you growing accustomed to the penetration of your backside; tonight I want to take you. Will you deny me?" His voice was gruff, commanding even to his own ears. He was on the razor's edge of control he had always feared, but somehow with Kat it seemed right. There was no fear in her steady gaze. All he saw was a love and desire that matched his own.

"I am yours to command." She confirmed for him.

He leaned over to the night stand and found a jar of salve to smooth his way in. He tipped her hips up just a fraction more, scooping some of the cream up he rubbed it against her rear entrance. Her cheeks were still red from his spankings as he slid one finger inside. She gasped at the intrusion, ever tight back there. He was going to hurt her, but they would both find pleasure for the pain.

Shoving aside any doubts, he worked the finger in and out until she relaxed. He added a second finger, spreading them to stretch the ring of muscle. She moaned as he added the third. He was amazed by this woman. She was more than he'd ever expected, more than he could have imagined of Lady Drummond the wallflower. Having discovered the strong, intelligent woman she hid, it was difficult to remember the mousy woman he first knew. Found it impossible not to be drawn to her beauty and unconditional acceptance of his primal essence.

He supposed she was as ready as she'd ever be, and so slathered the salve on himself and set it aside. Rising up on to his knees between her legs, he positioned the head of his throbbing cock at her opening and pushed against the tight ring. Her body tensed with a sharp inhale as he penetrated her with the wide head of his sex.

Bloody hell she's so tight. His mind reeled with the grip her body had on him. Gritting his teeth against the surge of lust, he edged forward bit by bit, deeper into her bottom. She moaned again as he sank further into her until his thighs were nestled against hers. He could go no further as her body quaked around him. His cock rippled in response, aching to finish.

He took a long slow breath and looked at Kat. Her eyes fixed on him, wide with awe, and so much more. "Are you all right, Kat?"

"Yes, Sir. So much better than all right." Her breathy response made his balls tighten up and his mind scream: *more.* Carefully he withdrew until just the head was inside her back passage. Then he slid forward again with a guttural groan. Soon he was pumping in and out of her tight hole, the friction of her body clamping down on him had him close to being over the edge faster than he'd have liked. He reached down between her thighs and shoved three of his fingers inside her as he worked his cock in and out.

Her body shuddered and she cried out louder than ever before as she burst, her juices flooding his fingers and running down her ass to surround his cock. He yelled out as his balls drew tight and he shot his cum inside of her. Racked by physical and soul deep spasms, he collapsed forward onto her body. His control shattered, he felt like a single exposed nerve. Love for his woman seemed to spill over from his body to hers.

They laid there panting and replete for quite a while.

Sated, and more entranced than ever before, Heath wanted to clean up so they could talk.

Wrapped in robes and each sipping a glass of wine as they sat before the fire, Heath cleared his throat. "Kat, these past weeks have been more than I could have hoped for. I can't imagine my life without you in it, now I have found you." He set his glass aside and dropped to one knee, legs shaking in fear of her rejection. Taking her wine and setting it next to his, he continued. "Would you honor me by becoming my Countess?" He pulled a carved wooden box from his robe pocket and opened it to reveal a huge sapphire surrounded by diamonds. Still emotionally raw from their joining, he clenched the box and waited.

Her breath caught as she stared at him, her gaze fathomless. Would she do forever? Could he survive without her? No. He would fight for her to his last breath. She was his.

"Kat, if you'll let me, I'll always protect you." His jaw tensed and his heart squeezed.

She shook her head. "No. I'll not have you any more tarnished by me than you already are in society. They'll never accept me again. I am ruined by my profligate husband. I don't want anyone else touched by his poison." She stood and shifted toward the fire, hiding her face.

His primal self screamed and clawed in denial. With a Herculean strength of will, he restrained the instinct to lash her to the bed and master her body until she recognized that she belonged to him. He trembled with the effort, and the pain of the rejection of his love. "Kat, please, don't deny me out of hand. It's my choice to risk the wrath of society, my choice whom I marry. I choose you. You or no one." His heart pounded as he prayed he could convince her to listen to her heart.

Turning, she pulled the lapels of her robe closer together, clutching them at her neck. "How can you say that? Until you have experienced such isolation you cannot know of what you speak."

"Ha! I do know it. I've always been isolated from them, if not in an obvious way. Do you not, like them, wonder why I have never married?"

"I assume you have your reasons, which are none of my business."

He drew a slow deep breath. This was his opening to convince her. "Not true. In a strange twist you are central to my reason. Tell me, do you enjoy the time we spend together? The nature of our interactions?"

"Very much. I feel safe, cared for, protected when I am with you."

Pleasure at her words pierced his heart and strengthened his resolve. "I'm glad. I feel strong, needed, and desired when I'm with you. I don't feel the shame and confusion I often experienced as a young man when the need to be with a woman, as I am with you, called upon me. For years I refused to consider marriage for fear of terrifying some poor girl. Not until you did I feel normal, balanced, at ease. Last week at the lecture and then during tea, I found the same peace with you in public as I do at The Market. I need that in my life. I need you."

Her eyes widened, giving her a wild look. Then she sank into the chair, still mute.

Hope burbled in his chest, made him ache to hold her and sooth the turmoil in her eyes. "Kat, I love you. I love that you share the same ideas as I on botany. I love how you feel right in my arms as we waltz. I love that you have strong opinions and are willing to share them with me. I love your smile, the way your eyes sparkle both when you argue and when I make love to you." His breathing had changed to a deep drawing of air.

Her body shook as the first tear slipped down her cheek. The moisture remained a moment before evaporating. Then there were too many, and they trickled together to form rivulets down her face. Heath reached for her. Pain and fear curdled his belly, made him desperate. "Please. Tell me you feel something, anything for me. Tell me you'll be my bride." He drew her against him and squeezed, burying her face against his chest.

She squirmed in his arms a bit, then cleared her throat, and leaned back. "Yes. Yes, I will. I-I'm not sure when or how but I fell in love with you, with Sir, and then I was so confused by it I wanted to run away. But you invoke calm in my life, a peace unrivaled in all my days. I need you, too. I love you."

Heath felt the fear dissipate as love rushed in to fill his heart. His woman. They drew together, their lips meeting in a deep soul stirring kiss that held the power to last forever.

~The End~

LOVE REDEEMED

BOOK 2

DEDICATION

To my husband, thank you for being my own personal hero. Without your support and tolerance of this writing addiction I'd still be turning the pages of somebody else's book. I love you.

CHAPTER ONE

Brennan cringed as a high-pitched squeal grated across his eardrums. He much preferred visiting the tailors. Squealing was not permitted. However, in a modiste's shop such behavior was expected. He sighed and reminded himself he made a very good living by catering to every desire of the rich and entitled. Well, their every desire for sumptuous textiles and fabrics to decorate their homes and adorn their bodies.

He specialized in exquisite silks from the Far East and fine laces from France. He never allowed himself to imagine how those fabrics might appear against the creamy white skin of the noble ladies. Those kind of women, as a general rule, would not deign to acknowledge a man like himself, a man in trade. But rules were made to be broken, weren't they?

Shaking himself from his reverie, his gaze drifted to the order lying on the counter. A review of the list of fabrics confirmed everything sat in one of three warehouses around the city. Satisfied there would be no issues fulfilling the order, he turned to Madame Le Fleur's shop assistant. "Mrs. Keeling, I should be able to provide the fabrics by Thursday without a problem."

"Very good, Mr. Whitling, thank you for stopping by today." She smiled and disappeared into the back room. Brennan knocked the edges of the parchment together and tucked them into his leather folio. Another peal of delight rang through the small shop and shivered down his spine. He placed his hat atop his head and gratefully departed. Pleased with his client visits for the day, he headed to his main warehouse and office by the wharf.

A rare day in London found a blue sky, sunshine, and the air almost warm. Tucked neatly in his folio, Brennan had the biggest set of orders collected in months. All seemed right with his world except for the loneliness of his bed. While on occasion he took up with a woman or visited one of the pleasure houses, he had yet to meet the one woman who would stir his blood and maybe even his heart. His sister had discovered love. He'd seen the joy it could bring. He craved it in his own life, but all the social climbing women he met were of little interest. Particularly since he'd been ruined for most women when he spotted the most beautiful woman he'd ever seen walking down the street. None of the simpering misses who aspired to join the ranks of the Ton, or at least live as they did, could compare. Reining in his unproductive musings, he headed down the street toward his office.

There she was.

The mystery girl he had seen on Bond Street for the last few months. The sightings were always random, yet nonetheless impactful for their haphazardness.

Her bright auburn hair glinted in the sunlight, mimicking the first rays of sunset caressing the hills. Her gentle curves called out to a man's hands in a way a lithe woman's figure never did. Her corset hugged her silhouette, exaggerating the nip of her waist and flare of her hips in the most sensual way. Heedless of the grossly inappropriate time and place Brennan's cock rose to attention.

The strategic placement of his folio over his groin provided immediate cover and allowed him to think about each order taken that morning. In itemized detail. Despite his best efforts at distraction, he marked her progress until she ducked into a milliner's shop.

He decided this was going to be the day.

The day he introduced himself to the most beautiful woman, ever. No reason not to meet her when the worst-case scenario was she would dismiss him and the best was he might learn her name. By the time she emerged from the shop he had his body back under control and a plan in mind.

A few feet away, Brennan drowned in her big brown eyes set under a thick fringe of bangs. Her grin teased the corner of her lips as men stopped to tip their hats. He stepped forward to introduce himself when calamity struck.

Serena secured the band around the hatbox holding her newest acquisition before picking up her other purchases. The little top hat with a veil and trailing ribbons was a perfect match with her riding habit. She waved to the girl behind the counter and scooted out the door excited to try the hat on with her dress. The bright sunlight blinded her as she paused on the stoop of the store. In the glare of the brilliance the most handsome angel drew her eye. His blond hair glowed, a nimbus around his head, as he lifted his hat in greeting.

Serena questioned her own vision until the sun shifted, confirming there was, in fact, an incredibly handsome man staring. She started to smile at him, but became distracted by another gentleman who saluted her as he strolled by giving her an appraising eye.

She shifted her weight and quickly found herself off balance. The world reeled. Her feet were no longer solid underneath her, and her limbs waved in a wild display. Her hatbox flew off her flailing arm as her other bags dropped to the ground. Guided by the solid feel of a steady arm around her waist, she righted herself.

Her breath caught in her chest. If she did not know better, she would have thought Lettie, one of the housemaids, had laced her corset too tight. But that was not the case. The very solid and very male chest pressed against her argued the inappropriate truth of the situation. She stood on the street in the arms of a strange man.

Serena slowly peeled herself from his warmth. Hands braced on his powerful shoulders, she took a moment more to be sure her feet were steady before stepping back to see her angel had rescued her. Her heart pounded as he bent to retrieve her packages from the ground.

"Are you all right, Miss?"

For a moment, for this moment, she was a normal young woman experiencing the attentions of a handsome young man. Heat crept up her cheeks as he held her hatbox out, and the burning had nothing to do with the sun. "I-I— Yes, I am. Thank you." His blue-gray eyes seemed to bore into her.

"I am so glad. I was sure you were a goner there for a moment." He flashed a brilliant grin liquefying Serena's insides instantly. "Please let me introduce myself. I'm Mr. Brennan Whitling of Whitling Textiles Importers and Wholesalers."

"How do you do, Mr. Whitling?" Serena allowed her lips to curve up ever so slightly. "I am Miss Serena Freemont."

"It is a pleasure. Might I interest you and your"—he glanced around the bustling street as his grin faded in confusion— "chaperone in a cup of tea?"

A wave of horror swept over Serena. Chaperone? Harlots did not require one of those. "Oh, Aunt Henrietta is in the bookstore, and I fear she will be in there a very long time. I am certain she won't notice if we slip off for a quick spot of tea."

"Excellent! There is a lovely little shop just up the street." A beautiful smile spread across his face, causing her pulse to quicken.

He escorted her up the block where they stopped at a quaint little teashop. They settled in at a table and ordered a pot of tea.

"What has you on Bond Street today, Mr. Whitling?" They sat in semi privacy at the back of the shop.

"Oh, I was visiting some of my customers and taking new orders. I am very glad I was there to help you, and by virtue of said assistance make your acquaintance." Did his already deep voice grow huskier? Their tea service arrived, dispelling the moment.

"As am I. Landing on my backside in the middle of the street would have been rather embarrassing. But in truth, thank you for your assistance today, and now the tea." She lifted her freshly prepared cup to her lips and took a dainty sip from the delicate china. Through lowered lashes, she watched his graceful movements as he prepared his own.

"It is my pleasure on both accounts. You seem familiar to me. Have we met somewhere before? A ball perhaps?"

"Oh, I think I would remember that. No, but I do find myself on Bond Street on a frequent basis. Mayhap you have seen me there?" Even if he were a customer of The Market, the notorious members-only brothel, there is no way he would associate her with the establishment. Most customers wouldn't if they met her outside of the house. Then again, most customers wouldn't want to be recognized themselves, which was why they wore masks. No, he couldn't know her from The Market.

"Of course, I'm sure that's it." His voice wobbled hinting at a bit of nerves. "Tell me, Miss Freemont. Do you enjoy reading?"

"I do. I enjoy the classics and of course a good gothic tale, as well. It can be quite titillating to read about all those old musty castles chocked full of ghosts and monsters." Not so titillating as being near such a handsome and kind specimen of the male species.

"Oh, well now, why doesn't that shock me? I haven't personally read a gothic novel, but I do enjoy the classics. You can't go wrong with Shakespeare. What would you recommend as a first time gothic read?"

"Hhhmmmm...." Serena considered him with his gentle manners, quick wit, and well-muscled form. He resembled the image of a man most of her customers attempted to portray. Her angel smacked of everything she would want in a man if given the choice. "Do you enjoy a love story? Maybe something by Elizabeth Gaskell? She has a new gothic out full of thrills and chills in between stolen kisses." He raised an eyebrow. "No. Maybe something more masculine, less romantic. You should read G.W.M. Reynolds's newest gothic. It is very dark and sad with lots of ghosts and monsters and no less than three moldering castles." She nodded, sure of her final recommendation.

"G.W.M. Reynolds it is. Why don't I escort you to your aunt and then I can stop at the bookstore and pick up a copy today."

Panic. Pure panic swamped Serena's senses muting the bustling sounds of city life. She had no aunt. He would learn the truth and look at her as everyone else did when they learned who she was. What she was. After enjoying the brief respite in her otherwise secluded existence, she did not think she could stand to see her angel look at her in such a way. No, far better to disappear and leave him wondering than to witness his perception of her colored by the reality of her life.

She drew a calming breath.

"Oh, Aunt Henrietta will be quite cross already. I dare say appearing with a strange man in tow would be the death of me. If you don't mind, I will leave you here and find my own way back." She grew certain her fragile facade would crack at any moment. A bittersweet pain fisted in her chest where her heart should have been. Regret for all she would never experience washed through her, coming very close to breaking her right there.

"Very well. I wouldn't want to get you in any trouble. How will I see you again?" He appeared so hopeful it pained her to lie.

Her body stiff with her determination to escape, she rose and grabbed her packages. "I am sure we will run in to each other again soon. Good-bye, Mr. Whitling," she called and disappeared into the crowd.

No sooner had she faded into the flow of traffic on the sidewalk than the wetness trickled down her cheeks in little rivulets of pain. Not that she had any great feeling for the handsome man, she assured herself. After all, they'd only just met. But, the realization she did not even have the option made her sad. Her life offered very few choices, and love was not one of them. A suitor, a man like Mr. Whitling, could never be for a woman like her.

Serena walked the five blocks to The Market and climbed the front stairs. The unassuming portico sustained their deception as much as her proper dresses and hats. The veneer of propriety allowed them to survive in a world that frowned on all things immoral, and at The Market all things immoral were bought and sold.

One just needed to name the right price.

CHAPTER TWO

Brennan departed Madame Le Fleur's after checking on the delivery of Mrs. Keeling's order. His warehouses were efficient and always delivered the orders, but customers liked the extra attention he paid them. It also made resolving any issues quick and easy. Mounting his phaeton, he scanned the street hoping to see Serena again. He had been disappointed when she vanished from the teashop. He had spent the last two days lamenting that fact to his best friend, Andrew Johnston. Today he hoped to see the young lady so he could rectify his mistake.

Seeing neither hide nor hair of the enchantress, he settled on the bench and took up the reins. Lurching away from the curb, he encouraged the horses into the stream of traffic when a flash of color caught his eye. He eased the rig forward and passed Serena. Thrilled to have spotted her for a second time so soon, he pulled the phaeton over and tossed the reins to a boy standing nearby.

A few feet away, he knew she spotted him when her chocolate eyes widened in surprise. He strolled toward her and raised his hat in greeting, his stomach tightening with nerves. "Good day, Miss Freemont." He scanned the nearby crowd, searching for her aunt. All he saw was a woman who looked a bit older than she did. Not the usual chaperone for a lady, but perhaps she, like him, came from a more working-class background.

"Good day, Mr. Whitling. Imagine running in to you twice in one week. This is my Aunt Henrietta." She gestured to the young woman with her who gave her a queer look.

"How nice to meet you, Aunt Henrietta." Brennan tipped his hat.

"Hello," she replied.

"How fortuitous to run in to you, I wanted to invite you to a dinner party I am hosting tomorrow evening. I realize it is rather short notice, but I hoped you, and your aunt, might join us."

"Oh, I...." Serena peeked at her chaperone as though unsure of her reaction.

"I don't believe we have any plans that evening." The other woman smiled, despite seeming a trifle incensed.

"Yes, dinner would be very nice." A timid grin flashed across Serena's coral lips, disappearing as soon as it appeared.

The tension gripping his chest relaxed with her agreement. "Excellent, may I pick you up?"

"Oh, I wouldn't want to take you away from any guests. We can manage to find you on our own if you will provide your direction," Serena assured him.

"It would be no bother." He wanted to have a way to contact her.

"Oh, we live quite far from here, and in truth we will be busy all day before we can arrive." With such urgency in her voice, Brennan decided not to push any harder. She'd agreed to dinner.

"Very well. Here is my address. It will be just a few friends, nothing too formal." He handed her his calling card with his address scribbled on the back. How fortunate he had come prepared. "Please come at eight o'clock."

Serena tucked the card into her reticule. After a regal nod, she and her Aunt were on their way.

Brennan watched them walk away and reveled in the excitement of finding her again. All that was left was to arrange for his friends to join them for dinner. Who of his acquaintances were married?

Serena dragged Miranda away from Brennan with a firm yank to the arm before she said something inappropriate.

"What were you about, Serena? You're Aunt Henrietta? Do I really look so old?" Miranda's vanity had taken a direct blow, which left her annoyed and far too curious.

"No, I apologize for such an inference. He was just a man I bumped into last week. Nothing more. I certainly won't be going." Serena lengthened her stride to an unladylike gait. Her skirts spread around her as she barreled down the sidewalk. She ignored the warmth pooling low in her belly and the pounding of her heart.

"Why ever not? He seemed perfectly nice, and very handsome to boot." Miranda tugged her arm in an attempt to slow their pace.

"He has no idea what I am. He sees only a lady, not a whore." Serena shortened her step and drew a deep breath.

"I see, hence the Aunt Henrietta." Miranda paused. "Still, it might be a nice treat to meet with a man and not have it be business related. I think you should go, if not for yourself, then for all of us who will never have such an opportunity."

"Really? D'you think I should?" Serena stopped, surprised by her friend's emphatic response.

"I do. Please go and come back to tell us what it is like to not be a whore. I think I have forgotten." A bittersweet smile slipped across Miranda's face as she linked her arm in Serena's and dragged her up the steps of The Market.

"Maybe I will." Serena sighed as they entered the house. As far as being a whore went, they had a very good life. They could have ended up gin-soaked trollops who fucked men against an alley wall for enough change to fill their mugs.

Brennan stared at Andrew. Every muscle in his body strung tight with an intensity he had never experienced before. The lunch he'd devoured a short bit ago curdled in his belly as he dangled on tenterhooks waiting for his friend's response.

"Are you kidding? I wouldn't miss an opportunity to meet the lady who has you all tied up in knots." Andrew smirked and clapped Brennan on the shoulder.

"Excellent. I shall have my sister, and her husband, attend as well." Happiness and excitement coiled within. He lifted his post-meal brandy, took a small sip from the snifter, and paused. "You know, her aunt is hardly older than she is. Perhaps you two will become better acquainted."

Andrew sputtered, his own sip of brandy spattering his vest. "Are you attempting to saddle me with her chaperone? I will remind you, I am but two years older than you are. Barely even counts."

Brennan laughed at his sensitive friend's reaction. "I only mention it as she was also attractive. I would never wish an old maid on you."

A short while later Brennan rose and stretched. "Excellent repast, but I must stop by and see my sister you know."

"Good luck with the Dragon." Andrew stretched his legs out and settled deeper into his chair.

Brennan headed over to his sister's home where he explained needing her attendance for dinner the following evening. She agreed as soon as she learned the party included a female of interest to him. The matchmaker in her overrode her inner dragon much to his relief.

Serena sat in the coach chewing her lower lip in nervous distraction. She could not help but worry arriving without a chaperone would be suspicious. In the end, she resigned herself to indulging her curiosity. Butterflies fluttered in her stomach when the coach drew to a stop outside of Brennan's townhouse. It had a sedate facade consisting of whitewashed brick, a blue door, and matching shutters. Taking a deep breath to calm her agitation before she alighted from the carriage bought her only a moment's respite. She found herself standing before the door far too soon.

Reaching out with a hand racked by tremors, she slapped the knocker against its brass plate. Her fingers had scarcely released the handle when a tall immaculate man opened the door.

"Good evening. I am here to see Mr. Whitling." Serena presented her card, willing her hand to cease shaking.

Taking her card, the butler all but hustled her into the foyer before he glanced at her card. "He is expecting you. May I take your wrap and reticule?"

Serena slipped her shawl off her shoulders and let the overeager butler whisk it away. She held on to her small bag in case a quick escape became necessary. Turning from the butler, she bumped into Brennan.

"Excuse me. I thought I heard you come in." His baritone flowed over her like warm caramel.

"Oh, I did not hear you walk up." Her face simmered with an inexplicable blush. *I am a woman of experience, not some simpering debutant.*

"I am very glad you came."

His proximity wreaked havoc with her ability to think, but the smile he bestowed made it worth the trip. "I am as well." Butterflies created a sudden knot that grew heavy like a bucket of coal. She would never be able to choke dinner down if the gastric acrobatics did not improve.

He glanced past her with a quizzical look. "Is your aunt not with you?"

"She uh...." *Damn and blast, I was a fool to come without a chaperone.* "She had a megrim and sent me on alone."

"Please, wish her a speedy recovery for me and thank her for sending you on." He turned and presented her his arm. "My other guests have already arrived. Shall we go meet them?"

She tucked her hand into the crook of his elbow and prayed he did not notice the tremors continuing to plague her. He led her into a cozy sitting room that contained a small group. A woman sat on the settee next to a handsome man who appeared absorbed in what she said. Another gentleman stared into the flames of the fireplace, brooding alone. He stood taller than Serena, but not by more than a couple of inches.

"Miss Freemont, I would like you to meet my sister and her husband, Sir Harry Thornton and Lady Caroline Thornton. Harry, Caro, this is Miss Serena Freemont."

His sister was a Lady! Serena bit back her gasp and curtsied. The evening, without a doubt, would be a disaster of epic proportions.

Brennan continued the introductions. "And this disreputable specimen is my best friend, Mr. Andrew Johnston."

The dark, dashing man kissed her hand, let his lips linger a tad too long, and straightened up. A lock of chestnut hair flopped into his deep blue eyes. "It is very nice to meet you, Miss Freemont." As expected, he edged past her in height, yet still came up shorter than Brennan.

"It is lovely to meet you all."

They sat and chatted for a bit before the butler announced dinner. Caroline, as she had been instructed to call Lady Thornton, was escorted into the dining room by her husband, leaving Serena with both Brennan and Andrew to accompany her. They settled at the table and dinner was served.

"I am sorry to hear your Aunt Henrietta is not feeling well this evening. How very kind of her to allow you to attend without her." Caroline picked up her glass to sip her wine and eyed her suspiciously.

Serena choked on a bite of food as she swallowed. "She felt so poorly, and Brennan had mentioned there would be other females. Although, she did instruct me to leave should that turn out to be false." She fluttered her lashes at Brennan in the hopes her flirtation would act as a distraction.

"I do believe I have been insulted." He barked a laugh that startled everyone.

Dinner carried on with Caroline and Andrew regaling them with childhood stories of the scrapes Brennan seemed to always find himself in. A footman presented a note to Brennan's sister with her dessert. She gave the note a quick perusal and darted a worried glance at her husband. "Oh dear, it seems my youngest is ill. Harry, I am afraid we must go."

"What a shame the lemon tart shall go to waste." Brennan rose to escort his sister out.

"I should go as well." Serena made to leave.

"I feel terrible about this." Caroline paused. "At least stay and have your dessert before leaving. No one shall know." She looked fondly at Brennan. "My brother will be a perfect gentleman."

"Indeed, I will," Brennan vowed as Andrew stood.

"I am lodged not far from you, Sir Thornton, could you drop me on your way?" Andrew winked at Brennan in a not quite sly aside.

"Of course," Harry agreed as they departed in a rush.

The group bustle out of the dining room. Upon Brennan's return, she grew unsure what to say, or more accurately, what a proper young lady would say in such circumstances.

"Well, we seem to be left on our own to enjoy our desserts." Brennan sat down and took a bite of lemon tart.

Serena followed suit and tried to focus on her plate. She managed a few bites before the knots returned. Somehow, Brennan's friends and family had put her at ease, but with their departure and that of all the servants, she'd lost her buffer. Alone with him, her body seemed to have one thing in mind. The juncture of her thighs heated, her core moistening in anticipation of taking him within.

His fork clinked against the china as he set the heavy silver utensil down. "Would you like to join me in the study? I could use a brandy."

"So could I."

Brennan's jaw unhinged halfway as he stared at her. Finally finding his voice, he sputtered, "You drink brandy?"

"My father lets me sip it?" Serena's skin stretched with a weak smile. She had misspoken with no way to cover it.

"How singular." Brennan shook his head and stood, extending her his arm.

CHAPTER THREE

S urrounded by wood and leather, Serena grew certain her handsome host must have guessed the truth after her slip up about the brandy. His intense blue-gray eyes focused on her from across the room as the door clicked shut.

"I am sorry my friends had to leave so early. If you need to leave, I can call my carriage around for you." He looked so earnest and yet all she could see was hope. Hope she would stay or hope she would go?

"Not at all. I thought you wanted a nightcap?" Comfortable in this pseudo-hostess role, she eased over to the decanter of cognac, or perhaps brandy? She lifted the lid. A delicate sniff told her the crystal contained the promised brandy. Excellent. She splashed two fingers of the amber liquid into a set of glasses and carried them toward her host who remained plastered against the study door.

She handed him a glass, transferring the smooth cool container to him before taking his warm free hand. A gentle tug got him moving so she could lead him to a nearby couch where they settled together. A heady, lightheadedness heightened the pulsing sensation of her blood thrumming as her body warmed to an uncomfortable temperature. Her breasts felt trapped by her corset and gown, and yet balanced in the most precarious way at the lip of her bodice. Serena had never experienced such anticipation before.

"Tell me, Mr. Whitling. How did you end up in the textile business?"

"Tell me, Miss Freemont. How have we not met before now?" He leaned in close and traced her ear with his fingertip.

Little shivers raced up and down her spine as though a breeze had stolen into the room. Tamping down the baser instincts demanding his touch, she focused on sipping her brandy. The dear man thought her a debutante. Not the practiced harlot that she was. He would be shocked were she to stand, strip, and proceed to manipulate both him and the situation with her usual finesse.

"I cannot imagine. Honestly, I am on Bond Street quite regularly. But" —she hesitated— "well, I shouldn't say it. It just isn't proper." She blushed.

"Please, you may say anything you like to me." He set his brandy on a side table and took her hand in his to offer her assurance.

Unsure how to respond Serena bit her lip. The truth of her next words rang clearer than the voice of a choirboy. "Well, I am glad I ran into you." She was glad she could at least be true to her feelings if not her story.

It took but a moment for her snifter to disappear under Brennan's power before he swept her into his arms. The comforting band of bone and sinew surrounded her as his chest pressed against her sensitive breasts. Even through five layers of clothing, her nipples tightened and pressed forward seeking his heat.

Warm lips claimed her soft moist ones, and his tongue demanded entrance. She willingly opened to him, accepted him, and welcomed him into her body.

He probed her mouth and caressed her teeth with his tongue as his hands sought out her precariously positioned breasts. It took ever so little coaxing and the loosening of her bodice for her to spill out over the top of her dress. He treated her to more attention than she had known in recent memory.

Her pebbled nipples grew harder as his teeth worried one nub and then the other. He cupped her breasts and lifted them, leaving her to hang on to him as he licked and suckled. Heat and moisture pooled low in her belly and between her thighs. She reveled in the tingling ripples radiating out from her pussy to her breasts and down to her toes. Normally a man did not take the time to treat her to such pleasures.

A low groan escaped him as he pulled away from her glistening breasts. "My apologies, we should stop this immediately." His voice rumbled with desire.

"No." Her body's demands left her legs like jelly and her mind fogged.

"Serena, this—" He leaned back farther, attempting to put more distance between them.

"I want this, Brennan. I want this with you." She stood and unhooked the rest of her dress letting it pool at her feet.

Brennan's mouth dried out as he stared at her breasts resting over the edge of her midbust corset. She wore the sheerest underclothes he had ever seen on a flesh-and-blood woman. They may as well have been transparent. Had he ever seen anything so erotic? He could never have imagined this moment when he invited her and her aunt to dinner. His cock gave an eager twitch against the fall of his trousers as a reminder of the matter at hand.

She raised her chemise a bit more and straddled him on the couch. Between her black hose and white chemise, her creamy thighs were exposed. He placed his hands on either leg and caressed the irresistible delicate skin there. She shivered, whether in reaction or anticipation he remained unsure. He no longer cared as electricity shot through his fingers and down to his painful erection. Need pulsed deep in his groin as he hauled her against his chest and plunged his tongue into her mouth.

Heaven. Her warm wet tongue caressing, exploring. Her hands skimmed down his neck and chest to push his jacket off his shoulders. Next, she peeled away his shirt and let her delicate fingers trail little patterns over his flesh. It seemed he would expire of want. Not to be out done, he reached up, took the tip of each breast between his fingers, and rolled the points to hardened tips. She moaned and ground her mound against his cock.

Uninhibited. She was naturally uninhibited. It was the only explanation he could come to in the fog of lust.

He drifted away from their kiss and turned to ease her down on to the sofa. Levering himself up, he shed his pants. Ever eager to join the interlude, his cock sprang out and stood at attention. A drop of clear fluid leaked from the tip. Serena stretched out and wiped it off with a finger she then sucked between her full pink lips. Brennan's body shook as he worked to control the lust coursing through him. Where had an innocent learned to do such a blatantly sexual thing?

"Please," she said, her voice a breathy whisper reaching out and caressing his tortured nerves. Innocent or not, he needed to be inside her warmth.

He kneeled between her legs and spread them wider. The urge to savor her, to see if she tasted as sweet as she seemed was driving him to the edge of madness. But his body ruled the day. Resting the tip of his cock at her slick entrance, he pushed onward in slow agonizing bits. Her hips lifted to try to meet him, but he pressed her into the couch with his weight. "Let me do this, love. I don't want to hurt you."

Confusion flitted across her face but disappeared with a small nod. Relieved, he surged forward again. Seated to the hilt, his balls against her ass, the realization dawned there had been no barrier. She felt tight, but he was larger than the average man. Again, something eluded him, but when she ground her pelvis against him, moaning, he lost all ability for critical thought.

He drew back and plunged again. Pleasure engulfed him as his cock slipped out of her tight sheath. A gasp escaped her only to be followed by a sigh. He set a steady pace as he pumped in and out of her body. With her legs wrapped around his hips, she settled her hands on his arms. Her skin a living flame as the heat radiated off her body. He braced her hips to give him the leverage he needed to fuck her properly. Determined she enjoy their joining, he stroked a fingertip over her clit. She sucked in a sharp breath and her eyelids flew open. Their gazes locked as he continued to stroke her with both his cock and his finger.

The shudder racking her was of an intensity he had never experienced before. Not even with the one mistress he kept for a short time the previous year. She cried out her pleasure as her channel rippled around his throbbing erection. Picking up the pace, he pistoned into her without a thought as to how he used her body. Her noisy orgasm ended as his own release gripped him. He withdrew from her heat and stroked his cock with his hand coming on the nearby pillow.

The languorous afterglow of sex still enveloped them as Serena sat up. Brennan seemed a little abashed as he sorted out his trousers and her dress. She decided he needed to relax. "Brennan, are you all right?"

He stopped and turned to her clutching their clothing. "I-I should apologize for taking you like this." He flailed his arms in an attempt to encompass the whole room, but ended up waving their clothes around instead.

Forcing down a giggle, Serena rescued her dress. "Brennan, stop. I wanted this as much as you."

He pulled on his pants. "Yes, but here? On the couch? What kind of man am I that I could not control myself long enough to at least take you to a proper bed, much less wed—"

"We could correct that oversight now." She cut in, desperate to avoid the awkward conversation. Her blood heated as her gaze swept his muscular arms and chest. She needed to feel those arms wrapped around her and wanted nothing more than to be beneath him again. One more time before reality intruded.

"Get married? Yes. We'll need a special license...." He paced, no longer speaking aloud.

"No," she shouted. Her heart pounded as fear swamped her. The situation called for a diversion. Her tone turned seductive. "I meant we could go upstairs."

"Won't your aunt wonder where you are?" He looked worried as he drew his shirt over his head.

"I am sure I will be in all kinds of trouble when I get home, so I may as well make it worthwhile." She flashed her naughty leer, the one always sure to excite her clients.

"Are you—are you sure you are ready to do it again?" Brennan's brow creased.

Serena stood, reached over, and stroked his growing cock through his pants. "I'm quite sure. Come, take me upstairs and ravish me." She leaned in and kissed him, gliding her tongue deep into his mouth to taste his warm brandied flavor. He slid his arms around her, lifting her into the air, and relief rushed through her. Hopefully he'd forgotten the wedding plans.

She lifted her legs and wrapped them around his waist as he unlocked the door and exited the study. Grateful she still clutched her dress in her hand, she hung on as he broke the kiss to dash up the stairs and down a hall. She tucked her face into the crook of his neck as another door opened and closed behind them. He pressed her down into a soft mattress. Cold air assailed her when he disappeared to step over to the washbasin. She heard water pour and a rag dip in just to be wrung out.

Brennan returned to the bed. "Don't be nervous. I am going to clean you a bit from our earlier encounter."

Serena thought she might swoon there on the bed. Most of the time, she cleaned and fussed, always the perfect mistress. Never did her clients take care of her the way Brennan did. The attention more alluring to her than anything else he could have done. She spread her legs with the knowledge he would not find what he expected. His gaze narrowed for a moment, but he said nothing. Perhaps he chalked it up to horseback riding? Nevertheless, the coolness of the cloth came as a shock against her heated, swollen flesh. He wiped her with gentle swipes before setting the rag aside.

After helping her to sit up, he set about unlacing her corset. In a matter of minutes he had the restrictive garment loose and off her small frame. Its absence left her with naught but a sheer chemise. Next, he gripped the hem of the fabric and raised it over her head fully exposing her. An attack of shyness seemed ridiculous, all things considered, but nonetheless she found she had to resist the urge to cover herself. It dawned on her she could count on one hand the number of times she had appeared fully naked in front of a man despite her profession.

"Beautiful."

One word uttered with such reverence. Serena's heart melted around the edges. She had been called beautiful more times than she could count, and by some of the most experienced men in London. But never, not once, had it been said with such heartfelt emotion. His sentiment more than she could take, a single tear slipped down her cheek leaving a cool, damp track. "Thank you for making me feel beautiful. Now come and make love to me."

Brennan shed shirt and trousers to join her on the bed. He laid her back and kissed her with an unmatched thoroughness before tracking down over her breasts and across her belly. Still moving lower, he parted her thighs and looked at her pussy. Most men took from her, but this one was different.

He gave.

A single finger traced her labia, sketching over her skin in a chill-inducing sweep. Then he let it glide straight up her center and over her clit. The worshipfully erotic gesture caused her body to grow wetter and more demanding. As though he could read her mind, he slipped his desire inducing finger into her body and worked it in and out in a gentle pumping, a wonderful sensation and yet not enough.

He added a second digit causing her to moan with need. Lightning shot through her body when he flicked her nub with his tongue. "Yes, Brennan." She encouraged him until he used the flat of his tongue to full devastating effect. Her orgasm broke over her with the impression of shattering into a million pieces. Despite her certainty the flood of sensation was more than she could stand somehow he knew she could take it. He replaced his fingers with his tongue as she came back together, merely to be overwhelmed again. She cried out and ground her hips against his mouth as he devoured her. His gentle licks and strokes eased her back down to earth, to him.

He rose up over her, his lips slick with her juices and kissed her, long and deep. The desire to take advantage of the moment and roll him over rocked her control. She wanted nothing more than to kiss her way down the hard planes of his chest and stomach and find the target of her interest. To take his cockhead into her mouth, swirl her tongue around it and sink down his length until he moaned and buried his hands in her hair. Draw back then sink down again, allowing her lips to stretch around his girth and her throat to relax. Finally, he would grip her head in silent command and pump into her warmth.

Instead of allowing her to act on her desires, he leaned away. "I want to bury myself inside you again." For a second time, she straddled him, but this time with far greater success. "Rise up and lower yourself on to me, love, like you're riding a horse astride." His gentle guidance sent a jolt of desire pulsing through her body.

Following his instructions, she placed the tip of his penis at her opening and sank down his hard length. The stretching sensation alone drew her near the edge. Orgasm would not be far behind. Seated on his cock, she stopped and waited to see if he might tell her what to do again.

"Now, rub yourself against me here." He placed his hands on her hips and showed her how to grind against him. "Then you can rise up and slide down again. You're in control."

She did as he showed her, reveling in both the feel of his body and the rare experience of having a man take care of her, see to her pleasure. She continued to grind her mound against him creating tingles that rippled out from her sensitive nub.

"Here, now bring your hands to your breasts." His voice hitched. "That's it. Make yourself feel good." He surveyed her while he reached back down between them to rub against her clit.

His free hand clutched her hip and encouraged her grinding. The feeling of fullness was exquisite as she rode him in earnest. Pinching and rolling her own nipples while he watched with a heavy lidded gaze, the stirrings of her climax twined through her. He groaned. "Beautiful. You are so bloody beautiful." The sweetness of his words caused the first crack in the armor of her heart.

Then the world as she knew it bent and twisted as wave after wave of pleasure overwhelmed her senses. Her body clutched his cock, gripping and releasing in spasms around him. He pumped into her twice more then pushed her off him to spill his cum on his stomach. She watched his body arch up off the bed as he stroked his cock. Replete, they lay side by side on the bed, until she drifted off to sleep.

CHAPTER FOUR

S erena awoke in a strange bed in a strange house. The sun streamed in through the windows cheerily showing, to her dismay, morning had arrived. She should have left hours ago. Madame Marchander would be furious if she knew Serena had not returned from her night off. A glance over her shoulder showed Brennan still slept. They remained nude from when he had woken her sometime in the dark of night to make love for a third time.

The strong planes of his face were peaceful in repose, yet not boyish in any way. She bit her lip finding it difficult to slip from the bed, but deep inside the knowledge she had to leave before he woke up took root. There were too many questions, too many conversations, all of which could reveal her lies. Calling herself a fool, she slipped from the soft Egyptian cotton sheets, so like the ones she slept on at The Market and yet different for the fact they graced his bed. Her feet sank into the plush rug beneath as she looked for her clothes. In rumpled heaps on the floor lay her chemise, corset, and dress. Her stockings were strewn nearby, so it did not take long to set herself to rights. She eased the bedroom door open and ducked back into the room when a maid walked by carrying a stack of sheets. Alone again, she darted out of the door and down the hall to the stairs. Another short dash downstairs and to the study yielded her shoes.

Feet shod and reticule in hand, she forfeited her wrap in the name of a quick and anonymous escape. Since the butler was absent, she headed out the front door and found herself on the sunny street with people strolling by. A glance down at her wrinkled dress, a hand on her head, and the shocked stares of the ladies passing by illustrated her shameful appearance rather well. Tipping her chin up and refusing to be cowed, she stepped down on to the sidewalk and turned left. The Market was not far of a walk.

Brennan rolled over and reached out for Serena. His hand came up empty and caused his eyelids to pry open. The crisp morning sun invaded his sleep-drugged mind leading him to wonder where she was. He sat up and called softly. "Serena, love?"

Beyond his cracked bedroom door the hustle and bustle of his staff going about their daily routines filtered in. Why was his door ajar? Certain he had closed it when they came upstairs; he climbed out of bed and looked at the floor. Her clothes were gone. The pit forming in his stomach told him she had gone too. The sinking sensation gripped his belly and nauseated him. He pulled on his trousers and a robe so he could step out into the hallway. Downstairs, he went to the study and found her shoes and reticule gone as well. He sighed, but reminded himself she must have left to sneak home. She was not a woman who could stay out all night without consequences.

Nor was she a woman to be able to sleep with a man without ramifications. A moment of panic seized him. Was he ready to marry anyone? Last night, he'd intended to offer marriage until she distracted him with the notion of going upstairs. He stopped to reflect over their time together. He had enjoyed their conversation as much as he enjoyed making love to her. The truth was he would have preferred to court her and get better acquainted, but his cock had taken over and done all his thinking.

He knew what he had to do. He'd known it last night. "Green," he summoned his butler.

"Yes, sir?" The poor man stood shifting from one foot to the other as thought the floor was too warm to stand upon.

"Have my phaeton brought around. I need to go out." Brennan turned and ran up the stairs taking them two at a time.

A few hours and a special license later reality dawned. He had no idea where to find his bride. He decided to go home. Surely her family would call on him once they realized what had happened. He sat in the study watching the time tick by. The first few hours he had been nervous and fidgety as he waited. He argued with himself back and forth about why he should or should not marry her. In the end, he acknowledged he knew little concerning her, but something about her spoke to him. She belonged to him.

By dinner, when no relatives had appeared demanding he do right by her, he grew utterly ornery. Andrew showed up at midnight to see why he had not appeared at the club. Brennan had become downright drunk and had no desire for company.

"Get out, Andrew." He sat sprawled in his chair behind his desk.

"What happened to you?" Andrew dropped onto the sofa and extended his legs.

"Nothing. Absolutely nothing. Not a blasted thing has happened to me. That's what."

"What's wrong with nothing?"

"Everything." Brennan poured himself another brandy.

"Everything is wrong with nothing? I am not sure I follow." Andrew yawned and stretched.

"I bedded her and nothing happened." Brennan tossed back the contents of his glass. "No knock on the door, no angry father. Nothing."

"Well, I'd say you escaped and be happy! You can't mean you wanted to be caught in the parson's trap, can you?"

"No, not wanted, but prepared. I am ready. Even got a special license so I could make good." He rose and waved the useless piece of paper in the air as he headed for the brandy decanter.

"What an auspicious result. Any chance you'll see the girl again?" Andrew sat up, concerned.

"Not bloody likely," Brennan mumbled.

"Then you're in luck! You had a nice tumble with the trollop. Be grateful for escaping the shackles."

Anger surged through his alcohol-muddled brain as he stumbled toward his friend. "Don't talk about her like that, you sodding bastard!" Brennan swung at Andrew and missed. Face planted in the cushions of the settee, Andrew's weight settled on top of him.

"Are you quite done? I would prefer it if you left my handsome face arranged as it is."

Struggling with his friend, the last thing Brennan remembered was muttering a no before exhaustion and alcohol took over and darkness consumed him.

Serena had been happy with her life before she met Brennan Whitling. Nothing seemed as rosy as it had before. The Market was heaven compared to the brothel her mother worked in until the pox took her. Left alone at thirteen with very few options available she'd known she could do better than Gran's bawdyhouse. She went in search of a good quality place to auction off her virginity. The Pleasure Palace, run by Madame Richmond, had seemed very elegant to a poor little girl who wore rags. At least until Madame Marchander offered her a position at The Market as a live-in girl. That was when she understood what elegance was. For the first year she did not go near the customers. She had to learn to pass for a lady in order to command a man's attention. Eager and smart, she absorbed everything she needed to succeed.

Six years later, she did not regret her choices so much as her lack of them. It had been a month since she had dinner with Brennan, and still she struggled to find contentment in sex with anyone. She went through the motions, but the small bit of pleasure she once found eluded her. It had become a problem, and she did not quite know what to do. She could not go to Brennan and tell him who she was.

A knock on her door drew her attention. She opened it to find Miranda standing there with a dress in her hands. "Madame sent me up with this dress for you."

"For me? Why?" Serena looked at the jade-green silk and dredged up a modicum of excitement about it.

"She's noticed you are not yourself lately. She thinks a new dress might cheer you up." Miranda shrugged and held out the beautiful gown.

Serena took it and fingered the sleekness of the material. "It is beautiful."

"I suggest you wear it and do your best to act like you are happy again. Madame is not cold, but I am not sure she would understand you pining for a man. In particular, one you saw in secret."

"I know. I will push past this. I promise." Serena attempted a smile, hugged her friend, and hung the dress on a hook by her armoire.

"Good. It should be busy tonight; you'll enjoy yourself more if you try to pick your spirits up." Miranda turned and shut the door on her way out leaving Serena alone again.

Her friend was right. The time had come to let go of an impossible dream and return to reality. She would never be Mrs. Brennan Whitling.

Either hunting for Serena or drunk, Brennan searched high and low for her, but came up with nothing. Not one of his associates or their wives knew of Miss Serena Freemont. She was a ghost, a phantom, a figment of his imagination. He slumped into his desk chair again and swallowed a slug of brandy. The alcohol helped to stop the wild imaginings he concocted in his brain. He imagined her snatched on the way home from his house and carried off by some villain, dead in a gutter at the hand of a footpad, or clad in rags selling her body for a swig of gin in the stews. But worst of all, he envisioned her sitting in her drawing room as though nothing changed and he never existed.

Andrew had given up on him and his sister refused to receive him in his drunken state the few times he stopped by. Therefore, he was quite surprised when his best friend sauntered into his study and proceeded to sit down as if nothing were wrong.

"Hello there, old chap." His friend grinned.

Brennan should have known something was up his friend's sleeve when he showed up. "What is it? I am not really up for company at the moment."

"Oh, I think maybe you will change your mind after you hear what I have to say." He glowed with an unsettling giddiness.

"Why is that?" Brennan took another drink.

"I have two tokens to the most exclusive brothel in London. The Market." He tossed one of the large, gleaming coins in the air.

"What good is a brothel to me?" Brennan slumped lower in his chair. How could he even be sure he could get a cockstand anymore? The damned redhead had ruined him for all other women.

"Come on, we'll find you a woman who can put the other one out of your head. A good grind and you'll be back on your feet." He stood up and walked out of the study.

Brennan sighed. Maybe the time had come to give up the hunt for Serena. Half hoping his friend might be right about replacing her with another woman, he followed him into the night. A short drive later they were at the door of a sedate, stodgy-looking home. A small brass plaque, bolted on the front, had four numbers on it matching the address on the tokens.

"Remember to keep the mask they provide on at all times. It's the house policy." Andrew knocked.

"Seems rather silly."

"Well, not everyone would want it known they frequent this place; bad for the business of politicking."

They entered, presented the passes to the man at the door, dropped their requisite masks into place, and soon found themselves in a salon full of stunning women. Even Brennan could not deny his interest in the ladies on hand.

Despite their beauty, he was not prepared to tup one of them. Spying one of the liaisons standing around, he asked if they had any redheads. The man nodded and disappeared behind a tapestry. A very elegant older woman appeared a few moments later with her bosom all but tumbling from her bodice and her shrewd green eyes assessing everyone and everything. She approached him with a warm smile gracing her still beautiful face. "Good evening, *Monsieur*. I understand you requested a redhead?"

"I did. I have a particular fondness for petite redheads." Brennan hoped this might help get him moving.

"I believe I have just the girl for you. Philippe, please take him to the Green Room." She nodded for him to be led upstairs. Following the bewigged liaison, he walked down a hallway and into the aforementioned room. The walls were a pale sage with a multicolored rug in the middle showing a mélange of sage, emerald, olive, and a little brown for balance. The furniture had all been done in variations of the colors found in the rug, as were the bedspread and sheets. There could be little doubt why they called it the green room.

He looked at the sheets closely, then the drapes. Fingering the sumptuous fabrics, he experienced envy for the lucky man who had this textile account. No expense had been spared on the luxuriousness of the fabrics adorning The Market. A soft knock at the door interrupted his examination. He turned as an all too familiar redhead entered the room. "Serena?" He stripped the infernal mask from his face and still could not credit what his own eyes told him. She was here, in a brothel.

Her gasp provided confirmation, but when she blanched sheet white and blindly reached out to grasp a nearby chair no doubt remained. The jade-green silk of her dress swished as she moved. He could not help but notice how beautiful she was, an exact replica of his memory.

"How did you find me?" Her voice cracked.

"What the hell are you doing in a brothel and where have you been? I looked all over London for you!" Anger boiled deep within.

CHAPTER FIVE

"I owe you an explanation." Serena's shoulders slumped.

"Is Serena even your real name?" Brennan's head pounded making her voice sound small and faraway.

"Yes. I told you my real name." Silent tears tracked down her cheeks as she looked up.

Anger warred with the desire to comfort her and sooth away her tears. Compassion won out, though he refrained from touching her. "Tell me what is going on. Please, I must understand."

"I'm a prostitute. I live and work here at The Market. My mother was a prostitute. I have no idea who my father was." She sat down in the chair she had been using for support.

"Why did you not tell me before I had you to dinner with my friends?" Embarrassment and anger bubbled up again and the edge had crept back into his voice.

"I should have, but you looked at me in a way I have never been looked at by any man. You treated me differently. For a moment I felt like a woman attractive in her own right, not because I had been purchased like a mare from Tattersalls. I wanted to know what it would be like to be with someone and not have it be a business transaction. You were handsome and earnest, and I was selfish." She stared at her hands clasped tight in her lap.

"And when you lay with me? What was that? Payment for my services rendered?" He tried to tamp back the fury burning in him. He could not abide liars. His father had lied to his mother throughout their marriage, and each time she discovered the lies it killed him to see how hurt she was. This whole conversation was too reminiscent of similar arguments he'd listened to as a child.

"No!" Serena's head snapped back, horror etched on her face. "That was something shared and beautiful between us. I had no idea it could be like that between a man and a woman." Her breath hitched.

"Then why did you leave? Why not stay and tell me?" Brennan needed to know, to understand. Her dishonesty pierced his soul like an arrow to the heart.

"I had lied! I deceived you and felt dirty for it. But in the end, I could not bear to have you look at me as all men look at me. I wanted to remember how it felt to be seen and respected. Leaving was the only option." She rubbed her hands up and down her upper arms.

Brennan drew a deep breath and paced across the room away from her quiet weeping. Her perfidy smothered him, made it hard to think, to trust. But, they barely knew each other for all that had passed between them in such a short time. She lied, but she also showed real regret for her actions. Unlike his father, who had never shown remorse, the deceit tore her to pieces. A small sniffle drew his attention back to her and he turned. She rose from her chair, stiffened her body, and held her head high.

"I understand how deeply I have wronged you. All I can do is apologize for any harm I have caused you or your family. I do hope in time you might forgive me or at least understand why. Good-bye, Mr. Whitling." She curtsied and moved toward the door.

"Stop right there." He strode across the room and halted before her. Once in proximity to her lush form and delicate scent of lilies, he realized he would forgive her. The burgeoning emotions deep in his heart swept his doubts and fears away as a savage need to restrain her physically from leaving whipped through him. She could not leave like this. Distancing herself was intolerable. "Mr. Whitling? After the intimacies we have shared, I do believe the formality is rather misplaced. Promise me you will never lie to me again. I can't tolerate a liar." His voice came out rough, as though he had gravel trapped in his throat.

"Never," she averred on a whisper of breath.

He pulled her into his arms and kissed her. Kissed her with all of the longing he had repressed for the past month. His tongue plundered the warm cavern of her mouth, tasting and stroking. He wanted to know her, know all of her with a bone-deep desire he could not explain.

Relief washed through Serena when he deepened the kiss. Her body flattened against him as his hands gripped her shoulders causing her toes to curl in her slippers. A deep-seated desire to pleasure him with the full range of her skills drove her hard as she was no longer bound by his notion of virginity. Edging away from his heat, she worked to strip him of his clothing.

He placed his hands over hers on the buttons of his waistcoat. "Stop."

"I want to do this for you. This and other things I could not do that night." Serenity in the rightness of taking care of him stole through her.

"Very well, but go slow. I want to savor the feel of your hands on my body." He released her letting her finish stripping him. Arousal spiked through her veins with the weight of his gaze tracking her every move. "Remove your dress." His rich tone caused chill bumps to burst over her skin as she reached back and made short shrift of removing the green gown. Beneath she wore a black sheer chemise and under bust corset. She sported stockings with garters, but no drawers as usual. Aware of the erotic picture she presented, her breathing grew shallow to the point of panting.

He groaned. "On your knees."

Feeling her control of the moment slip away left her unsure what had changed, but the natural compulsion to obey his demands drove her. She sank before him, took hold of his rising cock with a firm hand, and proceeded to lick from the back of his balls, over the glans, and to the glistening tip. His body shuddered in pure pleasure she needed no words to interpret.

With practiced ease, she took his entire length in her mouth and proceeded to let him slide down into the back of her throat. She wanted to bring him to completion once before he touched her. This pleasure was for his enjoyment and hers. Swallowing as he worked in and out of her mouth and throat intensified the sensations for both of them. He moaned, threading his fingers through her hair, and proceeded to fuck her mouth with utter abandon.

"Serena, I'm close." He tried to retreat, but she wanted this. Pulling him closer and taking him deep spawned his orgasm. A guttural noise erupted from him as he pumped until the last drop hit her tongue. Reveling in the saltiness of him in her mouth, she released his softening penis.

With his assistance, she rose up and pecked him on the cheek. "I wanted to do that for you the first time."

"Thank you." He turned his face, kissing her, a velvet caress across her lips, and then led her over to the bed. There he stepped back to stare until she grew uncomfortable. "Beautiful." He repeated his comment from their first time with the same reverence.

Warmth centered in her chest unlike anything she'd ever experienced. His treatment of her had not changed with the knowledge of her profession. This was a good man. He kissed her again, letting it trail down her jaw to her neck and over her collarbone. He reached the neckline of her sheer chemise and opted to suckle her nipple through the material. Shivers of pleasure radiated out from her breasts to her pussy and everywhere in between. It continued as he switched to her other nipple and bore her back against the coverlet.

Moving down her body, he spread her thighs, skating his tongue along her slit. Shivers of delight cascaded up and down her body, matching the swirling patterns his tongue traced over her sensitive flesh. Then he drove a finger into her channel, sliding it in and out. She moaned, "Brennan, mmmm...." Her hips pumped against his hand and tongue. He stopped, moving back up her body to kiss her, and this time she slicked her tongue over his lips to taste her essence.

"Roll over," he commanded. She obeyed, happy to please him in any way. He situated her on her stomach, hips toward the edge of the bed, and on her hands and knees. Her breasts hung, rasping with delicious friction against her chemise. With her ass in the air, she waited as he drove his finger into her sheath, working it in and out. Then he placed his cock at her entrance and plunged into her body. He withdrew to repeat his thrust and pressed his slick finger against her anus.

She stiffened. This was new territory for her, something she had never done for her clients.

"Relax," he whispered against her skin. "Focus on the sensation of my cock sliding in and out of you."

As his finger eased past the tight ring of muscle, she wriggled at the discomfort. Once he slid in, while still fucking her, she realized it wasn't bad. As he timed the rhythm of his finger and his staff, she appreciated why some enjoyed the sensation. The pleasurable, yet intense, feeling of fullness had her pressing back into both his hand and his cock.

"That's it. Let me make you feel good, as good as you've made me feel." His voice sounded gruff with desire.

The double penetration was a powerful decadence that pushed her over the edge and into the abyss. Her body spasmed all around him with an intensity she could never have imagined as she came apart. He removed his finger from her backside but continued pumping into her pulsing heat until he cried out and withdrew. The warm splatter of his cum hit her backside as he released.

In the predawn darkness, as they lay together tangled in the green sheets of the bed, Brennan could no longer deny how right it was to be with her. To hold her in his arms. To love her.

"I love you, Serena Freemont." The words escaped before he thought about them, about the repercussions.

Her gaze hardened, revealing her cynicism. "Don't, Brennan. What we have is lovely, special even. But, love? Love does not exist. Not for women like me." She pulled away from him and rose.

"Do not make light of my feelings, Serena. I care for you. I was worried sick when I could not find you. Now I have, and I will not let you escape from me again." He climbed off the bed and took her by the shoulders from behind to press her against his length.

"I'm sorry, but all I can offer you is time here at The Market." She paused. "I have responsibilities and rules I must live by."

"I will not share you with all of London." Jealousy ripped through his gut and shredded his control. He spun her around and kissed her with all the ferocity contained within. "Mine. You are mine," he said as they broke apart.

Serena stared up at him, her breath coming in panting gasps. "I am. In any way that counts, I am yours. But, my body is not mine to give to you alone. Even if it were, I don't know anything about you." Her chin tilted up in stubborn determination. "I could not take the risk of walking away from my sole source of income."

"Then I will arrange it so your body is mine. I intend to have all of you. Heart, mind, body, and soul." He wanted her as his wife, but their conversation told him she would reject the idea out of hand. He needed to speak to Madame Marchander about exclusivity and the future.

A short while later, Brennan found himself sitting across a delicate writing desk from Madame Marchander. Her blond hair glinted in the gaslight as her green eyes assessed him once again. "I take it the young lady I sent you was satisfactory."

"She was the precise woman I wanted. I would like to arrange an exclusive contract with her. She will be unavailable to anyone else, and she will come to me in my home when we spend time together." An experienced businessman, Brennan knew a shrewd negotiator when he saw one.

"Mmm, that will cost you. Are you prepared to pay for those rights?" She made notes on a sheet of paper in front of her.

"I am prepared to pay for those rights and the right to marry Serena when I can convince her to accept me." He decided he needed to lay all his cards on the table.

"I see. After just one night with her?" Her gaze rested on him full of questions.

"No. A month ago, she and I met by accident. I did not know who she was when I invited her to have dinner with a few friends and myself. She came and after everyone left, we got to know each other better. I expected to see her again, but she disappeared. I found her tonight purely by accident, but I have no intention of losing her again." Brennan produced his checkbook and set it down on the desk. "I have no idea how this works, but I would like it resolved tonight.

"And do you believe she wants to marry you?"

"I believe she will if given time. I love her, but she claims not to know what love is. I need the time to show her so she might come to understand what we share. I do not wish to rush her, but I will not share her in the meantime, and I do not wish to make her feel trapped. I want her to choose me."

"Very good. I believe we can come to an arrangement which will satisfy both of our needs. You will be required to join The Market, until such time as she agrees to marry you. Should that happy event occur, you may choose to end your membership or continue it as you see fit. Our contracts run in six-month segments. For the duration, Serena will be bound to you as a mistress, and will be yours to do with as you please. You may of course feel free to gift her with anything you wish, keeping in mind it is a gift and will not be returned, nor will you be reimbursed at any time. I do not own the girls, so no fee is required should she choose to accept a proposal from you."

Brennan nodded. "And what of her staying with me?"

Madame looked up from her note taking. "She may spend the night with you, but is required to have at least one night a week off. She may choose to spend that night here or under your roof as long as she is not obliged for services, unless they are freely given. If she stays with you regularly, I will expect her to visit with me once a week alone."

"Fine. How soon will this agreement be put in place?" Brennan needed to restrain himself, too eager to have it done.

Glancing at the clock on the wall she replied, "You may return this afternoon to collect Serena and her bags should she wish to go with you. I will have the contract ready for you to sign at that time." She eyed his bankbook. "A check to cover your membership is all that is left tonight. I will be conducting an investigation into your reputation over the next week and if I find anything objectionable the contract will be null and void based on your failure to disclose such issues."

Her gaze bore in to him with an intensity that made him want to squirm like a young boy before the headmaster. It seemed she could see every mistake he had ever made. He wrote out the check and passed it across the desk. "I foresee no issues. Might I see Serena before I leave? I would like to be the one to tell her of our arrangement."

"Of course. She should still be in the green room." Madame nodded in dismissal. Without a backward glance, he rose and departed to inform Serena.

CHAPTER SIX

Alone in the green room, Serena waited to find out her fate. Brennan had left her, determined to find Madame, but she could not be sure he had the financial wherewithal to accomplish his goal. Besides being paid well there were other fees involved in being a member of The Market. More private club than public brothel, Madame Marchander catered to a very exclusive clientele. Most of the members were peers of the realm or the ridiculously wealthy from around the world.

A single knock was the lone signal she received before the door rattled and swung open. Brennan's jaw locked tight, his body stiff and tense as he closed the portal. Serena's throat tightened and her mouth dried out. *He failed.*

"I spoke with Madame Marchander." Brennan crossed over to the bed and sat on the edge.

"Brennan, it is not your fault if an arrangement could not be reached."

"True, but irrelevant. You are now under an exclusive contract to me. You will not entertain any other men."

Surprised by the ferocity with which he spoke, Serena took a moment to absorb his words. Brennan had been so gentle before. This possessive side was a new development. She liked it. "Really? That sounds perfect. Will you be returning to see me tonight?"

"I will be returning tonight to collect you and whatever you will need while you stay with me." He reached for her hand and took it in his much larger one.

"Stay with you? I do not understand. My clients have always visited me here. How is that possible?" Her heart sped up as fear Madame might throw her out clawed at her.

"Part of the arrangement we reached includes you staying with me. You are to have one night off a week, you may choose to stay at my home or come back here to rest. You are to visit with Madame once a week without my attendance, so she may be assured of your welfare. And, of course, whatever gifts I choose to give you are yours to keep." Brennan beamed at her.

"Oh my. I had no idea...." She rose and paced. "How long is the contract for?"

"Six months." He crossed the room, stepped in her way, and stopped her. His brow creased. "Is this not happy news?"

How could she explain her fears of being replaced at The Market, of becoming a two-bit dockside whore? "It—it is. Will I have a place to return to here if you no longer want me?" Fear squashed down on her chest, a leaden weight of worry.

"Not want you? Are you mad? I shall always want you." He pulled her against him and kissed her soundly. His tongue slid past her lips and teeth to twine with hers in a velvety caress. The kiss ended with sweet nibbles on her lips.

"You say that now, but after six months of me, day in and day out, you might find you feel differently. I might find I feel differently. What will I do if Madame will not have me back?"

"You are still in her employ. I have simply paid for the pleasure of your company when and where I choose and for exclusivity." His words should have soothed her, but there was an unmistakable annoyance in his tone. He resented having to pay for her time and services.

"I'm sorry. I know how repugnant it must seem after I gave myself to you so freely." Serena jerked from his hands and traversed the room. Reflexively, her arms crossed over her body. Was this a mistake? Would he come to despise her for what she was, as she had feared originally?

A sigh slipped from his lips as he followed her, pressed his chest to her back, and cradled her in his arms. "It is unsettling, but I understand you need time to accept that my affection for you is real. I do not want you to feel trapped. Madame assured me, when I inquired, that a clause will be included in the contract allowing you to end the agreement at any time and for any reason."

"Oh my. Thank you, Brennan, for asking for that." She squeezed his hand resting on her arm. Perhaps this would work, as long as she kept her heart well-guarded. He would see soon enough that his infatuation would wane, and she would still have her livelihood.

"Now, I must go and prepare the house for your arrival and you must gather your things. I will be back at four o'clock to retrieve you. Will you be ready?" Brennan turned her to face him.

"I will. Thank you." Serena leaned up and kissed him, a gentle press of her lips against his. The urge to giggle and spin with joy so unusual she had a hard time holding it back.

"You're welcome. I will see you later." He departed the room, leaving her alone again.

A quick twirl and a laugh escaped from her before she composed herself.

Brennan couldn't cease smiling. Finally she stood in his home. Not the exact way he had imagined it over a month ago when acquiring the special license, but he had bought himself some time. Precious time he would need to convince her to stay.

"Serena." He nudged a small woman-child toward her. "This is Maggie. She will act as your maid, help you dress and whatever else it is maids do for women. Her aunt is Mrs. O'Keef, the housekeeper."

Serena smiled kindly at the girl. "Hello, Maggie."

The girl curtsied and mumbled, "Mum."

"That will be all for now. Miss Freemont will ring for you when she has need of your assistance." Maggie curtsied and trod silently from the bedroom, closing the door behind her. "Now. Come here, Miss Freemont." He towed her into his arms, unable to resist the lure of her body. Tilting her head back, he feathered his lips over hers in a gentle caress. As she opened to him, surrendered, he deepened the kiss, sweeping inside to claim her mouth. Their tongues tangled, twisted together in an intimate caress. Her body molded to his, his cock nestled between them.

Desperate for more of her, but unwilling to wait long enough to remove the many layers of clothes, he turned toward the bed and bent her over. Her torso splayed across the mattress as he rucked up her skirts, covering her head. Finding easy access through the split in her drawers, he let loose his hard cock and slipped through her slick, swollen folds. Her tightness clutched him in a silken grip that threatened to push him over the edge as soon as he entered.

With a slow retreat, he let his hard length tease her engorged tissues before slamming back into her body with a sure, swift stroke.

"Yes." Her soft moan, muffled by her skirts and the mattress, floated up to him.

He repeated the tantalizing rhythm, trailing out in a slow drag and abruptly driving into her body. Brennan wouldn't last much longer as her moans increased with each powerful thrust. Desperate for release, he reached down and searched her clit out through the opening in her under things. Ruthless, he flicked the sensitive nub and pushed her over the edge as his tempo increased. The silken walls of her passage clamped down around him then released. Over and over, the spasms squeezed him and pushed his control until he needed to explode. He pulled out to shoot his hot cum onto the linen drawers covering her bottom. Complete and relaxed, he drew the soiled garment down her legs and used them to clean himself up. Tossing them aside, he sat on the bed and tucked her into his arms.

Serena lay in bed sipping her hot cocoa when Maggie appeared bearing a folded note. Setting her drink down, she read the missive in which Brennan explained that a modiste would be arriving within the hour.

"It seems we will have company soon. I should get dressed." She stretched and sat up, her chocolate abandoned on the bedside table. "I'll wear the navy blue dress with the white trim."

Maggie scampered to find the dress and left Serena to see to her morning ablutions. Refreshed with her hair brushed out and her undergarments in place, Serena finagled the dress over her head with Maggie's help. After a few moments of struggling the gown fell into place and the girl could work on buttoning the back of the dress. "Thank you, now do you know anything about fixing hair?"

"Yes, mum." She watched Serena move to the vanity.

"Come then, how would you style my hair for a meeting with a dressmaker?" The girl was painfully shy, not something Serena was accustomed to dealing with. At The Market all of the girls tittered and chattered like sisters, even the maids.

"Perhaps a simple knot at the nape would be best if you'll be in and out of your gown." Maggie walked over to where Serena sat and picked up the brush from the table.

"That sounds like an excellent notion. I leave it to you to sort out." Serena sat still and waited for the stroke of the brush through her tresses. Soon her hair appeared coiffed into a neat knot. A knock at the door heralded Mrs. O'Keef's entrance.

"Miss Freemont, Madame Le Fleur has arrived. She is in the front parlor."

"Thank you. I will be down directly. You may go get your breakfast if you have not eaten yet. I shouldn't need you again until later." Serena rose and left the two women. Nerves got the best of her on the way downstairs. Brennan had left no instructions regarding what he expected her to buy. She entered the parlor, her hands damp with sweat and her stomach full of butterflies. She could do this. She could act like a lady as well as any gently reared daughter of the Ton. Pasting a pleasant expression on her face she greeted her guest.

"Thank you for coming, Madame Le Fleur."

"Ah, at Monsieur Whitling's behest I would travel to the far reaches of the earth," the flamboyant woman drawled in her fake French accent, laced with slips of Cockney.

"Well, shall we look at some designs? I am in need of a new gown." Serena strove for a calm she did not feel. How many dresses should she order? Stupid man left no instructions, no clue about what or how much.

"*Oui*, I have many beautiful gowns for you to look at." She presented a thick stack of drawings for her to peruse.

After an hour of discussing the merits of various designs, Serena found four that she wanted. Without any direction she placed her order. "Please send the bill for two of them to this address." She scribbled an address on a piece of paper and handed it to the dressmaker. She would send a note around to Madame with instructions to pay for the dresses out of her personal account. Madame's man of affairs handled all the finances for the girls who chose to save their pennies.

"*Non*, I cannot. *Monsieur* Whitling insisted the full bill be delivered to him."

"But, I wish to pay for these two myself." Frustration rankled her composure.

Madame Le Fleur's chin took a stubborn tilt. "*Non*, he gave strict instructions."

"Fine. Reduce my order to the green baize and the dark blue riding habit." Serena rose to leave the modiste and all her wares.

"But, *Mademoiselle*...the other two gowns—"

"Will not be ordered unless the bill is sent to the address I gave you." Serena carefully tensed the muscles in her face, taking on the superior mask Madame Marchander had taught all her girls to use when dealing with recalcitrant servants and rowdy patrons.

"As you wish, *Mademoiselle*. I will send the bill for the other two gowns to that address." The woman shrugged in defeat. Serena knew she would give with the threat of losing the sale. Money always won in the end.

Brennan fought for control of his fury. Two dresses. He had ordered the modiste to provide a complete wardrobe and the fool woman had billed him for two dresses. Two! He took a deep breath. This must be Serena's doing. He crumpled the insufficient bill in his hand and stalked upstairs. He found her in the sitting room she had taken over. She perched at a small writing desk bathed by the sun's rays, her hair a nimbus of living flame. Despite the arresting vision, Brennan stormed into the room and slapped the bill down in front of her. "Please explain this."

She gasped and jumped at the thump of his palm on the desk. She glanced down at the paper and up to his face. Her mouth drew down and her gaze narrowed in anger. "I ordered two dresses because you neglected to give me any direction regarding what I should order or how much I could spend. If I overspent, it is your own fault." She rose and pushed past him.

A fool. He was an utter fool. He thrust his fingers through his hair and cursed roundly under his breath. "Stop right there." His command rang out and she stopped, which caused her skirts to swish around her trim ankles. "You are right. I should have told you what I wanted you to do. I assumed telling the modiste would be sufficient. It is clear I was mistaken."

"I see. She tried to have me order more, but I believed...." She sighed and turned to face him. "I believed she was pushing for a sale. It never occurred you would have given her instructions."

Brennan laughed so hard his shoulders shook. "I can just imagine how that exchange went. Madame Le Fleur is very tenacious when following instructions. However did you convince her to only make you two gowns?"

"It wasn't an easy fight. I purchased two others in addition to those two. She departed rather unhappy about our arrangement." Serena giggled.

"I only received a bill for two though." Brennan's mind raced. What happened to the other gowns?

"Oh, I had her send me the bill for the other two. They are all quite lovely."

His temper flared to life anew. Bloody hell, she paid for the clothing herself. "Serena, you will give me those bills so I may pay them. I intended to furnish you with an entire wardrobe, not just four dresses. Now, please send me those bills, and then I would like you to order at least five more gowns."

"No. I have no need of a new wardrobe. The four dresses, two of which I will pay for, is more than sufficient." Her brows drew together in a scowl.

She dug in, her body stiffening, and Brennan had no clue how to prevent it. "Serena. Now come, sweetheart. I want to buy you a bunch of beautiful things. Why won't you let me?"

Her chin tilted up in defiance. "It is not necessary. That is not why I am here, and it's ridiculous to spend so much money on clothing. Obscene really."

Recognizing defeat, Brennan let the issue of the two frocks go. However, the modiste had her measurements, he could order additional items without her agreement. "Very well. I will deal with Madame Le Fleur. Do you like what you selected?"

"I do. They are quite lovely." Her smile eased his irritation.

"Excellent, we should take you out and let all of London see you."

"Oh." She appeared daunted by the notion of venturing into society on his arm.

He hauled her against his chest and ravished her mouth. Driving his tongue into the wet cavity, he stroked her teeth and over the hard palette.

Separating to catch their breath, he looked deep into her eyes and experienced a wave of pure emotion unlike anything previous. Sweeping her into his arms, he walked to the settee and lowered her legs. Her breath hitched, causing her chest to rise and fall in a sensual heave designed to torment him. His gaze wandered over her collarbone, and the urge to nibble and taste her there made his knees weak.

Lowering his head, he sprinkled light kisses from her jaw down to that oh so tempting ridge. He sucked on the prominent edge as though he could draw the marrow through her skin. Her moan cut through the haze of lust and helped him resume his oral exploration. Deft fingers unlaced her bodice letting it droop to expose her linen-clad breasts. Such lush curves on his woman. He molded one with his hand, while the other one gripped her bottom and pinned her to his hips.

With a slow, taunting grind of her pelvis, his control snapped. He loosened her petticoats and shoved them down her hips. "You women wear too many bloody clothes," he mumbled in frustration as he ripped at the laces of her corset. If he had a knife, he'd cut the damned thing off.

"One could say much the same of men." Her breathy rejoinder slithered over his ragged patience. At last, the corset came loose leaving nothing but the fine linen chemise as a barrier. In a single swift motion he ripped the fabric right down the center leaving the frayed edges at her sides and her breasts exposed. "Brennan!" She pushed at his shoulders. "That was my good chemise."

"I'll buy you another one." He growled and trapped her arms at her sides ceasing her feeble display of resistance. *Mine.* He latched on to one breast and sucked the hardening peak into his mouth. Still, she writhed in his arms as though struggling until a sexy little whimper escaped. He released her arms to better hold her while she gripped his head and urged him closer.

Yes, she belonged to him. She responded like no other. He switched to her other side to lap and nibbled the twin tip. She had such fantastic nipples, long and made for a man's mouth. His cock throbbed as it chafed against his trousers. After retreating a step, he peeled off his clothes in the span of a few heartbeats.

She shed her ruined chemise and sat with her legs splayed on the settee in an obvious erotic pose. He lunged toward her, crazed with lust. Dropping to his knees, he spread her glistening folds and slipped his tongue over the engorged flesh. Her tangy sweetness burst over his taste buds zinging straight to his groin. The tightening of his balls was painfully exquisite.

"Play with your nipples while I sip from your body...your deliciously sinful body."

She groaned, but followed his directions. A heady rush of pleasure at her small submission flowed through him as he returned to licking her pussy. Surrounded by her sweet smell and decadent flavor, he knelt and immersed himself in the woman he loved with no place else he'd rather be. Sliding two fingers into her soaked core, he fingered her in time with the pulsing sucks of his mouth on her clit. Her hips thrust into his hand and face as she sought to quicken the pace. No. It was his orgasm to gift her, and he would not let her take control. He used his free hand to press her hips into the cushion and still her movements. Her panting evened out as he waited for her to settle.

"Slide to the edge of the couch."

She complied again. Moving her bottom to balance at the edge of the cushion, she leaned her head against the back of the furniture. Satisfied, he resumed his ministrations. Collecting as much of her cream as he could, he removed his fingers and dragged them down to the tight sphincter of muscle. He swirled the tips of his finger over it, causing it to ripple in awareness. Desire snaked through him as he slid the first finger in causing him to groan at the tight grasp on the digit. He could imagine how snug she would feel when wrapped around his cock.

She moaned and urged him on, so he added the second finger. With a gasp, she tensed then relaxed at the intrusion. Working the two fingers in and out of her forbidden entrance, he resumed tormenting her swollen nub. Her cries escalated and she exploded on his tongue with very little encouragement. Her backside clamped down on his fingers, grinding them together as he worked to pump them in and out to prolong her orgasm.

She floated in the aftermath of release, very relaxed. Limp on the couch. He spread the fingers still lodged in her rear to open her wider for his cock.

He wanted to bury himself in her and claim her in a way no other had before him. He burned with the selfish need to imprint himself on her so thoroughly she could no longer deny their connection. When he added a third finger, a moan ripped from her. His desire surged from the ashes of her climax.

Realizing he had no salve available to ease his entry, he slipped his fingers from her bottom, rose, and slung her nakedness over his shoulder. Peeking into the hall, he spied no servants and made a quick dash to his chamber. There, he dropped her face down on the bed and dug into the drawer in his nightstand. A jar of salve awaited this moment. He pulled it out and slathered it on his cock. Using the remains on his fingers, he pushed past the rosebud and worked to stretch her a bit more. Satisfied he'd made her as ready as possible, he raised her up on hands and knees and nudged her opening with the tip of his rigid cock. He shoved forward slowly, working the crown of his erection past the tight grip of muscles. With the head in, a burst of lightheadedness whipped through him at the intense heat of her body. Shaking it off, he drove deeper until she gasped.

"Wait." She panted and squirmed, forcing him a bit deeper. "More." Her husky demand made his toes curl and his balls draw up. He took a deep breath and plunged the rest of the way in as she pushed back against him. Fully seated, he savored the moment, reveling in the tight clutch of her channel around his cock. The snugness was even better than he had imagined.

In a slow, delicious slide, he withdrew until just the glans remained within. Then, he pushed back inside. With each stroke, he increased the pace and power of the thrusts. Reaching down between her legs, he sought out her clit and stroked it. Once. Twice. Three times and she exploded. Her back passage clamped down around his cock, squeezing and releasing in a rhythm that gave no quarter. The first wave washed over him in a gentle caress, but as he continued pumping into her, it grew into a tidal wave sweeping the breath from his lungs and thought from his mind. He grunted and groaned, burying his cock in her ass to the hilt. The burst of semen into her body only added to the searing warmth surrounding him.

Withdrawing from her, he fell over and lay there panting. Stretched out on her stomach, she nestled up to him and sighed.

"I could never have imagined how wonderful that could feel."

He slid his arms around her. "I didn't hurt you?"

"No. It pinched at first, but the pleasure wiped out all sense of discomfort. I just felt so full, fantastically full."

He kissed her. A long, lingering kiss that said everything he couldn't express with words.

The following weeks were a blur of activity as Serena settled in to life with Brennan. He treated her to a new wardrobe, replete with shoes, gloves, hats, and all the sheer unmentionables a girl could desire. They spent every evening together, often times making love, and her days were her own to command except when he came home to lunch with her. Without question, life was good.

They had spent four blissful weeks together when reality set in. In the library retrieving another book, Serena heard a female voice in the foyer.

"Good day, Green. Is my brother at home?" Lady Thornton's voice rang out.

"No, my lady. He is at his office, I believe," Brennan's butler said.

"Very good. Is the woman staying here with him available?"

"Oh—um. I...uh..." he stuttered and sputtered.

Taking a deep breath, Serena stepped out of the relative safety of the library and into the sun-drenched foyer. "Why hello, Lady Thornton. It is nice to see you again."

"You? Why Serena, I had heard that some trollop resided with my brother. Whatever are you doing here?" Lady Thornton looked truly confused while the servant turned beet red.

Serena took control of the situation. "Green, will you bring tea into the parlor for Lady Thornton and me?"

"Yes, ma'am." He nodded and left the two women.

"Lady Thornton, why don't we sit in the parlor and I can explain."

"I think that would be best." The veritable dragon Brennan often described followed Serena into the parlor where they sat across from each other.

Serena set her book aside and faced the very proper woman. She hesitated, wishing Brennan was there and yet glad he would not witness what was to come. Taking a deep breath, she steeled herself for the inevitable storm. "I am in fact the trollop staying with your brother."

Lady Thornton blinked once very slowly. "I fail to see how that could be true. Both you and Brennan know better than to do something like this. Clearly there is some explanation."

"The night I met you, your brother, in all innocence, invited me to dinner after meeting me on Bond Street. I was...curious what it might be like to be treated as something other than what I am."

Green entered the room bearing a teacart with mini-tarts and finger sandwiches. He bowed to both ladies and made a quick departure. Serena gathered her composure and continued.

"As I was saying, Brennan had no idea who or what I was. After that night, I disappeared, as you might know, because I avoided Bond Street. I doubt any of your family's acquaintances would know me or acknowledge knowing me." She poured two dishes of tea. "Cream or sugar?"

"Just one lump of sugar, please." Lady Thornton reached out to take the beverage. "True, I doubt they would know you under those circumstances."

"Just so." Serena nodded and took a sip of her own tea. "It happened that a month later Brennan appeared at the establishment where I work."

She drew a sharp breath, her eyebrows nearly meeting her hairline at the notion of her brother's activities including a visit to a brothel. "Never say. I cannot imagine him doing such a thing."

"Yes, well he did. It turned out he requested a redhead, which led him to me. He was, of course, stunned to find me there and quite confused until I explained the truth to him. I lied, deceiving him the night of the dinner party. I have apologized to him, and now owe you one for having knowingly exposed you to someone of my background. I am sure it is quite inappropriate for you to associate with someone such as myself."

Lady Thornton's eyes snapped with a steely glare. "So you deceived my brother and everyone he introduced you to."

"Yes." Serena stared at her hands clutched in her lap.

"This is disgraceful. Have you no shame, taking advantage of him like this?" Her tea abandoned, Lady Thornton rose to pace the floor.

Heat bloomed in Serena's cheeks; her shame swallowed her whole, and yet she would not allow Lady Thornton to believe she took advantage of Brennan. "No! Never! After your brother found me, he arranged a contract for my services for six months and installed me here. I at least managed to keep him from his original notion." Serena held her hands out, begging the angry woman to understand.

"His original notion?" Lady Thornton looked surprised. "Are you suggesting he might have married you? Absolutely unacceptable, that would destroy this family's reputation. No upstanding merchant would do business with Brennan." Horror etched on her face as she considered the idea. She continued to pace, muttering to herself all along.

Serena caught bits and pieces of her monologue, including one troubling bit about canning someone. Whether such punishment was meant for her or Brennan she was unsure.

Then the pinched quality relaxed from Lady Thornton's face, replaced by a thoughtful look. "I am a member of the Women's Improvement Society. We help prostitutes get off the streets and start a new life. I am sure I could assist you, but you will leave my brother alone." Lady Thornton stopped and locked gazes with her.

Striving for a calm soothing tone so not to upset the woman any more, she tried to explain. "Lady Thornton, I will not leave my life. It is all I know, all I have ever known as the daughter of a prostitute. Everything I am I owe to Madame Marchander. She taught me to be a lady. She gave me a place to live and work where I am treated fairly and earn more money than I ever could working in a factory or selling flowers on the corner."

"I do understand. I have seen too many of the women we try to help return to that life for those very reasons. But surely we could provide you with a better situation." She returned to her seat.

"Yes. We could, but the stubborn chit we are dealing with would refuse. Wouldn't she?" Brennan stalked into the parlor as the clock struck two in the afternoon.

"What are you doing home at this hour?" Surprised, Serena's face warmed as he bussed her cheek in his customary greeting and sat down.

"Green sent a note around when you invited the dragon to have tea and discuss our living arrangements." Brennan helped himself to a dish of tea and relaxed back.

"Finally that bumbling butler of yours shows some promise," Lady Thornton snapped at her brother.

"Yes, well. Regardless, I would not have accepted any arrangement but the one we have. Your brother knows me too well." Serena darted a glance at Brennan. His expression remained perfectly neutral. Was he angry?

"The current situation is not acceptable. Word is getting out, and I will not have you sullying the family name by keeping this woman in your home." The dragon had made her pronouncement. She rose from her seat and sauntered across the room to the door.

Brennan rose and faced his sister's back. "I'm afraid, Caroline, that our living arrangements are none of your concern. May I suggest you find someone else's life to interfere in?"

"Brennan, you will heed me on this." With her parting words, she swept from the room and out of the house.

Damn his sister to perdition. He had been planning for over a week on asking Serena to marry him that night over dinner. With his sister's judgments ringing in her ears, Serena would never accept. "That was an interesting visit."

"Quite." Serena sniffled and dashed out of the parlor.

"Bloody hell," Brennan cursed, rising to follow her.

He took the stairs behind her two at a time and found her bedroom door locked. He detoured into his own room and tried the connecting door. Unlocked. He slipped into the room and found Serena stretched across the bed, her body shuddering as she cried.

"Please love, don't cry." Brennan eased onto the bed.

She sniffled and started to sit up. "I'm sorry, I know it is not a mistress-like thing to do, but I fear I have disrupted your life and made your sister angry with you."

Brennan handed her a handkerchief. "Do not be silly. She is a veritable fire-breathing dragon who only looks like a woman. If it were not this, she would be huffing and puffing about some other perceived failing on my part. Now settle down." He rubbed her back as she hiccupped and sniffed her tears into submission. "I have a lovely evening already planned, including attending the masked ball at Vauxhall Garden. Will you feel up to going?"

Serena nodded and sighed. "I will. I don't want to ruin the evening you planned for us."

"Good. Now I am going back to the office for a bit to wrap up my business. I'll be home to clean up and change later." He kissed her nose and headed out of the bedroom door. Maybe he could salvage the night and get her to see he loved her.

CHAPTER SEVEN

S erena sat at her vanity. Well, the table was not really hers, was it? She peered into the glass and coiled the last rope of hair into place. Warm hands came down on her shoulders in a gentle squeeze. She glanced up meeting Brennan's heated gaze in the mirror. His hands slipped down to cup her exposed breasts through the sheer material of her chemise. He took each nipple between his thumbs and forefingers and rolled them. Waves of pleasure fired down into her belly. She leaned back into his body as he continued the attention.

"You look lovely this evening." His voice was a sensual growl as if disused.

"I'm not even dressed." She let her eyes slide close while enjoying the pleasant sensations.

"Ah, but lovely nonetheless." He chuckled. "Turn around for me."

Serena did as directed. He stepped between her legs, spread them wide, and kneeled down. He ran a finger across her slick opening and rubbed it up over her clit. Then, he dipped it back down and plunged into her pussy to work in and out. A soft moan escaped at his erotic assault on her senses. He added a second finger to his effort and tipped forward to suckle one nipple through her chemise. The tingles tightened and grew more focused as the pace of his fingers increased.

As she drew near to cresting that peak, he stopped. He withdrew his fingers, licked them clean, and sauntered toward the door between their rooms. "I suggest you get dressed to go."

Her body was alive with all the sensations he had stirred up. The slightest brush against her nipples caused a deep throbbing between her thighs. Every movement carried torture, exquisite torture that would continue for quite a while. With a resigned sigh, she stood and called for Maggie to help her finish dressing for the evening.

A short while later she swept down the stairs. Brennan waited below looking dashing in his dark evening clothes, matching domino, and mask. The perfect foil of Night to her Day, with her bright blue gown and matching mask adorned with peacock feathers.

"Good evening, Master Night." She curtsied once on the floor of the foyer.

"Good evening, Mistress Day." He bowed to her. "Your carriage awaits."

They departed for Vauxhall, every bump in the road causing her nipples to rasp against her chemise. She squirmed in her seat while rubbing her thighs together for some kind of relief.

"Stop fidgeting, Serena." Brennan's implacable tone left no room for argument. This was that dominant side he was slowly revealing, and she found she liked it as much as she liked his more tender side.

Adept at role-playing, she bit her lip and stilled her body. "Yes, Master Night."

Brennan settled back against the squabs of the carriage and relished her flexibility and resilience. She could follow as easily as lead, and she had not let his sister's visit spoil their evening. He thought back to their interlude in her bedroom. How she opened to him and how responsive she was. His original intent had been to give her release and help her relax for the evening. But he changed his ploy when he found her so responsive and relaxed already. Perhaps having her anticipate what would come later would be good for her. Help her see they belonged together.

The carriage stopped and the door swung open to reveal the glittering lights of Vauxhall Gardens. He climbed down before assisting her in alighting. The voluminous skirts of her dress fell out around her to a graceful drape. His eyes snagged on the expanse of cleavage exposed. He bit back a groan, grateful the domino he wore would hide his rampant erection.

"I have a private table reserved for us right off the orchestra." He grasped her arm and led her to their spot. As requested the candelabras were half lit and the champagne chilled.

"This is excellent, Brennan—I mean, Master Night." Her lips tilted up at the corners as she took the seat he offered her near the railing.

"I am pleased you like it, Mistress Day." He sat across from her and poured the champagne. "Have you never been to Vauxhall?"

"I've never had the opportunity to visit." She peeked up through a fringe of lashes. "Had I known it had so much to offer I might have tried to attend sooner."

"Ah, but then I would not have had the pleasure of bringing you." He sipped his drink before opening the curtains to reveal the colorful swirl of dancers gliding by.

"It is amazing all the colors and people." Pleasure shone on her face as she leaned forward to gawk at the display. She paused and drew in a long deep breath. Brennan grinned in satisfaction at the turmoil he created. She cast him a glance full of desire. It emanated from her in palpable waves.

"Are you well, Mistress Day?"

She nodded.

"Perhaps you would like to dance with me?" He stood and presented his hand. Silently, she accepted the offering and rose from her chair. He maneuvered her down a step onto the dance floor and swept her into an effortless waltz. He clutched her closer than proper so that her belly rested against his hip allowing her to feel the rigid shaft along his thigh. The intimate embrace crushed her pebbled nipples into his chest. He wanted her melting into a puddle of need by the end of the dance.

When he led her back to their private table and drew the curtains for privacy, he tipped her into his lap and fed her one of the hors d'oeuvres that had appeared on their table while they had danced. She nibbled the bite of toast and caviar and licked the crumbs from his fingers. A growl escaped him as the tip of her tongue darted out from between her lips to caress his finger.

Tilting her head more toward him, he kissed her and popped one of her breasts from the confines of her bodice. Their tongues dueled while he squeezed her nipple between his fingers. Hearing her moan and then feeling her grind against his lap in need, he released the hard nub and gathered the front of her skirts up to her thighs. Gaining access to her damp cleft, he tugged her clit, much as he had done with her nipple. She lay her head back on his shoulder and squirmed in his lap.

"Mmmm, Brennan," she murmured, her voice almost inaudible over the music.

He stopped. "Who is this Brennan fellow?"

"I mean, Master Night." She bit her lip and pressed against his hand. He resumed his attentions, though he thrust his finger inside of her heated channel. She rippled around him, soaked with her own desire, as he added a second finger and pumped them in and out of her body. She reached up to caress her own breast, freed the other, and plucked and twisted both her nipples as he slid his fingers deep inside her. Gorgeous. She straddled his lap with her thighs splayed wide for his attention. Enticed by her wanton display, he feared he might come without her ever touching him.

He stopped. "Stand up and turn around. I find I must be inside you this instant." He opened his domino and his trousers to reveal his throbbing erection. Easing her back into his lap, he guided her over his cock and pulled her down. She gasped and her eyes widened in pleasure.

An importunate knock on the servant's door broke the moment. "Not now," he barked. His patience was nonexistent as he held back his release. Her heat alone could set him off, but paired with the gentle clutching of her sheath he was very nearly unmanned.

After a moment, he allowed her to move. Strong thighs helped her rise and fall, impaling her on his erection. Over. And over again. She ground into him until she came with a shuddering spasm designed to milk his seed from his body before he was ready. Spying a small bench, he rose up and carried her to it. He set her down and stayed between her legs to drive his cock back into her heat. He could fuck her properly with unfettered access, allowing him to pump in and out in a rhythm that synchronized with the beat of the country-dance that played. A few more strokes and he withdrew to come in his handkerchief.

He straightened, stuffed the soiled cloth in his pocket, and helped Serena sit up. "My apologies for attacking you like a randy schoolboy."

"No apology required." Serena flashed him a seductive smirk promising more.

He nodded and strode to the door of the booth. He opened it to find a ruddy-faced footman camped outside. "Please have dinner brought in."

The footman nodded and disappeared. He returned a short while later with a cart bearing their meal.

Brennan had reclaimed his seat, observing her with an uncomfortable intensity. A wave of gratitude rolled over her when the waiter served their meal. Food allowed her to focus on something other than the man across the table. Her heart raced as she suspected him of screwing up the courage to ask for her hand in marriage. That would be an utter disaster. How could she, a prostitute, marry him, a successful businessman? No, without a doubt, after Lady Thornton's reaction that afternoon it would never be possible. She would have to end their arrangement. She should have ended it when she realized she had developed deeper feelings. Madame Marchander had always warned her girls about fancying themselves in love with a customer. Brennan was a customer, and she remained bought and paid for, for six months, or until one of them ended the arrangement.

The waiter laid her napkin in her lap, letting the material drape over her skirts. The tension grew palpable as neither said a word. Each studied the other until the man departed the private booth and Brennan cleared his throat.

CHAPTER EIGHT

"Serena, I wanted to thank you for the last few weeks. I cannot begin to tell you how much I have enjoyed having you with me and a part of my life. I find it hard to imagine life without you."

She released the breath she did not realize she'd been holding. No! He could not do this. It would ruin his life, his business.

Panic surged through her causing her stomach to contract and release in time with the pounding at her temples.

Brennan eased forward in his seat. His hand slipped into his pocket and produced a small elaborately enameled box. The violets painted on the lid were remarkable in their detail and her favorite flower. How did he know? Then the box opened to reveal a stunning pair of sapphires encircled by diamonds. *Oh goodness.*

"Serena, I don't give a damn what my sister or anyone else thinks. I will not release you from our contract, and I will not move you out of my house." His gaze locked with hers, saying far more than his simple statement.

Her heart cracked a little. No one but a fool would think he'd propose after his sister's visit. And even if he had, she would have had to reject the man she wanted more than any other because it would never work. She would never be accepted by his family or his friends.

Breaking their gazes, she looked at the dazzling display of jewelry. "Oh, Brennan...." She drew in a deep breath and settled her whirling thoughts. "I cannot accept such an expensive gift. It is beautiful, but too much."

"Why can't you accept them?" His pleasure dimmed a bit as the sparkle in his eyes faded.

"It is too extravagant. Besides, I think—" She bit her lip and glanced around the small space as she willed her hands to cease shaking. "—your sister is right. I should not be staying in your house. If your clients hear of my presence, they will refuse to do business with you and of course the scandal is shameful for your family." Refusing to cry, she blinked rapidly.

"My business might suffer a bit, but I am certain I can rebound. Many of my clients will never know nor care. I love you, Serena. If you would marry me, I'd spend my life with you regardless of the consequences. But, for now I will be content with you sharing my bed." He turned his stubborn gaze on her, chin tilting ever so slightly in defiance.

"Brennan, I cannot allow you to ruin your life like this. Your future. I would happily become your mistress, warm your bed, and give you comfort all my days tucked away in a small house not too far from you. But I should not continue to live with you. I will not steal your future and be labeled a social-climbing whore, for that is what I would be." Wet tracks of tears trickled down her face.

Brennan reached across the space and offered her his handkerchief. "My sister is damn near intolerable. All my life I have listened to her strictures, honoring her as I would a parent. But no more. In time she will come around and see how happy you make me. Please, grant me a short while, and I promise any uproar will fade into the cacophony of other, juicier scandals."

Falling in love was a cruel twist of fate considering her origins. Pain lanced through her chest as the truth set in. He had not said he loved her since the night he found her. Could she trust that the continuance of their arrangement wasn't a ploy to aggravate his sister? Yes, the man she had come to know would never be so callow. She had to believe deep down he cared and spoke the truth. She would be willing to live with that for now.

Brennan sat, still clutching the ear bobs, and stared at a thoughtful Serena. They never spoke of love, even in the afterglow of sex. They cuddled and talked of their childhoods or friends. He often told her about his business, but never once did either of them mention love since the night at The Market. Having said it, he would not call the words back, but he wished she would return the sentiment.

He sighed and closed the jewelry box, slipping it back into his pocket. What a complete and utter disaster. He'd made his plea, now he had to wait and see how she would respond.

The tip of her pink tongue slipped out to moisten her lips. "Brennan, I-I'll stay on a bit longer. But, please know if I feel you are suffering because of my presence, I will not hesitate to end the contract and return to The Market before our time is up."

He nodded, relief having tied his tongue in knots. The revelry forgotten, he rose silently, and took her arm. He led her from the box, out the servant's door, and through the warren of back halls. Finding a side door, they bolted into the cool night air and made haste for his carriage. Once alone, he pulled her into his arms and simply held her on his lap as they drove home. The house had become home because she was there, would continue to be there.

The vehicle halted, forcing him to release her. They retired to his room. The signs of strain were evident around her eyes and mouth. It dawned on him that he'd said nothing since before leaving the masquerade. He cleared his throat, causing her to jump and gasp. "I'm sorry I've been so quiet. I am very glad you are staying on." He reached out to drag his knuckles along her jawline.

"As am I." Her lashes lowered hiding her thoughts from him.

"Look at me, Serena." The compulsion to let her hide nothing from him caused his hands to tremble with the need to force her chin up so he could stare into her eyes.

Her compliance required no physical action from him as she submitted to his command without question.

"Never hide your feelings or thoughts from me. I always want to know what is going on inside that pretty head of yours. Hiding from each other will do nothing but get us into trouble."

"Yes, Brennan." Her gaze remained locked with his.

"Now I am going to strip you bare so I may enjoy all of your charms." He smiled a bit in an attempt to ease the apprehension lurking in her eyes.

"Please." Her whole body trembled with anticipation. The unholy fire dancing in his eyes and the steel edge of his words combined to unleash a storm of need unlike anything she had ever experienced. She vibrated with the desire to please him. On the ride home, he'd held her with such tender possessiveness he melted her heart. How could she keep her emotions from him when it seemed she came under constant assault from his love?

At some point between her agreement to stay and arriving in his chamber, she came to understand that he loved her, and she was terrified. The more time they spent together, the more possessive he became, the more commanding of not only her body but her emotions. It seemed he would settle for nothing less than baring her inner landscape for his inspection.

"Turn around." His deep resonance sliced through her introspection.

She presented her back and he unlaced her gown, making short work of the many layers of undergarments. Standing gloriously naked in front of a warm fire, she waited, caught between her desire to please him and her own need to feel his flesh beneath her fingertips.

"My turn. If you will assist me, this will go much faster."

"Of course." She stepped forward, eased his jacket off his shoulders, and loosened his neck cloth. Parting the front panels of his shirt, her fingers glided over his warm skin, seeking out his pebbled nipples.

He trapped her hands, groaning like a wounded animal. "Cease. I said undress me. I did not say to torture me. Behave or I promise you will be punished like the naughty little girl you are. Now, finish the task at hand."

With a short nod, she tamped down her own wants long enough to strip him of his shirt and stockings. Once she got his breeches down she tackled his small clothes, but could not resist a quick grope of his buttocks as they were exposed.

"Madame, you will pay for that stray caress. I hope it was worth it." He stroked his stiff rod and flashed a chilling grin promising retribution. His dominant side surged to the fore again, and her body responded to him in spades.

"I assure you, it was well worth it." Her mind had a different response, desiring to push and challenge. How far would he let this game go? Would he spank her? A shiver of anticipation snaked down her spine.

He quirked an eyebrow up. "I see." He took her wrist and towed her over to the chair before the fire. There, he sat and proceeded to pull her body across his lap. She was in trouble. Biting her lip to keep from begging his pardon, she recognized she'd provoked this. That she craved this. The first blow landed across her bottom and sparked a small dull flame. The next two, alternating between cheeks, fanned the flames into a full burn. "I think we need to come to an understanding. You belong to me, Serena. I love you, and I will convince you of this before our time is up. I will prove to you love exists and it can be trusted, as I can be trusted."

He landed two more blows causing her to whimper as she tried not to cry out. Her body shuddered at the delicious heat spreading from her backside to her pussy.

"I will take care of you. I will see to your every need and desire. But sometimes, those needs and desires will be met at a pace set by me. You will accept this, as I am coming to accept this. You are too headstrong by half, but you will learn to allow me to take care of you. Do you understand?" He paused, and while she understood what he wanted her to say, she could not find the words in the jumble knotting her brain. He smacked her twice more.

"Yes! I understand," burst from her lips before her brain could rein the words in.

"Very good." He helped her to sit up and then to take a seat on his lap.

Her bottom burned from his attentions, even as she worked on rebuilding her defenses.

"Are you all right, Serena?" He stroked her face before starting on the pins in her hair.

"I think so." Her response again came from somewhere deep within that her brain appeared to be cut off from.

"I can't explain my reactions to you. I have never been this way with a woman before, but something about you drives me to it. I cannot explain nor ignore this desire to protect you, to care for you. I will not let anyone stand in my way. Not even you." He gripped the back of her head and kissed her with a ferocity that stole her breath and puddled her insides. Had she not been sitting in his lap, she surely would have collapsed to the floor.

He broke their kiss leaving her gasping for air and words to express the turmoil of desire raging within. She had never been spanked so she was ill prepared for the desperate need that swamped her. "Brennan, I—"

"No, I want no declarations from you tonight. Too much has happened. In time the opportunity for you to express your true emotions will come. You must be sure of what you are feeling before you can share it with someone else. Now, I feel the very great need to bury myself deep within your heat." He helped her stand. "Get on the bed and on your back to start."

Serena scrambled onto the coverlet and lay down as directed. Her submission was the best way she could show him the depth of emotion she was experiencing. He crawled up between her legs and forced them to spread wider. Her pussy throbbed for want of him, any part of him he might grant her. Anticipation sensitized her skin until little jolts of electrical current zipped back and forth. His finger slid between her moist lips and spread her open for his perusal.

"I believe spanking agrees with you. I have yet to caress you anywhere, nonetheless you are sopping wet." He slid a finger deep into her channel and curved up toward that magical spot.

"Oh! Oh, Brennan."

He added a second digit and began stroking her inside. "That's it, love. Take what you need from me."

Her hips pumped against his hand as her need increased. When his tongue swiped across her clit, she groaned and sank her fingers into his silky hair. "Please," she begged.

He continued to caress her sensitive nub with his tongue as he pushed her toward climax with unfailing accuracy. Frantic and needing release, the first wave broke over her sending tingles down her arms and legs, but then he switched his hand and tongue. Lapping at her entry and driving in with his tongue to taste her. He massaged her clit in firm relentless strokes that burst through her like the fireworks display at Vauxhall Gardens. With slow, measured licks and suckles, he eased her down until she lay on the bed a boneless mess.

"I can't be sure which I prefer more. Watching you come for me or tasting you when you do. We will have to explore this further so I can make a decision." His mischievous smirk desecrated the meager fortifications she had rebuilt. Feeling raw and vulnerable, she raised her arms to him.

"Come into me, Brennan. I wish to feel you buried deep within me."

He growled at her invitation as he slid between her thighs and drove his cock deep into her pussy. He thrust into her and filled every nook and cranny of her body. If she weren't such a practical girl, she would swear he had been made for her. Each push into her core stroked across her swollen tissues. She quivered around him as he took her over and over until cognizance slipped beyond her ability and she became one giant hyper-sensitized bundle.

He suckled a nipple as he plunged into her and she exploded. Awareness of the room, the bed, anything except where their bodies linked no longer mattered. His weight anchoring her down kept her from floating away on a tide of bliss. When he did join her, crying out her name in benediction, she realized what it meant to make love to a man. But where did that leave her?

A month slipped by before Serena realized it and her unspoken love for Brennan grew until it stretched the boundaries of her heart. She could not remember when she had been as happy, and it had everything to do with the kind, caring, and demanding man who shared her bed every night.

Peeking out the window, she spied the bright sunshine and decided today would be perfect for a picnic lunch with him. She shot out of bed and sent Maggie hurrying around to get everything ready for her to pick up Brennan.

A few hours later, arrangements all made, she headed off to his warehouse to coax him into playing hooky with her for the afternoon. She wore a sprigged muslin dress topped off by a jaunty straw chip hat with the loveliest green ribbons trailing from it. Spirits high, she sailed into the enormous building and strolled about looking for Brennan. She had never been to his warehouse, but she had no doubt he would be happy to see her.

After wandering for a few minutes, she found a door that appeared to lead to a smaller office like space. She opened it and stepped in to find a desk and a second door sitting ajar. Stepping toward it, raised voices caught her attention and she hesitated. Perhaps this had been a bad idea. Closer, she could make out words.

"Mr. Whitling, orders are down. Many of the merchants who cater to the wealthy are canceling long-standing orders. We have to do something to stop this." The speaker, a broad-shouldered man with salt-and-pepper hair, slumped into a chair across the desk from Brennan.

"I understand, Robert. I am working on some new clients, but I will not bow to societal pressures. My private life is none of their business. I provide them quality fabrics at reasonable prices. Who is living under my roof should be no concern of theirs."

"But, Mr. Whitling, Brennan, having such a woman in your house is costing us business. How much longer can you keep the doors open with the dwindling orders? We've already lost three men who refuse to work for you."

"I love her, Robert. She stays. I will work the rest of the issues out in time. I am very close to landing a new client, and once I do others will follow. I promise I can and will turn this around."

Serena's excitement and joy slithered from her person leaving her shoulders slumped. She had to leave Brennan or watch his world crumble around him. He was too stubborn to see letting her go was the right thing to do. One last night to take with her, to store away with all the other memories she had been hording for just such a day.

Turning, she slipped from the anteroom and through the warehouse cloaked in silence and weighed down by her decision. Back in the carriage, she let the tears flow as the driver returned her to Brennan's home one last time. She readied the two new gowns she bought and a few other things she had brought with her from The Market. Later, Brennan's footsteps rang through the house as he arrived home. Pasting on a smile, she greeted him wearing nothing but her wrapper.

A single knock heralded his entrance. He beamed at her from across the room. "Good evening Serena." He closed the door and swept her into his arms kissing her soundly.

As they parted, her heart raced, pounding in her chest. Pushing down her sadness, she tried desperately to affect a cheerfulness she did not claim. "Hello."

"Why don't you get dressed? Dinner will be ready soon and then I want to stroll in the garden." He stepped away and headed toward the door that joined their rooms.

Stiffening her resolve, she watched him disappear and then rang for Maggie. She needed to dress and the quicker the better.

The sun had set, blanketing the sky in darkness. Stars twinkled overhead as she wrapped her shawl tighter about her shoulders. Brennan draped an arm about her hoping to offer her a bit more warmth. Excitement left him a little breathless as he anticipated proposing to Serena, and her accepting. Deep in his bones lie the knowledge she loved him; he saw it in her eyes every time their gazes met or they made love.

They rounded the corner following the hedges and a small gasp loosed from the feminine body next to him. "Oh, how lovely."

They took in hundreds of candles flickering in the dark, casting a warm glow on the garden. Everywhere one looked sat a candle, except for a bench in the midst of it all. His confidence grew by leaps and bounds. He led her to the bench and lowered himself to one knee. A trembling hand came up to cover her mouth.

"Serena, I have made no secret of how I feel about you. You bring me joy and laughter and make me want to cosset and protect you from all that is wrong with the world. I cannot imagine our contract coming to an end and you no longer being here, in my bed, in my arms, or in my heart. I love you to distraction and most humbly beg you to please make me the happiest of men by becoming my wife."

He opened a small jewelry box, identical to the one that had held the earrings she'd refused. The difference being, that nestled inside lay a sapphire-and-diamond ring. Her gaze sought his, but instead of joy he found heartbreak and sadness lacing her eyes.

"No." A small, pitiful cry escaped from her as she stood.

A denial of his suit or something else?

"No, Brennan, I cannot marry you. I will not be responsible for ruining your life...your business. I came by your office this afternoon to invite you on a picnic." She drew a deep breath.

"Serena, please!" He rose up from his knee.

"No, Brennan. I know. I know you are losing business, just as your sister said you would, because I am here. I told you before I would not tolerate being your downfall. I'm sorry, I cannot marry you. Please consider our contract severed." She moved around him, leaving him rooted to the spot unable to move or object.

He was stunned by her speech as he groped about his mind for an argument. Precious little came to mind beyond the truth. "But, I love you," he called out to her retreating back.

She paused, looking over her shoulder, the soft glow of the candles casting a halo about her. A single tear tracked down the soft skin of her cheek. "Good-bye, Brennan."

And then she was gone.

Brennan collapsed to his knees and cried, surrounded by candlelight and alone in the garden. Sometime later, he picked himself up from the ground and resolved to find her. Make her see reason. Upstairs in her room, he found all of the gowns he had paid for, but no sign of her. All her trinkets from the vanity were gone as well.

He stalked downstairs, ordered his carriage and headed to his club. He needed a stiff drink and some masculine company.

Settled into a comfortable wing chair by a roaring fire with a brandy in his hand, he could almost pretend the disaster of a proposal had not happened. But Andrew appeared, confused as to why Brennan sat in their chairs.

"Weren't you proposing to your ladybird tonight?" Andrew settled in the open chair.

"It did not go as hoped. She was less than enthused by my offer." Brennan frowned and swirled the snifter of amber liquid.

"I see. She refused you?"

"She fled into the night. She refused to be the cause of my financial failure."

"She does have a point. You're losing business now that word's got out you are living with a whore. I cannot imagine what would happen if you married her." Andrew shrugged.

"If you ever refer to her as such again, I will wallop you where you stand." He issued the threat and sipped his drink, relishing the burn from his tongue to his gullet.

"Very well. Give her a day to calm down and then visit her. Bring her flowers and chocolates, you know the usual things." Andrew nodded sagely.

Brennan grunted in acknowledgement and pondered his options.

Serena arrived at The Market, unable to stop the flow of tears. After slipping in the back door, she crept to her room and shut herself in. Tomorrow she would figure out how to go on; how to continue to live with a gaping hole in her chest. Madame had warned all the girls that while sometimes their customers would take them as mistresses, might dote on them, and play the besotted swain, it was foolish to fall prey to any semblance of love. Falling in love with your protector was a certain path to misery. And Serena could personally attest to the validity of those warnings.

Still unsure how she arrived at such a disastrous end, Serena crushed her face into the pillows and sobbed. She mourned all that could have been had she been born to different circumstances, and she mourned all that would never be. No man would ever touch her as deeply or stir her soul in the manner Brennan had. Her existence would be a solitary one, always giving pleasure, never experiencing it, for all things paled in comparison to the joy she had found in Brennan's embrace and in his love. As she drifted off to sleep, she recalled the feel of his arms around her, the heat of his breath on her skin, the slide of his firm muscular frame against her softer one. In her dreams, she would take solace in his memory and the love that burned so strongly between them.

Rising stiffly from her bed, Serena went in search of Madame Marchander. A light knock was answered, calling her in to the office.

"What are you doing here so early, Serena?" Madame sat by the fire sipping her morning cocoa.

"I have ended the contract with Mr. Whitling."

"Oh? Why is that?"

"He fancies himself in love with me. It seemed better to end it now rather than allow the situation to drag out to the inevitable end."

"What end would that have been?" Madame quirked an eyebrow up.

"Why, the end of the contract."

"Did he not propose to you while you were with him?"

Serena's hands shook with nervousness. "He did."

"Do you not love him then?"

Confusion whirled through her head. Why was Madame asking these questions? "Yes—but, it cannot be. I am a whore, and he is a gentleman. All he worked for was crumbling around him. I refuse to be the cause of his ruin. He would ultimately hate me for it one day when he woke up and realized that not only was his business failing but he had tied himself to such an unsuitable woman."

"I see. Are you sure this is what you want?"

Serena gathered the fraying bits of her resolve. "I'm certain. I am ending the contract as I was told I could."

"Very well, I will send a note returning the balance of his fees. Take a day or two for yourself, then you may return to socializing in the salon. You may refrain from servicing any customers until you feel you are ready, but don't be too long about it. I doubt it will become easier with time."

"Thank you, Madame."

A week later Brennan and his friend sat considering their options. "Andrew, I called on her bearing flowers and candies, but she refused to see me. I had flowers delivered with a note, they were refused. I had a boy watch the house to alert me if she came out so I could have a word with her on the street, but she has not left. If she won't see me, how can I convince her to marry me?"

His friend looked thoughtful. "Perhaps you could try a different approach to convince her you two should be together."

"What do you suggest? I must say I am at a loss."

"What of a healthy dose of jealousy?"

"Jealousy? How can I make her jealous if she will not see me?"

"She might not see you, but she will hear things. Perhaps Madame Marchander could be of some assistance?"

"I see. I make her believe I have moved on, and she will come to me begging for another chance? Do you honestly believe that will work?"

"Women chase men they want all the time. Why shouldn't it? You simply need to find a woman to carry on with and ensure she hears of it."

"Would your sister be willing to let me court her?"

"Hold on there now. I did not say to drag Melanie into this."

"Come on, Andrew. I wouldn't want to bring some chit into this plot that would have an expectation of an unrealistic outcome. We would tell your sister what is going on."

"Unacceptable."

"Why don't you at least let her hear me out and see what she thinks?" Brennan sat forward, hope blossoming anew.

"Silly chit would go right along with you all in the name of love," Andrew grumbled.

"Come, don't make me remind you who helped you out when you needed someone to escort Melanie to the Shaferton soiree last season?" Brennan hated bringing it up, but he needed her help and he needed Andrew to agree.

Andrew sipped his own brandy. "I knew your help would come back to haunt me. Very well, we will speak to her tomorrow."

Brennan sat across from Melanie over tea with Andrew on his right. He had not heard from Serena since her flight. He was certain this remained the best way to get her attention. The three friends sat awkwardly over tea and shared a stilted conversation about the weather. Not one of them cared the sun had not been out for the last four days.

Within a short time, they realized they had much to explain.

"I do not understand why you do not simply tell the woman how you feel about her," Melanie urged.

"I have. She does not believe she is worthy of becoming my wife, and she believes she is ruining my business." Brennan grew more frustrated every time he explained the situation.

"I must say, I would advise against this little plot you two have hatched." She looked from her brother to Brennan. Disapproval creased her forehead, drawing her brows together.

Brennan took a deep breath and refused to let go of hope. She would come around. Melanie always had a soft heart.

"However, if you really believe this is the only way, I will help you." A smile dissipated her earlier frown.

"Thank you. I cannot tell you how much this means to me. If ever there is anything I can do...." Brennan came forward to the edge of the chair and grasped her hand.

"Oh, I am sure I will think of some way you can help me in the future." She winked and took her hands back. "In the meantime, we must plot a way for you to be seen with me and have word get back to Miss Freemont."

"We shall go for a drive in Hyde Park and perhaps do some shopping on Bond Street. Then Andrew here will be responsible for ensuring word gets back to her that I am having dinner with you at my home, alone." Brennan nodded, pleased with the plan.

"Obviously, I will not be there when she arrives, but by that time it will be too late, and she will have shown her hand." She clasped her hands and sighed.

Andrew stood. "Well, I suggest you two go for that drive while I work on my part. Brennan, I assume shopping tomorrow and dinner tomorrow evening will give her time to react?"

"Indeed. I imagine she will be quite angry once this all unfolds, hopefully just angry enough to make her realize we belong together." He shook hands with Andrew then turned to his accomplice. "Shall we go for that drive? I believe it is the fashionable hour."

"Yes, let's." She rose from the settee. "I'll be just a moment." The golden-haired girl floated out of the parlor leaving Brennan alone with her brother.

"You will be able to secure a token for The Market? My agreement did not include any or I would take care of it for you." Brennan and Andrew walked into the foyer to wait.

"I should have no problem. Tomorrow night I will drop by there and plant the seed. I imagine she will hotfoot it over to your townhouse once she hears." Andrew clapped him on the shoulder.

"We shall see." Brennan took his hat from the butler and turned to take Melanie's arm as she rejoined them ready for a drive.

CHAPTER NINE

S erena could not stand the misery any longer. He continued, relentless in his pursuit, and if he came to see her once more, she would fall apart. There was one person she believed could help her bring this siege to an end. Lady Caroline Thornton.

She took a huge risk. The lady would likely slam the door in her face before she got two words out, but she had to try. For her sake and for his she stood before the imposing door of Lord and Lady Thornton's townhouse. She lifted the heavy brass knocker and tapped it against the matching plate. The door opened to reveal a starchy butler with bushy eyebrows and a bit of a sneer on his face.

"How can I help you?" He sniffed with disdain.

Serena handed a calling card to the formidable figure. "Miss Serena Freemont to see Lady Thornton." She strived for the brisk, no-nonsense tone that usually got her what she needed with recalcitrant servants.

"Wait here." He disappeared and the door thumped shut.

Serena remained on the stoop working to rein in her temper. She needed to be calm for the coming discussion. Shortly, the door opened again and swung wide. "This way, please."

She followed the crusty old man into a sumptuous sitting room where Lady Thornton sat perched on a delicate settee.

"Please come in, Miss Freemont." Lady Thornton waved her over, indicating a seat near her.

"Thank you for seeing me, Lady Thornton. I will not take any more of your time than required to beg you for your assistance."

"Do you wish to take me up on my original offer?" she inquired and sipped her tea.

"It is about your brother. As I am sure you are well aware, I have severed all ties with him in an effort to salvage his professional reputation. I came to learn he lost business because of our association. Then he proposed to me and I said no before leaving. However, since then he has hounded me. Sending flowers, candies, notes, and he even had a boy sit across the street to watch for my comings and goings. I am a prisoner in The Market!" To her great mortification, tears slipped down her cheeks. She had sworn she was done crying over Brennan Whitling, but once again her wretched emotions had gotten the best of her.

Lady Thornton perused her as though she could peel back the layers of skin and bone and see deep within. "Do you love him? Do you love my brother?"

Indecision gripped Serena, would she be appalled to know the truth? "God forgive me, yes. I do love him, and if he does not cease this onslaught, I will have no ability to refuse him. My heart breaks anew every time I send him away."

"Then don't." Lady Thornton calmly sipped her tea then took a delicate nibble of a scone.

"I beg your pardon?"

"Don't refuse him. It is clear he loves you. Enough he has refused to acknowledge my guidance, and he has entirely restructured his business. He has acquired customers who have no interest in who he spends his nights with, so his business will recover before any lasting damage is done."

Thunderstruck, Serena gaped at the serene lady across from her. Her heart pounded as the blood rushed to her head. Spots formed before her eyes, so she drew a deep breath and blinked. "But I'm a whore! You said it yourself, Lady Thornton. He has no business marrying someone like me."

"Pish. I was being a ridiculous, closed-minded prude. It is unfortunate I tend in that direction more often than not. But, having seen how happy my brother was with you and how miserable he is without, I am left to conclude he is better off with you in his life irrespective of your past. I have known enough women like you to know they are often strong of character, ethical, and most important they are survivors. Brennan needs someone like that in his life. I want my brother to be as happy as I, and you seem to make that happen."

"You are wrong, Lady Thornton. I am terrible for Brennan. I will ruin his life. I am sorry if I bothered you. Good day." Stiff with shock and despair, she rose and exited the house as if she strolled through grand homes of the nobility every day. She was doomed. She would make one last effort to dissuade him, and if she failed she would speak to Madame and see about leaving England. Nothing else she could see would stop the persistent man.

The previous day's drive in Hyde Park had been uneventful. Today, Brennan intended to take Melanie shopping on Bond Street where he met Serena. With any luck she would see him, and once Andrew stopped by The Market that evening, would be goaded into appearing at his door. He placed his hat atop his head and clambered up into his phaeton.

An hour later, he walked into a milliner's shop with Melanie on Bond Street when a flash of auburn hair caught his eye. He looked again but could not spot her, despite his certainty he had seen her. The increased thump of his heart told him she must be near.

Melanie tried on a few hats before settling on a lovely light green *chapeau* she declared would best match one of her riding dresses. She handed it to him to carry for her, and they left the shop. Next stop, her dressmaker's where she was due for a fitting. Brennan found himself sitting in the shop and waiting on her when he spied another glimpse of red hair through the window. All proceeded according to plan.

Serena dragged Miranda past the modiste's after seeing Brennan waltz down the street carrying a box for the pretty little blond chit he strolled with.

"Damn him! How dare he ask me to marry him and then not two weeks later be out on Bond Street shopping with some chit barely out of the school room!" Her blood drummed in her veins and battered against her temples. This was a drastic improvement from the melancholy she had wallowed in since leaving Lady Thornton's the day before.

"Well, you did say no and run off. What else did you expect the poor man to do? Moon after you forever?" Miranda shrugged and towed her past the window.

"No, but I—well, I simply didn't expect to see him with someone." Serena stomped down the sidewalk brushing past people oblivious to the ruckus she caused.

"Do you love him?" Miranda's tart question drew Serena up short. Damn everyone to perdition. Why must people insist on asking that blasted question?

She whirled around to face her friend. "I do, which is why I said no." Serena's heart twisted inside her chest.

"Does he love you?" Miranda's arms were crossed over her chest as she stood blocking the walkway.

"Yes. He has said as much." Serena stared at the ground.

"Then why did you say no?" Miranda queried as her exasperation became evident.

"I was scared and reasoned I was protecting myself, and him, at the time. I couldn't stop myself from falling in love. Madame has always warned us about mistaking lust for love in our profession. When I learned he lost business because of our association, I couldn't allow that to continue." Serena shrugged and turned back toward The Market, which meant passing the modiste's window again.

"I know it seemed the right thing at the time, dearest. But perhaps you should consider fighting for him?" Miranda linked arms with her, and they strolled down the path.

"How could I ruin his life by letting him marry me?" Serena was near to tears again as she pondered the same question she had asked herself every hour since he proposed.

"Serena, he is an adult. He asked you to marry him. Don't you think you should let the man make up his own mind what is or is not best for him? It is clear he thinks you are."

"But his family." Serena slowed as they approached the shop.

"Is no longer a problem by your account of your visit with Lady Thornton yesterday." Miranda smiled encouragingly. "Don't let a chance at happily ever after slip through your fingers. Women like us don't get those opportunities very often."

They started past the shop as Brennan and the golden chit walked out. Serena's heart rose up clogging her throat when her gaze clashed with his. He tipped his hat and nodded. "Miss Freemont." Next, he nodded at Miranda.

"Mr. Whitling." Serena inclined her head and walked past the happy couple grinding her teeth. Three shops down she glanced at Miranda to see a knowing smirk. "What is running through that head of yours?"

"Not a thing." Miranda's face looked innocent.

"I doubt that. However, I do believe I may need to reconsider my decision to run away. It makes me sick to see that woman on his arm. He's mine." After uttering the words, the truth of them sank in and wrapped around her heart. He belonged to her, and she to him.

"I am very glad to hear that. What do you plan to do about it?" Miranda pulled her down the street.

"I do not know. Yet." Serena tilted her chin up and marched down the street, confident something would come to her.

That night, Serena sat down in the salon acting as hostess for Madame Marchander. Though technically her night off, sitting in her rooms alone had become cloying and uncomfortable. She lounged on a settee chatting with the masked Earl of Cornwall when a familiar presence entered the room. Despite the mask he wore, she knew him to be Brennan's friend by his easy manner, dark good looks, and deep voice. Only half listening to the earl, she tracked Andrew's path across the room. He disappeared somewhere behind her.

The Earl continued talking about his horses when she heard Brennan's name from over her shoulder.

"Good evening, Johnston. Where is Whitling this evening?" a gregarious baritone intoned.

"He is at home entertaining a certain lady friend of his. In private," Andrew replied.

Serena's whole body went stiff with anger. Entertaining at home? In private. "Excuse me, my lord. I must check on one of our guests." Serena rose from the couch and restrained herself from running out of the salon. She arrived in the foyer and found the doorman.

"Fetch me a hack. I shall return in a moment." Serena dashed upstairs to grab her cloak and bonnet and bumped into Celeste, one of the other girls who acted as hostess for Madame.

"Celeste, I must run out on an urgent errand. Could you stand as hostess for the evening?"

"Certainly, Serena. Is something wrong?"

"No, just a matter which cannot wait. Thank you."

Within a few minutes she settled into the vehicle barreling toward Brennan's townhouse. As they came to a stop she rushed from the carriage without waiting for help. She flew up the steps of his home and tried the door, the handle rotated unimpeded in a smooth arc and pushed inward.

Serena closed the door behind her and looked around. The whole downstairs lay dark and looked uninhabited, as though the staff were off for the night. The idea they were in the bedroom struck her with the force of a punch to the gut. *Mine*, rang through her head in time with each step she took up the stairs. At the top, she turned down the hallway and found his door cracked with a strip of light limning it.

She rushed ahead and banged through the door into his candlelit bedroom. He sat in a chair by the bed, reading and wearing a robe over his trousers. He glanced up at the sudden noise and looked, not surprised to see her. Confusion swirled, but her anger and jealousy still reigned. "Where is she?"

"Who?" He closed the book and set it down.

"That blond chit I saw you with. I know she is here." Serena marched over to his dressing room and opened the door. Nothing. She stomped back into the bedroom and over to the neat and tidy bed.

"What makes you think I have a woman here?" A smirk lurked in his eyes.

Unconvinced, she knelt down and looked under the bed. "I saw you with her today, and then your friend came into The Market. He said you were here, entertaining her in private." Serena's anger surged again as she got to her feet. She stalked up to Brennan and slapped him across the face.

The crack of skin on skin reverberated through the empty bedroom. The red imprint of her hand blazed an outline on his smooth cheek. She fisted her hand and brought it to her mouth as it dawned on her what she had let her anger drive her to do.

"I told you there was no woman here." He appeared angry but not as angry as he should be. He rubbed his pink cheek and stared.

"I heard your friend, why would he lie?" Serena retreated and dropped her fist to her side.

Brennan's irritation morphed into sheepishness. "Because I asked him to."

"What do you mean, you asked him to?" She glared at him, no longer feeling sorry about the slap.

"You ran off and refused to see me. I could not figure out how to convince you I wanted to marry you." Brennan shrugged.

"The blonde girl from today, who is she?"

"Andrew's sister. She agreed to help me in the name of love." A small smile hovered on his lips.

"Love? She's in love with you and you used her to try and trap me? This gets richer and richer!" Serena paced without ever having made a conscious decision to do so.

"No! She agreed to do it because she knows I love you, and I was miserable when you left." Brennan took a step forward interrupting Serena's path.

She glanced up and saw the sincerity in his gaze. He let her see the pain he bore in her absence and it wrenched her heart anew. "I missed you, too. I was miserable when I left and furious when I saw you two today. I wanted to scratch her eyes out and shred her pretty golden locks because you Brennan Whitling are mine." Serena's words tripped out over each other she spoke so fast. Then, without warning, she flung her arms around his neck and kissed him. A possessive instinct pummeled the last shred of her resistance. Dear God, she loved him and he would be hers. No more denial, no more pushing him away. He chose her, against all the odds, he saw in her someone worthy of redemption. Who was she to argue?

She slid her tongue past his teeth and over the velvety softness of his tongue. He moaned as his arms surrounded and crushed her body to his. He took control of the kiss, searing her, branding her with his mouth. She skimmed her hands inside his robe to find deliciously bare skin. Shoving it back off his shoulders, she exposed him to her exploring hands.

He hauled her so close he could have been trying to merge their bodies into one being for a moment. Upon spying her breasts, displayed by a precarious neckline, a crease formed between his brows. "My God, did you come here in that dress?"

"Yes. I left The Market as soon as I heard Andrew. I did not stop to change clothes." Serena looked down and realized she had left wearing one of the dresses she wore while visiting in the salon. The tops of her areolas crested above the neckline, which just covered the stiff peaks of her nipples.

He tipped her chin up so their gazes met. "You, madame, are only permitted to wear this dress for me, here in our home. Are we clear?"

"Quite." Serena agreed without hesitation, not missing the "our home" part. Her heart raced as her stomach flip-flopped.

"I have other demands I shall enumerate for you at our earliest convenience, but for the moment I think I shall investigate this gown further." He leaned forward and slicked his tongue over the top of each coral arc. Continuing, he slipped a finger inside the material and popped her hard nubs free of their confinement. "Very nice, my dear." He flicked each point with his tongue before raking them with his teeth. Heat converged between her thighs as he pressed his lower half closer.

Brennan let the surge of lust rip through him. With a jerk, he wrenched the sleeves of her dress down, fully exposing her breasts. He bent over, suckling one then the other when he realized the skirts impeded his ability to access the rest of her body. Righting himself, he spun her around and loosened the fastenings of the dress. He lifted it up over her head, tossing it aside, and released her petticoats. Satisfied with having stripped her down to her corset and short chemise, which left her breasts exposed, he dragged her against his chest. He kissed her neck as one hand toyed with a nipple. The other hand snaked down over her belly to dip between her moist folds.

He dragged his finger over her clit before slipping inside her warm sheath. A living flame in his arms, she branded him with her passion and desire. His cock had become a steel rod in his pants, aching for release. After leading her to the bed, he bent her forward with his body and kissed his way down her spine. Easing back, he opened the fall of his trousers. "I am yours, Serena, and you are mine," he said and slammed his staff into her heat.

Whimpering in need and desire, she pushed back farther against him. Her ass ground against his thighs before sliding forward. He required a moment or he would be unmanned by his own need. Clasping her shoulder, he stopped her forward progress holding her in place. The burning ache of denied release passed and he could move. Hands on her hips, he skimmed back and slammed forward again. An inexorable drive to be deeper in her core had him pounding into her body like a man possessed.

A compulsion to mark her rode him hard. Even as his balls slapped against her thighs and his fingers dug deeper, gripping her securely.

She groaned. "Yes, Brennan, I'm yours." Her glorious red hair tumbled loose from the force of his thrusts, and her hands splayed out to brace her body on the bed. A soft note of lilies wafted up to him combined with the musky scent of sex.

"Mine," he repeated as she peaked. Her body spasmed around his invasion, clutched his cock in a vise that felt too good. He continued pumping, fighting the resistance of her body as his own orgasm sparked to life. One, two, three strokes and he pulled from her to pump his own cock as he came on the creamy smoothness of her backside. Spent, he tucked his soft dick back in his trousers and found a cloth by the washbasin to wipe her off. He rolled her over and kissed her again.

Despite the physical satiation, emotional turmoil rocked him. She claimed to be his in the heat of the moment, but would she change her mind? He needed her to understand no other woman would do. Her love made him feel whole.

Breaking their connection, he reached to the floor and found his robe nearby. He slipped each of her arms into the sleeves and wrapped it across her body before tying the belt.

"What is this for?" She waved her hand at the robe.

"I need your delectable and distracting body covered while we finish this conversation." He settled next to her on the bed. "There are a few things we need to straighten out about our new agreement."

"Are there?" Serena arched a single brow in question.

"Indeed. You will henceforth be known as Mrs. Brennan Whitling because you will marry me. You will admit you love me. You will move all of your belongings here and sleep with me in this bed every night for the remainder of your days as befitting my wife. And, you will do all of this because you love me, you mule-headed woman."

"Well then, you sir will remember you are my husband and will refrain from gallivanting about London with blond-haired chits who could be your little sister. You will come home every day for lunch so you may see me. And you will end your membership at The Market as this will be the sole place you need come for pleasure. And you will do all this because you love me." Serena beamed at him and launched herself into his arms as they fell back on the bed and kissed as if only their love could offer redemption.

~The End~

LOVE RECLAIMED

BOOK 3

DEDICATION

To all the women who missed out on love the first time around but found their second chance.

CHAPTER ONE

T wenty years could be considered a long time to wait for any woman, in particular a whore. But, she wasn't just any whore. Jonathan had fallen in love with her as a young man and lost her to circumstances beyond his control. The brothel called The Market had been the last place he'd seen her as she escaped the bustling London streets and slipped through the front door. The momentary glimpse wouldn't be worth a tuppence now. She could be anywhere.

Jonathan settled back against the cracked leather squabs and tried to ignore the stench left behind from the hack's previous occupants. Palms sweating within his gloves, he attempted to take deep, calming breaths. Flashes of a towheaded beauty with her skirts rucked up around her knees as she waded into the stream merged into the same girl kneeling by a calf whose mother had abandoned it. Refusing to give up, the girl urged the baby cow to drink the milk from the bottle she held. A bump in the road jerked him from his memories and the dark of night collapsed around him, tangling with the fog to make the evening impenetrable. Fortunately, a short carriage ride from his townhouse delivered him to The Market. The brothel's convenient address situated it in the better section of London. Proximity to one's clients seemed to be as important as who your clients were. Cautious of the atmospheric pea soup, he landed on the pavement to climb the steps to the already opening front door. The golden token became a leaden weight in his palm as he presented his ticket into the exclusive establishment.

The Market consisted of three row houses. The main house in the center contained the common rooms. From the street, the house on the left was for the average customer who was there to see one of the girls. The right side catered to those with less average desires and the income to indulge them. Rumor had it, kinks of all kinds could be found on the right side. Voyeurs given something to watch, floggings could be both given and received, domination abounded, and orgies were not uncommon occurrences.

Beyond the immaculate doorman lay a sumptuous interior designed to appeal to the wealthy elite of the ton. Inside dripped with pictures in gilt frames, velvets and brocades, and marble floors. And he'd merely seen the foyer. A glance into the main salon proved the men dominated the ladies two to one. Most people wore masks to hide their faces, but a few brazen men defied society and revealed their identities.

He'd long since lost all fear of society's censure. A widower now, he lived life by his own rules, no longer beholden to his father or anyone else. Besides, what good could come of being in The Market if she didn't recognize him? He removed his cloak, handed it off to a bewigged servant, and strode into the crowded space. He held his head high, shoulders back, and allowed the confident swagger he'd cultivated in the military to carry him into the room. The tails of his coat swished softly behind him as he turned to take in the throng.

Women in low-cut gowns with hemlines that fell short of their ankles dotted the salon. Beneath their elegant skirts, he would find silk, both man-made and the natural silk of skin. Ignoring the parade of lovelies, he remained vigilant in his quest for a slightly older version of the women arrayed before him. One brunette sidled up, her nipples on the verge of spilling over the neckline of her gown. She twitched her skirts aside and nestled closer to him as he stood leaning against a long bar.

"Hello there, my Lord. I do believe you are new to our fine establishment." Her whiskied tone caressed him, even as she rubbed her breasts against his arm.

"I am, but I am here in search of a particular woman." He clamped his hands on her shoulders and set her back from his person.

"Who might that be, my Lord?" Her skirts tangled around his ankles.

"Her name was Marie." He left off her last name because it made sense she would have changed it in the course of discovering how unrelenting the world could be for a women who diverged from the normal path. No matter the reason.

The brunette paused to consider. "No, can't say as I know any Maries at The Market." She shook her head and pulled away from him to move on.

Undaunted by his initial foray, he determined to stay on and see if perhaps one of the older women might remember his Marie. He flagged the bartender and pointed to his empty glass. The staff seemed content he remain stone-cold sober. The bartender took care of every other patron before returning to tend his glass.

Sipping his refreshed brandy, he continued surveying the salon. Voices raised in congratulations drifted in from an adjoining parlor, which housed the gaming tables. Deciding to investigate what entertainment the room offered, he wandered in that direction. He found an amiable game of whist with modest stakes in need of a fourth.

"Baron Heartfield, come join us," one of the masked players bade.

Despite the masks, his keen eye for detail provided him a rather good idea of who sat at the table. The three introduced themselves using monikers from popular Gothic tales: Fogg, Hyde, and Holmes moving around the table from his right. "Thank you for the invitation," Heart agreed and took a seat. "Please, Heartfield will suffice gentlemen."

Over the next hour, he lost fifty pounds and decided luck had rather deserted him. Pushing away from the table, he bid his partner and opponents adieu. Strolling back into the main salon, he found his eyes drawn to a woman now holding court near the fireplace. His heart skipped three or four beats as his mind peeled away the layers of paint and finery, turned back the clock, and saw the young and vivacious Miss Marie Doring. Without conscious thought his feet carried him to the woman surrounded by masked admirers.

Hovering on the outer edges of the group, he found himself waiting for her to notice him.

Madame Marchander paused from the conversation to survey her packed main salon. A deep sense of satisfaction settled in her bones. Philippe had informed her most of the rooms were occupied at present, and the card room bustled as well.

Business remained excellent.

Her gaze drifted across the room and collided with the tall figure of a man who impeded her view as he stood over the small group of fawning gents arranged at her feet. Shifting directions, her gaze swept down and then up the masculine form. Arriving at his face, the blood in her head deserted her as an older but all-too-familiar face swam within her vision. Jonathan Pierce, currently styled the Baron of Heartfield according to her sources, had been her first love.

One of the men noticed her distress and patted her hand. "Madame Marchander, are you not well?"

Her head swam as the room closed in on her. Why was he there? What could he want? Was it presumptuous to assume he could be looking for her? She rose and the men parted so she could pass. "Please, I fear I am a bit warm with so many of you crowded around. I think a breath of air would be best."

"Madame, please allow me to escort you." Baron Heartfield slipped her hand into the crook of his arm and led her toward the French doors open onto the rear gardens.

"Do I know you, sir?" Hiding behind formality and time, she opted to continue pretending Marie Doring no longer existed.

"Baron Heartfield, Madame Marchander, or may I call you Marie as I once did?" Familiar blue eyes sparkled as he swept aside her deflection.

"Madame Marchander will do." Anger overcame her initial distress. What brought him to The Market? Why resurrect ancient history? She had not heard he was low on funds, so it was doubtful he intended blackmail. If the gentry of Coventry learned what had become of Miss Marie Doring, it might cause a ripple of scandal, but her sisters were long married and could weather the storm. They had little contact, the occasional bit of correspondence and the annual Christmas card being all she allowed.

Her skirts brushed past the doorframe as they attained the patio. The cool air, brisk and refreshing, snapped her back after the shock of seeing him for the first time in twenty years.

"I see." He paused. "Very well, I'll permit you to hide behind formality for now. You look beautiful as ever." Warm, strong fingers stroked the bare skin of her hand he held captive.

"You will permit me?" Her spine stiffened in indignation while she arched one eyebrow at the infuriating man. "My Lord, you may be a peer of the realm, but I am the queen of my domain. I could easily have you removed from the premises and refuse you entrance in the future."

"Don't get your feathers ruffled. It is good to see you again."

"Is it?" Still wary, she concentrated on his words and not gripping his arm too tightly. Blaming the cold for her sensitized nipples made ignoring the heat surging through her much easier.

He chuckled. "I remember you being far more talkative when I knew you."

"I learned quickly to guard my words. What brings you to The Market, my Lord? In all my years I have never seen you here before, nor are you a member." Breathing at a normal rate as she waited for his answer became a herculean effort. His long, drawn-out pause was brutal to endure.

After a few minutes of silence, he cleared his throat. It sounded as though gravel had gathered there. "My wife died two years ago. I am just emerging from mourning, and with so much time to ponder, I spent a great deal of it pondering you and what happened after I last saw you."

"Oh. Well, as you can see I am doing well." At least she had been until he strolled into her salon and back into her life.

"Yes, I can see you have surpassed anything I could have imagined for you based on circumstances. I am glad to see you thriving."

A foursome spilled out on to the patio on a burst of uproarious laughter as they passed a bottle of champagne around. Heartfield's arm tensed beneath her hand, and they stopped their meandering stroll. "May we speak someplace in private? Where we will not be disturbed or overheard?"

A shudder raced down her spine. This was the moment. Once alone, he would reveal what brought him to her. Deep down, did she want to know? Perhaps the wisest course of action would be to push him off, send him on his way. But some small part of her, which still harbored Marie, yearned to know Jonathan again, to hear what he had to say. "We will not be bothered here. Those four are too absorbed in their own pursuits to notice us." She looked pointedly at the two couples settling on a bench upon which to sample each other's charms. Each masked man had their female partner on their lap with their bodices pulled down to expose their breasts. One avidly suckled one nipple and then the other, while the other couple kissed in a rousing show of passion as his hands massaged the plump flesh of her arse.

"While I see your point, this is a rather private conversation which pertains to both of us. I would prefer a private room away from such intrusions." He waved his free hand in the direction of the licentious group.

Could she trust him alone? Could she trust herself? His mere presence stirred long forgotten desires. Marie sighed, her heartbeat thumping in her temples. "Very well. Come this way." She pulled away from his grasp and sailed back through the open doors and into the house.

Taking a brief moment to enjoy the retreating view of her swaying skirts, Jonathan hoped Marie might be amenable to his intended conversation. He drew a deep breath of the cooling air to slow his ardor before he caught up to the formidable Madame Marie Marchander. Miss Marie Doring no longer seemed to exist. Yet he found the enigma before him as alluring as the memory of the sweet girl of his youth. They entered what he assumed to be her inner sanctum hidden behind a curtain. A luxurious but cozy office awaited with a chaise lounge tucked near a fireplace. Across the room from the door they entered stood another door. Perhaps it led to her private quarters?

A vision of Marie in her chemise and hose, golden hair loose around her shoulders, and her emerald eyes glowing as she walked toward him caused an uncomfortable and rather awkward erection to press against his trousers. Turning away to shield his predicament, he heard the rustle of her skirts. A glance over his shoulder revealed she had retreated behind her desk. Not wanting the expanse of mahogany between them, he moved to the chaise in hopes she might be drawn closer to him.

"Please, have a seat here." She indicated an open chair across the desk.

"I find I am a bit chilled. I'd prefer to be closer to the fire." He lied as sweat trickled down his spine.

A low growl escaped her only to be cut off as she circled the desk to sit in the very seat she had pointed to only a moment ago. Round one, him. On to round two. "Marie, I feel I owe you an apology."

Confusion creased her brow and pinched her pretty face. "Whatever for?"

"I was not there when you needed me. I should have been there to save you from this life you were forced into." He raised a hand to indicate The Market.

She laughed. Not the full-bellied, youthful chortle he remembered of her, but still she was amused. Tamping her mirth down, she composed herself. "Dear man, you owe me no apologies. Even had you not been off with the army, I would have had to take this path to save my sisters. It was my sacrifice to make, and I made it. Your family was as close to being in as dire straits as mine. Our marriage would have accomplished nothing but compounded the problem."

"No." He stood and stared into the fire, his guilt at deserting her crashed through him with a surfeit of emotion. "I could have married you and spared you the humiliation of this life. If only I had known." His voice cracked on the last word.

The muted crunch of the carpet fibers beneath her foot alerted him to her movement a moment before her hand rested on his shoulder. "There was naught to be done. If it had not been me, then one of my sisters would have had to suffer this fate. You must not blame yourself for the hand life dealt me. I do not."

Her skirts swallowed his ankles as her body pressed against his back in what she meant to be a comforting gesture. Little did she know the contact did no more than exacerbate his insistent problem. "Thank you. You were always a generous woman, a lovely woman, and nothing has changed except perhaps you wear nicer clothes."

She chuckled, a deep, throaty, sexy sound that fed his unexpected yet growing need for her. He'd been driven by the urge to find her and see if any feeling remained from their youth, but he had not anticipated finding himself caught up in the throes of lust for this woman. And, she was without a doubt a different woman than the girl he had left behind. He turned and slipped his arms around her, caging her next to his chest. She gasped and glanced up at him, uncertainty etched on her face. Her hands rested on his chest as he leaned in to capture her lips.

Her palms pressed into him, searing his skin through the layers of his clothes, even as they stopped him halfway to his goal. "What is it, Marie? Don't you feel the pull between us?"

"That is not the point. This is a path fraught with disappointment and heartache. I see this coming to no good end."

"How so? You feel right in my arms, right against my body." He leaned down and pressed his lips to hers. A moment of resistance froze her, but faded away, freeing her to slide her hands up his chest where they twined around his neck and pulled him closer. Her lips parted, granting him entrance to the warm cavern of her mouth. Their tongues collided and tangled in an erotic exchange with the potential to push him over the edge.

He reached behind her, found the lacings of her gown, and worked them loose. The bodice released, and he eased it down over her shoulders to expose her corset-covered breasts. He groaned as he kissed across the tops of her cleavage before working one breast free. With a step backward, he sat on the chaise and drew Marie closer, twisted her so he could remove her laces. Her skirts puddled around her feet after the lower lacings were released along with the ties of her petticoats. Clad in nothing but her corset, chemise, and hose, real life mimicked his wanton thoughts of a half hour earlier.

Next, he pulled the corset laces, releasing the constriction from her hourglass waist. Need speared through him like a red-hot poker when she rotated to face him, and he realized her nipples showed through the sheer material of her chemise. She lifted her arms so she could release her hair, making his vision complete. Reality far outstripped the paltry image his feeble imagination had conjured. Drawing her down into his lap, he kissed her again and sought the breast hooked over the chemise's neckline. He moaned in pleasure as her warm flesh filled his mouth. The pebbled nipple rolled across his tongue, responding to the smallest stroke or nibble. Delicate hands clutched his head, urging him on in silence. He switched breasts, exposing the other one and her breathing grew rapid, shallow. The erotic sound of her soft little pants enflamed him more than the sight of her half-naked.

Withdrawing from him, she unbuttoned his coat and slipped her soft hands beneath the fabric to ease it off his shoulders. Next, she attacked his waistcoat, and then his shirt. Cool air hit his overheated skin. A vain desire to slip his shirt back on wiggled its way into his consciousness. After all the chests she'd seen over all the years, would his be found lacking? Would she turn from him in disgust of his no longer rock hard abdomen? Steeling himself, he waited.

"Very nice." Her whispered words relieved his moment of worry that a man of forty-five might not entice such an experienced woman. Without a doubt, time had changed her, leaving her less firm in places than the young woman he once knew, but nothing about her failed to please. Nothing failed to tantalize. He stood as she opened the fall of his trousers and removed them along with his small clothes. Naked before her, there'd be no hiding his cockstand, not to say he wanted to any longer.

"My, my, it seems you are eager to see me." A wicked smile flashed across her face as she sank to her knees before him. Taking him in a firm grip at the root with one hand, she used her other one to fondle his testicles with a gentle caress. The electric sensation of her tongue running from root to tip before swallowing him up came close to unmanning him. After two years of mourning with nothing but self-pleasure, it could best be described as a profusion of sensation to experience not only a woman's touch, but her eager mouth sucking him with such single-mindedness.

Pumping the base of his shaft with her hand while her mouth sucked and licked the upper part, brought him to the edge with unreasonable haste. The precipice loomed before him. A bit of gentle pressure on the spot behind his balls had him exploding like a boy with his first woman. Her relentless grip on the base of his member thwarted his attempt to withdraw from her mouth. He understood her message quite clearly; she had no intention of letting him go anywhere until she finished taking his seed.

Releasing his softening penis, she rose up and walked over to the mystery door he had spotted when they first entered. She opened it and disappeared with a come-hither glance over her shoulder. Left to stand there or follow, he opted to see where she had gone. In the next room, he found an elegant bed draped with silks and satins in various shades of green. Near the fireplace burning brightly with a crackling fire Marie stood holding a glass of brandy.

She waited on pins and needles to see if she had appalled Heartfield—or enticed him. The latter appeared to be true since he followed her into her *boudoir*. He retrieved the brandy and hesitated as though waiting for her to take the lead. A sip of her own drink allowed her to ponder the options. To her delight, he tired of waiting for her to decide. Brandy abandoned on the mantle, he took her glass from her hand and pulled her into his strong arms for another plundering, soul-stirring kiss. Being with him would be dangerous to the emotional armor she long ago erected upon agreeing to her father's plan.

Her blood thrummed through her veins, pulsing at her woman's core with the need to feel him buried within. It had been a long time since she experienced the stirrings of hunger with any man. Damn near five years. Not since her last long-term engagement had she reveled in the heady rush. The decision to focus on business and not entertaining was an easy one when no one could fan to life the flames of her desire. No reason to waste her time on men she did not want. But Heartfield remained a different story altogether. Every past stroke from other men paled in comparison to what his touch did to her.

Ending the kiss, he stripped off her chemise and lifted her into his arms like a groom with his bride. He laid her out on the bed and took his time with his inspection. The weight of his gaze dragged over her flesh in an erotic and far too intimate caress. More than aware of the ravages of time, she struggled to suppress the urge to cover herself. Normally, she was more than proud of her physique. Careful about what she ate, she ensured sufficient activity to keep her figure healthy and curvy as it had always been. Despite her best efforts, her skin looked less youthful and her breasts less perky. She was not the young girl he might remember.

He, on the other hand, had held up well for a man his age. Not in the first blush of youth, his chest still contained enough muscle to make a younger, less active, man envious. With a stomach tapered to lean hips, a firm derriere, and legs well-muscled from years of riding and controlling horses without the reins, he proved more than she could have expected. In particular since many of his peers sported potbellies and florid faces from years of overindulgence.

His big hands parted her thighs letting him kneel on the bed. Leaning over her, he returned to her nipples, sucking and biting them to hardened peaks. As he ministered to them, he slipped his fingers between her thighs to delve into her wet folds. He groaned when he found the excess moisture signaling her need. Allowing the peak to pop from his mouth, his salt-and-pepper head dipped down the length of her body and let his tongue trace patterns across her skin, leaving chill bumps in its wake. He dipped his fingers into her pussy, working in and out of her as he descended.

Upon reaching his goal, he spread her thighs wider and exchanged his digits for his tongue. She gasped in pure pleasure, stabbed her own fingers into his close-cropped hair, and lifted her hips to meet his thrusts. Marie was certain she would come apart at the seams at any moment. The boy of the innocent kisses no longer existed. In his place existed a man who commanded her body's attention.

When he pinned her hips down with his hands, she released his hair and let him lead. She let her hands drift back up toward her aching nipples to roll and pinch them while he shifted his tongue up to flick over her clit in a relentless laving of her core. A loud moan rattled up and out of her body as the first waves of orgasm crashed down. He thrust his tongue back inside of her, his thumb rubbing her oversensitive nub. She arched up in a contraction of pleasure as a release unlike any she had provided to herself over the last few years racked her body. Spent, she collapsed back onto the bed, a puddle of bone and flesh.

Heartfield crawled back up her length to take her in his arms. They lay there spooned together, his growing cock wedged between them. How could she ever have imagined foreplay might be so incredible? He had yet to bury himself in her, and yet she knew a deeper satisfaction than ever before. He held her and caressed her back with his fingertips. His magical fingertips.

"Mmm. That was lovely." Her words were muffled by his chest.

"Indeed. It will be lovelier still in a short while. I want nothing short of burying myself in you and watching you come around my cock." His words were a rumble resonating deep in her still-pulsing core. Like a siren called to sailors in the tales of yore, his lust called to her. His lips sought hers again, and they kissed, renewing their ardor in a matter of moments.

The kiss deepened and he rolled her underneath him. The weight of his body pressed her into the mattress in the most deliciously wanton way. It felt good to bear a man's weight once again, to bear this man's weight in particular. Spreading her legs, she urged him to slide into her sheath, to join them in the way they had both been denied for twenty long years.

A single thrust seated him within her, his balls pressed against her ass, and yet she wanted more. She needed him pounding into her in the most elemental way. No slow lovemaking, she needed a base and elemental fucking meant to leave them sweaty and longing for more. "I won't break, Heartfield. Fuck me," she demanded.

"Christ, woman." He ground out before his assault began. Lifting up he pulled back and slid home again, a hard, solid stroke that shot a zing of sensation to her toes.

Such a delicious, sexy man, and he happened to be buried between her thighs. "Yes. That's it."

His movements became more rapid as he pumped in and out of her body. Her heels dug into the mattress so she could meet each thrust with her own. Their bodies slapped together over and over as he took her. Tingles skipped across her skin and pooled where they joined. She could feel her need building and reveled in the way his cock worked her soaking pussy. Mad with desire for him, all self-control lost, she shouted his name as she shattered around him. He drove into her, unstopping as she came until his own release shot deep inside her. He, too, shouted her name as his climax took him. Their bodies, still joined, pulsed in an animalistic rhythm that wrung every last drop of energy from her.

CHAPTER TWO

Jonathan woke up from a nap to find Marie still asleep. The fire had burned to a flickering flame, and in the soft glow of the low light he stared at her. In a slow, sleepy sweep, her lashes revealed her eyes and her wakefulness. He rose from the bed and added some wood to the fire, as much a stalling tactic as a need for warmth. He'd searched her out with the intent of discovering what still lay between them, if anything. The crystal-clear answer left a lone course of action as far as he could see. Despite her sordid life, she'd been raised a gently bred young woman. She'd wound up living the life of a whore through no fault of her own. He could never condemn her for sacrificing herself to save her sisters.

If her wastrel father had done right by his family, she would have become his wife when he returned from his first campaign. Instead, he'd had to marry Miss Jane Landing, a young missish heiress, whose dowry bailed his family out of the poorhouse. All he'd been asked to do was to marry a plain but sweet and wealthy girl. By any reckoning, he'd gotten off lucky.

"Tell me, Marie." He stood and turned back toward the bed. "If I had returned from my first campaign, and your father had not been so in debt, would you have considered marriage to me?"

She lay silent on the bed, still snuggled under the covers. He returned to her side and slid between the sheets, but left her alone to ponder the question. "What could that possibly matter now?"

He pulled her into his arms, enjoying the feel of her soft woman's curves against the harder planes of his male body. Beneath the covers he stroked the underside of her breast with a lightness that elicited a purr of contentment from his partner.

She angled herself more toward him. "What is this about?"

"I have always remembered our time together with fond memories. Summers in the fields chasing the cows, wading in the creek between our properties, and Christmas caroling. You always had the loveliest voice." Obvious discomfort at his remembrances caused her to tuck her face into his shoulder.

"I, too, have fond memories of our times together. Learning to jump fences, swimming in the pond on your property, and the sled races we always held after the first snow." Her husky tones wove deep inside him and wound themselves around his heart.

"What if we could be together? As we should have been." He tossed the dice and waited to see how they landed.

The warm woman in his arms stilled before pulling away. Rising from the bed, she donned her dressing gown while turning to face him. "Heartfield, what precisely are you suggesting?" Her eyes narrowed and seemed to bore into him.

He sat up, dragging the covers with him. "I am suggesting exactly what it sounds like I am. I wish to marry you. To spend the rest of my life with you as I should have from the beginning."

She shook, a visible clue of the emotions simmering beneath her cooling exterior. Her eyes turned a dead mossy color, which did not bode well for the outcome he desired. A pit formed in his stomach in anticipation of her coming refusal. "That is ludicrous. Beyond the obvious issue of everyone in the ton shunning you, there is your familial duty. You owe your line an heir."

Familial duty. He somehow managed to contain the need to snort. *But wait.* "I have not mentioned the absence of heirs. How exactly would you know that if you had not seen me before now?"

"I traffic in gossip as well as pleasure. It is almost as lucrative a commodity." Her hands knotted and unknotted over and over again in an unconscious gesture he remembered from their youth. The rest of her tall form stood as still as a statue.

"Bollocks! I am a low-ranking baron of little to no consequence. There is not one man or woman in the ton who would be interested in whether or not I had successfully gotten children on my dear departed wife except for our own mothers who are long since gone to the great beyond." He rose from the bed, angry she would not admit the truth. She had been keeping abreast of his life.

She still cared.

With a dismissive wave of her hands, she stalked toward the fire. "I must have heard it mentioned in passing by someone. Regardless, what I said still holds true unless you have some heir tucked away I've not heard about. Not that you could recognize a bastard."

"No. There are no bastards and no legitimate heirs. I was a good and faithful husband while Jane lived." Anger over her lies and casual dismissal of his character burned through him. "As for my family line, there is a cousin who can inherit. I can marry when and where I wish."

"Heartfield, we do not even know each other. Yes, we enjoyed a physical exchange. We reminisced about our childhoods. But we only know the boy and girl we were. I am a very different woman than you might ever have imagined me becoming."

"All surface layers to be explored and peeled away. At your core...." He came behind her and pulled her against him until her buttocks nestled against his groin. "Here." His fist pressed against her chest and over her heart. "Here, you are the same person I knew. Kind, generous, and self-sacrificing."

A bitter laugh rumbled from her as she pulled away from him. "Kind? Just yesterday I threw one of my girls out on the street with nothing but the clothes on her back."

Doubt assailed him. Did he know her? His confidence resurged to the fore. "She must have been a thief."

"She broke one of my rules." Her face hardened around eyes like green ice. "Generous? I do not help anyone who cannot help me. Nothing is free, my Lord. And the last time I committed the sin of self-sacrifice—nearly twenty years ago—I allowed myself to be auctioned off. After that night, I swore every act I made would be for my benefit alone for the rest of my days." She prowled toward him, a mocking smile on her face.

Horror washed through him as he gained a peripheral understanding of the differences between the woman before him and the girl he had known. Shoring up his reserves, he dug deep for his belief in the innate goodness of people. Of her. "You have been forced into a hard life which required hard decisions and a need to look out for yourself to survive. But, Marie, it does not change who you are at the core. I cannot believe you are not still fundamentally the same loving person you always were. And none of what you have said changes my desire to be with you. Forever."

Turning away from him, she faced the fire, but her words carried in biting clarity. "Get out. Put on your clothes in the office and leave. Your money is always good at The Market, but I have no desire to personally indulge you again. Good evening, my Lord."

Jonathan's heart crawled up his chest to lodge in his throat. Could she not want him in truth? Perhaps he had pushed too hard, too fast. He'd go and give her a little space, but he would be back to claim his Marie.

The door closed behind him, and Marie let her shoulders slump. Holding them up had been more wearing than everything else they had done together. She raised her hand to her face and discovered the wetness from her silent tears. She wiped it away. With a ragged breath, she straightened up and went to her vanity. There she tidied herself up and repaired her hair to some semblance of order. Draped in her dressing gown, she rang for Phillipe.

"Madame." He bowed.

"Has Baron Heartfield departed?" She sipped a fresh brandy.

"About five minutes ago, Madame. Is he to be allowed to return in the future?"

"Yes. As long as he appears with a token or a member and pockets to let, the door is always open to him. But if he asks for me, I am indisposed."

"Very good, Madame. You should be aware Lord Bethany became too rough in the dungeon. We escorted him from the house and I took the liberty of barring him for a fortnight with payments." Her client liaison looked concerned.

"He had been warned previously. One more incident and he will be banned from this establishment for life. When the fortnight is up send around a note inviting him to return with the understanding his outbursts of violence will not be tolerated again without permanent repercussions. Who did he attack, and how is she?"

"Yes, Madame. It was Celeste. Some of the other ladies are caring for her with a poultice Cook prepared. A few days rest and she will be right as rain. Some of the men in the room restrained Bethany before he could inflict any lasting damage. Is there anything else I may do for you before I close the house up for the night?"

"No. That will be all. Thank you." Exhaustion swept over her as the door clicked shut. Emotionally wrung out and sore with a physical ache from the tension riding between her shoulders, she longed for the oblivion of sleep. Her day had been up and down like a yo-yo.

Five days later, Jonathan decided to try a different tactic with his siege. A frontal assault seemed in order. If she would accept his blunt, then he would spend it in her establishment and prove to her he could be as hedonistic as the next peer. He was, after all, single and his actions should serve to show her he could play by her rules since she no longer seemed interested in playing by society's after so many years living outside of them.

Sauntering into the room, he spied his prey sitting in the corner by the fire holding court again. Elegant in a bronze silk gown, she glowed with beauty and inner light. The green-eyed monster seethed below the thin veneer of politeness, even as he chastised himself. Of course, he would not be the lone man drawn to her flame. Their eyes met, and he inclined his head in greeting. Her eyes widened and then returned to normal as she turned to laugh at something the man next to her said.

Turning away to hide his desire to rip the doting fop to shreds, he approached the bar. Two quick slugs of brandy bolstered his courage, and he approached the client liaison to inquire after an arrangement. "Good evening." The man looked surprised to see him.

"Good evening, my Lord. I am Phillipe; how may I be of service to you?"

"I am hoping to find one of the ladies of the house available this evening." Jonathan imagined his brow must be dotted with beads of sweat his nerves were strung so tight.

"Ah." He glanced at Marie, who must have nodded. "I believe I have one or two available this evening. Do you have a preference?"

"No blondes." Jonathan picked at some phantom bit of lint on his sleeve.

"Of course." Phillipe nodded. "If you will wait here, I will have Celeste join you."

"Very good." He returned to the bar to wait for the heretofore unknown Celeste to join him. He did not wait long before a svelte brunette sidled up to him.

"Good evening, my Lord. I'm Celeste. Phillipe sent me."

"Yes." The bartender appeared, and Heart ordered a brandy before glancing at Celeste for her order.

"Champagne please." She smiled a sultry grin, which promised untold delights.

Their drinks appeared, and she took his hand. A short walk upstairs led to a room decorated in various shades of blue. She turned to face him, having set her glass down as the door snicked shut. "Now, my Lord, is there anything in particular you would like to request this evening?"

"Actually, yes. I would like to sit and chat with you. That's all I wish to do, and I would prefer you not mention it to anyone, including Phillipe or Madame." He sipped his drink and considered the beauty over the rim of his snifter.

"That's all you want? Dirty talk." She winked at him.

"No, just conversation. No sex, no discussing sex."

"Just conversation." She blinked. "Well, I've had far stranger requests."

"Excellent. Let us sit by the fire." He showed her to a chair and handed her the abandoned champagne before taking his own seat. "So, Celeste, where are you from?"

Afternoon sunshine caused the dust motes to shimmer and dance in the light. Marie focused on breathing and framing her questions for Celeste. Tall with her dark hair hanging loose, Celeste settled across the sitting area on the opposite settee.

"I'm sorry to wake you so early, but I need to speak with you about a client." Marie strove to project her normal cool and confident persona despite the inner turmoil she fought.

"It is of no issue, I was already awake."

"Excellent." Marie attempted to smile. "How is your back doing?"

"Very good, Madame. I am healing well and it does not pain me overly."

"Good. I am very sorry you had to suffer such an unpleasant and unexpected episode."

"Thank you for asking, Madame. Is there something else you wished to ask me about?"

"There was. You entertained a gentleman last night. Tall, broad shoulders, dark hair with a bit of salt streaked through."

Yes, I remember him." The softening of Celeste's gaze ate at Marie.

"Did he have any strange requests of you?"

"No, Madame. He was very kind."

"I see." She groped for what to ask next. "Did your back upset him?"

"Not at all." Celeste glanced at the floor and then the art on the walls, her gaze never settled on anything.

"Did he do anything inappropriate?"

"Inappropriate? Madame, we cater to so many unusual requests. What might you be referring to?"

"He didn't have any desires outside of our normal bounds?"

"No, Madame. As I said, he was very kind."

"Kind." Marie couldn't find a way to ask what she wanted to know without feeling like a meddling hussy. "Did he...satisfy you?"

Celeste shifted in her seat. "He is one of my new favorite clients."

Madame wanted to growl her frustration at the non-answer. She still didn't know if they in fact had sex, bloody hell. "One of your favorites? Is there a particular reason why?"

"Of course. He is a consummate gentleman, very concerned about my comfort, tender, and of course he is very handsome to gaze upon all night."

"Yes. Well, such a list would recommend a fellow."

"Indeed." The clock in the hall chimed ten in the morning. "Oh my, Madame, if that is all I must go dress. Miranda and I are off to Bond Street for a few items. Is there anything I could fetch for you while I am out?"

A powder for the headache you created? "No, dear, I am quite fine. Thank you."

Celeste disappeared and left Marie alone to mull over the obtuse responses she had received. Why couldn't the girl have been more forthcoming? The whole situation was damned awkward.

Marie watched as Heartfield once again came to The Market, selected a girl, always a brunette or a redhead, and disappeared upstairs for the evening. For the fourth night in a row! The man had the stamina of a bull in rut. A very few of her regulars came on so frequent a basis and they were the young pups. The typical men of Heart's age attended The Market a couple nights a week and sometimes with the sole intent to gamble.

Something strange and foreign gnawed at her insides as she considered whom he had taken upstairs the last three nights. First Celeste, who looked radiant the next day—a woman well catered to. Next came Caroline, and then Sally. Tonight, he had selected Celeste again. Bordering on physical illness with the malady she refused to name, she departed the salon to retire to her room.

Despite her questions of Celeste, and each subsequent girl, she had come away with no better sense of what might be happening. If she had been asking for business purposes, she would have put things more bluntly. But, this proved to be such a personal concern she could not summon her normal steely reserve.

In the safety of her most private space, she could be honest with herself. Jealousy ripped at her guts. Pacing in long, angry strides, knowing Heartfield lay upstairs in her house burying himself in one of her girls came near to driving her over the edge. It should be her body he took and used. She had ached for him for twenty long years and now, with a maddening lack of control, she grew desperate for more of him after their one night. Frustration rode her as she rang for Phillipe, who appeared in short order.

"Before Baron Heartfield departs, please see he is brought to my office."

"Very good, Madame." Phillipe bowed and departed.

If the ridiculous man insisted on continuing to visit The Market, he would have to see her. Otherwise, he would need to find a new establishment. Tolerance of his frequent visits was too much to ask, and the damn insufferable man knew this.

Picking up a book of poetry, she settled in to wait for Phillipe to let her know Heartfield had descended. She suspected a long night lay ahead of her.

A knock at her door woke her from her doze. Bleary-eyed, she glanced at the clock. Three in the morning, that must mean Heartfield waited in her office. Excellent. She rose, tidied up a bit, and swept into her lair. His gaze followed her path across the room and stayed with her as she settled behind the desk. She needed all her armor as she prepared to wage battle.

"I am afraid I misspoke the other night when I said your money would be welcome here. I find it intolerable to have you appearing at my establishment so regularly." Drawing a breath to calm her racing heart, she let the silence reign for a moment.

His eyebrows rose in question. "Are you barring me from The Market because of our personal differences?"

"No. Not entirely. I am simply limiting your selection of companions to me." There, she said it, and with some modicum of credibility.

The blasted man smiled. "I see."

"I would suggest we negotiate the terms of the contract now and have done with the business end of this deal." She attempted to pull the tattered edges of her business persona around her in defense.

"Well, what terms do you seek in such an arrangement?"

"First, you will be required to seek out a wife while our contract is in place. If for some reason you fail to do so, our arrangement will end and you will be barred from The Market. Second, you will be required to keep your name clear of scandal, and will therefore immediately begin wearing a mask while in the public rooms as the majority of my other patrons do. In the privacy of the room we use, a mask will not be required. And I will deal with the prevention of conception, though you are welcome to use skins should you choose. Finally, you will not be permitted to invite friends or have guests at The Market as our normal members do. The contract will be for the term of six months and is severable by either party at any time for any reason." She slid a half-blank page over to him with a pen.

"And what of my demands? Am I permitted any terms?" He ignored the page and the pen and waited for her response.

"Very well, what terms would you add?"

He picked up the pen and wrote his stipulations. "First, you will be mine exclusively. You will entertain no other men, and you will cease all flirtations. Second, you will entertain me any time I wish to see you as long as it does not interfere with your ability to conduct the general business of

The Market. Finally, you will indulge my every desire, and in return I will indulge yours." He finished writing and then signed the bottom of the document.

"Keep in mind I will make the determination on what might interfere with my business and as for your desires, as you know, there are certain practices we do not permit in this establishment."

"I believe I recall the rules."

She ignored his droll comment. "No defecating on the girls, no cutting the girls, and certainly no raping the girls. I will allow a forced seduction fantasy to play out under strict control and with a monitor to ensure the girls' safety. Otherwise, we accommodate any reasonable request."

He stared at her for a moment and then blinked. "I do not foresee any issues."

Marie took the document and pen from him and signed her own name below his. They had an agreement. She tucked the paper away in her desk drawer and stood. "Good. Now, if you do not mind, I will retire for some much-needed rest. Please send around word when you intend to visit."

"I shall be here tomorrow evening at eight." He eyed her and then turned to leave.

No quarter would be given and none asked. This meant war, and she wasn't certain who'd won the first skirmish. Closing the door behind her, she listened for the sound of retreating footsteps. The room remained silent for a bit before she heard him move over to the door she pressed her ear against. The steps stopped. He hesitated, and then retreated without knocking or saying anything. It was as though he could sense her there, on the other side, but he withdrew without further comment. A small part of her wished he had opened her door and taken her in his arms. With a ruthlessness born of years spent as a prostitute, she tamped down the kernel of hope and went to bed.

CHAPTER THREE

M arie tried to control her restlessness as she waited for the clock to toll eight, the delay almost more than she could bear. As the last chime of the clock sounded, reverberating through the halls of The Market, a knock sounded on her office door. "Enter."

"Good evening, Marie." Even with the mask obscuring half of his face, Heartfield looked handsome in his somber suit with white cravat.

Forcing herself not to stare, she stood and circled the desk to welcome him. "Good evening Heartfield. If you will follow me, I had a room prepared for us." She took his arm and led him upstairs to the quieter side of the house with private rooms.

He selected a seat near the fire as she poured him a brandy and herself a glass of Madeira. "I shall be right with you," she offered as she slipped behind a screen. With an efficiency born of years of practice, she shed her gown, corset, petticoats, and chemise in order to don a red Asian inspired robe made of the finest silk. Easing from behind the screen, glass back in hand, she settled by his feet on a cushion he had placed for her. He silently worked the pins from her hair to let it fall down around her shoulders and to her hips. His fingers were magical as they rubbed and massaged her scalp in between long strokes of her hair. Her eyelids drifted closed as all the tension left her body.

She'd almost left behind her earlier anticipation letting the knots in her stomach unsnarl. Then his stray hand skimmed down her robe and cupped her breast, flicking the nipple through the silk. Delicious shivers ran through her in response. Her nerves vibrated with need and expectation.

"This is very nice, Marie. I am feeling more relaxed by the moment." His voice stroked her jangled senses in a gritty caress. The roughness sexy as hell, and when combined with his nimble fingers on her breast and head, came close to undoing her then and there.

"As am I. Some gypsy must have charmed your fingers once upon a time." Her contentment had edged away as need pooled low in her belly. She lifted her head, took a sip of her drink, and tried to bring her wits back under control. She had a plan to execute, and it did not include being seduced by him from the start of their liaison. Rising from her knees she walked to the little chest nestled by the bed on a nightstand. Within the box lay a large jade ring with a dragon's head on top waiting for retrieval. Far too large for a finger, yet not big enough to be a bracelet. It was easy to imagine he had no idea what it was, so she sought to both enlighten him and teach him how to use the circlet.

"What are you hiding over there, Marie?" He asked the question even as he returned to watching the fire.

"A cock ring." A knowing smile slipped across her lips as she waited for him to respond.

"Whatever for? I can't imagine wanting one of those torture devices near my penis." He shuddered.

Laughter bubbled up from inside her. "Don't be ridiculous. This is a house of pleasure. Even the torture devices are intended to bring pleasure to those who wield them"—she paused—"and those who submit to them." Her measured tread carried her closer to his side. "Those rings created by the puritanical types are hideous contraptions. This is an Asian ring designed to enhance pleasure for both you and I." She knelt before him and watched his reaction through lowered lashes. "If you'll trust me, I assure you it will not disappoint."

His brow quirked, giving him the air of a skeptic, even as he took the ring from her and inspected it. Running his fingers over the smooth stone surface, he paused to appreciate the dragon's head and tongue. "How does it work then?"

"You slip it over your cock and balls now, and once you grow hard it will create a pleasurable sense of engorgement, lengthen our time together, and provide me with additional stimulation. Asians have been using these for thousands of years." Grasping the fall of his trousers, she unbuttoned them for removal. He worked on his shirt and tie as his drawers followed his pants leaving him naked and exposed. Her tongue slicked over her dry lips while she concentrated on easing the ring down his semi hard shaft and over each of his balls. With the ring in place, she stood up and disrobed for his perusal. She massaged her own breasts until her nipples rose up in stiff peaks for him.

He stroked his length as he watched her pinch and roll her own tips. Abandoning his cock, he stretched up and pulled her down. She found herself in his lap in an unceremonious tumble. She arched into him as he suckled first one breast and then the other. The heat of his mouth on her sensitive nubs sent erotic jolts of pleasure to her core. His shaft, hard and beautifully engorged, rubbed against her slit and drove her to distraction. She wanted—no needed—to come. Lifting up over him, she located his cock, sheathed it in a skin, and pressed the head to her entrance. He filled her in a slow assault until she found her clit pressed against the tongue of the green dragon. A short rub and she came near to exploding. Little gasps escaped as she pressed against it harder, she rose up, and came down on him.

He groaned while he continued to feast on her breasts, sucking and licking her nipples into tight little berries. Up and down she rode him while the dragon's tongue rubbed her swollen bud over and over with each stroke of his cock. She impaled herself on him and ground against the jade sex toy until her body shattered, seeming to fragment in a million pieces. She pumped his shaft, letting her body clench around him until he too joined her in release. He called her name as he pumped into her, meeting her stroke for stroke. A second orgasm ripped through her, less intense, but just as satisfying as her first.

Slumped over him, awareness returned and she lifted off his shaft, removed the ring, and the spent sheath from him. He sat boneless in the chair and stared at her.

Shaken from such an intense orgasm, Jonathan found it hard to believe the pleasure she had shown him. He had not imagined sex being so explosive with anyone. His whole perception of the world and the principles he tried to live by shifted with the experience. How could that ever be wrong? With Marie, it seemed so right, so beautiful. How could there be anything evil in what they had shared? Nothing that brought so much pleasure could be wrong.

"Thank you for sharing this with me." He couldn't wipe the grin from his face.

"You're welcome. We can certainly use it whenever you would like." She had cleaned the semiprecious mineral and placed it back into the box. Then, in short order, she replaced her robe and refreshed his brandy from the decanter on a small table. Her drink also refilled, she sat across from him and they talked of life and how they each had arrived where they were.

Much time, and a few more orgasms, later he departed The Market a happy man. She had shared a bit of her world with him, and despite the path her life had taken, and her rather spurious claims, the woman and the girl he knew were not so very different.

The next couple of nights he spent attending balls and afternoon recitals in search of perspective brides. Keeping to his promise, he spoke with some of the girls who had debuted a few years earlier. He could not stomach courting the young girls out for their first season. He sought a wife not a broodmare despite Marie's notion he must carry on the family name.

He decided to attempt to court one of the ladies, a sweet-toned, plain girl who seemed eager to please. Miss Felicia Blackstone was no great beauty, but she had proven kind and generous in the few meetings they had and he hoped he could manage courting her without hurting her if it did not work out. He feared he'd already lost his heart to Marie.

The next day, he appeared at noon to escort Marie for a walk. She agreed because of the unfashionable and early hour he suggested, and they were limiting their jaunt to Maple Park near The Market. As they strolled, he sought the words to tell her he had held up his end of the contract. It seemed odd to him to be assuring one woman he courted another.

"Marie, I wanted to tell you I have begun courting a young lady as you stipulated in the contract. I am taking her out for a drive later this afternoon during the fashionable hour." Her body stiffened next to his for the briefest of moments. Certainly that had been his imagination.

"I am happy to hear that, my Lord. I hope you continue to do so in earnest. It is for the best." She gazed up at him with such longing it caught him off guard.

Hope bloomed in his chest. "Marie, if you decide to cancel that clause of the contract please feel free to inform me. I will gladly cease looking among the debutants for a wife."

"No. No. You must continue," she assured him as they arrived at the front door of The Market. "Thank you for the afternoon stroll. When might I expect you again?"

His heart leaped with the knowledge she wanted to see him again. "Tonight. I will be here at eight again. Until then." He raised her hand, but at the last moment turned her palm up and planted the kiss there. With a tiny flame of hope flickering in his heart, he departed.

Bloody hell! Marie couldn't credit that she'd actually asked him when he would be coming to see her again. Foolish woman. He did not belong to her, nor would he ever. He deserved better, and he needed an heir whether he would admit it or not. More importantly, she refused to be courted out of some misguided sense of guilt for not having been there when fate and her father forced her down this path.

Apparently, the time had come to cease the kid-glove treatment and prove to him she had become far too cynical to make him a good wife. She needed to counteract the damage her wayward tongue had caused as they parted. In her chamber, she strolled to her toy chest and lifted the lid. Over the years, she had collected a number of strange and very useful objects designed to enhance sexual pleasure while also being quite beautiful to view. Reaching into her box, she withdrew a smaller one that held the companion piece to the cock ring she had introduced to Heartfield during their last interlude. Opening the hand carved square, she pulled out the exquisite phallus one of her protectors had gifted her with. Made of Chinese jade with a dragonhead carved at the base, the other end consisted of a few inches of smooth stone that mushroomed at the tip replicating a penis. The dragon, worn to rounded edges from a few thousand years of use, remained a beautiful piece.

How would Heartfield feel about adding this to their bed play? Would it shock him more than the cock ring had? She certainly hoped so once she showed him how she preferred it to be used. She smiled thinking of the surprise she planned to deal him and in anticipation of where the night would go should he prove to be game. Putting the toy away, she decided a hearty lunch was in order and then a nap.

If all went well, she would be awake into the wee hours of the morning.

By seven, Marie struggled to control her nervous energy. She alternated between pacing her office and shuffling the papers on her desk. In another hour, she would be a simpering idiot if she didn't settle down. Deciding a stiff drink would be helpful, she poured herself a finger of whiskey and tossed it back. After a few moments, the burning settled into her belly and the warmth radiated out from there. She relaxed enough the next hour seemed far more bearable than the previous one had.

She returned to her desk and focused on reviewing the week's expenses while she waited. As the clock in the foyer chimed eight times, a knock sounded at her door. He had arrived. Rising, Marie shook out her skirts and paused before a mirror to check her coiffure. Not a hair dared to be out of place, so she made her way into the salon. There she found Heartfield waiting at the bar. Handsome as always, he dressed in somber black and gray. His mask hid his face, but she would have known him from twenty paces on a foggy night by the way he carried himself. His shoulders back, head high, he displayed a proud but not cocky tilt of his chin.

"Good evening, my Lord." Executing the perfect curtsey, she displayed a dazzling amount of cleavage. It amazed even her she did not spill from the neckline; it cut so low.

"Good evening, Madame." His expert bow over her hand allowed him to breathe in the dab of perfume she had traced between her breasts earlier.

"Would you prefer to remain in company for a bit or retire to our private room?" Her breath hitched as she waited to see if her torment would end or be extended far longer than she thought she might manage.

"You are the one I am here to see; please lead me astray." The seductive smile he displayed both excited and worried her. This side of him not one she experienced as a girl, but a part of the man she must learn.

"You flatter me, my Lord." Heat pooled between her legs in response to his words and rather obvious desire to be alone. Upon reaching the room, he followed her in and locked the door behind them. She poured their usual drinks, brandy for him and Madeira for herself. They settled by the fire to begin their night in what was becoming their ritual. First they discussed their days and then drifted on to their respective histories.

"Where did you find the cock ring? Aside from the pleasant side effects, it is quite beautifully made." The amber liquid swirled around the bowl of his snifter.

"A protector gave it to me as a gift. It is part of a set he claimed were used in ancient Chinese fertility rituals." A low chuckle escaped.

"You doubt his claim?" His brow winged up in curiosity.

"I am no scholar, but I know a sexual implement when I see one." Rising, she retrieved the matching jade dildo from the box on the bed and presented it to him. "Now explain, if you will, what a dildo has to do with fertility."

He looked at her and then at the bauble in his hands. Marie waited for the next obvious question.

"I suppose from a scientific perspective we would need to assess the number of times you became with child after using one or both of the implements." He eyed her with a charming leer.

"Never." She sipped her wine to steady her nerves. This part of the evening would take a turn for the worse or the adventurous.

"And how often have you used this particular device?" The husky note in his voice skittered across her skin, puckering her nipples.

"I have easily lost count." Her legs gave out amid her nerves and desire, and she sat in her chair.

"Mmm." He paused considering the hunk of mineral he held. "And you are sure you used it correctly?"

The time had come. The moment of truth. "It is difficult to use it incorrectly as it can go almost anywhere you choose to insert it."

His gaze jerked up from the device. Confusion flashed first until it dawned on him what she meant, then surprise, followed by curiosity. The various emotions crossing his face spoke volumes about his life experience and his determination to accept her as she was. It would seem things were going to take the adventurous route in lieu of the abrupt ending she half expected.

"And you have used this other than in the traditional sense?" His throat sounded parched beyond reason as his words rasped out.

"I have and I enjoyed it." She paused letting the tension crackle in the air as the silence drew out. "I could show you."

He nodded, despite his obvious shock, and he gave every appearance of being excited at the naughty prospect. Rising from their chairs, they each stripped off their garments.

He undid her laces, placing kisses along the way as he revealed each bit of flesh. Little shivers of bliss rippled over her skin in his wake. Both nude, they stretched out on the bed. The toy lay on the nightstand as they kissed and petted. He eased his hand between her legs and stroked her sensitive tissues until she writhed in his arms. He retracted his seeking fingers to reach for the jade piece, but paused to look at her in question. She rolled to her other side, produced a jar of salve from the dildo's box on the side table, and opened the lid. With the thick, oily substance she coated first the colorful mineral and then reached around and coated her rear entrance.

"It has been a while so you need to ease it in slowly. I will tell you when to stop and when you can press deeper." She smiled at him over her shoulder in encouragement.

The mushroomed tip of the stone nudged against her backside. The tight muscle resisted the initial invasion. "More pressure," she said.

He pressed harder, even as he dropped kisses along her shoulder, and the head slipped past the ring. She drew a deep breath in and exhaled as he continued to press it deeper. "Hold." Her body shook with the pleasure pain crests as her anal passage adjusted.

"This is hurting you." He reversed directions, withdrawing it.

She fumbled behind her to still his hand. "No. It feels good, but I need to adjust to it. I have not been breached there in a rather long time." Another moment passed. "Now, press it deeper."

Reluctant, his hand remained motionless until she wiggled back against the phallus trying to impale herself farther. At last he drove it in as far as it could go and she gasped, her body rippling around the jade cock as her pussy pulsed with emptiness. He pulled the implement out. Then with no additional direction, and using a smooth motion, he slid it back in causing her to moan in pleasure.

Damn him for a fast learner.

His hand worked it in and out of her body as though he had been doing it for years. "Stop." Her breathless plea came as she neared the precipice. "I want to feel you inside me with this in my bum. Please, I have never had the chance to—"

"On your knees." A glance over her shoulder revealed him pausing to sheath himself with a skin before he moved behind her. He held the tip of his cock to her damp folds and dragged up and down her slit. Then, with a languorous shove he sank his cock deep into her pussy.

The unique sensation of fullness from both him and the phallus had her trembling as intense waves of pleasure buffeted her body. When he shifted the dildo deeper into her backside she physically shook with the carnality. "Take my cock," he demanded grabbing a fistful of hair and slamming into her core. His free hand worked the jade in and out opposite of his thrusts.

"God that feels good." He groaned as the green rod slid over his cock in the opposite direction. His shock and surprise were replaced with overwhelming sensation. Her silky warmth wrapped around him, while the hardness of the stone contrasted against the softness of her body. Her inner muscles clenched around him, and he decided to try a different rhythm. He drew the phallus out and reversed direction so he entered her sweet pussy in a dual plunge. She gasped at the sensation, as did he. The feeling like nothing he had ever experienced. Soon the pace increased as she pushed backward into his thrusts, and he met her stroke for stroke with his cock and the toy.

When she came, he could only compare it to watching a roman candle explode up close. He pumped into her working both channels until he joined her in final ecstasy. His orgasm rocketed into her with more force than he could remember since being a young man. In short, it was the most incredible sexual experience in his entire life. She amazed, even mesmerized.

She pulled away from him and the stone and proceeded to again tidy him up, remove the sheath, and whisk the bauble away for cleaning. She paraded around in the buff much to his delight. "You have the most delectable backside, Marie."

"Why, Heartfield, I had no idea you were partial to a woman's rump." She flashed a coquettish smile and disappeared behind the screen in the corner of the room. When she emerged a few moments later she brought a rag and some water over to the bed. She sat and bathed his penis. "So, how are things going with your Miss Harrod? Might she be an appropriate new wife?”

“I’d prefer not to discuss my courtship of another woman with you while nude. In particular, we should not do so while you are handling my cock.” He repressed the urge to growl at her.

Marie sighed. “Very well, but I expect to hear if she will be suitable soon. You are not getting any younger.”

“Well, now that you have reduced me to my dotage perhaps you might like to also emasculate me?” He shot her a baleful glare.

“I did not intend to....” A pretty pink suffused her face as she tried to recover her composure. Then he ruined the whole effect and chuckled as he watched her reaction. “Why you insufferable man! You shouldn’t tease a body like that.”

“But I do so enjoy teasing your body.” He grabbed the damp cloth from her and tossed it aside as he tumbled her back to the bed. “I’ll show you who isn’t getting any younger.”

CHAPTER FOUR

J onathan climbed down from his phaeton and cringed. His entire body ached from his exploits with Marie the night before. Of course, she would never know that little truth. Bad enough she teased him about being old, heaven forbid she discovered the truth of those words. Straightening up to his full height, he tossed a coin to the boy holding his reins and climbed the steps to the overstated abode of Sir and Lady Blackstone. A baronet, he sought to have his daughter marry up both in title and wealth, which made Jonathan a good prospect.

Not the best prospect possible, but they were happy to have him noticing their daughter who had otherwise been languishing in relative obscurity. He rapped a smart tattoo on the door with the knocker and waited for the portal to open. A gray-haired, stout man dressed in simple black garb greeted him at the door.

"I'm here to collect Miss Blackstone for our outing." Jonathan presented his calling card.

Taking the small square, the stoic man peered at the print and nodded. "Very good, my Lord."

Stepping into the dim foyer, Jonathan paused to let his eyes adjust as the butler closed the door.

"This way please."

Jonathan followed the servant into a garish parlor. Putrid green upholstery clashed with the decidedly bloody-red walls, all of which was punctuated by spots of mustard fabric. The nightmare kaleidoscope was enough to put a man off eating. He shut his eyes against the visual assault as he waited for Miss Felicia Blackstone to join him. With any luck she would arrive with a promptness that failed most women.

"Good afternoon, Baron Heartfield." Her soft voice served as a balm to his soul. He would be able to depart the torturous salon forthwith.

"And to you, Miss Blackstone. Are you ready for our drive?" He stepped toward her and escape.

"Mother thought we should have tea before we departed." She stared at the floor, but could it be out of shyness, submissiveness, or to spare her daily punished eyes?

Dear God! Tea in the front parlor? He'd rather be drawn and quartered. "It's a warm day. I thought we might stop by Gunter's for an ice."

Her face brightened as she raised her eyes. "Oh, that would be lovely. I am sure mother will understand."

"Excellent, shall we?" He held his arm out for her while she rested her hand on his elbow with a delicate touch.

A short while later they sat on Berkley Square in the shade of the Plane trees, with their maple-like leaves. "How is your ice?"

"The lavender ice is delicious. How is the chocolate?"

"Very good."

Silence reigned. Jonathan tried very hard not to dwell on the notion that if Marie sat at his side they would be chatting away as the old friends they were. Instead, he sat with a young woman whose intelligent eyes hinted at far more than her demure bearing offered.

"Have you been to the latest exhibit at the British Museum? There are some wonderful antiquities on display."

"No, Mother and Father fear I will become too bookish should I entertain such pursuits."

"I see. What do you do for entertainment?" He hoped she would not say shopping. He could not abide such flighty women.

"Shopping." The word flew from her mouth as though she had to struggle to expel it from her lips.

His interest withered like a boiled noodle. "What precisely do you shop for?"

"Oh, dear." She mumbled and shoved another scoop of ice into her mouth. She swallowed and glanced up at him and smiled. "Parasols. I have quite a collection of parasols."

How strange she did not carry one with her at the moment and the freckles dusting her nose were unmistakable, a clear indication she did not carry a parasol. Peculiar. "Do you read?"

Her eyes widened at his sudden switch in topic. "Books?"

"Well, yes. For one thing."

"I do." Her hands clutched her empty ice cup as though she'd never let it go.

"I recently read a fascinating booklet 'Practical Remarks on Aerial Navigation' by Sir George Cayley. The author provided a wonderful discussion on the principles of flight. Can you imagine people soaring through the air like birds?"

Felicia smiled and let her hands relax around the dish. "That would be ever so amazing. How about Mr. Hancock's steam phaeton? I saw him once in Hyde Park."

Jonathan eased back into his seat and passed their ice cups off to the footman who came around to collect them. So, he'd found a bluestocking in debutant's clothing. "I have a copy of his *Narrative of Twelve Years Experiments* and have taken a ride with him."

"Oh! You've ridden in his steam machine? How exiting! What was it like?" Her eyes sparkled and her cheeks took on a rosy blush.

"It was a rather loud and juddering ride, but amazing nonetheless." He took up the reins and steered them toward Hyde Park. "Perhaps we will run in to him today while on our drive?"

Who could've guessed she had a tinkerer's soul? The rest of their drive she chatted about all things mechanical with an animation most women reserved for fashion. As they left the park to return to her house, she grew subdued again. It became clear her parents did not encourage her intellectual pursuits, and the typical men of their class would not wish to court a woman with such interests.

A small pang of guilt stabbed at his conscience since he knew he was not truly interested in courting her either. Damn Marie and her ridiculous stipulations. He had to prove to her once and for all they belonged together. Perhaps a night out would help her adjust to the notion. Maybe attending a masquerade would give her enough anonymity to relax and enjoy herself and help her see how well matched they were?

"Thank you for the enchanting afternoon." The meek little mouse had replaced his animated companion and reminded him he was not alone.

"You are quite welcome. And, truly, don't let your parents douse your interest in mechanical things." He helped her alight from the carriage and escorted her to her door.

"Thank you, my Lord." She curtsied and dashed through the door in a flurry of skirts.

If he wasn't already in love, Miss Felicia Blackstone might have made a delightful companion despite her parents. He shrugged and climbed back into his vehicle. Heading home to change, he decided to stop by his club for dinner and some masculine companionship. Tomorrow he would make arrangements to treat Marie to a night she'd never forget.

Jonathan pulsed with excitement as he arrived at The Market. In his hand he clutched a feathered mask that matched the simple black one he wore. Before he could knock, the butler swung the door open and greeted him. "My Lord."

"Good evening. Please tell Madame Marchander I am here." He headed into the empty main salon and ordered a drink. Tilting his glass, he downed the amber liquid in one swallow. He enjoyed the penetrating warmth of the alcohol as he waited for Marie.

"Good evening, Heart." Her melodious voice carried over to him from the left. She'd shortened his title, could it mean something? Perhaps she had softened toward him?

"Ah, you look bewitching as always." He bowed to her.

"Please, join me in my office for a moment while I wait on Karen to bring my cloak." She disappeared behind the tapestry that hid her office door.

Following her inside, he determined to take a moment to steal a kiss before they left for his surprise. She stopped and turned around to find him close behind. So close she ended up captured within his arms. Soft, feminine curves pressed against him in delightful contrast to his masculine form. His gaze drifted to her parted lips, and he swooped in to capture the pink softness. Delving past teeth to find her tongue and the warmth of her mouth, he slid his tongue over her inner landscape. Probing, exploring, tasting.

A sigh of a breath escaped her as she melted into him. His chest rumbled with the growl of desire he could not contain. Finally, he pulled away convinced if he did not end the kiss they would never make the evening's entertainment. "Turn about so I can tie your mask."

"A mask?" Marie sounded breathless from their kiss.

"I am taking you to the masked ball at Vauxhall. We shall have great fun eating and dancing in anonymity, and then we shall escape just before midnight and the big unmasking."

She could not hide her delight, even as words to the contrary crossed her luscious lips. "We should not take such a risk. What if someone recognized us, even with the masks?"

"They will all be far too busy dancing and drinking to care who we are." He placed the mask over her eyes and tied the ribbons behind her head taking care not to disturb her perfectly styled hair.

"Very well. We shall go. But I warn you if we recognize anyone I shall insist we leave."

"We will consider the options should the need arrive. I have a private dining box reserved for us." A knock on the door preceded Karen's entry with said cloak.

Jonathan took the garment and slipped it over Marie's shoulders. Arm in arm they left the office and then The Market.

Alone in the carriage, Marie looked at Heart. *When had he become Heart and not Heartfield? And what possessed this bit of lunacy of his?* "Why the masked ball?" Her question broke through the comfortable silence.

"I'm selfish. I want to see you dance and smile as you once did at the balls we attended. Before I left...."

"I have not danced like that in many years, but I will endeavor to enjoy myself to the fullest this evening." Her smile felt freer than any she'd granted in the last four or five years. The weight of being the perfect hostess and mistress lifted from her shoulders in an unexpected twist.

The carriage halted and Heart, because he was still her heart after all this time, assisted her in exiting the vehicle. Arm in arm, they found their way down the shadowy winding paths through the flora and fauna from which

Vauxhall Gardens received its named. The ball was already a crush. They surged through the crowd, hands linked. Arriving at their box, Heart swept her to safety and into his arms again. He straightened her mask, which had been knocked askew during their dash through the press of people. Then, he kissed her. A swift brush of lips before the service door opened and their waiter arrived.

A lavish six-course meal left them secluded in their semiprivate box, free to touch and caress each other at will.

"I remember the time you broke your arm trying to ride your father's stallion." Heart grinned, letting his gaze rest on her face as he drifted back in time.

"I was so determined I had outgrown my pony. Papa grew terribly angry with me." An ache in her chest took up residence. "That happened before the gambling problem started. Or perhaps he just had it under control then. Who's to know what was happening."

"I'm sorry, Marie. I did not mean to bring up painful memories." Concern creased his brow above the mask.

"No, don't apologize. I love remembering good times, even if there are negative memories associated." She patted his hand that lay on the table between them. "Perhaps it is time we danced?"

"I think it is." He rose, held out his hand to assist her, and led her onto the floor as a waltz struck up.

Feeling the strength of his arms about her, she reveled in the moment of contentment. Then he swept her into the music and they whirled around the dance floor. They danced song after song, never leaving the floor. Enjoying themselves immensely, they lost track of the hour and before they knew it, the reveal waltz floated across the assembly. Every so often, partners were swapped and passed from one person to another. At the end of the song the clock struck midnight and Marie realized they had stayed too long. She found herself in the arms of a man who unabashedly leered at her bosom. He pulled off his mask, revealing a drunken Lord Bethany.

The fates were not only against her, but had conspired to punish her for some perceived slight.

On the ran-tan, he reached for her mask with an unstable hand and tried to pull it off. She smacked the appendage away, refusing to reveal herself.

"Come now, love, show me your face so I can get my due." He swayed toward her and then stumbled back pulling her with him. Bracing himself, he grabbed her breast and smiled as he stabilized. "Well, now that's nice, too."

"Unhand me, you bug hunting nobbler!" She slapped his hand away, but in the melee knocked her mask off.

"I know you! Madame Marchander!" He announced so loud those around them turned to gawk at the disturbance.

Feeling as exposed as she had the night of her auction, she cringed away from the drunken fool, but he would have none of it.

He gripped her arm with brutish strength and pulled her against his pudgy body. His hand dove down the front of her bodice to fondle her breasts. His beefy limb didn't quite fit resulting in his own thwarted frustration. He jerked his hand back tearing the dress so it drooped and left her corset exposed. "I've never had such a fine piece as you." He proceeded to attempt a kiss.

His moist mouth crashed down on hers. Shocked, she opened her mouth, allowing him to swipe at her with his tongue. She struggled to push him away, to no effect. Then he vanished. Staggering back, she looked up to see an avenging angel in the form of Heart. Mask gone, he landed his fist square in the sot's face leaving him out cold on the floor of the ballroom. Everyone around them stared in shock as he turned and took her hand. Silent, he led her away from the scene and into his carriage.

"I-I..." she stammered at a loss for words.

The carriage moved out posthaste as he pulled her into his arms. "I am so very sorry, my dear. By the time I realized the time, the music began playing and someone had whisked you away. I looked for you but couldn't find you before the music ended."

Moist tracks of tears dampened her face as she pulled away from his chest. "You must not blame yourself." She sniffed. "I did not realize either. And who could have predicted I would end up with that horrible Lord Bethany?" She shuddered.

"I should have been there. Are you sure you are well?" He looked her over and noticed the state of her bodice. "That dirty whoreson. He molested you?"

"Not very successfully. Between his drunken state and my tightly laced corset he merely managed to tear my dress, which can be repaired." She glanced down at the ruined fabric. "Or at least I hope it can be mended."

Heart's jaw ticked with repressed anger lending him a menacing air. "I'd very much like to go back and thrash the rotten bastard."

Deep inside Marie thrilled at the protectiveness he displayed. Despite that, she tried to temper her words. "I don't believe that will be required."

"It might not be required, but it would bring me deep satisfaction." He pulled her closer to him again and held her until they arrived at The Market.

"I'll see you inside." He hopped down and helped her out.

"Heart, would you mind terribly if I retired? I think I am rather worn out after all the dancing and then the tussle at the end."

"Please, Marie. Just let me hold you. Nothing else."

The need in his voice won out against her better judgment and she nodded, letting him follow her inside.

Alone in their room, they stripped down and climbed into bed. She sighed on a soft exhale as he pulled her into his arms and held her until she drifted off to sleep. Her defenses lay in a pile of rubble around her heart.

CHAPTER FIVE

M arie awoke surrounded by Heart. His arms, his smell, his very essence seemed to encompass her. Needing to extricate herself, she eased out from between the sheets without disturbing him and tugged the bell pull to call Karen. After tending to nature, she drew on a robe as Karen bustled into the room with a tray of hot chocolate and the morning paper. Beneath the news lay the gossip rag.

Heart slept on, oblivious to the tinkling of silver and china as she poured herself a cup of steaming chocolate. She cracked the curtains enough to light her paper. After perusing the news, she picked up the gossip rag. It often contained more tripe than not, but the occasional bit of information, when paired with her more reliable, sources had become very useful. She stared at the front page and scanned the bits deemed most news worthy.

A certain Lady F— was seen in the company of Lord K— who was supposed to be home ill in lieu of attending the soiree at Blake House the previous night.

A credible bit of information, too bad his wife would be the last to know. She scanned farther down past trivial bits and then a line on the inside page caught her attention.

Lord H—was seen to wallop Lord B—in the face over the notorious Madame M—at the Vauxhall Garden Masquerade last night.

"Damn! Damn! Damn!" She set her chocolate aside and rose to approach the bed. "Wake up, Heart. You silly fool. Wake up this instant."

Sleepy and tousled, he sat up, letting the covers bunch around his waist. His smooth chest a distraction to her line of thought until he flexed his hand and inspected it more closely. "What is the matter, Marie? I was having the most lascivious dream about you." He sported his naughty grin, a slightly lopsided smile paired with his twinkling eyes. It left no doubt as to just how carnal his dream had been. The evidence was irrefutable when his hardened cock tented the covers.

"Yes well, while you were dreaming, Madame Gossip had her way with us. Your little display last night was spotted and reported in the gossip column this morning." She slapped the paper against his chest and set to pacing. "I warned you our association would come to no good."

"I hardly count a vague reference to three people as 'no good.' He got up and came toward her naked as a babe. "Stop fretting about a single line buried on the last page of a gossip rag. Come back to bed. I wish to feel the silk of your skin against mine."

Marie joined him, though she continued to worry about the ramifications of that single line. She had seen greater men than Heart ruined with less.

After a morning round of making love, Marie managed to send Heart away so she could attend to business matters. He was blind if he thought he would survive unscathed. At the very least, there would be talk of his defense of her person. Worst case they would be linked and his chances of securing the kind of woman he should have as a bride would be ruined. He would have to settle for a world-wise widow or some merchant's daughter instead of the heiress he deserved.

Frustrated, she decided she needed to up the ante. He had not batted an eyelash at the cock ring or the dildo. She wondered how he might feel about another partner in bed with them. Would he share her with another woman? Perhaps that would be the final straw. Resolved to finally prove to him how unsuitable a baroness she would be, she set about making arrangements for the evening's entertainments.

The clock showed four after nine when he appeared in the salon wearing his mask and de rigueur dark clothes. Marie reminded herself she needed to push him away not try to attract him, so she had no business fixating on him. Even less, allowing her heart to soften in the face of his persistence. She must be strong or they would both be hurt in the long run.

He smiled at her from across the room. As he stalked toward her, slow and steady with sensual intent, she felt her core grow warm and begin to dampen. Her nipples puckered and chafed against her clothing as desire threatened to overwhelm her good sense. He extended his hand and helped her rise from her seat. "Good evening, Madame. You look stunning as always."

"Thank you, my Lord." She curtsied. "Phillipe has made your usual arrangements if you will follow him." She waved her liaison over.

"My Lord, if you please." He bowed and gestured toward the stairs. Heart seemed confused for a moment, but then went along with Phillipe without issue. Marie returned to her seat for a few minutes before rising and retreating to her office. There, she slipped into the servants' hall and scurried upstairs to their room.

Darting in through the door, she turned around and found Heart sitting by the fire sipping a brandy without his mask on. One sardonic brow lifted in response to her frenzied entry to the room. "I take it that little charade was done for my benefit?"

"Indeed. I did not warn you for fear you would object. After this morning's gossip, we must be more circumspect. I will not meet with you in the salon any longer. You will come here in the future to meet with me."

"Very well. If it soothes your concerns, then I will concede the point. But, not because I believe what we do matters one whit to anyone outside of this room. I'll do it for you, Marie." He set his glass down and gestured for her to come to him.

She sighed, but accepted his reluctant compliance with her wishes and joined him by the fire. "Thank you. Now, I have a little surprise planned for tonight."

"What might that be?" He tugged her down in front of him and worked the pins from her hair, letting the heavy, silken strands cloud around her shoulders.

"Mmmm. I can't remember with your hands in my hair like that." She settled against his legs, enjoying the sensuous feeling of his fingers massaging her scalp. Relaxed and drifting she almost missed the gentle *snick* of the door closing. Heart remained oblivious, but her pulse raced as she anticipated his reaction.

Focused on the silky slide of his fingers through her hair and the retrieval of all the pins, it was rather shocking when a pair of hands slid down over Jonathan's shoulders and a vaguely familiar feminine scent engulfed him. "What the devil?" He sat forward out of the woman's reach.

"It's okay, Heart. You remember Celeste. She is one of my best girls, and I asked her to join us this evening. I believe most men fantasize about having two women at one time, and I intend for you to have that experience with me."

His jacket seemed to slip from his shoulders as Marie's words penetrated his confusion. She had arranged for another woman to join them? What would a man do with two women? How could he manage them both? "Marie, really this is not—"

"I want this. I sometimes enjoy the charms of my own sex as well as men. Is that so hard to accept? I thought you might enjoy this with me." Marie stared at him as though his rejection of this would be a rejection of her. He would not do that. He could accept all of her in order to have her in his life again.

"Very well, ladies. I will expect you two to show me the ropes." He smiled tentatively, unsure how the evening would turn out.

Celeste moved forward at his consent and helped Marie undress him. They peeled his many layers of clothing from his person and then sent him off to the bed. He sprawled across it and settled back to watch as their new friend disrobed Marie. With each bit of clothing gone his cock grew harder. By the time the two women had stripped each other bare he sported the hardest cockstand he could remember having in his adult life.

Celeste's fair complexion, willowy build, dark hair, and pale blue eyes offered an enticing juxtaposition with Marie's curvier figure and fairer skin with blond hair. They were a sultry study in contrasts. Nude at the side of the bed closest to him, they stopped and kissed. Marie's tongue drove into Celeste's mouth in a possessive, comfortable way. It was easy to imagine they had done this many times before.

He fisted his shaft and stroked it as their hands roamed over each other's breasts, mouths fused. Finding it incredibly erotic to watch their display he wanted to be in the midst of these two beautiful wanton women. As though they sensed his desire, they broke their kiss and turned to him. Marie crawled around him to kneel on the bed while Celeste perched between his legs. She nudged his hand out of the way and took over fondling his length while Marie swooped in and kissed him. Her tongue traced the seam of his mouth and demanded entrance.

His mind fogged with lust while his woman nestled in his arms and another sucked his cock. Celeste's mouth covered the head and then eased down the length of him until he could feel the tightness of her throat. With still a bit of length to go, he expected her to stop, but she kept going. The tightness of her upper throat intoxicated him as Marie nibbled at his lips. Then she shifted lower to suck on his nipples as Celeste reversed directions. While Marie explored every inch of his torso, their companion continued to work his shaft over as though it might be her last. His muscles tensed and shivers of pleasure racked his body. The woman's mouth was nothing short of amazing.

Her free hand slid under his balls to fondle them as the suction became more intense. His hips pumped, pushing his rod deeper into her mouth, in answer to the ache signaling his peak neared. Finally, Marie kissed him again and his body exploded. Spasm after spasm of ecstasy rolled over him as his cries were swallowed by Marie and his cum by Celeste. She milked him until nothing remained but his softening manhood.

Rising up, she smiled and joined Marie at his side.

"I'm afraid you two have put me out of commission." He looked ruefully at his spent penis.

"I'm sure we can help you get back in to the thick of things." Marie winked at him and turned to kiss Celeste. Heart found himself astounded and completely turned on by the idea they were sharing the taste of him as they kissed. Fascinated that another woman touching Marie did not bother him in the way a man's touch would. Drawn back to the tableau before him, Marie pressed the dark beauty back onto the bed and sucked her nipples. She seemed as enthralled with the dusky medallions as he. Then she kissed her way down Celeste's body, nibbling every curve and indentation until she arrived at the apex of her thighs.

As Marie dipped her finger into Celeste only to lick it clean, he experienced the first twinge of interest in his staff. When she did it again but offered to let him lap Celeste's juices off he rose to attention. "She tastes so sweet, doesn't she?"

She tasted sweet, but not as sweet as his Marie.

"Yes," he croaked, his throat dry as dust. He glanced around and found a pitcher of water by the bed. He poured a glass and turned to find Marie facing him with her nipples glistening in the light.

"Lick them." Her voice came demanding and husky.

Obediently, he swirled his tongue around one areola and then rolled the nipple with his teeth. Dear God, she had swabbed Celeste's moisture on her nipples. Enthralled, greed had him moving to the other nipple to taste it as well. Hands pressed him back from her honey-dipped bounty. Then she turned from him and lowered her face into Celeste's pussy. Marie lapped at the other woman, sliding her tongue up and down her length and drove back into her sheath. His cock grew rock hard within moments of watching their display. Celeste laid, legs spread with her own hands pulling and pinching her nipples. Marie balanced on all fours to nibble, suck, and stroke Celeste's clit.

Inspired, Jonathan retrieved the semi-precious dildo from the box on the nightstand and handed it to Marie. "Use this on her, too."

Marie looked up, surprised by his directions. Good. He needed to keep her on her toes. She slipped the jade piece into Celeste and worked it in and out while she flicked her clit relentlessly. The cock-filled woman writhed on the bed and moaned in pleasure. Excellent, it was Marie's turn. Shifting his position to line up behind her, he pressed his cock against her sopping wet pussy. Marie jerked up for a moment, stopping her attentions as she glanced back at him. He smacked her on the ass. "Don't stop. Celeste needs more."

Marie smiled and returned to her duties as Heart seated himself until his thighs were plastered against hers. She pressed back and ground against his cock. Yes, she wanted him to fuck her, and so he would. Pulling out, he left the crown in her channel and then slid home to his balls. He settled into a steady rhythm. He pounded into her from behind as relentless as her own attentions to the sobbing Celeste. Finally, Celeste's orgasm ripped through her, as she cried out in release. Marie continued lapping at her, tasting her until the last ripple had passed. Heart continued to impale Marie from behind, his hands gripping her ass as he worked in and out of her body. Her sheath rippled and squeezed around him, trying to grip him even as he continued.

He watched as Celeste shifted and angled her head so she could lie beneath Marie and suck on her nipples. Marie knelt there, her breasts being adored, but somehow managed to meet him thrust for thrust as her climax came near. With the added stimulation of Celeste's mouth on her breasts, Marie was lost right away. She moaned and her body shook. His entry became more difficult as her orgasm ripped through her, her sheath gripping him relentlessly. His own release pounded through him as Marie's body clutched at him until he shook with the effort of kneeling. Exhausted, they collapsed on the bed next to their partner.

Marie found it difficult to comprehend what had just happened. Instead of being shocked to his core, even repulsed by what they had done, he had been turned on and a full participant. He'd gotten the bloody dildo out for her! Even as he lay stroking her thigh, Celeste got up and quietly left them. Not a man who frequented establishments like hers, his eager response was beyond her comprehension. He came from the conservative quarter. How could she have known he had such a hedonistic streak?

As much as it foiled her plans, his pleasure-seeking side turned her on and made her love him that much more. Double damn. Her ability to deny the truth increased in difficulty after the respective displays, each more decadent than the last. However, what they shared did not mean she wouldn't continue her campaign to get him married to a proper heiress. He needed someone who could bear him a child, whether he knew it or not. But, what it did mean is she would have to be prepared for the inevitable pain when he left.

Sometime in the early dawn, before the first pale streaks colored the sky, she roused him. "Heart, you should go now before anyone is about on the street."

"Must I?" His words were garbled by sleep.

She shook him awake. "Yes, dearest. You must leave before anyone can see you. Please. I will see you again in a few days."

"All right then." He sat up and rubbed his eyes to clear the fog of sleep. At a painstaking pace, he dressed and then kissed her good night. Alone, she returned to bed where she pretended she wasn't lost and her heart wasn't aching for the one man she could never have.

Jonathan arrived home and retreated to bed. To his great dismay, his butler awakened him in short order.

"My Lord, Miss Felicia Blackstone is downstairs with Sir and Lady Blackstone. They demand to speak with you immediately."

Eyelids like sandpaper scraped open and closed as he blinked to clear the dregs of sleep. "Tell them I will be down directly. By the way, what time is it?"

"It is eight o'clock in the morning, my Lord. I will bring tea and coffee to the salon for your guests." The stoic butler bowed and departed.

Damned lucky to have such an unflappable and competent butler since it appeared his own wits had deserted him. What did Blackstone want at this bloody hour? They weren't supposed to meet until next week for the formal signing of the contracts. He'd put the betrothal off a bit so he could spend more time with Marie before he had to decide things one way or another. He held on to the tenuous thread of hope he might still convince her to marry him, so he could escape the loveless marriage he had begun to arrange. Besides, it was deuced early for a social call, even by his future bride and her family. Standing he set about cleaning up and getting dressed. Fifteen minutes later, he stood at the entrance of his front salon.

"Good morning, Miss Blackstone, Sir and Lady Blackstone." He greeted them and then seeing they each held tea poured himself a stiff cup of coffee. No cream. No sugar. He needed the bitter brew to get his wheels turning and fast because the lack of a smiling faces in the room did not bode well.

"Let's skip the false pleasantries. We are here to find out the veracity of the news that you have been traipsing around town with a notorious madam. I understood you were a widower who had been faithful to his wife and now sought a new woman to bear your children and set up a home with you. What is the meaning of this rakish behavior?" Sir Blackstone had turned red as his jowls flapped during his impassioned speech.

Jonathan cringed inside. Blast it. He sighed, seeing no way around the issue. "I take full responsibility for the situation. I believed myself ready to settle down, but it seems I am not. Please accept my profound apologies. Miss Blackstone, I understand if you feel the need to sever our acquaintance publicly in any way you see fit. I am quite prepared to take the brunt of whatever public censure you and your family feel is warranted. I had not intended to hurt you." He bowed to the lady who, while not smiling, held no anger in her eyes.

"Thank you, my Lord. I am sure you understand if I no longer speak to you publicly." She rose from the settee and nodded to her parents.

"Felicia, stop where you are." Sir Blackstone demanded as his daughter reached the salon door. "This is not finished. This man led you on and then behaved abominably. He has shamed you and this family."

"Oh, Father. Do shut up. I never wanted Lord Heartfield's attentions. You were the one currying his favor. I consider this an important lesson learned. I will marry for love from here forward. I want a man who loves me, quirky interests and all. Neither you nor mother will bully me into a loveless marriage again." Back ramrod straight, Felicia Blackstone strode from his salon and left her stunned parents gaping in her wake.

For a brief moment Jonathan again considered there might in fact be more to the woman he had courted than initial perception allowed. She would have made a superior baroness between her intellect and her spirit, but she could never be Marie. "If you will excuse me, I believe your cloaks will be waiting for you at the door." He bowed and departed the room. He had to find Marie and make her understand his intentions in no uncertain terms.

CHAPTER SIX

Jonathan retreated to his bedroom and considered his options. How much longer should he play Marie's game? Grateful the sham of a courtship had ended, the time had come to convince Marie they belonged together. She belonged to him. He'd lost her once, but not again. He would reclaim the woman he had always loved.

Glancing at the clock, he cursed the uncivilized hour that made it far too early for a visit. A gallop in the park would clear his head before he made his argument to Marie. After a bruising ride along the quieter paths in Hyde Park, he sat down to a light luncheon since he'd missed breakfast.

Still working out his argument in his head, he made his way to the familial safe and retrieved the Heartfield Emerald. A stunning green stone surrounded by tiny table-cut diamonds it had belonged to his grandmother and then his mother. The family ring had always been presented to a beloved Heartfield bride.

His wife had never worn the ring.

Tucking the jewel into his pocket, he dashed downstairs and out to the stable to saddle his horse. Within the hour, he found himself tossing the reins to one of the stable boys behind The Market and slipped in the rear entrance. Karen bustled down the back hall loaded down with a basket; he stopped her. "Where is your mistress?"

"In the main salon with some of the ladies of the house." She bobbed a curtsy and scurried away.

Jonathan smiled and made his way to where the women gathered. There he found a bevy of beauties in various states of undress lounging and chatting over tea. Marie sat regally amidst the women, wearing a simple day dress in a shade of pale green that reminded him of the girl he'd once known.

She rose and crossed to where he hovered just inside the room. "Heart, what are you doing here at this hour?"

"I needed to speak with you, and I felt certain if I sent a note, you would refuse to see me in the light of day." He couldn't control the smile tugging at his lips. She was beautiful.

"Of course, I would. You will ruin yourself being seen here. What of your potential bride? How would she feel to learn you were seen here? We have discussed this before." She ushered him into her office even as she scolded him.

"I have no fiancée."

"Well, not yet, but you will be asking for her hand soon." She sat in one of the chairs near the fire.

"I will not—"

"Oh, Heart! Stop this instant. You agreed to pursue her if I signed the contract."

"Let me finish. I did pursue her, but she learned of the masquerade and became dissatisfied with the idea of marrying me. She chose to end our courtship." He raised a shoulder indicating the decision had been made.

Marie shot to her feet. "I knew this would happen. It was pure folly to think we could hide the time we spent together." She paced, wringing her hands and chewing her lip in apparent consternation.

He stepped in front of her, bracing her shoulders with his hands as he ended her forward motion. "Marie, I have no interest in a young girl for a wife. I have room in my heart for one woman. I knew her once long ago, and I have been fortunate enough to have a second chance at making her mine. You are the woman I want, the only woman who can make me happy."

"Please, don't." Her voice cracked and tears welled in her eyes, making them sparkle like the rarest gemstones.

His chest constricted until he couldn't draw breath knowing what she would say next. Despite his knowledge, her next words struck like a lance to his heart.

"We can never be. The girl you loved does not exist any longer. The woman you see now is older, wiser, and, I'm sorry to say, too world-weary to believe in love. It is too late for what could have been, but you have a chance at your future. You have a chance to ensure your family line and perhaps even snatch a small bit of happiness from the reminder of your life." A single tear slipped from her eye, leaving a wet track down her cheek.

"Why? Why can we never be? Why can't I find happiness with you?" Jonathan's world crumbled around him with naught he could do to stop it.

Her face hardened, her eyes turning to chips of green ice. "I'm sorry. I should never have agreed to the contract with you. I had hoped you would see how inappropriate I am for a wife. I do not remember my genteel education including the arts of cock sucking, ménage à trois, or cunnilingus. I am quite certain husbands do not fuck their wives' asses, nor do they share them with other women. Consider our contract severed. Your payment will be returned as soon as I can arrange it. And I think it goes without saying you will not be welcomed in this establishment as long as I am the owner. Good day, my Lord."

A wash of heat smothered Jonathan as he stared at the woman who retreated to her desk and shuffled paperwork with a disturbing calm. Desire, stoked by the images painted with her raw words, warred with anger at her rejection. Together they bolstered his determination. He would have her. Beating a strategic retreat, he departed The Market without another word.

With the soft *click* of the door closing, Marie surrendered to the despair that had eroded her self-control during the conversation with Heart.

She loved him but knew she shouldn't.

She loved him but could not change a hard-learned lesson. Men were never there when she needed them, and to count on them only led to further humiliation and betrayal.

Whether in a public display, such as an auction, or a more private experience such as heartbreak, the end result never changed. The Market was real, solid, and a dependable source of income. Without that security she might find herself once again humiliated and betrayed, left to her own ends. Frankly, she didn't have enough spirit left to rebuild if Heart married her and then decided he'd made a mistake.

His desertion would be a killing blow and a risk she wouldn't take, no matter how bad she wished she could. As long as she remained unmarried, The Market belonged to her. With her security assured, the future, though bleak, would be steady and predictable.

Resigned, she dashed a note off to her bank directing Heart's funds be returned immediately. They had been sitting in an account waiting for her to decide what to do with them. Keeping the money had never been an option, but she had not figured out how to convince him to take it back either.

Tears blurring her vision, she retreated to her room and allowed her misery free rein. She'd allow this short period of mourning for what was and what could have been, and then it would be over. She would have to tuck it all away deep inside and forget about him.

Jonathan let the anger and hurt of her rejection cloud his thinking. So much so, he departed by the front door and walked halfway home before he remembered his mount. He jammed his fingers through his hair and cursed. For a brief moment, he grappled with the overwhelming desire to go back to The Market and paddle Marie's bottom for her stubbornness. Then he wanted to do all the naughty things with her she spoke of and more. With a groan, he turned around and returned in her direction. He wouldn't go back in just yet. He swore he merely intended to collect his horse.

Around the corner from The Market, two rather disreputable-looking men approached him. The taller of the two, had on trousers stopping well short of his ankles and a ratty-looking, threadbare shirt. The shorter man dressed as shabbily as his partner, but with no socks.

Jonathan made to move around them after realizing not another soul could be seen in the immediate vicinity. "Excuse me."

"I don't think so. A bloke like you ought to have a bit of blunt on him," the short one said, his tone almost affable.

The barrel of a revolver poked Jonathan's stomach, emphasizing their point. With a resigned sigh, he pulled out his wallet and retrieved the bank notes he had tucked inside. "There, that's nearly twenty pounds to split between the two of you. Now out of my way."

"Not so fast there. What else you got in those pockets?" The hammer cocked, a loud *click* in the sudden silence.

Jonathan made a mental catalog of what he carried. He pulled his pocket watch from his vest and yanked the chain, freeing it from his vest. "Here." He reached in his pants pockets and pulled out the empty linings. "See. You have everything of value."

The short one took the watch and then shifted as though reaching for Jonathan's coat pockets. Losing the ring he would give to Marie was not acceptable. Without a second thought, he knocked the gun away from him and punched the shorter man. As he turned around to deal with the taller one, he heard the loud *pop* of the revolver. A searing pain sliced across his left shoulder.

The taller thief paled and backed up. "I didn't mean to shoot you. Please, sir, I swear it were an accident." And then he dropped the revolver and ran. By the time Jonathan could gather his wits enough to check on the shorter man, he had disappeared.

The throb in his shoulder drew his awareness to the hole in the sleeve of his coat. Somehow still on his feet, he took a stumbling step forward and managed to avert collapse. His heart raced while pain sizzled along his arm clouding his ability to think.

A few more steps forward and he found a railing to lean on. He wasn't far from The Market. If he could make it there, then someone would help him. It seemed to take forever to reach the familiar building. The few steps up to the door almost defeated him, but with a final surge of energy he pushed past the pain and reached the door. Pounding on the solid surface with his good fist, he continued beating on it until it seemed to disappear. His body gave out and he collapsed into a faceless pair of arms.

Distant voices filtered into his brain. Male voices followed by an achingly familiar female one.

Afternoon light filtered past the cracks of his eyelids. Jonathan hesitated as he heard Marie's voice again.

"Dr. Westfield, thank you for coming so quickly. He apparently stumbled onto our door step in this state." Marie sounded worried.

"Yes, Madame. Of course. Let me take a look at his arm and then I can patch him up."

"Thank you, Doctor." A door closed and Marie grew quiet.

Footsteps muffled by carpets grew closer. Unable to stand not knowing what happened around him, Jonathan let his eyes slide open. An older, graying man hovered over him.

"Well, it seems our patient is waking up. That's a good sign. Now can you tell me what happened?"

Glancing around the physician's shoulder, Jonathan tried to spy Marie, but had no luck. "I was shot by a footpad. I believe it is my left arm." He waved at it with his right hand distracted by his search for her, and winced at the pain the movement caused.

"Best to sit still for a bit," the doctor cautioned.

Marie stood in the hall pacing as the doctor tended to Heart. Stupid man, to go and get himself shot. After an eternity, the door opened and the doctor emerged. "How is he?" She hoped the anxious feeling constricting her heart couldn't be heard in her voice.

"He'll be fine, but he needs to rest. Looks like the bullet grazed him. I am sorry, but I must ask if he can remain here for a day or two."

"Of course. I will see he is cared for until he can depart. Thank you." Marie watched as Phillipe escorted the doctor down the hall. Alone, she took a deep, steadying breath and opened the door.

Heart lay on the bed, propped up by pillows, his torso bare but for a swath of white bandage around his upper arm. She paused and allowed the relief to swamp her senses. Her heart pounded as she grappled with the feeling of having nearly lost the man she loved. Of having been a fool to push him away.

"Heart, you foolish man. How could you let yourself be shot?" She tsked and moved toward the bed to pour him a glass of water.

"I seem to remember trying to avoid that very thing, but my efforts were thwarted. For the second time today."

Marie's gaze snapped to his face as heat suffused her cheeks. "Well, thank goodness you managed to make your way here. And it seems here is where you will stay for a bit. Is there anything I can get for you?"

"No, not at the moment." His gaze guarded, the wariness put Marie on edge.

"Well then, I'll leave you to rest. Someone will check on you later." She stalked from the room, annoyed with having created such distance between them. After all, he was the man she loved.

She saw that the room across the hall was readied for her so she could check on him in the middle of the night. Restless with the knowledge Heart slept but a few steps away, she paced the confines of the chamber. Periodically, she would sit and attempt to read the book of sonnets that lay open on a chair by the fire. The unfortunate truth was no distraction seemed sufficient to pull her wayward thoughts from the man across the hall.

None other than the sweet Jonathan of her childhood memories would still see her as a worthy candidate for marriage. He'd always been too soft hearted, letting her run roughshod over him. On more than one occasion, he bent to her stubborn nature and as a result he wound up taking a whipping or some other punishment because she had begged him to teach her to swim, to ride astride, or to show her how to climb a tree. Her heart swelled with love for the man she'd known and for the man she had come to know more recently.

There were not many men who would have defended her as Heart had at the masked ball. And if she were honest, it thrilled her to her toes to have him protect her from Bethany, a known brute, in such a physical way. Absorbed in her own recollections and the brush of her nightgown as it swished over her legs, she missed the first sounds of movement across the hall.

Sometime after midnight, she heard a loud curse from his room. She rushed in and turned up a light to find Heart holding his shin as he leaned on a chair.

"Perhaps if you kindled a light, you might maneuver in a strange place a little better." She shuffled over to him and knelt to look at his shin. Gentle fingers probed the spot feeling for a knot. "I am sure you'll be fine."

"Quite. If you don't mind, I think I will finish what I was about." He nodded toward the bathroom and walked away from her.

Sitting on a chair by the fire and gathering her patience around her, she waited for him to return. Once he settled back in the bed, she turned to leave. But he took her hand and held it. "Can you honestly say you don't love me?"

She was trapped by her own feelings and his unrelenting drive to have her. But, she knew she would not lie to him. "No." She fled his room before he could do or say anything else. Her resolve to save him weakened every moment she spent with him. Lesson learned.

The next day, Jonathan lay in bed and waited for Marie to appear. He had scared her. The stubborn woman just wouldn't admit they belonged together, but at least she acknowledged she loved him. He tried to console himself with that small victory.

The ability to understand her refusal eluded him. Having made it clear he had no regard for society's rules and the financial wherewithal to take care of her for the remainder of their days, her reluctance was baffling. Deep in his heart he had let go of the girl he knew in favor of the woman he had met upon coming to The Market. What more did he need to do to prove that he loved and accepted her as she was?

His door opened and the focus of his ruminations strode into his room bearing his breakfast tray. Her spine held ramrod stiff and her face a blank study. Her gaze refused to meet his.

"Good morning, Marie."

She hesitated at the husky timber of his voice. "Good morning, my Lord."

"So formal? Please, I promise to behave myself today."

"Sit up, please." She stood holding a breakfast tray destined for his lap.

The distinct tap-tap-tap of her slipper-clad toe could be heard despite being muffled by the rug and her skirts. Momentary forgetfulness led him to using his injured arm to lever himself up. He winced as pain lanced through his appendage. Yet, he caught her stricken look right before she snapped her façade back in place. The decision to play the moment up was made in the blink of an eye. He groaned and cradled his injured arm.

"For heaven's sake." She turned and set the tray down on a nearby table. Returning to the bed, she leaned over him, encompassing him in her lavender scent. She gripped him under each armpit and hauled him upright in the bed with his assistance. Her breasts brushed against his arm, eliciting a groan from him that was soul-deep and utterly out of his control.

She moved away, but came back with the tray while ignoring what they'd both heard. "I will return later to collect your tray."

"Perhaps you'd stay and talk with me? It is rather isolated in here."

She paused. "I'm afraid I have things to attend to."

"I see. Perhaps later?"

"Perhaps." She disappeared.

Jonathan awoke to discover that not only had a few hours passed, but he was alone and his tray gone. Damn. He'd try again around suppertime when she brought his next tray. His arm was already feeling much better, but perhaps he needed to let her believe it still hurt him as he had earlier? Could he get past her cool exterior with a little sympathy? It was worth a try.

Later that night, when she returned with his dinner tray, he took pains to warm his face using his bedside light and sprinkle a bit of water on his face to offer a clammy feel. She came near, and he moaned.

"Dear heavens," she exclaimed as she clapped the tray down on the table again and rushed to his bedside.

"Heart? Heart? Can you hear me?" Her cool hand slipped over his forehead and then along his jaw.

"Marie?" He fluttered his eyes open. He was beyond having any shame, and with a ruthlessness he would have never credited himself with, he played on her weakness.

"You foolish man. Why didn't you call for me?"

"I didn't wish to be a bother to you any more than I am." He licked his lips.

"No, this is my fault. I should have come here sooner to check on you. Can you ever forgive me?" Distress caused her voice to crack and guilt to slap at Jonathan.

"There is nothing to forgive. If you'll help me sit up, I can eat, and I am sure I will feel better."

"No. I will sit here and feed you," she stated as she helped him sit up. "It's the least I can do letting you relapse like this."

She brought the tray over and set it on his lap. She cut the meat into tiny bits and fed him one bite at a time interspersed with mashed potatoes and cooked spinach. As she fed him they reminisced about childhood ailments and injuries until silence ruled. He relished every bite despite his guilt at perpetrating his deception. When he swallowed the last bit, she whisked the tray away. The tension in the room had thickened while he ate.

Sitting up farther, he resettled the covers using both hands and froze as he felt her regard.

"Heart, I thought your arm was still hurting you."

"It is sore." He tried to temper the sheepishness in his voice with a trace of humor.

"And your fever?"

"Marie, I just wanted to have you sit with me for a while."

"So you faked the fever?"

"Yes. I thought you might let your guard down if you thought I was weak."

"Well, aren't you the clever one?" She drew a shaky breath. "That was too bad of you, Heart." She turned on her heel and departed leaving the tray behind.

The next day she avoided him entirely, which wasn't difficult since by Celeste's report he slept for most of the day again.

Still choosing to sleep across the hall from him, she settled in and ignored the various sounds emanating from the dark recesses of The Market. Business could survive one more night without her eagle eye. Exhausted from a fitful night's sleep, a busy day reviewing bills and dealing with vendors, and ignoring her heart, she fell into a deep, dreamless slumber.

Upon waking in a different room than she had gone to sleep and disoriented by her unusual positioning, a moment of panic ripped through her sleepy haze. A silken tie tightened around one wrist as she acquired her bearings. Without question, she remained in The Market, but in one of the other rooms. She tugged on the binding and looked up to see Heart tying her other wrist with another tie.

"Heart. What are you doing?" Fear pressed down on her, but common sense reminded her who she dealt with. Heart would never hurt her. At least not physically.

"Marie, you will address me as 'my Lord.' Do you understand?" His voice held a command she had not heard before. Tingles raced down her spine.

"Heart, you'll hurt yourself. Your arm." She wiggled and realized she'd been bent over the high bench at the foot of the bed where a pillow cushioned her hips and belly, and left her breasts dangling. Arms stretched out, were lashed a little less than midway up each of the bedposts. Her night rail still covered her body, but for how much longer?

"Incorrect response, Marie." He smacked her bottom through the thin material stretched across it.

"Yes, my Lord."

"Very good. You have been a very bad girl, Marie. You have lied and been disingenuous with your true feelings. You will learn to not lie to me again."

"Yes, my Lord." Her blood pounded through her veins as she took in the situation. They had not visited the dungeons during her attempt to show him how unsuitable she was, but it seemed Heart had a natural knack for taking charge. Somehow, with his military background and being a peer, that didn't surprise her.

The thin cotton material was lifted in a slow, torturous drag and tucked under her belly so it would not be in the way. Every inch of her skin tingled as though electrified by not knowing what to expect. Then the first strike landed across her bottom. The blow put her in mind of a riding crop with the extra snap from the popper. She shivered as it fell again. The harshness of his words matched the burn in her backside. "Repeat after me, Marie, I will never lie to you again, my Lord."

"I will not, *my Lord.*"

Two more strikes of the crop landed across her ass. "Say it, my dear."

"No." Her heart pounded in her chest, her bottom sizzled from the crop, and she wasn't quite ready to tell him the truth. She liked this new Heart, liked how he commanded her body and owned her desire.

"Say it, Marie. Say, 'I will never lie to you again. I will always be honest with you, my Lord.'" He landed four more blows across her backside, and she knew the time had come to give in. Her heart melted, and the love she'd struggled to lock away exploded in her chest.

"I will never lie to you again. I will always be honest with you, my Lord." She knew no way to hold him off now. He would insist on marrying her as soon as he got her to tell him she loved him. There would be no turning back.

He smoothed his palm over her enflamed ass. "You're mine, Marie. You will never deny me again."

"Yes, my Lord. I belong to you." Her arms and shoulders were beginning to ache, but the warmth of love, radiating through her body, eased the pain.

"That's a good girl, Marie. For your quick response, you have earned a treat."

Marie remained draped over the bench as his hands moved down her backside to pull her cheeks farther apart. His finger slipped between folds of her pussy and slicked through the wetness gathered there. She groaned as pleasure assaulted her senses.

"Ah, yes. You like that. Don't you?"

"Yes, my Lord." Her hips strained to press back, but could not move.

"Such a pretty pussy you have. So wet and ready for me." His voice shifted coming from lower behind her. Then his tongue plunged through her slickness.

Her body trembled with need. Desperate for more of his intrusion, she attempted to shift her feet and hips closer to him. A quick swat of his hand on her heated bottom ceased her movements.

"Do not move again." He pressed a hand on her lower back, pinning her in place.

She groaned as he drove deeper into her slit and lapped at her juices. When he slid his tongue forward and raked it over her clit, the first ripples of an orgasm broke over her. Relentless, he drove two fingers into her cunt as he flicked and teased her sensitive nub. The second orgasm followed on the heels of the first and left her spent and panting where she continued to be restrained.

"Nicely done, Marie." He rose up and disappeared for a moment. When he returned, he held the jade implement in front of her face. "Do you want this inside of you?"

"No, my Lord. I only want you." Her voice sounded breathless with anticipation even to her own ears.

"Not yet. You have not earned that reward." He moved behind her and shoved the phallic stone deep inside of her. She moaned, her body stretching to accommodate the sudden intrusion.

He fucked her with the rod, working it in and out of her pussy as he flicked her clit with his finger. Just as she neared the precipice once again, he stopped and withdrew the trinket. "No, my Lord please!" she begged, desperate for the release he now denied her.

"You have more to say to me, Marie. Say you are mine."

"I am yours, my Lord. I have always been yours." Caught between her raging emotions and the desire coursing through her veins, tears shimmered just below her thinning control.

"Very nice. Again, you have earned a reward." He moved around near her head, and the dildo came into her vision. It glistened with her essence as he held it before her. "Suck it. Lick your sweet juices off of it."

With a nod, she opened her mouth and he carefully inserted the stone between her lips. She liked the way she tasted and knew he must as well since he shared it with her. His eyes glowed with want as he watched her tongue swirl around the head of the phallus. While he held it for her, he reached down with his free hand and opened her nightgown exposing her dangling breasts. Pulling and tweaking her swollen tips, he sent jolts of pleasure from her nipples to her core. As he teased her, she grew desperate to have him buried in her heat again.

"Well done. My sweet, biddable Marie." Still rubbing her nipple, he sighed. "I love you so much, my dear. I have always loved you." He moved away and circled behind her. There, he dropped the fall of his trousers and pressed his cock against her slick, swollen folds. "Now, tell me the truth. No more lies. No more deceit."

He shoved into her body, impaling her on his cock and she broke. "Yes. Yes. I love you, Heart. I will always love you." He continued driving his cock into her soaked heat and then she felt the cooler salve against the rosette of her bottom. Without missing a single, delicious stroke, he slid the jade dildo deep into her dark hole.

Her orgasm erupted in an instant. It roared through her body in racking waves of intense pleasure as he fucked both holes, filling her completely. Her physical bliss seeped away leaving an intense sense of connection and love with the man impaling her body. He relentlessly plunged into her until his own release came.

"Mine. You're mine!" he yelled as he released his cum inside of her, marked her in an animalistic way that spoke to her blighted soul.

After a moment, he withdrew and then released her wrists. He cradled her in his arms and moved her to the bed.

"My dear, sweet Marie. I cannot go on if you are not part of my life. There will be no other women. Only you. Please say you will marry me. We can run The Market together or it can stay yours. I simply want you to be my wife."

Want ripped through her body, but doubts still assailed her. She needed to explain the reality of her world. "Oh, Heart. I want to marry you, but if I do, I must give up The Market. The terms of sale require I turn the establishment over to a new girl in the event I choose to retire or I am wed. I am scared to give up my source of income. If you changed your mind, I don't think I could rebuild my finances, much less recover from the emotional devastation. You have shredded every defense I erected to protect my heart."

"Oh, my dear, I would never turn away from you. I have loved you all my life. Why do you think I took all those punishments in your stead as children? I was crushed when I returned home from campaign to find you were not just gone, but sold to the highest bidder to settle your father's debts. I failed you then, and in my pain and confusion, much to my shame, I let my parents guide me. As a man I want nothing more than to love you as I always have. I will always take care of you. For the rest of your days you will want for nothing."

Fear and hope warred within. How could she doubt his love? Yet, leaving herself so exposed terrified her. "If I do this, I need you to stipulate the money I bring to the marriage will remain mine and in my control. It is a very large sum of money, but I need to know I can take care of myself should you renege or worse, should something happen to you."

"Anything you want, Marie. I will take care of all our needs and your money will remain yours. I love you. That is all that matters to me. Please, make me the happiest man on earth and marry me."

"Yes. Yes, Heart. I will marry you!" Tears rolled down her face to soak her breasts as his lips crashed down on hers.

~The End~

LOVE REQUITED

A Short Story

CHAPTER ONE

Magnus Pendersen, III looked at his cards and cursed. He'd already lost five thousand pounds, a small fortune, though it felt better thinking about the number in pounds rather than dollars. He looked at the green felt table with a rather large pile of money in the center and once more at his cards. He had no shot at bluffing his way into winning so he decided to cut his losses. As the bid came around the table he laid his cards face down and rose. "Gentlemen, it has been a passable evening, but I fear I cannot stomach further losses. If you will excuse me."

"Grand having you with us, Pendersen." One masked man chortled.

"I'm certain it was." He smiled indulgently and stepped away from the table.

The need to douse the pain of his bad luck at the tables led him into the main salon. He found the bar and requested his preferred whiskey. A cut crystal glass appeared and was promptly filled by the liveried servant. He turned to absorb more of The Market's décor.

The brothel reminded him of New York City's Hoffman House in its elegant décor dotted with risqué touches such as nude art and more than a few rather phallic statues. The most resounding difference between the two establishments lay in that most of the long-term residents of Hoffman House were American tycoons, the giants of industry, not prostitutes. Though he supposed they were all for sale in their own way. He was one of the lucky ones who could afford to own a floor of the hotel so that when he stayed in the city he had all the comforts of home. And better than home, there was always a ready card game in the common rooms of Hoffman House. Just the previous month he'd taken Randolph Hurst for ten thousand dollars in a friendly game.

Unfortunately, tonight the cards at The Market had not fallen in his favor, but perhaps some of the establishment's other offerings would. As he scanned the room, the Earl of Northampton approached him as he stood near the fireplace. "Pendersen, enjoying our little corner of the world?"

"I am indeed, Lord Northampton." He nodded his head as he spoke.

Lord Northampton clapped him on the shoulder. "Please, call me North."

"Then, by all means, call me Magnus. I've never been much for formality." He tipped his drink and drew a sip of the warm amber liquor.

"Yes, well even if you were, I imagine all of that would be shed the moment you entered these hallowed halls. Madame Celeste de Pompadour only stands on ceremony when in the throes of a lively contract negotiation."

"Contract?" Magnus was curious, but as he asked the single word question a flicker of sea blue caught his eye. He turned a bit to better locate the source of the distraction. Two men crossed his vision and parted ways to reveal the most breathtaking beauty he'd ever seen. Golden hair piled on her head accentuated the long creamy column of her neck. Her companion must have said something amusing because she didn't merely giggle with lady-like demureness. No, the beauty threw her head back and laughed a full-bodied laugh. Blue eyes danced with merriment from behind a black mask as she straightened up pressing her hand to the delectable swell of her breasts. A man could dive into the plumpness and choose to never leave.

"Magnus." North snapped his fingers before his face.

"My apologies. But, do you know who that enchanting creature is?"

His companion looked in the direction he had indicated. "Afraid not. I've seen her here a time or two, but I generally stick to the ladies of the house. Much easier that way."

"So she's not a prostitute? What the devil is she doing here?" Magnus couldn't have explained his indignation that a woman of quality, and she clearly was not born of the gutter, would be found in such a place.

"I imagine much the same as we are. Enjoying the company, possibly looking for more intimate entertainments." North shrugged as though women often frequented brothels.

"But it's a brothel."

North chuckled. "The Market is more a private club that caters to all of its members' needs, however deviant they may seem."

Magnus peeled his gaze off the woman long enough to cast a dubious look at his companion.

"But, even should you tend toward less exciting interests, they are happy to make arrangements that suit your needs." North tipped his head toward a masked couple slipping from the room. "That is a pair of nobles who might not otherwise seek each other out. Neither is a professional."

"And how do they come to slip off together? Mutual agreement?" Magnus was curious, and not just because of the beauty across the room.

North nodded. "That or Madame de Pompadour will negotiate an agreement of some duration. All depends on the needs of the parties involved."

"I see." Magnus couldn't resist the pull of the woman from across the room. "I believe I shall go and make myself acquainted with the lady."

North slapped him on the back, "Best of luck, my friend."

But lost in his desire for the sultry beauty, Magnus did not reply. He simply drifted away from the bar and into the milling crowd.

As he neared the woman in blue, her friend was pulled away by a masked man who seemed to have more to say with his lips than with words. The object of his recent obsession turned to walk away and landed smack in his arms. Exactly where he wanted her to be.

"Excuse me, sir." Pink dusted her cheeks beneath her mask as their gazes met and locked, her breath hitching as she pressed her hands to his chest.

"My pleasure, I assure you." He held on to her, unable to make his arms obey his command to release her as propriety dictated.

She stared a heartbeat or twenty longer...long silky lashes lowered over her mesmerizing eyes as she shifted her focus to his arms wrapped around her. Then she shifted her gaze back up to his face. "I am quite capable of standing on my own two feet, sir."

"That may be, but I seem unable to let you go." The words rattled around in his throat like the last coals in a bucket.

"Quite the conundrum. But, being two rational adults I am certain we can negotiate a compromise." The imp had the audacity to wink at him!

He couldn't help but laugh. "And what is this compromise you speak of?"

She paused as though considering her options. "I could promise to remain here for at least ten minutes if you released me."

"No." He pulled her in closer until her hands were all that remained between them. "I fear that may not be enough." His instinctive response surprised him.

She chuckled. "What could a big strapping Yank like you have to fear?"

An infectious grin stretched his mouth. "What if you're a fairy? If I let you go you'll simply flit away and then I'll never know your name."

"If I were a fairy I wouldn't tell you my name. It would give you too much power over me."

"Then tell me your name and I'll promise to let you go if you'll remain here for no less than a quarter of an hour." He watched surprise, and a glint of something he couldn't quite put a name to, flash through her brilliant blue eyes.

"Whitney. My name is Whitney."

"Whitney." He repeated her name and his heart seemed to do a hundred and eighty-degree rotation in his chest. "And do you promise to remain for a quarter of an hour?"

She looked up into his eyes again, seemed to search for something, and then nodded. "I'll promise if you'll also tell me your name."

"Magnus."

"Hello, Magnus." She offered a winsome smile and fluttered her lashes like an experienced flirt.

He made his arms release her slowly so she wouldn't take a spill. But as she withdrew from the embrace a chill crept in where she had previously heated his body, his blood, and possibly even his soul. Not a man prone to flights of fancy, he shook his head at that last notion and ensured his hands found his pockets lest he reach out and grab her again. "Would you care to sit a spell?" He motioned at an available settee.

"I'd love to, Magnus."

And with a sweep of her skirts she spun about and sat down leaving enough room for him to join her, though his rather large thigh would be pressed against her own more delicate one.

Whitney Merriman's head spun. She'd heard about this sensation. Studied it in her self-guided human sexuality curriculum. But, she herself had never experienced such a physical response before. And my, what a response Magnus caused. Her body waffled between flashes of hot and cold. Her breasts had grown sensitive, almost achy as he held her, and her legs had turned as soft and wiggly as aspic.

As he settled next to her, despite the layers of petticoats and sundry layers of fabric between them, she swore she could feel the flex and release of his muscles along their adjoined legs. Her pulse skittered wildly as she grappled for something intelligent to say to the handsome devil.

He leaned closer, pressing his arm against hers. "Don't grow shy on me now, Whitney."

"Never." Where was her fan when she needed it? For once she cursed her lack of decorum, which her mother described as her tendency to leave off the accouterments of a well-dressed lady. "Where in America are you from?"

"Yes, you did suss that out rather quickly. I am from New York, the City specifically." His deep voice rumbled against her and sent a jolt of desire through her body. An interesting phenomenon. She made a mental note to record all of her symptoms later when she returned home.

"I see. And are you here for business or pleasure?" She had to dig deep to find the inane conversational elements her mother often assured her were critical to social interaction.

"Both I hope." His boyish grin charmed her despite the obvious lusty undertones of his response.

Her cheeks grew more heated as she imagined what he might mean by pleasure. And as the images flashed through her mind, all rooted in her study of current and historical pornography, as well as the hours spent in The Market's salons and hall of mirrors watching how humans interact, she suddenly wanted to step out from behind the glass and experience all she had spent the last year studying.

But could she? Did she have the nerve to allow a man, one unknown to her beyond the last few minutes of interaction, to touch her so intimately?

And then she imagined when she might have a future opportunity. One word came to mind. Never. Without the mask and her spectacles, she was simply another plain-faced woman with more brains than most men could manage. She had come to believe it was the primary reason her parents had encouraged her studies. Her distinct lack of marriage options was not something she had the dowry to remedy. Without means, most eligible men wouldn't be able to look past her bluestocking ways.

Magnus—whoever he was—might be her one chance to experience her area of expertise first hand. To be able to speak with the authority of one who truly knows versus one who has studied what others have known. She couldn't pass up the chance. With determination, she looked up at the man beside her. Examined his strong, distinct features. Chiseled jaw, high cheekbones, slashing eyebrows over clover green eyes, and all topped with a mop of sun-bright blond hair. He was beyond handsome, and then when she added on his body, which was huge in proportion and covered in what felt like honed muscles from her limited exploration of his arms and chest, she knew a finer specimen would not be made available to her ever again. If he sought a bit of pleasure, she was certain she could provide him exactly what he needed. "Indeed, you've come to the right place for the latter."

One brow rose in surprise at such a double entendre. "Have I then?"

"I believe you have. The Market is notorious for catering to the pleasure of men..." she drew a breath, "and women." Her face flamed, but she captured his gaze with hers and refused to look away. She would do this, damn it.

"And what of you, Whitney? Are you one to cater to men's pleasure?" At a glance, one would think Magnus was calm and cool in asking her such a scandalous thing. But since she was trained to note even small nuances of human response, she saw the pulse pounding in his neck, the strain hinted at around his eyes, and the fine tremble of his lip as though he worked hard not to say more.

"Honestly, no. I am not one to do such a thing. But for reasons of my own, I am inclined to do so tonight."

"And do those reasons have anything to do with another man?" His mouth tightened as he waited.

"Not in the least. There is no one behind my decision beyond my own needs and interests. No man I wish to strike back at. No husband who might hunt you down. No one at all." She groaned when she added the last little bit. As usual, she offered up more than was seemly.

He snorted at that. "I find that difficult to imagine. But I shall take your word. Would you prefer to make an arrangement through Madame de Pompadour?"

"No need. Celeste will keep an eye on me regardless of a formal arrangement or not. But, I would like a drink to toast our agreement and then I can arrange a more private place for us to retire." She rose from the settee.

Magnus popped up, surprise written across his face. "Please, allow me to manage what we require. You have proven more than capable of handling this conversation, but some things a man does like to take care of." He winked and stepped over to where Madame Celeste de Pompadour held court. The regal brunette waived her lead manservant over and Magnus stepped aside to speak with Phillipe. It seemed he was the third or even fourth Phillipe to work at The Market. Whitney had been fascinated that though the Madame's name changed with each new owner, the second in command, her manservant, always retained the same name.

After a few moments more, Magnus strode across the room and placed a hand against her lower back. A ripple of sensation rolled through her as she luxuriated in the possessive gesture. The warmth of his big hand against her back paired with the size difference between them made her feel more dainty and feminine than she had ever experienced. At five foot eight, she often met her male colleagues eye to eye, which they found disconcerting.

"Phillipe will bring a bottle of champagne to our room. We will be in the red room, one of the mirrorless rooms you are likely aware."

She grinned, pleased that he had instinctively known she would prefer not to be observed. "An excellent choice, sir."

"Just Magnus." He leaned closer as they climbed the stairs and whispered, "That is the name I want on your lips as I make you come tonight."

And just like that, her core grew superheated and her thighs wet with her desire. Would she survive her own curiosity? She wasn't sure, but she had not been wrong that this was the man who could show her all she desired to know about sex and intimacy.

CHAPTER TWO

Magnus led the golden-haired beauty into a room that looked as though it had been dipped in a vat of red dye. From the walls to the carpet to the drapes and bedding, every surface was red with a few contrasting touches trimmed in white. Yet somehow it did not overwhelm. Then again, perhaps the woman by his side drew his focus?

He looked his fill, taking in the nip of her waist where it flared out to her hips and the fullness of her skirts. He continued his perusal upward where her breasts were pushed up and put on display in a most inviting manner. And then he moved higher to her delicately feminine chin and her full lower lip topped by a perfect bow. But the black mask disrupted the rest of the picture except for where it framed long lashes and shimmering blue eyes, though if he staked a guess, he'd say she wore glasses beneath. "Will you take off your mask?" He couldn't help but ask as his fingers itched to do it.

She pressed the tips of her own fingers to the edge of the covering. "Why?"

"Because I am curious about the rest of your face and I am not inclined to be intimate with a woman whose face I have not seen. It's impersonal."

She seemed to consider his response and then she nodded slowly. "I suppose it doesn't matter. It is not as though you and I will ever meet again." She hesitated. "Though you should be warned you may find the rest of the picture less appealing without the mask."

He blanched, his stomach plummeting to his toes at the idea she might have experienced some trauma leaving her disfigured. "Did something happen to your face?"

"Nothing but unlucky genetics I'm afraid," she said with a rueful tone.

"Yes, well I doubt you are too hideous to behold. Please, show me." He was sure the pleading was unmanly, but he feared she might renege.

"Very well." She sighed and reached for the mask.

"Thank you." The rush of relief flooded him as she pulled the black from her face.

To his delight, he found delicately arched cheekbones supporting intelligent blue eyes over a pert nose. Her dark-blonde brows lent an exotic air to her features as they slanted upward with her eyes. But of course, she must think her spectacles distracted from all that giving her a bookish appearance. He reached up to run a fingertip over her cheekbone. "Goodness, you're lovely. Why ever would you be afraid to remove your mask?"

"I've been told I am rather plain and bookish in appearance. My spectacles magnify my eyes giving me an owlish appearance." She blushed again, though this time for less enticing reasons.

"Whoever told you such utter nonsense should be horsewhipped." He took the mask from her and tossed it aside. Then he stepped into her space, pulled her close to him and kissed the tip of her nose. "You are beautiful. Intelligent and lovely beyond words." Then he snagged her mouth in a kiss that started gently before it morphed into a hungry devouring of her lips. He found himself ravenous for the sweetness of her mouth as he explored.

Then, as though he triggered a chain reaction of some kind, she moaned and responded to his kiss with a fervor that had his shaft hardening in his trousers until the pain threatened to buckle his knees. The feel of her delicate fingers tangling in the shaggy strands of his hair made him grateful he'd skipped the barber earlier in the day. He pressed against her, letting her experience what she did to him and reveling in her own curvaceous treats. As he suspected, her hips sloped to a fullness that enticed a man and was likely the envy of many a bustle wearing female.

A knock at the door interrupted what had become a scorching kiss and they broke apart, both heaving for breath.

Whitney stumbled toward a chair where she steadied herself as her head spun from the headiness of Magnus' kiss. Behind her, the door opened and a servant rolled a cart in. She turned to find Magnus—who looked far too collected for her liking—escorting a manservant into the room. She must have looked overset because he paused to look at her as though he might intervene if she gave any indication she was in need of assistance. With a subtle shake of her head, she let him know she was fine and he stopped the cart near the chair she leaned on for support. The conveyance bore champagne, glasses, and strawberries. He'd considered everything.

As the servant departed Magnus closed the door and strolled over to where she stood. He dropped a kiss on her lips in a casual gesture of affection. "Thank you for not siccing the servant on me. I thought for a moment he might take action."

Mortified, she moaned and desperately wished there was a secret exit she could use. "Madame de Pompadour's servants are trained to intervene in any situation if required.

He laughed and smiled as he pulled the top off the champagne and poured them each a glass. "Actually, I'm happy to know someone here is looking out for you. I was rather shocked to learn a woman who is not a member of the household was permitted to enter the establishment."

Suddenly, she found her starch as she took affront to his rather arrogant comment. "Why should I not be permitted here? Do I not have the right to partake of the fleshly pleasures just as a man?"

Magnus turned to her and held out a glass. "Well, now, I suppose you should have that right. I'd say it's merely the Neanderthal in me who was more interested in grabbing you by the hair and claiming you than any rational response." He looked chagrined as he waited for her to take the drink.

She found it hard not to laugh at his admission, and from an intellectual perspective, she found it a fascinating response deserving more exploration. "And did you feel the same way about Lady Atherton who was also wearing a mask? Or perhaps Mrs. Davenport?"

She took the glass from his hand, and his body seemed to sag almost in relief. "I did not. In fact, I barely noticed their presence."

"Interesting." She strolled over, closer to the bed, to examine a portrait of a nude woman. "And I assume the women of the house also did not elicit such a response from you?"

He followed her and closed the gap between them. "They did not. Inquisitive little thing, aren't you?"

"I am always intrigued by the relationship between human emotion and intimacy." She took a sip of the champagne and studied the generously curved woman in the picture.

"And do you always question the men you are intimate with on these topics?" He nuzzled the back of her neck just above the neckline of her gown.

She wavered in that moment, indecision striking her like a hidden assailant. Should she tell him the truth? Would he continue with this endeavor if he knew? Still not sure, she prevaricated. "I question everyone I meet on these topics. It can make for rather awkward moments at times. In fact, my mother laments my inability to set my studies aside long enough to make polite conversation."

He set his glass down and then wrapped an arm around her waist. "I can see how some people might find it awkward to discuss their every emotional reaction during an intimate moment. Perhaps I can find a way to distract you?" He took her glass and placed it beside his as he turned her around and plundered her mouth once again.

Whitney's heart did a slow roll in her chest as she squeezed her thighs together to alleviate the throbbing sensation taking up residence at the very heart of her sex. And then, all thoughts fled her head as her desire was set loose to tangle with his in the most erotic of kisses. Their tongues slipped and twisted together as hands roamed up and down their bodies in a restless motion set to drive their need higher.

Lips still fused, his hands worked her laces loose and the bodice of her dress sagged around her breasts, trapped by her arms. Frustrated, she released her hold on him and helped him tug the dress down as he pulled back and shifted his kisses to rain down on her shoulders and the tops of her breasts. Next, he reached behind her gown and released her petticoats and hoop with a few strategic tugs. All the while his lips never ceased moving over her flesh, driving her to wriggle in a most undignified manner. "Please, Magnus."

"I'm going as fast as I can." He murmured against her shoulder.

Then the bulk of her clothing fell to the floor in a whoosh of satin that left her standing in her corset and pantaloons. He stepped back, casting an appreciative gaze over her as she resisted the urge to hide. It took all her courage to stand before him in her skivvies with her head held high. If he found her unappealing, it would be his own failing, she assured herself. Then he slid his jacket off and tore at the buttons of his vest as he stepped toward her again. "You make a man's mouth water with all those curves, Whitney."

Emboldened by his praise, she reached up and unhooked the front of her corset and let it drop as she stepped out of the pile of her clothes. Wearing nothing but a sheer linen under-blouse and her bloomers, she watched Magnus shed his shirt revealing a muscle-packed torso that met all her expectations.

"My, you are a specimen." She stepped toward him now and reached out to run her fingertips over his chest as he met her partway.

"Up." He whipped her linen blouse off and then tugged her bottoms off as well, leaving her standing in her stockings and garters as he circled around her planting more kisses on the newly exposed parts of her anatomy.

Once he made his way to her front again, he flicked his tongue against each nipple and moaned as he sucked one then the other. The iron band of his arm wrapped around her waist as her knees gave out with the electric sensation of his mouth on her breasts.

Her head spun with the overload of new sensations. She had touched herself before, trying to understand her subjects drive for intimacy, but it had never felt like this. So encompassing. Excitement bubbled deep inside her in the most unladylike way. Made her want to do things...unspeakable things.

He growled as he pulled away and picked her up. A surprised squeak escaped her mouth, as he carried her the short distance to the bed and placed her on the edge. There he ravaged her mouth as his deft fingers found the wet heat between her legs. And as he kissed her senseless, he plunged a thick finger into her pussy with a sureness born of experience. And she reveled in his confidence, his surety that she wanted what he had to offer.

As he pumped in and out of her body, he licked, nipped, and ate at her mouth until she felt crazed with the need for release. And while she'd heard it described in colorful detail, she had never experienced the unrelenting need that now governed her body and her every thought in an all-consuming conflagration.

She broke their kiss and begged. "Please, Magnus. Make me come."

He groaned at her demand and dropped to his knees. "Anything you wish, my Whitney."

When he spread her thighs and planted a kiss on her cunny, she nearly fainted with need as all the blood left her head to gather where his tongue now explored. Her sex throbbed with her lust for the man between her thighs. And as he tasted her obvious desire, she gave in to the urge to grind her pelvis against his face in search of the bliss she knew awaited based on her own self-exploration.

He pinned her hips to the mattress in a firm grip and swirled his tongue around her nub as pleasure assaulted all her senses. He continued to alternately lash and lave the swollen bundle of nerves until the tingling burst into a firestorm of blissful proportions and swept her away off to oblivion. She cried out his name over and over again, a litany as he continued to lick her folds until she shuddered and slowed her thrashing. All sense of time was lost as she lay there in a desire induced haze and attempted to catalog each sensation. The issue was, as quickly as she identified a sensation she forgot it as a new one crowded in. At this rate, she'd never be able to recount them all.

Perhaps she could convince him to repeat his rather fabulous performance enough times she could remember each detail to later record? It was the last coherent thought she had for a while as the very fine specimen she had found stood between her legs naked with an impressively large erection jutting from between his thighs.

CHAPTER THREE

Magnus looked down at the sated beauty, who still managed to have her spectacles on, and repressed the growl rumbling in his chest. For some unknown reason, he wanted nothing more than to beat his chest and claim her as his. She had been stunning in the throes of her orgasm as she called out his name. He'd felt like a damned God sipping ambrosia as her essence burst over his tongue. And he wanted more, but first, he needed to bury his cock inside of her. A fucking shame he had to don a French Letter, but he refused to put himself at risk when he knew so little about her. Though he suspected she was far less experienced than she presented herself. And with all the questions and analysis, he had a sneaking suspicion that both tantalized and terrified him. Her virginity certainly wouldn't stop him—she was no young chit—but he wouldn't want to surprise her too much. And by the wide-eyed way she currently stared at his shaft, he wondered just how much she really knew about intercourse.

He stroked his shaft. "It will fit."

She bit her lip. "I'm well aware the female body is designed to accommodate a man, it just seems rather daunting in comparison to the other examples I have seen."

An emotion, too similar to jealousy for his taste, swelled up within him and had him hovering over her on the mattress, hands on either side of her head as he demanded, "And whose cock have you seen before now."

Her mouth flopped open and closed a few times before she uttered a high pitched answer. "Pictures. I've seen many pictures." Pink stole over her cheeks as she refused to meet his gaze. "I've never seen one..." She sighed. "I'm a virgin."

Satisfaction crashed over him like a tidal wave. He would be her first. "Then we'll go slow for this part." He reached up and smoothed the wrinkle in her brow and then lifted her spectacles from her face and set them aside. "But these might get damaged once we get moving."

"They might? And you aren't unwilling to continue?"

"Oh no, sweetheart. I plan on relieving you of your virginity and I'm humbled that you'd chose me when you barely know me." He rumbled the words.

"I'm quite a good judge of character, and you seemed a reliable upstanding sort. Not at all pompous or unsavory," she informed in the most straightforward way as though her assessment was fact.

He chuckled, "Well, lucky for me you think so. Now, stop talking sweetheart. I have an aching need to be inside you."

She sighed and smiled brightly. "Do let's get on with it. I am ever so curious."

In the wake of her blindingly innocent statement, he swept in and captured her lips in a kiss meant to steal any further words from her mouth and distract her from the pain that was to come. He pressed the tip of his cock against her opening and pushed forward a bit. She stilled. Digging deep, he waited for her to adjust to the sensation, and then he resumed his forward motion. While he slid inside of her a bit more, he knew a swift strike would serve her better, so he slammed his rod deep inside her in a single stroke that had her crying out with the pain. He kissed her forehead and murmured nonsense to her as they both waited for her to adjust to his invasion. He desperately tried to ignore the encompassing heat of her pussy that pushed him to withdraw and slide back inside.

Beneath him, her breathing evened out and her eyes were no longer clinched tight. "Whitney, look at me."

Slowly she lifted her lids to reveal watery blue eyes.

"I promise this is the last of the pain. All that comes after is pleasure." His heart thumped a slow steady rhythm in his chest as he waited for her assent.

"Very well." The wobbly sound of her voice pierced his chest, a clean shot through and through.

Dying to pull back and slip into her again, he waited a moment more. Kissed her brow and then her sweet lips. A small lick and then a nibble. He slid his tongue past her lips and she opened to him immediately. What started as a sweet kiss quickly turned hot and demanding. As the woman under him moaned and writhed with renewed desire he pulled back and stroked into her with careful precision. Their lips parted and he focused on ensuring her pleasure before seeking his own. As he pumped into her tight sheath his toes curled in ecstasy and he began recounting the name of every ship in his fleet to stave off his own orgasm.

"Magnus, please," she cried out and thrust her hips up to meet him.

Balancing on one elbow, he slipped his hand between them and flicked her clit as he filled her with his cock once more. She screamed his name again and exploded around him as he carried her through her climax. Then he continued shuttling in and out of her slippery hot core until the tightening in his balls turned into a rush of sensation that shot through his body and curled his toes. He groaned as he surrendered to the pleasure and then collapsed on top of her.

Whitney lay there, smothered by the hulking male body on top of her. Her head spun and her body buzzed with pure pleasure. Add to that the unadulterated masculine smell of man, sweat, and something faintly spicy, and she suddenly understood the lure of sex. Or perhaps it was simply the allure of a man named Magnus.

He leaned up, balancing on two hands as he looked at her. "Are you well?"

Confusion warred with the absurd desire to laugh. "Am I well?" She managed to choke the words past the laughter bubbling up.

"It was your first time. Women are often overwrought after, or so I've heard." He seemed as flustered as she was confused.

His concern was both sweet and amusing. "Lucky for you I am not most women."

He looked at her warily, as though she might begin leaking tears at any moment. "You're sure you're well?"

Laughter pealed out as her whole body shook with it.

"I'll assume that is not a sudden case of hysteria." He withdrew from her body and rolled away.

"Oh please don't be offended." She reached out toward him, laying her hand on his arm.

He glanced down at where their skin met and then up to meet her gaze. Heat and desire flared in his green eyes. "Give me a moment to clean up."

He disappeared behind the privy screen only to return a few moments later. Before joining her on the bed he collected the wash basin and a strip of cloth. Curious as to his intention, she watched as he set it all down beside the bed and then crawled back between her legs. "Um, Magnus. I don't think I could..."

"Of course not, silly woman. Let me take care of you."

And then to her surprise, he wet the cloth in the basin and dabbed it between her legs. The cool water soothed the soreness between her thighs and cleaned up the small mess that represented her maidenhead. Strangely, she held no lingering attachment to her virginal state. Giving it up in the moment, and to the man she had chosen, seemed more than natural. With a contented little purr, she stretched and leaned back against the pillows.

Once he finished cleaning her up he set it all aside and then climbed into the bed beside her.

"Thank you for making my first time so wonderful." She smiled at him feeling particularly sleepy.

"You are a conundrum, Whitney. In some ways, you appear experienced and worldly, and in others, you are as fresh as the country air."

"Yes well, most people have a difficult time relating to me. It's why I study human intimacy..." she yawned. And then drifted off to sleep.

Whitney awoke to find the room draped in shadows as the lowered gas flames flickered in the lamps. Beside her, Magnus lay with the sheets twisted around his legs. In the dim lighting, she studied his body and wondered how a man who could afford to avail himself of The Market also possessed such a fine physique. She lightly traced the ridges of muscle along his stomach, entranced by the smooth skin over hard muscles.

Emboldened, she nudged the sheets draped over his hips lower until his soft shaft lay exposed. With a quick glance at his face to assure herself he still slept, she reached out and touched the appendage she had heretofore only read about, discussed, or seen in pictures. And while she'd seen it in various states of erectness, she had never had the chance to touch it in any of them. As she ran her finger along his length, it stiffened slightly. Intrigued she continued to explore his cock as it hardened before her eyes. But then it jerked in a sudden motion and she snatched her hand away with a gasp.

"Well, don't stop now." The rumble of Magnus' sleep-garbled voice had her gasping again and her cheeks flaming to life.

"I-I-..." She blushed even harder and pressed hands to her cheeks.

"I was enjoying your touch, Whitney. You are welcome to look your fill, to touch me, to explore." He laid there looking much like she imagined a magnanimous Sultan would.

She scooted closer. "You don't mind?"

"Not mind? Your touch feels good. It is what made my shaft grow hard. Why it jumped under your fingers, wanting more." He grinned devilishly.

"What kind of more?" Curiosity got the better of her shyness.

"You could wrap your hand around the shaft and stroke it up and down." He helped her wrap her fist around his erection and then showed her how to pump the length. At first, fascinated by the contrasting feel of such softness and hardness, it wasn't until he groaned that she realized the effect her ministrations were having on him. The same time she noticed the drop of moisture seeping from the tip. Again, her analytical side drove her to use a finger and scoop the wetness up and stick her finger in her mouth. He tasted salty with a faint hint of something sweet in the background. Needing to identify the elusive flavor, she leaned over and plopped the head of his cock in her mouth looking for a more accurate assessment.

He groaned and bucked his hips, pushing his length deeper into her mouth, and then slid out. She glanced up to see his eyes were wide open as he watched her every move. On the one hand, she was well aware that men found fellatio pleasurable, it was one of the more frequent images she had found. But once again, knowing a thing and experiencing it were two very different states of awareness. And she found she liked the latter far more than she might have imagined.

"That's it. Suck my cock nice and deep." He made a noise that she thought might be more growl than anything, and then he lifted her mouth from his penis and helped her rise up to her knees. "Are you too sore for me to be inside you again?"

She considered his question and quickly decided even if she were too sore, she wanted to feel that fullness she had enjoyed so much the first time. Well, after she got past the stabbing pain that came with breaking her hymen. "No, I'd like very much to have you inside me again."

"Good," he mumbled as he reached over to the night table and took what she assumed was a French Letter out of a small packet. "Give me a moment." He placed the contraceptive over his erection and then reached for her hand again. "Now straddle me as though you were riding a horse astride."

She followed his guidance and found his rod poised to slide back inside her.

"Excellent. Now you're in control. Lower yourself down over me and then it's all in your hands. You can ride me fast or slow. You set the pace." Magnus placed his hands on her thighs as she sank down.

A bit tender from their first foray, she found the twinge passed once she fully encompassed his length. Oh my, the fullness was exquisite as she ground against him wanting more. Unsure, she stopped and rifled back through her mental notes. She had read a section of Fanny Hill where the heroine had ridden a man astride and as Whitney recalled, a slight bounce was the key. So she lifted up and sank down on him, which elicited a moan from both of them. Before long she rose and lowered like she was born to the saddle. Then he pulled her forward, changing the angle of penetration and giving him access to her breasts.

When he sucked one nipple into his mouth, even as she continued to slide up and down his shaft, something sharp and wondrous occurred where they were joined. She knew with the added stimulation she would come again in short order. Encouraging him, she pressed her hands flat against the mattress on either side of his head. "Don't stop, Magnus."

He grunted in response, and only let go of one nipple long enough to switch to the other. Her pussy convulsed and then an explosion the likes of which she had yet to feel ignited within her as she came. And to her delight, as she screamed her pleasure out, he followed right behind her with a shout of his own. Exhausted, she slumped over on his chest and sighed. "That was amazing."

"Indeed it was. You, my dear Whitney, are a fast learner." He rolled her over and slid from her now sore body. "Don't disappear on me." He dropped a kiss on her left nipple and then scrambled from the bed. When he returned they lay together until he drifted off to sleep. As she lay there, images of the two of them entwined flashed before her eyes, except they were older. Her heart stuttered and she immediately pushed away the sentimental notion of them having a future. This was one night. One night to experience that which she had only studied.

Scared by the emotions her new experience had stirred up and determined not to lose her objectivity, she slipped from the bed, dressed as best she could and tiptoed out of the red room. Celeste would help her right her clothes and make her way home before Magnus awoke. As lovely as the night was, she couldn't allow herself to fall prey to any womanly notions of marriage and children. It simply wouldn't do.

CHAPTER FOUR

Magnus awoke alone. With sexy images dancing through his dreams, he reached for the source and found her vanished. The sheets were cold where she should have been. With a curse, he flew from the bed and grabbed his trousers. Damn it, he knew he should have asked her last name before he fell asleep that last time. Asked to see her again, to have tea, to talk more.

Heart pounding in his chest, he ran downstairs, trousers flopping open, shirt-tail streaming behind him, and feet bare, to bang on the only door that hadn't been opened or mentioned during his tour. He assumed it was Madame Celeste de Pompadour's rooms. He waited. One heartbeat, two heartbeats, and he pounded again on the solid wood door determined to rouse the lady.

When she did not respond, he took to pounding and calling her name. Thump. Thump. Thump. "Madame de Pompadour!"

Finally, after what could have been an eternity for as long as she took, the door opened a crack. "What in bloody hell are you on about?"

"Whitney, the woman I spent time with last night, is gone. I need to find her." His blood pumped through his veins, a rush very similar to the one he normally experienced when just setting sail or before a battle when he'd been a soldier.

The woman looked at him and yawned in the most unladylike fashion. Not as though she were tired, but to suggest she had grown bored of the conversation. "You may leave whatever trifle she deserted with Phillipe." She moved to close the door, but he wouldn't have it. Not one bit.

With a big meaty hand, he blocked the move and pushed his way in. "And what if that trifle is my heart?" The words had escaped before he'd even considered the truth of them. But in his heart, in his soul, he would not deny the raw honesty. He realized she had won his heart over the course of the night. It was a wager he had not intended to make, but if he played his hand right he would undoubtedly win.

The jaded proprietress of The Market chuckled. "I doubt seriously Phillipe would know what to do with that, let alone Whitney. Perhaps you would like to reconsider such a declaration before word gets out that the great and mighty Magnus Pendersen, III has lost all his marbles." She raised a brow and waited for his reply.

But every bone in his body protested. No, he did in fact, love her. He'd never experienced anything like this, he simply needed the chance to tell her. To convince her of his feelings. To show her.

"Please, Madame. Help me find her. You may think me a fool, but I am a fool in love with the most intelligent, inquisitive woman I have ever had the pleasure to encounter."

Madame de Pompadour sighed and pressed her fingertips to her temples. "There must be something in the water in this building. Love keeps happening here." She waved her hands about as though flummoxed.

Magnus, well versed in the art of negotiation, refrained from speaking another word. The woman would relent or she wouldn't.

"Come inside. I believe I'll need a draught of brandy for this discussion." She led him further into the room after closing the door behind him. A wash of relief crashed through him as all his muscles relaxed and he prepared to get his answer.

She poured a drink for herself and offered him one. "No, I prefer to keep a clear head at the moment."

"Suit yourself. Remind me why you are here in London?"

"Steam engine technology. I want to build the best trains possible."

"I see. And who are you planning to meet with while you are here?"

"Madame, I do not see the purpose—"

"Of course you don't. Answer the question or leave. Your choice Mr. Pendersen." She stared at him with the steely-eyed assurance of one who has the upper hand in a negotiation.

He held out for a moment, then grudgingly answered her question. "I still have two appointments, one with the London and Southwestern Railway and then Dr. Merriman, who I've been corresponding with for months." Confused and just a bit frustrated, Magnus resisted the urge to pace.

"I see. And tell me, Mr. Pendersen, do you believe in fate?" She reclined back on a divan close to the embers in the fireplace.

"Madame, I am a rational, successful man. I make my own fate," he growled slightly.

She laughed at him. The woman had the audacity to laugh as though he were not one of the richest men in America. As though he couldn't buy and sell a Dukedom four times over should he so desire?

"Well, then. You must not need me." She arched a brow and pinned him with a haughty stare.

Beyond frustrated, he turned on his heel and strode to the door. The conversation accomplished nothing except wasting his time. Time that could have been spent tracking Whitney down.

Whitney slipped into the house and up the stairs to her room on stockinged feet. She was nearly inside when her mother appeared in the hallway, an oil lamp in hand. "Whitney?"

She wanted to groan and curse. She should have slipped away sooner, but by the time Madame Celeste had roused and assisted her in righting her clothes, it was much later than she had expected. "I was just getting a glass of water from the kitchen."

"While wearing your gown from last night?" Her mother might be unobservant at times, lost in her studies, but she was no fool.

"No, Mother. I'm afraid I stayed out a bit later than planned last night. I ran into a rather interesting subject and wanted to be sure I captured all the observations I could before they disappeared." She prayed her mother didn't ask too many more questions.

"You should be more careful, dear. It is very late for a young woman to be alone on the streets." While her mother sounded vexed, she did not seem so upset that Whitney feared she'd tell her father.

"I will be more careful in future, mother."

"Get some rest, dear. I believe we will be having a guest for dinner tonight. One of your father's colleagues or some such." Her mother yawned mightily and then retreated.

"Goodnight Mother," Whitney whispered and slipped into the welcome familiarity of her room. The pang in her chest had grown with each stair tread as she climbed, with each heartbeat as she spoke to her mother, and still with each breath as she worked to remove her gown. With each layer, a memory returned bringing the ghostly tingles of a man she would never see again. And while at that moment, leaving had seemed the thing to do in order to protect her heart, alone in her room the decision appeared flawed.

After struggling with all her clothing alone because she refused to wake Beatrice, she slipped into her nightgown and lay wide awake. Considering all her research on intimacy and sexuality, she was well aware of the initial infatuation people often felt upon meeting someone new who they found attractive. However, in direct opposition to the theory of fleeting attraction, she had met several couples who claimed to have met and fallen in love at first sight. If they were to be believed, which until her own experience, she did not, then she should have remained with Magnus to see what would have happened in the morning. If she subscribed to the theory that the initial attraction either faded or grew into something more, then staying would also have been deemed the logical choice because then she would know whether her attraction would fade or grow for Magnus.

But, if she subscribed to the theory that most of society believed, only a long-standing acquaintance could engender tender feelings and emotions upon which love could blossom. Until walking into the arms of Magnus earlier in the evening, she fell strongly in the latter category. But, with the fluttering wings of butterflies in her stomach, as she gazed into his deep green eyes, she had begun to question her stance. And now, alone in her room in the dark, missing the feel of his arms around her? She believed, had she remained, she might have been able to discern if the attraction would fade or grow.

Bloody hell. How had she tossed away her one chance to test the second hypothesis? How had she lost her scientific focus so easily? Now, while she knew the third theory remained viable, she could not, in fact, rule out either of the other two which is one of the goals of all her studies. She needed to understand the laws of attraction and intimacy in order to figure out why she was still alone.

Feeling defeated and unsure, she rolled over and started counting backward from one hundred. It was one of the easiest ways to clear her mind when she needed to sleep.

Magnus had considered canceling his dinner plans with Dr. Merriman so that he could return to The Market or some other likely establishment where his Whitney might appear. But, in the end, he needed to get answers on his business matters as much as he wanted to find the elusive woman. He decided that one did not necessarily cancel the other. After dinner, he could haunt the hedonistic halls of London. So, he knocked and rang the bell at the address he'd been given in the invitation.

A man wearing basic livery consisting of a simple dark suit and cravat opened the door and bade him enter. He was deposited in the study and told someone would be with him shortly. It seemed odd that the man had not even requested his invitation or asked any questions. So either it was a rare occasion for the doctor to have guests, or the household, in general, was a bit abnormal.

After ten minutes alone, he rose and began perusing the shelves. He found an odd array of books covering everything from mechanical principles to genetic splicing. He continued to look and found a few books on human emotions offering some rather wild theories. He had just returned the book when Dr. Merriman entered the room.

"My apologies Mr. Pendersen. My wife and I were discussing her latest thesis on the hybridization of roses, and I'm afraid, as usual, I lost track of the time." He crossed the room to a decanter. "May I offer you a pre-dinner drink?"

"Thank you, but I'm fine at the moment. Your wife has a garden, I take it?"

Dr. Merriman laughed. "She has an entire greenhouse and is writing a thesis on the viability of hybridizing particular roses in order to create stronger more resilient varieties."

Surprised, Magnus refrained from making any untoward comments, though he wondered how a woman who ran her husband's home might also have time for such extensive endeavors. "I see. That must keep her quite busy."

"Indeed it does, which is why we so rarely entertain. In fact, because it is such a rare occasion, I've asked my wife and daughter to join us for dinner." Merriman took a drink of his brandy and smiled. "Perhaps we can manage a game of cards later."

He wanted to groan. He had hoped to have a short dinner, discover more about Merriman's research into more efficient steam engines, and then head out on his hunt. But, all things considered, he did not want to risk offending the man who seemed poised to help him launch a faster, lighter engine design.

"Perhaps we can." He sighed and glanced around the room. "Perhaps I will take you up on that drink."

His host poured him two fingers of brandy and they settled in to talk engines. Before long, his glass was empty and his head was full of ideas for Merriman's concept engine. Of course, the lightheadedness may have had some small bit to do with the fact he skipped breakfast and lunch as he tried to find his elusive Whitney.

A knock at the door interrupted their discussion of alternate methods of creating steam. Mrs. Merriman entered dressed in a simple, but elegant, lavender gown. With dark blonde hair silvering at the temples and blue eyes, he found himself imagining her to be an older version of Whitney. Certain the drink had gone to his head, he set his empty glass down and rose to greet their new arrival.

"Magnus, my wife, Harriet."

"Good evening, Mr. Pendersen. I apologize for my delay. I do hope my husband and daughter have been keeping you entertained." She then took that moment to glance around the room. "Winston, where is your daughter?"

"I assumed she was with you, my dear." He looked abashed at his oversight of her whereabouts.

The elegant older woman sighed. "Please excuse me. I'm sure she will be down any moment. She must still be dressing." And she slipped from the room.

Winston snorted. "More like she's hiding somewhere with a book or her notes. My daughter is not your typical society miss. Despite her mother's excellent lineage, our daughter generally abhors most social gatherings."

Magnus wanted to groan at the idea of having some socially awkward young girl trying to make conversation with him all night. "If she'd rather not—"

The study door sailed open and Harriet swept in with the recalcitrant daughter in tow. "Mr. Pendersen, my daughter, Miss Whitney Merriman."

Without a doubt, the liquor had gone to his head. Whereas before he had imagined his colleague's wife resembled the woman he'd taken to bed, now he was imagining their daughter as the one he sought. He shook his head and looked again to find the brilliant blue eyes he'd stared into all night staring back at him in wide-eyed surprise.

She looked as shocked as he felt to be standing in the same room. Her parents stood there for a few more moments as the silence drew out to an uncomfortable length for everyone.

"Whitney, do be polite and greet our guest," Mrs. Merriman said with a nudge of her daughter's shoulder.

Finally recovering himself, Magnus stepped forward and reached for the hand she seemed to present as though the appendage responded to her mother's command wholly without her consent. "My apologies, such beauty is known to steal a man's tongue." He pressed his lips to her hand as he gently squeezed it. He needed to be sure she was real and not a mirage.

"Mag-Mr. Pendersen." She glanced back and forth between her parents. "A pleasure to meet you."

Harriet stared first at her daughter and then at him. He realized belatedly, that he still held Whitney's hand. "Please, excuse me." His face heated as though he were a child caught with his hand in the cookie jar.

Her mother peered more closely at her very pale daughter. "Whitney, are you feeling well?"

CHAPTER FIVE

"No. I don't think I am." Whitney pressed a hand to her head. "I believe I shall go lie down. I am terribly sorry."

And Whitney fled the room. Magnus stared for only a moment before he flew after her without a word to her befuddled parents. "Whitney, wait."

She stopped at the bottom of the stairs but did not turn to face him. One hand pressed to her chest, the other forgotten at her side she stood there ramrod stiff.

He took hold of the hand left at her side. "Please, don't run. I merely wish a word with you."

"How did you find me?" Her question sounded stiff, scared.unlike the vibrant, inquisitive woman from the night before.

"While I looked high and low all over London, and I begged Madame Celeste—"

She spun around and pulled her hand from his grip. "Do not say her name in this house! Are you mad?"

"She would not tell me who you were. But I knew your father from a mutual friend who had suggested we correspond about steam engines."

She looked green, muttering to herself more than to him, but he pressed on. "How can this be?"

"It was merely coincidence that we had arranged to have dinner this evening. I planned to resume my search for you later." His heart pounded in his chest. What if she did not feel for him as he did? Admittedly it was an instant reaction to someone he did not know, but his heart told him it was love. That no other woman would do. He learned long ago to follow his instincts after making his first million on a shipping company others had told him would fail.

"You've had your word. I'm afraid—"

Pure desperation, of a sort he had heretofore never experienced, bombarded his thought processes and stole his ability to argue logically. "Wait. I have more to say. Whitney, however sudden it may seem, I dare say I am falling in love with you."

Her big blue eyes widened in surprise before she spun on her toes and fled up the stairs. With her departure, he knew the sour taste of defeat. What did a man do to win the heart of the woman he desired? He considered what he knew of Whitney and immediately dismissed a bouquet of flowers. She was a far more intellectual sort of woman. Not to mention, she seemed to share earthier tastes than most genteel women.

Turning to leave the scene of battle, he thought to retreat and regroup. But first, he had to get past the fire-breathing dragons that had once been Whitney's parents.

"What is the meaning of all this, Mr. Pendersen. How do you know my daughter?" Dr. Merriman demanded from the door of his study where he and his wife hovered. Gone were the welcoming smiles and friendly banter.

"I made her acquaintance yesterday, but I dare say I was enraptured by her the moment I set eyes on her. When she slipped away from me without getting her last name, I was desperate to find her. A mutual acquaintance of ours refused to give me her direction. As it turned out I came here for dinner and unexpectedly ran into her again."

"And why does she appear so reluctant to welcome your suit?" Mrs. Merriman asked the very question he wished to understand.

"I'm afraid I am not aware of what is causing her distress. I do wish I knew." He sighed and mentally cursed himself a fool for likely scaring her off with his foolish declaration. "Could I impose upon you to speak with her on my behalf?"

"I am afraid that won't be possible until I understand what has upset her. If you will excuse me, I shall check on Whitney now." Mrs. Merriman swept up the stairs and left Magnus alone with a glowering Dr. Merriman.

"I believe you should go, Mr. Pendersen." The man who only a short time ago had been friendly and forthcoming with information now had a shuttered air about him. Wariness gave his gaze a hardness that contrasted with the earlier friendly glint. It was likely past time for him to retreat from the Merriman household.

Whitney rose with the sun, which in and of itself was not unusual, but considering she had tossed and turned all night long dreaming of the very man she had discovered in her father's study, it seemed wrong not to still be sleeping. With a yawn that did nothing to dispel her exhaustion, she crossed to her basin, poured some cold water into the bowl and splashed her face.

The question she grappled with throughout the long dark hours of the night was, why? Why did the magnetic man draw her so inexorably? Why did he find her so attractive when so many had seen only the oddity of an intelligent woman? Could he be after her inheritance? While no King's ransom, upon her father's passing she stood to inherit a reasonable annual income of two thousand pounds per year. It was certainly enough to see herself and the man she chose to marry live comfortably through their lives. Of course, most men never looked past the spine of the books she typically held.

But Magnus had seen beyond her intelligence, beyond her socially awkward conversation, and deep into the soul of the woman who stirred beneath. The hot-blooded, adventurous woman who had wanted to know the touch of a man. And what a man she had chosen. She could not deny that he had made her cry out in pleasure over and over, playing her body like a fine musical instrument. But then she'd realized if she stayed, she would not remain objective in her examination of the experience. Of course, she figured out far too late that once she became the subject of her study she could no longer maintain her detachment. Her heart and soul had both been stirred and while he had stood in her parent's foyer and declared himself in love with her, how could she trust her ability to decipher the difference between truth and fiction when she could not separate sex and love?

A knock on her door announced the arrival of her mother and their housekeeper, who bore a breakfast tray.

"I was about to dress and come down for an early breakfast."

"Come, Whitney. Sit." Her mother motioned to the table and chairs nestled in the small nook by the tall window overlooking the house's rear garden. "Just set the tray there, Martha. That will be all, thank you."

Martha departed leaving them sitting alone with a pot of hot tea and scones.

"Martha's scones?" Oh dear, this couldn't be good. Martha's scones weren't trotted out in the Merriman household except for special occasions, such as celebrations...and deaths. Her stomach gurgle in anticipation of the delicious treats despite are concerns.

"You were clearly upset last night when you refused to see me, so I thought you might need a little something to lift your spirits." Her mother poured tea as though they sat below stairs in the front parlor.

"What makes you think I had an upsetting evening?" Whitney tried to pretend that all was well with her, but she should have known better. While her mother was often lost in study or thought, she knew her daughter and her moods.

"Dearest, did I ever tell you the story of how I met your father?" The older version of herself sipped her tea and waited patiently.

"I believe you met at Hatchards booksellers." Whitney smiled, pleased with herself for remembering.

"Quite so, but what I have not shared before are the details of what happened. I was in the back stacks of the shop looking for *Clinton's Compendium of the Genus Rosa* when your father walked past. He stopped and stared at me for a few moments, an almost awkward length of time. Then he disappeared. Nearly an hour later I went to the front counter to settle my tab, I noticed your father hovering just outside of the store. As I stepped onto the street, my heart raced as the sunlight glinted off his golden brown hair. Without a single thought for propriety, he walked right up to me and introduced himself. He explained that he had waited for me to come out because he was certain I was the most beautiful woman he had ever seen and he had fallen in love the moment he saw me."

Whitney could not reconcile the rational man she knew with the portrait of a lovesick fool her mother painted. It simply did not equate.

"I blushed furiously, stuttered and stammered. Then he begged to know my name. Caught completely off guard I answered and then turned and fled. As I ran off I could not determine if my heart raced from fear or excitement. The next week, I returned to Hatchard's and found him waiting for me in the front of the shop. Once I clapped eyes upon him again, I knew the truth, he made my heart race and my body ache in ways I was not prepared for. He followed me up and down every aisle that afternoon until I agreed to let him call upon me at home. Within a few weeks, he proposed. A few months later, my parents refused to allow us a quick wedding due to the unconventional way we met, we were married. That was twenty-eight years ago."

Whitney released a breath, her muscles slightly more relaxed than a moment prior. At least the fact she was not a bastard remained unchanged. "But, did you feel the same as him? Was it truly love at first sight for you?"

"Another truth I have held back from you is that the women of our family all have experienced this very phenomenon. I decided long ago, when you were born, that you would not live with such knowledge hanging over your head. I wanted you to experience life and possibly love through your own eyes. Part of what scared me so badly when your father approached me was the knowledge of The Gift, as we Brantley women have come to call it. I had found myself terrified that I would look at the wrong man and fall in love, so I viewed every man I met with suspicion and fear."

"So you tried to spare me the fear of men, when in fact, I had begun to fear I would never find love," Whitney said and then picked up a scone.

Her mother's brow crinkled. "You feared never finding love?"

"Mother, I am twenty-seven and I have never had a beau. Not one. Did you not find that odd?" She added a dollop of berry preserves to her treat and took a bite. She moaned in delight as the warm richness of the scone mingled with the sweetness of the berries.

"I did not, considering The Gift. But I suppose, since you were unaware, it might have grown distressful. But you never said a word to suggest concern."

Whitney sighed. "You didn't find my interest in human sexuality and intimacy strange for a young woman?"

"Darling, you've always been curious about what made people tick. Much like your father, who loves to unravel the mechanics of a thing, you have always had a penchant for unraveling the mechanics of a person. By the age of ten, you had poor Martha utterly sorted out. She made scones for you every day for a month before I interceded." Her mother laughed. "Human intimacy seemed a natural path as it was an area you had little personal experience beyond your platonic and familial relations. The question that concerns me at this moment is, are you in love with Magnus Pendersen?"

Whitney's stomach cinched tight like the drawstring of a lady's reticule. Could she be in love with Magnus after one single night together? The moment she walked into her father's study she panicked. Fear had surged through her body. But why? She considered her mother's story. Was it as simple as not being prepared? Feeling an instantaneous connection so strong that she was drawn to him like metal to a magnet? A bee to nectar?

A knock on the door interrupted her train of thought as Martha entered bearing a bouquet of hothouse flowers. A dozen deep red roses had daffodils interspersed within a ring of hawthorn. Trailing behind was their butler, and then her father, each bearing boxes.

Her mother rose from her seat and crossed to where Martha set the blooms on the dresser. "What is the meaning of all this?"

Her father answered, "Gifts from an admirer. For Whitney."

It rankled that he felt compelled to clarify who the gifts were for, but then again it was not as though she had ever had admirers let alone gift giving ones.

Her gut clenched and she knew before her mother looked at the card who they were from. Magnus. She leaped up in a most undignified fashion, not that she was ever terribly graceful, and tried to grab the card from her mother. If the man mentioned The Market in his note she was doomed. Because while her parents were more than supportive of her studies, she knew they would have drawn the line at her visiting a brothel.

"The card says: Dear Whitney, I hope you find these flowers as beautifully enchanting as I find you. Sincerely Magnus Pendersen, III." Her mother sighed dreamily and handed her the card.

"Harriet, are you feeling well?" Her father looked concerned as her mother gazed at the flowers.

Her focus returned and her cheeks turned rosy, "Quite well thank you."

Whitney was unsure what to make of it all, but she turned to her father and their butler, "Please set them on the bed."

Martha and the butler quickly departed. Her father looked as eager to bolt as the servants had been, so she excused him and encouraged her mother to go with him. Instinct told her some, if not all, of the gifts should be opened in private.

Alone with the boxes, she eyed them warily for a bit longer as she considered her previous line of thought. Considering her mother's revelations about both The Gift and her own experience, it seemed that her fear might stem from the sudden shock of such abundance of emotion. Though she did not subscribe to the idea that women were delicate creatures, one need only look beyond their noses to see that women all about them were able-bodied and strong of constitution. However, she must admit that for one, such as herself, who had begun to see romantic love as something foreign, the shock of experiencing it for the first time in such an unexpected manner would be disconcerting if not outright fear-inducing.

Certain now that she had come to the root of her reaction she felt she could examine the gifts beyond the flowers with some objectivity and possibly even record her thoughts for later analysis. With that in mind, she inspected the beautifully crafted boxes. Each one bore a tag with a number written on them. Logic dictated she start with the medium sized container bearing the number one.

Carefully she untied the beautiful blue bow and lifted the lid. Inside, nestled amid tissue paper, sat a gorgeous pair of bronze inkwells and a carved ivory pen. The pots were a man and a woman sitting with their legs crossed upon a pillow, but when she tipped the lids back to open them she was delightfully scandalized to find their sexual organs displayed. Curious after that wonder, she picked up the pen for a closer look. While at a glance what appeared to be a carved design of curves and various lines, turned out to be a pair of lovers entwined each with their mouths on the other's sexual organs. A memory of her taking his cock in her mouth had her body warming as she imagined enacting the image on the pen. She set the items aside and selected the next box, larger in size and flatter. Again she carefully opened the gift, pushed aside the tissue and discovered a tooled leather journal. The cover held a damask design punctuated by a budding flower that was, in fact, a depiction of a woman's quim. She opened the book and found a short note scribbled inside.

A place for your darkest desires, with the hope, I may assist in their realization.

Love, Magnus.

She looked at the third box and decided to continue exploring the gifts. She set the journal aside and opened the container. Inside a beautiful mask embellished with jewels the likes of which she had never seen before. It was a sumptuous gold color encrusted with what appeared to be rubies and garnets. The fourth and final box proved much larger than the others. She opened the final blue bow and pushed the tissue paper aside to discover a stunning red gown and another note.

Whitney, My Love—

I request the honor of your presence this evening at the place where we first met. While I can only hope you will indulge me in this so that I may prove to you both the depth of my feelings for you, as abrupt as they may seem and the honorableness of my intentions. I shall await you until the hour strikes midnight.

Humbly Yours,

Magnus Pendersen, III

She lifted the gown from the box and stroked over the golden stitching that detailed the deep red silk bodice. The skirts cascaded down to end in a flounce of delicate gold and red ruffles. She gasped as she realized it was a design from the House of Worth.

Looking over the extravagant collection of gifts and considering the sentiment behind each item, she realized any notion of objectivity disappeared like the setting sun. Along with the laughable notion that he might be after her meager inheritance. Considering it was still morning, she wondered how she might while away her day as she waited to meet her lover at The Market. And then she remembered his wish that she scribble her darkest desires in the journal. Determined to do just that, she set her breakfast tray aside and set to work.

CHAPTER SIX

M agnus sat in the daffodil room in The Market…and waited. And waited longer. An hour into his wait he grew restless. The need for action of some kind gnawed at him. Worry seeped in along with the itch to move. Would she accept his gifts? His invitation?

He imagined her wearing the red and gold gown with the matching mask. Then he imagined stripping the dress from her delicious curves and quickly found he needed to think of other things lest he develop a premature erection. Withdrawing his Patek Phillipe pocket watch specially designed with his monogram on the inlaid mother of pearl cover, he monitored the sweep of the second hand as he willed Whitney to appear.

With each tick of the minute hand, his gut drew tighter, more painful as though it were twisting in on itself. No longer able to remain still, he rose and allowed the need to pace take over. He walked the length of the room, some twenty steps and then turned to retrace his path. He was on his tenth or maybe twentieth pass when a knock at the door announced the arrival of someone. Someone he hoped was Whitney.

"Enter," he said as he stepped over to the decanter and poured himself a much needed, but previously denied drink. He had feared one drink might lead to two and before he knew it he'd be stinking drunk when she arrived.

The door opened, and Phillipe escorted in a woman who wore a cloak with a deep hood. "Your guest, Mr. Pendersen." Then he bowed and left them alone.

The woman pushed the hood off her face to reveal her shining deep blonde hair and a face obscured by a golden mask studded with red jewels. The mask he had given her. Next, she unclasped her cloak and allowed it to simply slip from her shoulders into a puddle of fabric on the floor. Stunned by the voluptuous vision before him, he moved to set his glass down on the table and missed the surface entirely. The amber liquid sluiced out of the glass to soak the rug, but it barely registered on his consciousness as he took a step toward the woman who had captured his heart and owned his every waking thought.

"Whitney, you look stunning," he said, his voice a raspy mockery of his usual tone.

"Thank you, Magnus. It is a beautiful dress and were I a more proper woman I would have refused such extravagance. But I will tell you I could not put on another gown while this treasure remained in the box." She reached up and removed her mask, her breasts threatening to spill from the low scoop of the neckline.

"Then I am glad of your impropriety, for it would have been a tragedy for you not to wear such finery." He remained where he stood for fear any sudden movement might send her fleeing, or worse yet make her evaporate like an enchanted mist. "I am so pleased that you came."

"After such a lavish display with your request, how could I not? Though truth be told, the flowers alone would have compelled me." The apples of her cheeks reddened as though it were cold in the room.

"I enjoyed selecting each gift especially for you." He dared a step forward and was happy to note she did not retreat. The rounded mounds of her breasts drew his gaze and made his mouth water with the memory of loving that very flesh. "I hope you found them as stimulating as I."

"Indeed, I was delightfully scandalized by each gift in turn." She held up the journal he had sent, though he had not noticed it before. "In fact, I spent all afternoon thinking of things to write in my naughty book of desires."

Both his curiosity and his libido were piqued. "And do you plan to share what you have written?"

She nodded.

"Very good. Before I come any closer, I should like to speak with you." He fought his body's need to touch her because once he did, he knew he would not stop until she screamed his name.

"I believe you are speaking to me." She stared at him and blinked slowly.

He chuckled. "Right you are, but I refer to the need to discuss what this is between us. I shall not have you imagining this is something other than what it is. I realize my feelings for you would be considered sudden by anyone's measure, but they are nonetheless real. I can accept that you may not share these feelings as of yet, but you should be aware it is my intention to do everything in my power to make you feel that way."

"Magnus—" she attempted to speak, but he would have none of it.

"No. I shall lavish you with gifts, pleasure you with my body, and make your every wish my command. I shall win your heart, your body, and your mind." There. He'd said his peace; made his position clear so there could be no question in her mind. He was not after a short romp. He wanted her. She was his, he knew it deep in the depths of his soul and he would not leave England without her.

"You do make it hard for a lady to refuse you. Which is why it is a good thing I came here to tell you I feel the same. The night before last, as you lay there sleeping I became overwhelmed with a tenderness toward you I could not credit. I have lived twenty-seven years without having experienced anything of the sort and it warred with my analytical turn of mind. Scared, I fled and told myself all would be well once I was away from you. The truth was, the feelings remained. And then when you appeared in my father's study, they overflowed the walls I erected to contain them. I was terrified by it all. By you."

"And now?" Hope leaped within his chest as solid as the thump of his heart.

"And now, after some discussion with my mother, I realized I have nothing to fear. That while sudden and unexpected, the love I feel for you is returned and together it will grow stronger."

Relief flooded through his limbs and lifted the weight from his chest. She loved him. Somehow, by some miracle, she loved him. "Whitney, I shall love you for an eternity. Both now and from beyond the grave." He crossed to her, hauled her into his arms and kissed her as though it might be their first and last kiss. She looped her arms around his neck and clung to him, her breasts smashed against him, their tongues entwined.

He pulled away from her, in need of air, and to ensure he did not ravish her straight from the start. "I should like to see your writings, why don't we sit on the settee for a spell?"

"The bed would be far more comfortable." She batted her lashes at him, a seductive smile dancing over her lips.

He shook his head. "The bed would be far more dangerous as I would be likely to attack you rather than learn of your desires."

"Perhaps you are right. The settee it is." She led the way.

Her heart raced more now as she waited for Magnus to read her darkest desires than when she'd proclaimed her love for him. Their conversation had been so calm considering the powerful emotions involved. But they were both rational beings who knew when to allow their passions to rule and when to keep them in check. They'd both had things to say, and now that they were agreed on the general course of their future, he wanted to know more about her sexual desires. Fear coursed through her veins as she hoped he shared some of her interests.

He opened the book and flipped to a random page.

"Did you not wish to start at the beginning?" She resisted the urge to snatch the book from him.

"No, I wish to delve into the mysteries of your mind and your desires." He looked at the page and read the words.

From her sprawling script, the word anal seemed larger than any other word on the page. She nibbled her lip as she waited on pins and needles for him to say something. Anything. Would he be repulsed by her knowledge? Her awareness of all things sexual?

After a few moments, perhaps minutes, regardless it felt like hours, he looked up from the pages where her inner self was scrawled across the page. Magnus' face held no hint of his thoughts. No clues about his response to her words. "You should strip."

Whitney blinked, not sure she understood his words. "Pardon, me?"

"I strongly suggest you begin disrobing before I decide to rip every last layer of clothing from your delicious body." He growled in punctuation, and heaven help her she damn near melted into a puddle of need.

Determined to follow through on his request, well, demand, she rose and reached behind herself to feel for her laces. A flicker of a grin stretched his lips. "Come, let me help you."

She hesitated. "But I do not wish the gown to be ruined."

"I shall not damage the dress. I need you naked and in my arms, but I fear I may have distressed you." He pulled her toward him and spun her around. With quick, well-practiced movements he loosened the back of her dress.

With each brush of his skin, even through all the layers she still wore, her desire grew stronger. More demanding. Soon, it was she who urged him to go faster. "Hurry! Please hurry!"

In the next breath, her dress and petticoats puddled at her feet and he started on her corset. As he worked those laces free he dropped kisses along her exposed skin above her under clothes. And he continued until he had her stripped down to nothing but her hose and garters.

"On the bed, my love." His gaze burned with need, as he stared at her puckered nipples.

The desire within her rose up making her quim ache as he quickly shed his clothes. First, she studied his muscled chest and then he dropped his trousers and let his erect shaft stand long and thick. There were so many things she wished to try, to experience with him that she struggled to voice her desires. "I-I-," she paused, took a breath. "I do not know where I wish to start."

He closed the distance between them a feral grin on his lips as she tracked his progress. "Do you trust me, Whitney? Trust me to understand your desires and know how best to show you all that you wish to experience?"

Mouth dry from want she simply nodded.

"Excellent." He stopped by the bed and opened the nightstand drawer. When he arrived he'd placed a few potential necessities close to hand. After setting a small glass pot on top and a packet of French Letters, he crawled on the bed and leaned over her. She'd watched his every move both curious and nervous about what was to come.

Without further words, he claimed her lips with his. Eager to taste him again, she thrust her tongue past his lips and teeth and took what she wanted. He pulled back from their kiss and chuckled. "Greedy wench."

And then he plunged back into the kiss where he ravaged her mouth, exploring every nook and cranny. She reveled in his touch and taste, thrilled to the feel of his hand on her breast. Her head spun with all the dizzying sensations he created in her body.

He withdrew to leave a trail of small kisses down her neck, over her collarbone, and then across the tops of her breasts. A nip and lick of each nipple was all the time spent before he resumed his path south. When he settled between her thighs, shifting them apart to make room for his shoulders, she had to remind herself to breathe.

"Lay back and relax," he said.

As if that were possible. She repressed the urge to snort, and then his tongue traced the length of her wet slit and all thought ceased. There were only her pussy and his tongue.

On his second pass along her folds, he drove a trifle deeper, grazing her nub. "So damned sweet," he said, though his words were somewhat muffled.

Using his fingers, he spread her wide open and he dragged the flat of his tongue from bottom to the top of her quim. He lapped at her until she squirmed with the swelling bliss he created with his mouth. Her breath hitched in her chest as though her corset was laced too tight and her heart pounded.

"Magnus, it's too much." The raw pleasure overwhelmed her, almost scared her with its intensity.

"You can take more. You will take more." His low growl melded with the vibrations from her core and had her moaning mindlessly while she bucked into his mouth. As she whimpered again, he thrust two fingers into her channel opening her up.

"Yes...yes...yes..." The words strung together to become a mindless chant.

Her body caught in the maelstrom of sensation when he prodded at her rear hole she barely noticed. But as his finger worked past her tight ring of muscle, her whole body shook. With his finger stuffed up her backside and his mouth on her clit, she felt herself standing on a precipice for a single heartbeat, and then she was tumbling over the edge. "Magnus!" Her shriek of pleasure rang out in the room as he pushed her harder, further, and with a relentlessness she could never have imagined in her studies.

He slid the finger in her backside out part way and then he looked at her up the length of her body. "Again," he demanded.

And as he shoved his finger deep inside her, he plunged his tongue into her pussy, mimicking the movement of his digit as he pushed her over the edge for the second time in as many minutes. She exploded, coming on his tongue as she tried to shove her bum down on his hand. "More," she begged as she bucked against him. And he gave it to her, adding a second finger which stretched her even more. Her orgasm rolled on as the pleasure and the pain from his invasion of her virgin backside collided and became one intense wave of sensation. As the wave ebbed away, he slowed his movements until he held still resting his forehead on her thigh while his fingers remained lodged deep within her.

"Fucking beautiful." He pressed kisses to her thigh as it quivered beneath his lips. "Not tonight, but soon I shall stuff your delectable ass with my cock. And just as you described in your journal, I shall fuck you hard and fill you with my seed." He slid his fingers from her backside, creating a wake of ripples through her core. "But for now, I need to be inside you. To fill your sweet cunny."

A moan of contentment escaped her as he rubbed the head of his cock over her sensitive tissue. Then he donned a French Letter and knelt between her legs. Focused on the spot where his shaft spread her wide open, he pressed into her body. She found it fascinating to watch the play of emotion on his face as he slid within, and he without a doubt stretched her. Slowly her body adjusted to his size and accepted him until his sack bumped against her bottom.

"As soon as we are wed, we can dispense with the French Letters, but for now I'll not have you end up pregnant by accident. Now, look into my eyes."

The tight clasp of her pussy around his cock had his muscles straining as he resisted the urge to pound into her. As desperately as he wanted to, he refused to be so callous when she was still new to sexual intimacy. But soon he would fuck her exactly as she described in her journal. He pictured his hand fisted in her hair as he pumped into her ass from behind and damn near lost control right there. He pushed the lusty thought aside and started listing his ships in his head. As he named them one by one—all thirty of them—he slid out of her pussy and then shuttled back in. Over and over he worked in and out of her body as she wiggled and thrust up to meet him.

And then he ran out of ships to name right as she panted and pleaded, "More, Magnus. Fuck me harder."

In the blink of an eye, all chivalry was lost and he tossed one of her legs over his shoulder as he pumped into her body. Each stroke fired pleasure through his limbs powering him to piston into her body like a locomotive on full steam. "Yes!" Her strident cry urged him on until she came, her quim spasming around him and demanding he follow her. One, two, three more strokes, and he tumbled into one of the most powerful orgasms of his life. Blissful tingles covered his body from head to toe as his sac drew up tight, and then he shot his load as he continued to relish the hot wet slide of her body. As his pumping motion slowed, his cock softened until he lay on top of her, a human blanket.

Together they gasped and trembled as the power of their love swirled around them almost a tangible entity.

Magnus leaned up and stroked Whitney's cheek, "I love you, now and forever."

Her blue gaze locked with his as she smiled at him. "Now and forever."

~The End~

Thank you for spending some of your precious reading time with me. If you enjoyed any or all of the stories you've read, please be sure to post a review and help others discover them. Just a line or two will do to share what you loved most about the series.

OTHER BOOKS BY SORCHA MOWBRAY

The Lustful Lords

His Hand-Me-Down Countess

Lustful Lords, Book 1

His brother's untimely death leaves him with an Earldom and a fiancée. Too bad he wants neither of them...

Theodora Lawton has no need of a husband. As an independent woman, she wants to own property, make investments and be the master of her destiny. Unfortunately, her father signed her life away in a marriage contract to the future Earl of Stonemere. But then the cad upped and died, leaving her fate in the hands of his brother, one of the renowned Lustful Lords.

Achilles Denton, the Earl of Stonemere, is far more prepared to be a soldier than a peer. Deeply scarred by his last tour of duty, he knows he will never be a proper, upstanding pillar of the empire. Balanced on the edge of madness, he finds respite by keeping a tight rein on his life, both in and out of the bedroom. His brother's death has left him with responsibilities he never wanted and isn't prepared to handle in the respectable manner expected of a peer.

Further complicating his new life is an unwanted fiancée who comes with his equally unwanted title. Saddled with a hand-me-down countess, he soon discovers the woman is a force unto herself. As he grapples with the burden of his new responsibilities, he discovers someone wants him dead. The question is, can he stay alive long enough to figure out who's trying to kill him while he tries to tame his headstrong wife?

His Hellion Countess

Lustful Lords, Book 2

A duty bound earl and a jewel thief might find forever if he can steal her heart...

Robert Cooper, the Earl of Brougham must marry in order to fulfill his duty to the title. He's decided on a rather mild mannered, biddable woman who most considered firmly on the shelf. But, her family is on solid financial ground and has no scandals attached to their name.

Lady Emily Winterburn, sister of the Earl of Dunmere, is not what she seems. With a heart as big as her wild streak she finds herself prepared to protect her brother from his bad choices, even if it means committing highway robbery. But marrying their way out of trouble is simply out of the question. What woman in her right mind would shackle herself to a man, let alone one of the notorious Lustful Lords?

Cooper's carefully laid plans are ruined once he must decide between courting his unwilling bride-to-be and taming the wild woman who tried to rob him—until he discovers they are one and the same. And when love sinks its relentless talons into his heart? He'll do anything to possess the wanton who fires his blood and touches his soul.

His Scandalous Viscountess

Lustful Lords, Book 3

Once upon a time, a boy and a girl fell in love...but prestige, power, and a shameful secret drove them apart.

Julia fled abroad after the death of her husband, Lord Wallthorpe. She has finally returned to England, but little has changed.

Except for her.

As a dowager marchioness, Julia lives and loves where she pleases. And the obnoxious son of her dead husband does not please. But what can an independent woman do? Why, create a scandal, of course!

Viscount Wolfington is no stranger to the wagging tongues of the ton. Between being a Lustful Lord and the scandal of his birth, he learned long ago that society had little use for him. So when he walks into The Market and finds the woman who once stole his heart being auctioned for a night of debauchery, he jumps at another chance to hold her—even for just a single night.

As Julia and Wolf unravel their pasts, will villainy win again, or will love finally conquer all?

His Not-So-Sweet Marchioness

Lustful Lords, Book 4

He's shrouded in shame, fighting with his demons in the shadows. Until she sets her sights on him...

Mrs. Rosalind Smith once followed her heart and love to the battlefield and left a widow. Spending the remainder of her life alone is enough... until she meets a man who's need for pain sparks an answering flame deep within her *soul.*

Matthew Derby, the Marquess of Flintshire is a fighter, it is all he's known since childhood. Throwing his fists is the only way to keep his need for pain at bay, and a certain gentle woman off his mind. She deserves a better man than him—Lord or not. Though when faced with the prospect of losing Ros, Flint realizes he has found something to fight for... something to *live* for.

To Ros' dismay, everyone around her believes her demeanor too sweet for someone like Flint. When his world begins to unravel and his dockside violence bleeds into the drawing room, a shocking family secret won't be the key to all the answers. Questions remain, can he solve the mystery, tame his dark needs, and still win Ros' heart?

One Night With A Cowboy

The One Night With A Cowboy series is a set of short stories linked by cowboys and Soul Mates Dating Service, a dating service with an uncanny ability to match up soul mates. These sizzling little treats are perfect for a quick hot read.

<u>One Night With A Cowboy Books 1-5 (Boxed Set)</u>

ABOUT THE AUTHOR

Sorcha Mowbray is a mild mannered office worker by day...okay, so she is actually a mouthy, opinionated, take charge kind of gal who bosses everyone around; but she definitely works in an office. At night she writes romance so hot she sets the sheets on fire! Just ask her slightly singed husband.

She is a longtime lover of historical romance, having grown up reading Johanna Lindsey and Judith McNaught. Then she discovered Thea Devine and Susan Johnson. Holy cow! Heroes and heroines could do THAT? From there, things devolved into trying her hand at writing a little smexy. Needless to say, she liked it and she hopes you do too!

Find all of Sorcha's social media links at

link.sorchamowbray.com/bio

or scan the QR Code

Printed in the USA
CPSIA information can be obtained
at www.ICGtesting.com
LVHW050306170923
758428LV00009B/76